Kill me ONCE

Jon Osborne has been a newspaper reporter for a decade, most recently for the *Naples Daily News* in Florida, where he covered everything from bake sales to triple murders. He is a veteran of the United States Navy. He is currently at work on his second thriller.

Kill
me
ONCE

Jon Osborne

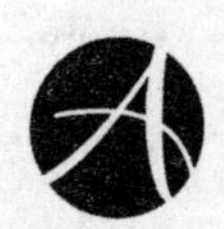

arrow books

Published by Arrow Books 2011

4 6 8 10 9 7 5 3

First published in Great Britain in 2011 by
Arrow Books
Random House, 20 Vauxhall Bridge Road,
London SW1V 2SA

www.rbooks.co.uk

Addresses for companies within The Random House Group Limited can be
found at: www.randomhouse.co.uk/offices.htm

The Random House Group Limited Reg. No. 954009

A CIP catalogue record for this book
is available from the British Library

ISBN 9780099550921

The Random House Group Limited supports The Forest
Stewardship Council (FSC), the leading international forest
certification organisation. All our titles that are printed on
Greenpeace approved FSC certified paper carry the FSC logo.
Our paper procurement policy can be found at:
www.rbooks.co.uk/environment

Mixed Sources
Product group from well-managed
forests and other controlled sources
www.fsc.org Cert no. TT-COC-2139
© 1996 Forest Stewardship Council

Typeset by SX Composing DTP, Rayleigh, Essex
Printed and bound in Great Britain by
CPI Bookmarque Ltd, Croydon, CR0 4TD

As everything, for Khloe

ACKNOWLEDGEMENTS

First thanks goes to my wonderful literary agent, Victoria Sanders, whose tireless dedication to this project provided the rock-solid foundation. She truly is the best, and I will be eternally grateful for everything she has done. Also to agency Editorial Director Benee Knauer – whose countless reads and structural suggestions were invaluable – and to up-and-coming agent Chris Kepner, who I know will have a long and outstanding career in the industry. Thanks, everyone, for hanging in there when the seas got choppy.

To everyone at Random House UK – especially Kate Elton and Georgina Hawtrey-Woore. From the first phone call to the final edits, Kate and Georgina embodied the genteel side of publishing I always imagined existed, and I couldn't ask for better editors or nicer people to work with. Thank you, ladies, for everything. Thanks also to Nick Austin for his wonderful eye for detail.

To author Jeff Shelby – who showed me how a true pro does it. Also to retired FBI agent James Jessee, who selflessly ensured that all the procedural elements were in place. I still owe you that dinner, Jim.

Finally, I would like to thank my family. My parents, Richard and Della, made me the person I am today – so please direct all complaints to them. Thank you, Laura Osborne, for changing my world for the better the first time I laid eyes on you. We'll always be like 'peas and carrots'! To Madison and Justin, for letting me in, and to my sisters – Kathleen, Elizabeth and Julie – for sharing my childhood and making it so much fun to be a kid.

Kill me ONCE

PART I

BECOMING RICHARD RAMIREZ

'I love to kill people. I love to watch them die. I would shoot them in the head and they would wiggle and squirm all over the place, and then just stop. Or I would cut them with a knife and watch their faces turn real white. I love all that blood.'

Richard Ramirez, aka 'The Night Stalker', who murdered at least thirteen people between 1984 and 1985.

CHAPTER ONE

Los Angeles – Friday, 12 November – 10:30 a.m.

Red, orange, yellow; green, blue, indigo, violet.

Of all the colours in the rainbow, orange was by far Nathan Stiedowe's least favourite, but on this morning it was making itself blessedly useful by warming his skin.

Thank God for small favours.

He stared directly up into the blazing ball of fire in the sky, not blinking, not feeling pain in his eyeballs like a normal person would. Then again, he'd always been different, hadn't he? Different and *weird* – or so he'd been told countless times since childhood by his parents and schoolmates.

Legend had it that he didn't cry upon receiving the painful round of inoculations all children received as one-year-olds. Not a single tear. The nurses were amazed – and horrified – by his complete lack of reaction when the sharp needle punctured his baby-smooth skin.

What the hell was wrong with him? they frantically wondered, fear in their voices as they scurried about. *We must run more tests immediately.* It was just plain *weird. All* babies cried.

Not Nathan.

Then there was the time in fourth grade when he'd broken his ankle in three places while playing soccer on the playground during recess. His terrified classmates had actually *heard* the bone breaking – or so they'd breathlessly informed the playground monitors – a loud crack that had sounded like a thick dry tree branch snapping underneath enormous pressure. But Nathan hadn't cried then, either. Not a whimper. Like everything else in life pain was only a state of mind and if your mind was strong enough you could simply block it out. Didn't anyone understand that?

The names had followed after that, of course. Names that would stick with him throughout the remainder of his schooldays. Freak. Nutcase. *Weirdo*.

Sticks and stones will break my bones, but names will never hurt me.

Nathan smiled sardonically. Who cared what they called him, anyway? To paraphrase old Billy Shakespeare, what the hell was in a name? Did a rose by any other name not smell as sweet?

These days the hopelessly childish nickname they'd pinned on him was 'The Cleveland Slasher'. For Christ's sake, how cartoonish was that? But as usual a press corps hungry to sell more papers had gone straight for the jugular. With Nathan's journalism background he understood that better than most, even if he knew that *he*'d have done a much better job chronicling a case that could surely land the right reporter with the proper motivation a goddamn Pulitzer Prize.

Nathan shook his head. *Fuck it*. In the grand scheme of things names were of little consequence here. The only thing anyone needed to know about him was that he'd soon be considered the most perfect serial killer who'd ever lived. And once he was done sharpening the thorns on this particular rose – sharpening them to the point they drew

4

gallons of blood – it was something they'd never forget. Not his parents. Not his former classmates. *Especially* not the thieving bitch in Cleveland, Ohio, who'd so carelessly stolen his life all those years ago.

But first there was work to be done, so that was the primary task of the day.

Nathan had already had a busy morning – an exquisitely beautiful fifth murder followed by the long plane ride back out to California – but a killer's work was never done, was it? Not for the good ones, at least. Certainly not for the *best* one.

Running was a strange way to prepare to kill people, but he knew he had to do it if he wanted to be the best there'd ever been. And he *did* want to be the best. God knew that much. Ever since he was a little boy (*freak*, *nutcase*, *weirdo*) he'd always felt the need to contribute his own special slant to the events of the past. To erase the jumbled chalkboard and start over from scratch. To make things better than they were. To make them *clean* again.

This morning it was hill repeats in Los Angeles's Griffith Park under the steady California sun. Hill repeats sucked ass, especially for a man Nathan's age. Spring twenty-five yards up the steep incline, jog down and repeat. The thighs would burn and ache like they were on fire, the chest would gasp helplessly for air and the sweat would pour in endless rivers down the back.

Most athletes would do this drill ten times, maybe fifteen if they were seriously world-class and really looking to build up a strong aerobic base. But that wasn't enough for Nathan. Never had been. He knew he had to push himself harder, faster and *longer* than all the others if he truly wanted to be the best killer of all time, so he forced himself through an agonising twenty trips up the steep hill before finally beginning the short jog back to the cheap motel he was temporarily calling home.

Running was the key for this one. It would establish him as a real player and set the tone for the other murders to come. And unlike most people out there running away from their own fucked-up pasts – *chickens running around with their heads chopped off* – he was running toward his future now. Running *for* his future. At least that was what he kept telling himself. Hell, one of these days he might even get around to believing it.

But it was fucking *hot* outside. Nathan had no trouble believing that. Over the past couple of days an Indian summer had slapped LA around like a husband would a mouthy wife, taking her by the throat and throttling hard. Eighty-eight degrees and air so heavy with humidity you could probably wring it out like a saturated washcloth if only you could get your fingers around it.

The sun was the sizzling yolk in the centre of a robin's-egg sky, beating down on his head like a solar jackhammer wielded by an especially malevolent god as he struggled out of the park on cast-iron legs a good ten times heavier than when he'd first started out this morning. But at least the exquisite fatigue in Nathan's aching muscles let him know that he'd accomplished *exactly* what he'd set out to do.

He knew there was no way in hell that Richard Ramirez had trained like this for *his* killing spree. Fat fucking chance. Wan and gaunt, with hollow cheeks sucked in around twin dead eyes, the only time when the Night Stalker had probably ever run was to the nearest corner store when he'd been looking for another pack of off-brand cigarettes to further pollute his wheezing lungs.

Nathan shook his head and chuckled to himself as he left the park. *The Night Stalker*. What a joke *that* was. When you really looked at things with a critical eye, it was amazing that Ramirez had ever been given a nickname at all.

Outside the park, his rubber-soled Nike cross-trainers slapped rhythmically against the cement and pushed the hot pavement back in consistent five-foot increments. Reaching up, he slid an annoying layer of perspiration away from his eyes and frowned suddenly. What the hell had been Richard Ramirez's problem, anyway? How could he have let himself be so fucking careless? So goddamn *unprofessional*?

If you wanted to become a master of your craft – to become a killer so far above reproach that not even your harshest critic would utter a single bad word against your work – all it took was a little bit of thought, a little preparation, a little goddamn *discipline* to get it right. What was so hard about that?

Absolutely nothing, that was what. If you wanted to be the best then you had to swallow your pride and become a student of the game first. That much went without saying. And if nothing else Nathan had always been an extremely diligent student, carefully studying even the tiniest details of how the heavyweights who'd come before him had operated inside the killing zone.

That was why he was going to be the best there'd ever been. It was as simple as that.

Lost in his thoughts, the bouncing breasts fifteen feet away knocked him out of his reverie and back onto the cracked sidewalk snaking its way along the boiling shore of the Pacific Ocean. Seagulls squawked noisily in the blue sky above and a strong westerly wind heavy with sea salt whipped hard through his full head of thick brown hair as he summoned up his best smile and nodded to the pair of attractive college-aged blondes jogging by in the opposite direction. Wearing matching sweat-soaked sports bras and barely-there Adidas running shorts, the little sluts held up their flawlessly manicured hands and smiled back at him in return.

Kill the right way, they seemed to be telling him.

Nathan chuckled again when they had passed and lowered his head, forcing himself to pick up his pace despite the fingernails of pain clawing at his sides. Hell, if even the stupid whores out here in sunny Southern California knew that much, just *what*, exactly, was so goddamn difficult about the equation?

Again, nothing hard about it in the least. Nothing to give him the slightest pause or reason for concern. There was no room for conscience here. Killers killed: it was what they did. It was their *job*, for Christ's sake. The good ones never got caught. The best ones were still talked about hundreds of years after they themselves had given up the ghost. But there was only room for one at the top of the heap – the unquestioned dominant lion of their special pride, as it were – and that was a title Nathan fully intended to claim for himself.

Now it was time for the dominant lion to show off his sharp white teeth and let out a thunderous roar.

Finally back at the run-down motel fifteen minutes later, Nathan couldn't help flinching at the building's outward appearance – dull, square, busted-up, a real shithole from ass to elbows – but he knew the anonymity that it provided was well worth the sacrifice of having to live there.

Waves of reflected heat shimmered up from the baking

pavement like a troupe of drunken belly dancers in a crowded bar while he carefully picked his way through the rusted-out cars littering the blacktopped parking lot. Datsuns, Cadillacs, Chryslers – even a forty-year-old Pinto featuring a smashed-in back window. Moments later Nathan's taut calf muscles were bouncing him up the concrete stairs on the outside of the building two at a time like a pair of stiff new pogo sticks until he reached the third floor, where he pushed open the rickety wooden door to Room 312 and locked it behind himself before kicking off his brand-new running shoes and tossing his room key onto the queen-sized bed that was covered by an especially garish paisley comforter.

Sweat poured down his temples as he sat on the bed and peeled off his ankle-length socks. He sighed contentedly. The lack of air conditioning provided a temperature exactly how he liked it best.

Hot.

It was one of the main reasons he'd come to LA, though certainly not the most *important* one.

His Oakley board shorts, plaid Armani boxers and soaking-wet Billabong T-shirt came off next. Completely naked now, Nathan rose to his feet and strode over to the full-length mirror in the corner to check himself out.

I look stronger, he thought, admiring a shredded midsection positively *rippling* with lean muscle. *I bet I could outrun an entire goddamn country if I really wanted to.*

But it would be just a small group of people he'd need to outlast tonight.

A cold rush of adrenalin flooded into his loins at the thought, and he felt himself begin to harden slowly. Only a few more hours left now until he'd find out if all his hard work and meticulous preparation were going to pay off. It had taken the laying of a lot of irritating groundwork, to be sure, but now that he had the attention of the thief back in Cleveland, tonight frightened little girls all around the Renaissance City could rest just a little bit easier as a result.

Nathan laughed out loud – a deep, throaty laugh that filled the room and vibrated his vocal cords like the strings on a perfectly tuned bass guitar. If they'd tried, could they have possibly picked a grander nickname for Cleveland – a city widely considered the shittiest place to live in all of the United States?

He shook his head to clear the thought away. No matter. As he'd established earlier, names were of no consequence here. And for better or worse he'd moved his one-man act on to the bright lights and fertile hunting grounds of LA. Soon he'd be recognised as the very best serial killer who'd ever lived. But for now it was simply time for the greatest show on earth to begin truly in earnest.

Lights.

Camera.

Action.

CHAPTER TWO

Cleveland, Ohio – 8 p.m.

What unspeakable things my eyes have seen.

The line from an old TV movie flashed through Dana Whitestone's mind as she slipped on a pair of paper shoe-covers and watched a balding forensic photographer named Doug Freeman lean in for a close-up of the little girl's spilled intestines. The flashbulb popped brightly once, followed by the electric sound of rewinding film. Not for the first time, Dana wondered how Freeman had the stomach for his job. How did *any* of them?

A uniformed Cleveland cop nodded to her and scribbled something down on a clipboard. As the first person at the crime scene he was responsible for establishing the perimeter, closely monitoring everyone who entered and exited. The fewer people inside the yellow tape the better the chance of maintaining integrity.

They were on the seventh floor of a Section-8 apartment complex on the east side of Cleveland, the hardest hit sector of a hard-luck city recently named the second-poorest metropolitan area in the country. Last year they'd been Number One but this year Detroit wore the tinfoil crown.

Dana had been on a dinner date downtown when she'd received the call but she hadn't been especially sad to leave. For all their silly commercials, Match.com had slim offerings

11

in the boyfriend department. Still, idly picking at a dozen mild chicken wings and washing them down with a quick succession of ice-cold Miller Lites while an overweight accountant from Parma stared at her breasts across the table had to be better than *this*.

She tied a paper mask over her mouth and nose and glanced around the apartment to make sure that everyone else was wearing the proper protective gear. Dana didn't want to miss out on the chance of catching a killer simply because somebody in the room had a cold. 'What's her name?' she asked.

The photographer looked up with his own mask tied on, making him look like a crestfallen surgeon documenting a hopelessly botched job. 'Jacinda Holloway,' he said. 'Eight years old.'

'Who found her?'

'The mother.'

'Where's she now?'

'Hospital.'

'Nervous breakdown?'

'You got it.'

Dana crossed into the room along the established entry/exit point – a crucial element in all crime scenes – and knelt beside Freeman for a closer look. Automatically shifting into investigator mode, she popped two pieces of Citrusmint Orbit into her mouth to mask the smell of beer and pulled on a pair of thin latex gloves.

She reached out a hand and lifted a slender wrist six inches off the floor, then did the same with a swollen ankle. No need for emergency medical care, that was clear, and Dana was thankful the EMTs had recognised that. Few people compromised crime scenes more than medical personnel. Not that Dana blamed the EMTs for their zeal. Saving lives *was* the most important consideration, after all – even more than catching killers.

She squeezed her fingers gently around the girl's ankle and frowned. Full rigor mortis had set in, indicating that she'd been dead for about twelve hours. Dana glanced down at her watch. At eight a.m. the little girl should have been in school learning her times tables, not lying dead in a pool of her own blood. Still, school wasn't always Priority Number One in this neighbourhood. That said – why hadn't the mother found her earlier? And why had the little girl been left unsupervised in the first place? She was only eight years old, for Christ's sake. Much too young to look after herself.

Doug Freeman read Dana's thoughts. 'Drug problem,' he said. 'Apparently the mother left last night and didn't come home until a couple hours ago.'

Dana shook her head. The killer had probably been watching the little girl for weeks to know that the mother would be gone all night. No doubt it was a common occurrence with the woman. But when she'd left last night she'd let the fox slip right into the henhouse unimpeded and that had cost her daughter her life.

Dana forced back the anger she felt rising in her chest and continued to examine the body. The undersides of the little girl's arms and legs looked bruised, a purplish colour where the blood – no longer circulated by a beating heart – had settled into dense pools beneath her soft skin. *Lividity*, they called it.

Dana glanced down at her watch again and estimated the time of death at eight a.m. before jotting it down in her notebook. Extensive documentation was a focal point of the US Department of Justice's *Crime Scene Investigation:*

A Guide for Law Enforcement – the research report that had come out in 2000 under the then Attorney General Janet Reno. Even though each federal agency had its own idiosyncrasies, as a general rule they all tried to follow the guide when it came to matters of evidence identification and protection. For her part, Dana considered it nothing less than her personal bible.

The manual was a step-by-step explanation of how to process crime scenes, and Dana had memorised it early on in her career. Some people kept diaries as a way of chronicling their lives. Not her. If anybody ever wanted to see a record of *her* existence, all they had to do was take a look at the cardboard box in the back of her closet – the one filled with a hundred notebooks similar to the one she was holding right now.

Shootings. Stabbings. Strangulations. They were all in there; all filled with questions pertinent to each case, some of them answered, too many not.

Where exactly had the bullet entered the skull? In the front or back? Which ribs did the knife separate before piercing the wildly beating heart? Had the killer used a cord to choke the life out of his helpless victim, or had he simply used his bare hands to get the job done?

The notebooks were what defined who Dana was now. Not much of a life, she knew, but at least she was still alive, which was a hell of a lot more than she could say for poor Jacinda Holloway.

The little girl's naked corpse had been posed, frozen in death in the middle of some perverse jumping jack: arms lifted in a *V* over her head; thighs forced three feet apart below her mutilated torso. A broken-off broom handle jutted from between her legs.

Dana gritted her teeth and slid her stare over the length of the defiled body. Viscous fluid leaked down from the little girl's split-open belly to the tiny hairless triangle between her toothpick-thin brown thighs. Her brown eyes were fixed and staring straight ahead, slightly rolled up into the back of her head as if she was trying desperately to look at her own eyebrows. The look of surprise etched on her small brown face would remain there for ever.

There had been a time in Dana's life when a horrific sight like this would have wrenched her perceptions adrift and caused the entire room all around her to melt rapidly away into some sort of surrealistic Dali painting. But those days were most decidedly in the past: she was a consummate professional now – right down to the point where it had robbed her of the ability to express even the most basic human emotions. Anger wasn't an option for her. Not any more. Neither was grief. Emotions only got in the way.

If you never cried, your vision never got blurred, right?

She stretched her neck and looked sideways at Freeman. 'You done yet?'

The photographer got the message at once. *Pound sand.* 'Yes, ma'am. She's all yours.'

Dana gave him a small smile that never quite reached her pale blue eyes – not that he could see it through the mask, anyway. 'Thanks, Doug.'

The room was buzzing with harried crime-scene technicians bumping shoulders in their haste to catalogue every last carpet fibre in the place, but a quick once-over told Dana everything she needed to know. Ritual child killing. Posed body. Grotesque sexual molestation.

The maniac who'd already murdered four little girls around Cleveland had struck again.

15

She slid her tongue across her teeth in disgust. They'd been after the Cleveland Slasher for three months now but hadn't come up with even a solid *clue* yet, which was highly unusual in serial-killer cases. Normally these guys were so focused on taking care of the raging hard-ons poking out of the front of their pants that they left more than enough evidence behind to point out their identities. But that wasn't the case here. Not with this guy. He was different. Something other than the overwhelming compulsion to control weaker people through sex was driving him to kill.

But what was it?

Dana shook her head to clear the thought away and forced herself to concentrate on the task at hand. Sighing, she quickly ran through the facts they knew: five dead bodies in ninety days. All five little girls under the age of ten. All five raped with a broom handle and split right down the middle like autopsy patients. As far as evidence went, the cleanest crime scenes she'd ever come across.

But maybe even this guy – as good as the bastard un-deniably was – was starting to get just the tiniest bit sloppy now. In his apparent rush to leave the apartment he'd left the murder weapon behind this time – a wickedly serrated hunting knife coated in dark dried blood that now lay on the uneven floor right next to the lifeless little body that he'd so viciously hacked to ribbons.

Transfixed by the sight of the weapon, Dana was imme-diately stung by just how *insignificant* it looked. No more than six inches long with a cheap plastic handle. Something you could easily pick up at Wal-Mart for the grand total of fifteen bucks.

How could something so mundane *do so much irreversible damage?*

She turned to a passing crime-scene tech and pointed to the knife. 'Has that been photographed yet?'

The woman nodded. 'Yes, ma'am.'

'Good. Could you bag it up for me now? I'd like for you personally to take it over to the lab for analysis.'

The woman bristled, looking slightly irritated at the assignment.

Dana lifted her eyebrows. 'Is that going to be a problem?'

The woman blushed. 'No, ma'am.'

'Great. Thanks a lot. I really appreciate all your help.'

As the female tech bagged the knife Dana quickly scanned the rest of the room. Five feet away from the eviscerated corpse a silver-framed photograph sat on a chipped mahogany end table next to a plastic-covered couch. Yesterday Jacinda Holloway had been an especially beautiful little girl. A tiny little thing with a toothless grin. No more than three-five or six, sixty pounds soaking wet. Big glossy brown eyes and a round angelic face accented by tight intricate hair braids and an array of colourful plastic barrettes that sprouted from her head like cornstalks.

Today was a different story.

'You OK, Special Agent Whitestone?'

Irritated by the interruption, Dana swivelled her head to the left and watched a Cleveland cop lean over with a pair of long metal tongs to pluck a bloody white surgical glove off the floor. Sergeant Gary Templeton straightened back up and held the glove in front of his eyes for a closer look. 'Sick bastard coated the inside with moisturising lotion again,' he reported grimly.

In his early forties, Templeton, a decorated fifteen-year veteran of the force, had been at each of the four previous murder scenes, finally requesting FBI assistance after the third one. Normally it was the smaller departments that asked for help from the feds – lab personnel and facilities were just too expensive for them to afford – but Cleveland PD was large enough to maintain those resources for itself. What they needed here was *investigative* help, so Dana had been assigned to the case, effectively taking control.

Following 9/11 the FBI's role had changed dramatically. They routinely worked more closely with local law enforcement now, partnering up even when there were no direct federal implications. One thing was for sure: they'd come a hell of a long way since the 1960s, when J. Edgar Hoover's guerrilla tactics had the Kennedy administration shaking in its boots. These days the feds and locals were at each other's disposal practically upon request, with little of the boundary-protecting or rancour that had defined their relationship in the past. There were still pockets of resentment on both sides, of course, especially when the FBI barged into local investigations uninvited, but that wasn't the case here: when Templeton had noticed the similarities at the Holloway apartment to the previous murder scenes it had been he who'd called Dana away from the crowded bar.

Dana looked him over again. Close-cropped silver hair framed a rugged face punctuated by piercing blue eyes. Hard muscles like croquet balls strained against navy-blue shirtsleeves. The first time she'd laid eyes on him three months earlier she'd instantly pegged Templeton as a pumped-up Richard Gere with a gun, spliced with a healthy dose of Clint Eastwood for good measure. An excellent cop and definitely not the kind who spooked easily. So when she'd heard his voice on the other end of the line when he'd called her to the scene earlier in the night she'd immediately known that the Cleveland Slasher had struck again.

The moisturising lotion the killer was using was an old trick. It had been the same thing at each of the four previous murder scenes. He always left one glove behind, always coated it with lotion to absorb the oil on his finger pads and prevent them from lifting prints. Normally fingers moved around inside gloves sufficiently enough to smear prints and make classification almost impossible, but this guy was obviously being very, very careful. Still, how was he managing to avoid leaving some type of print when he pulled the gloves *on*? A second pair of gloves? Tape, maybe? Dana didn't know, but his little measures had worked like a charm. So far they hadn't been able to lift even a smudged *partial*.

Templeton dropped the bloody glove into a large plastic evidence envelope and pressed the self-sealing flap into place. 'No doubt it's the same guy, right?'

Dana shook her head. 'None.'

'Other than that, what are your initial impressions?'

Before she could answer him, the flashbulbs started popping in the room. Dana turned toward the commotion and saw Doug Freeman standing in the middle of a pack of photographers, all of them huddled around a rickety prefab TV stand shoved against the south wall.

'What the hell's going on over there?' she asked sharply.

Freeman lowered his expensive camera in the middle of the fray and let it dangle from the leather strap around his neck. 'You'd better come over here, ma'am. I think we just found something.'

Dana's knees cracked as she rose to her feet and smoothed the black Malandrino skirt into place around her slender legs. The pack of photographers parted for her like the Red Sea on Moses' command as Doug Freeman lifted a shaking hand and pointed to a colour photograph wedged underneath the front of the VCR. Dana took a small pair of rubber-tipped tweezers from her purse and removed them from their plastic casing before plucking the photograph out. Her breath caught in her throat as she examined the find.

A huge palm in the centre of the frame dominated the majority of the photograph. Bony fingers were bent slightly forward, like those of an evil magician getting ready to hurl a ball of fire at his enemies. The fingernails on the hand were sharp and overly long, the centre of the palm coloured in with a crudely drawn pentagram.

Dana turned to Freeman and frowned. 'What *is* this?'

The photographer shook his head. 'No idea, but whatever the hell it is, it's definitely been cropped and blown up. Probably with Photoshop.'

'Why do you say that?'

'It's way too pixilated to be the whole frame,' Freeman said, studying the picture. 'It's gotta be a close-up of a larger photograph. I'm almost sure of it.'

'Do you have enough documentation yet?' Dana asked – photographs were always prime evidence in trial cases.

'Yeah.'

She nodded and slipped the photo into a manila evidence envelope before tagging it. 'Get the hospital on the phone and find out if it belongs to the family.'

'Right away, ma'am.'

As Freeman moved away, Dana tucked a loose strand of short blonde hair behind her right ear and savoured the sudden tingling sensation in her stomach. The dizzying rush of adrenalin she got from investigating murderers hadn't subsided in the thirteen years she'd been on the job and she doubted it ever would. Something about the psychology of a killer fascinated the hell out of her. It was like passing the twisted wreckage of a twenty-car pile-up on the highway. You knew you shouldn't look, but who could resist?

Freeman flipped his cellphone off a moment later. 'Photograph doesn't belong to the Holloways,' he said. 'The nurses got the mother to stop crying long enough to confirm that much.'

Dana chewed on her lower lip, unconsciously fingering the small gold crucifix hanging from a delicate braided chain around her neck. 'You said the picture was Photoshopped, right?'

'Yes, ma'am.'

'Is there any way of finding out what the larger photograph is?'

Freeman shook his head. 'There's no database for that kind of thing, ma'am. It isn't like plugging a search term into Google.'

'So there's *no* way of finding out?'

'Not unless somebody recognises it.'

'I don't suppose *you* recognise it,' Dana asked hopefully.

Freeman shook his head again, this time in an apology. 'No, ma'am. I sure as hell don't.'

Dana thanked him and moved away before finding Templeton and pulling him aside. The first four autopsies had been little more than quick visual checks since the cause of death had been rather obvious – not to mention that the Cuyahoga County coroner was a doddering old fool who hadn't quite warmed up to the notion of being told what to do by the feds yet – but Dana wanted to make sure they dug deeper on this one. 'Let's get a full workup this time, OK, Gary?' she said. 'I don't care what that asshole Johnson says. Go to a different ME if you have to. Just get it done.'

Templeton nodded. 'I'm on it.'

Dana took a deep breath as Templeton walked away, wondering what had happened to the nervous rookie agent she'd been more than a decade earlier. Back then she'd been half-afraid even to look anyone squarely in the eye, but now she was a woman used to having her orders followed without question. She considered it a blessing knowing that Templeton would execute her autopsy orders to the letter – which hadn't always been the case with some of the other law-enforcement personnel she'd worked with in the past – but she couldn't help worrying that she'd miss something if she didn't do the work herself. Still, the difference between her old self and the current version couldn't be starker. And thank God for that.

After those initial growing pains Dana's meteoric rise through the ranks had been the talk of the FBI, inspiring respect in some corners and deep resentment in others. First in her class at Quantico. Handpicked by the legendary profiler Crawford Bell to be his partner out in the field before his age relegated him to a teaching role and her ambition led her to strike out on her own and move back to the Cleveland of her youth.

Through it all, Dana had never been the type who delegated responsibility easily. It was her greatest strength, and also her greatest weakness. She might have been a hotshot according to some of her colleagues (and a royal pain in the ass who always insisted on doing everything by the book according to others), but even hotshots needed help sometimes, and she'd do well to remember that.

Dana felt another sudden thrill in her stomach. *The thrill of the chase.* Some senior agents might have considered her next task beneath them, but she actually *relished* what was coming next.

A little good old-fashioned police work to make sure she didn't miss a single clue in this case that was slowly beginning to drive her crazy.

CHAPTER THREE

Los Angeles – 8:25 p.m.

Nathan whistled softly to himself as he exited the cheap motel. The oddly comforting smell of warm asphalt floated up into his nostrils. A good kind of anxiety rippled through his muscles as he walked. He felt ready for the exciting night ahead.

An updated kill to start things off right.

Now that he'd finally gotten *her* attention back in Cleveland, the fun and games could really begin. Following tonight's festivities, no way in hell she wouldn't see all these murders were connected. She just wouldn't understand how or why yet. He'd leave *that* part up to her to figure out. After all, he certainly didn't want to make things too easy on the bitch, now did he? Where in the hell would be the fun in that?

Of all places, he'd found tonight's intended victim in the metro section of the *Los Angeles Times* – a fawning, retrospective fluff piece on how she'd been some kind of semi-famous dancer on the Chicago nightclub circuit back in the late 1940s, back in the days when a little burlesque had actually been considered racy.

A careful reading of the article was followed by a quick Google search that provided him everything else he needed from there. And judging by her photograph, her advanced years and general look would fit in perfectly with his intentions for the evening, which were to flawlessly mirror the Night Stalker's first and most horrific slaying.

AC/DC's 'Night Prowler' blasted over the beautiful rental car's stereo system as he slowly circled her block, in no particular hurry now while he deliberately scouted for his prey. Richard Ramirez was said to have been a big fan of the Australian heavy-metal group, and especially of this song in particular – the media's inspiration for his thoroughly chilling moniker – so tonight Nathan was a fan of the Aussie rockers as well.

He checked his mirrors and eased the wheel to the left before carefully pulling the car over to the side of the road across from her ramshackle apartment complex just as an emaciated black man wearing a pair of filthy khakis and a tattered wife-beater stumbled past on the cracked sidewalk. The black man stopped walking and leaned his head down, trying to look through the tinted window on the passenger side.

Nathan could almost *smell* the man's body odour through the rolled-up glass as he turned the music down with the steering-wheel control and activated the power window. When the window slid down and their stares locked, the black man recoiled like he'd just been slapped.

His bloodshot brown eyes widened into saucers. 'S – s – sorry, man,' he stuttered. 'I was jus' lookin'. I don't want no trouble.'

Nathan shook his head and reactivated the power window as the black man scurried away. 'Fucking crack addict,' he muttered.

He turned the music back up, plucked a small glass vial

from the glove compartment and shook a large pile of cocaine onto the webbing between his left thumb and index finger before lifting the drug to his face and snorting it up hard into his nostrils. The powerful cocaine took effect almost immediately, shooting sharp waves of pleasure throughout his entire body.

So *this* was what the big fucking deal was all about.

Although he'd never done any kind of drugs before – much less something as potent as cocaine – authenticity was paramount to what he was about to do, so he figured there was no time like the present. Richard Ramirez had been stoned out of his fucking mind on the night when he'd viciously raped and murdered Jennie Vincow, so tonight Nathan would dabble in a little bit of the stardust as well. Not a lot, not enough to make him do anything stupid, of course – just enough to cover his bases and ensure authenticity. Above all else, it was the *details* that mattered most.

Another ten minutes passed before the old woman finally came walking down the street, clutching a small beige change purse in her gnarled hands and hobbling slightly as she favoured her right side. She glanced around furtively to make sure no one was watching, then quickly inserted a silver key into the antique door lock and let herself inside the small ground-floor apartment.

Nathan smiled and gripped the leather-wrapped steering wheel tighter while a series of cold, almost *painful* goose bumps spiked across his forearms and shoulders, a thrill of adrenalin rolling so hard through his bones that he thought it might lift him right out of his seat. He was deep inside the killing zone now and all five of his senses suddenly felt sharper, more in tune with the world around him, more *reliable*.

This was it. The culmination of everything he'd been working so hard for. For the sake of updating history, this old woman would have to die a very violent death here tonight. There was simply no other way around it.

He waited patiently for a passing patrol car to turn the corner and drive out of sight before hopping out of the sleek green Audi and popping the trunk. Aimlessly wandering crack addicts and half-asleep cops aside, the quiet street was deserted at this time of night, so rather easy to prepare undetected. Still, he knew the empty street would be full of people soon enough. That was key. There had to be people around.

They had to *see* him.

The chords of 'Night Prowler' were still ringing in his ears as he dressed quickly in breakaway athletic pants and a thin black turtleneck before pulling an AC/DC baseball cap over his head. To complete the sacred transformation he used a blue ballpoint pen to carefully draw a perfect pentagram in the centre of his left palm.

Anticipation bubbled in his loins as he slid a sharp knife into the leather sheath on his belt and closed the trunk softly. Quietly – *oh so quietly* – he crept across the street under the cover of darkness.

It was time to get to work.

CHAPTER FOUR

After leaving Templeton with her instructions concerning Jacinda Holloway's autopsy, Dana walked out into the hallway of the Section-8 apartment complex and knocked on doors until one finally opened. Most agents usually delegated this sort of chore to underlings, but she'd seen that approach backfire enough times to know it was always better to do the work yourself. It was what had gained her the respect of most of her fellow agents and the resentment of others – individuals who didn't want to look bad in comparison. It certainly wasn't as easy as they made it look on television, but you never knew what vital clues might be hidden in the seemingly mundane tasks. Sometimes you just had to roll up your sleeves and get your hands dirty – all the way up to the elbows, if need be. Crawford Bell had taught her that much.

Three doors down from the murder scene a shadowy figure darkened the peephole before a chain rattled and a young black woman holding a sleeping baby eased the door open a crack.

The young woman narrowed her eyes when she saw Dana and shifted the baby on her hip. 'What do you want?'

Dana held up her badge and smiled. It was extremely important that an investigator's demeanor appeared non-threatening and non-confrontational from the outset, pretty much Questioning Techniques 101, as it were. Besides, she found that being friendly usually worked a hell of a lot better than pulling the old 'goodcop/badcop' routine. Another trick she'd learned from Crawford Bell early on in her career.

'Hello, ma'am,' Dana said in a cheerful voice. 'My name is Special Agent Whitestone and I'm investigating a murder on this floor. I'm sure you've heard about it by now. May I come in?'

The young woman studied Dana's badge, then glanced down at the sleeping baby. Not much older than a newborn, Dana noticed. Then again, Mom couldn't have been much more than eighteen herself. 'I don't want no trouble,' the young woman said warily.

Dana brightened the smile on her face. Even if her troubled past made her keep people at arm's length in her personal life, she never felt that kind of pressure on the job. No doubt it was the main reason she enjoyed working so much while her colleagues were off spending time with their families. Work was a *relief* for Dana, a place in which she could concentrate on other people's lives and problems, not her own. Still, lately she couldn't help feeling like maybe she needed something more in her life. A loving husband, perhaps. A couple of kids. A white picket fence edged with beautiful daffodils that the family dog would dig up half an hour after she'd planted them.

Maybe in another lifetime.

'Won't be any trouble, ma'am,' Dana told the young woman. 'I just need a moment of your time, that's all. It'll only take a couple minutes, I promise.'

The young woman opened the door further and shifted the baby on her hip again. 'You sure you got to?'

Dana nodded. 'Yes, ma'am, I'm sure. I really appreciate your cooperation.'

The young woman sighed and opened the door all the way. She stepped aside to let Dana in. 'Well, come on in, then – if you really have to.'

Dana stepped inside the apartment and looked around. The place was absolutely spotless, with the heavy smell of freshly baked cinnamon buns hanging in the air. Dana's stomach growled loudly, reminding her that she'd left most of her dinner on her plate at the bar during her mercifully brief date with the leering accountant.

The furniture inside the apartment was old but well maintained considering the fact it appeared to be mis-matched pieces hastily thrown together from a 1970s-era Sears catalogue. Pictures of Jesus and John F. Kennedy hung on the wall above the small table in the dining room, interior-decoration staples for black folks who'd come of age during the civil-rights movement in the 1960s.

Dana lifted her eyebrows in surprise. Truth was, she'd expected something shabbier. 'You live here?' she asked.

The young woman closed the door and motioned to the threadbare couch in the middle of the living room. 'Nah,' she said, crossing the apartment and placing the baby down in a playpen next to the television set. 'This here's my grandma's place. She's just letting us stay for a while until I can get back on my feet.'

Dana nodded and sat down on one end of the couch. 'Is your grandmother home?'

The young woman shook her head and took a seat on the opposite end of the couch. 'No, she's in the hospital right now. Cancer.'

Dana shifted away from a broken spring that was jabbing

her in the butt. 'I'm very sorry to hear that. My name's Dana. What's yours?'

Questioning Techniques 102: *Establish rapport with your subject early on whenever possible. Don't dive in too quickly with the complicated questions. Get your subject on your side and gently steer them into the topic of conversation, especially when they don't seem all that willing to cooperate.*

The young woman tossed an intricate braid over her left shoulder. Dana noticed that her elaborately styled fingernails were painted bright red. 'My name's Tyesha.'

'And your baby's name? She sure is a cute little thing.'

The faintest trace of a smile finally creased the young woman's lips. 'Tamara.'

'How old is she? Six months?'

'Five.'

'She your first?'

'Nope. Fourth. I got three others.'

Dana didn't ask where the other children were. None of her business. Still, she felt a sharp twinge in her heart. If she hadn't burned through a string of relationships with perfectly worthwhile men over the years she'd probably be on her fourth child herself by now. At thirty-eight, her biological clock wasn't just ticking any more. It was *thundering* in her ears like a goddamn runaway freight train.

'Listen, Tyesha,' Dana said, 'I need to know if you've seen or heard anything unusual around here lately. Especially around eight a.m. this morning.'

The young woman looked confused. 'How do you mean *unusual*?'

Dana waved a hand in the air, painfully aware of just how bad her own fingernails looked compared with Tyesha's. 'I

31

mean did you notice anything out of the ordinary today. Hear anything out of the ordinary? I want to know if you've seen any strangers on this floor lately. What the Holloway family was like. Where they went for fun. If they were a close family. If they were religious. If so, what church did they go to? Who came to visit them on the weekends? That sort of thing. It'll help give me a clearer picture of the family and of anybody who might want to hurt them.'

The young woman pressed her lips together. 'It don't pay much to notice strangers around here, lady. That family kept to themselves, like we all do. Other than that, I really don't know what to tell you.'

Dana nodded, feeling about as welcome now as a raging case of herpes in a monastery. Still, even though it wasn't the answer she was after it didn't surprise her in the least. Nobody ever wanted to talk, but who in the hell could blame them? In this neighbourhood, cooperating with the authorities quickly branded you as untrustworthy, a reputation that usually prompted a severe beating – or worse – to remind you to keep your big fat mouth shut the next time.

Dana took a deep breath and went on patiently, as if she was talking to a young child. 'Listen, Tyesha, a little girl was murdered here this morning. That's the fifth one in three months now. You're a mother so I'm sure you can understand how awful that must feel. Jacinda Holloway's mother is at the Cleveland Clinic right now, barely holding things together. So if you know something, you have to tell me. That's just the way it works. It's the only way I can make sure nothing like this ever happens to another mother.'

The young woman smiled thinly at her. 'First of all, I ain't no goddamn crack whore like that bitch. Second of all, that might be the way it works where you're from but it sure as hell ain't the way it works around here.' She waved a hand in front of her chest. 'Take a look around, Dorothy. You ain't exactly in Kansas any more. Like they say on the block, *stop snitchin'*. Ever heard that phrase before?'

Dana shifted on the couch again. Maybe the 'bad cop' routine wasn't such a bad idea, after all.

'Yeah,' she said, holding the young woman's stare. 'Ever heard the phrase "accessory to murder" before?'

Tyesha laughed out loud. A deep, genuine laugh that filled the room and caught Dana completely by surprise.

'What the hell you gonna do?' Tyesha asked incredulously. 'Haul me downtown? Toss me in a cell? Who's gonna look after my baby while I'm locked up? You? I don't fuckin' think so.'

Dana didn't answer her. She knew the young woman was right. Some people just weren't cut out to be mothers – and Dana happened to be one of them. Hell, she could barely take care of herself these days, much less look after a baby.

Over in the playpen Tamara was beginning to stir, making soft cooing noises in her sleep and trying to lift her head.

The young mother looked over at the playpen and let out a resigned sigh. 'Look, lady, I don't know nothin', OK? I ain't seen no strangers because I ain't been looking. Are we done here yet? I need to feed my baby.'

Dana stood and walked to the door. She was clearly unwanted here, but where was the surprise in that? In this part of town, law enforcement was just one step above the KKK in the social pecking order, if that.

Out in the hallway, she turned and handed Tyesha a business card. 'Thank you very much for your time. If you happen to remember anything – anything at all – please call me at this number. Any time. Day or night.'

The young woman took the card and glanced down at it, then looked back up at Dana. 'Like I said before, lady. I don't know nothin' about nothin'.'

And with that she simply closed the door in Dana's face.

CHAPTER FIVE

2250 Drexel Street – South Central Los Angeles – 9:39 p.m.

If there was one thing that Mary Ellen Orton knew better than anything else these days, it was that being old was no fun at all. Though her mind was still remarkably fresh considering her advanced years, her frail old body just wasn't up to the exhausting task of simple day-to-day living any more.

The heat only made things worse.

She'd spent most of the long, tiring day trying to ignore the unforgiving temperature all around her, but nothing had worked out very well. Like most people her age, Mary Ellen hadn't grown up with the unimaginable luxury of air conditioning, and as a youngster in Chicago each summer she'd read horrible accounts of the elderly citizens of the city literally *dying* from the heat.

Back when she'd been a fresh-faced girl, those sad tales had seemed little more than abstract concepts – nothing to worry about very seriously. But she had been *young* then. Now seventy-nine and still not fully recovered from a badly shattered right hip brought about by a nasty slip in the shower three years earlier, those old newspaper articles seemed to hit a lot closer to home.

Moving to Los Angeles in order to be closer to Jerry – her last living child and the only thing she had left on this

Earth in terms of family – had brought with it a certain sense of emotional comfort, but the City of Angels wasn't exactly known for its *mild* weather. And the cloying layer of smog always hanging over the city like a thick blue cloud of cigar smoke in a crowded bar certainly didn't help matters, either.

Mary Ellen sighed and wiped her sweaty palms against the sides of her thin yellow housedress, desperately trying not to cry despite her many frustrations. How she wished Ed were here with her now. If Ed were here he'd hold her close and kiss her face and tell her not to worry, tell her everything would be all right and that he'd never, ever let anybody hurt her. He'd just smile that little smile of his and pull her to her feet to sway to imaginary music. Oh how they used to dance!

But Ed wasn't here any more, hadn't been for more than ten years now, so these days Mary Ellen simply filled out her time the best she could. But it really was *lonely* being old. Nobody had ever warned her about that part of life when she'd been a little girl, and as a result she was finding the Golden Years badly tarnished. They seemed more like something suspiciously along the lines of tin.

Word Searches with oversized type helped combat the excruciating boredom for short periods of time. Reading was a tolerable activity for a while, too – just so long as the words on the page were large enough to save what precious little remained of her failing eyesight. The Social Security cheques and small pension from her deceased husband's job as a postal worker certainly didn't allow for such outlandish modern expenditures as cable television, but Mary Ellen made do just fine with her old black-and-white set equipped with its rabbit-ears aerial.

Sometimes the set-up managed to pick up a halfway decent signal, allowing her to stay updated on her soap operas and the latest news, but even that much had become a chore lately. Tonight, however, the television was picking up only a snowy-white static – not to mention the obnoxious buzzing sound accompanying the flickering picture – so she simply flicked it off.

Mary Ellen tried knitting for a while, but it wasn't very long before the arthritis shook the needles from her hands and they clattered down noisily onto the cheap TV-tray table in front of her. Old Arthur had been living with her for years now, and she'd be damned if he weren't just the *rudest* house guest she'd ever known – even if the folksy term for the crippling affliction was a bit dated even for her taste.

A bead of sweat slipped down the back of Mary Ellen's neck in the stifling heat of the apartment. The damn air conditioner had broken again and Jerry hadn't quite gotten around to fixing it yet. Although basically a good boy in most respects, her son had just as many issues as anybody else. Probably a few more than most.

Mary Ellen's gnarled fingers lightly brushed the Life Alert medical call hanging around her thin neck like a forlorn plastic cross. She'd never fallen before and been unable to get up, of course – as those silly commercials so condescendingly suggested – but neither had she ever been the type to tempt the fates. Besides, Jerry had absolutely *insisted* on it for the nights when he was out there doing whatever the hell he was out there doing and she'd grown fairly accustomed to it by now.

The heat rose high in her paper-thin cheeks as she struggled to her feet and crossed the living room in her small apartment to go do battle with the sticky window in the far corner. It was an *oven* inside the apartment and she knew she'd never be able to fall asleep if she didn't at least *try* to do something to cool the place down. But when she finally managed to wrestle the window up, the arthritis in her wrists immediately screamed at her for her foolishness. The weak breeze that followed hardly seemed worth all the pain and effort involved.

Sighing as she gently rubbed her tender wrists, Mary Ellen stepped inside her tiny bedroom and slowly slipped out of her clothes, neatly folding them up and placing them on the old wooden chair next to her bed. She would wear the same clothes tomorrow. It was just too much of a hassle to do laundry more than once a month any more. Besides, who in the hell did she have left to impress, anyway?

Her aching muscles throbbed in hot protest as she pulled a thin white nightgown over her wispy silver hair and squinted her watery blue eyes at the digital alarm clock on her bedside table. Almost midnight now – well past her usual bedtime.

Her ancient joints sang with pain as she carefully climbed up into the rickety double bed with its lumpy old mattress in the middle of the room and leaned over to switch off the bedside light. The metallic sound of squeaking springs filled the darkness as she covered herself with a thin sheet and closed her exhausted eyes, desperately trying to think about the good old days. Sometimes that helped her forget the pain. On good nights it even helped her forget the loneliness for a little while.

Soft strains of remembered music echoed gently in her mind as she floated slowly back in time and once again became the picture of grace on the dance floor, hovering over the wooden planks like a lace-covered ghost whom all the men desperately loved and all the women desperately envied.

As she gradually drifted off into the painless world of her dreams, a contented smile finally played across Mary Ellen Orton's wrinkled old face.

It would be the last smile in a very long, very well-lived life that once upon a time had been *full* of them.

CHAPTER SIX

Dana left the squalid apartment complex on the east side and fought her way through the insatiable press corps that had flooded into the parking lot. The questions rained down on her from all directions as she hurried to her Mazda Protégé.

A man with perfect hair in the middle of the pack stepped forward and shoved a microphone in her face. 'Special Agent Whitestone!' he shouted. 'Chip Hall, Channel Three News. Was this murder the work of the Cleveland Slasher?'

Dana squinted against the bright television lights. She focused on the man's perfectly plucked eyebrows, not wanting to encourage him by making actual eye contact but also not wanting to look evasive when they ran the footage on the eleven o'clock news. 'There will be a press release in about two hours,' she said, her voice steady and strong as she continued walking. 'That's all I can say right now.'

She unlocked the Protégé with the keychain control and hopped inside. Slipping the car into gear, she slowly backed the vehicle through the mass of humanity and out of the parking lot, being very careful not to run over anyone's toes. That was the last thing she needed right now.

As she hit Interstate 90 and headed for home, Dana felt guilty about the little white lie she'd just told. There would be no press release coming in two hours, of course, but sometimes you had to throw the wolves a little meat to distract them. Her comment would keep them satisfied for tonight and buy her some time, though, and that was the important part. Most of the reporters would probably be happy enough with her empty promise, and if she was lucky they might even forget about it for tomorrow night's broadcast and move on to chasing the next big story of the day.

One could always hope.

Half an hour later she was inside her own apartment on the west side of Cleveland, seated at her dining-room table with her notebooks scattered on the tabletop in front of her. She felt wired, unable to wind down after the events of the day as she tried desperately to map the case out in her mind. The MO for Jacinda Holloway's murder matched the previous four murders exactly, but none of the few clues that the Cleveland Slasher had left *pointed* anywhere. The pattern was clear – little girls were his targets – but to what end or for what purpose? And why had he left behind a photograph of a pentagram at the Holloway apartment? What exactly was he trying to *tell* them?

When her mind started to grow fuzzy from information overload, Dana went into the kitchen and grabbed a Corona from the refrigerator, leaving her notebooks abandoned on the table. That was enough for tonight and she needed the beer after the day she'd just had, needed a little something to take the edge off. She found that alcohol usually did the job quite nicely, even if she knew it was an extremely dangerous friend to lean on. But it was when she was here at home – when she wasn't actually out working in the field – that the seams started to show. For all its faults – and there were a lot of them, Dana knew – booze helped her keep the stuffing inside where it belonged, kept all the emotions from spilling out. She knew it was a crutch but she also knew it was the only thread keeping her tattered psyche together at this point.

Beer in hand, she went into her living room and curled up on the couch underneath a soft blanket with a classic text by Elisabeth Kubler-Ross – the Swiss-born psychiatrist who'd written the groundbreaking book *On Death And Dying*. Dana had always found the book helpful, both personally and professionally. It was comforting to know that other people had gone through the same things she had, soothing to know she wasn't all alone in the world and wasn't crazy for still feeling the way she did after all these years. Still, Dana wished like hell she could just let go of the terrible events of her past instead of endlessly wallowing in them like she'd been doing for more than three decades now.

She sipped on the Corona and tried to relax while the sounds of Regina Spektor played softly on her living-room stereo. The beautiful voice led viewers into Dana's favourite show each week – the hit series *Weeds* on Showtime. Most people around the country had professed their allegiance to *Dexter* or *True Blood* on HBO, but Dana saw enough blood and guts in her real life to make watching dramatisations of it on television rather pointless. When *she* watched TV, she wanted to *stop* thinking, not be reminded of how cruel human beings – or vampires, for that matter – could be to one another.

Dana glanced around her apartment and tried to feel a sense of home, but it didn't work. The furnishings were literally straight out of a Pier One showroom but she'd never been especially proud of them. Why should she be?

Who besides her ever saw it? But that was what you got when you didn't have anyone else in your life to spend your money on. You tended to buy the good stuff for yourself.

In addition to the couch there were matching plaid armchairs, a coffee table with a thick cut-glass top and an old-fashioned coat rack over in the corner next to the front door. The furniture was three years old now, but for all intents and purposes it might as well have been brand new. Material things aged slowly when you hardly ever used them. Emotional things, too.

Above the plasma-screen television – no doubt the most expensive *Weeds*-watching device ever constructed – a gilded frame hugged an old Sears portrait featuring a four-year-old Dana flanked by her mom and dad, Sara and James Whitestone. The four-year-old Dana smiled down without a care in the world on the thirty-eight-year-old version. The short blonde hair and fair skin were the same, making her a carbon copy of her mother – and most likely the milkman's daughter, considering her father's swarthy good looks. But there was something missing now in the current version's pale blue eyes. The sparkle was gone. Dana knew because she looked for it every single morning in the bathroom mirror.

Dana closed her eyes, missing her parents badly as the stereo kicked over to John Cougar Mellencamp's 'The Authority Song'. Opening her book to chapter five, she began to read. The five stages of death and dying had stuck in her brain since she'd first learned the catchy anagram in freshman psychology at Cleveland State almost twenty years earlier.

DABDA. Denial. Anger. Bargaining. Depression. Acceptance.

Over the years Dana had found that the stages could be applied to just about anything, and since there'd been a lot of death and dying going on in her world lately she didn't think applying Kubler-Ross to her current situation was going to hurt. She needed something – *anything*, really – to give her a better idea of just who exactly she was dealing with here in the Cleveland Slasher – a sadistic killer who'd already murdered five little girls around Cleveland and probably wasn't going to stop there if Dana couldn't catch him before he killed again.

She started with denial. What was he denying when he murdered his victims? His own mortality? Or was he simply denying them *life*?

Anger was pretty obvious. He was sure as hell pissed off about something, but what was it? Most serial killers had experienced horrific childhoods, so that might be it, but Dana's own childhood had been no walk in the park either and she didn't go around killing innocent little girls to make herself feel any better about it.

Bargaining was a bit trickier. An eye for an eye, a tooth for a tooth it wasn't. If nothing else, *he* was still alive, though he made damn sure none of his victims shared that particular trait for very long.

Depression was another obvious one. The killer had undoubtedly suffered more than most as a kid, like most serial killers, but the truth was that Dana really didn't give a shit. She only wished he'd suffered a whole lot more – like right down to the point of *dying* over it. If that had been the case, five beautiful little girls would probably still be alive today.

Lost in her reading, she was startled by the knock at her front door. She glanced down at her watch – a gold Rolex that had belonged to her mother. It had been a first-anniversary gift from her father, who wore a matching men's version and said that he and Sara matched so perfectly as husband and wife that the least their jewellery could do was the same.

Almost eleven p.m. already. Way too late for it to be anything good. Dana had learned the hard way over the years that late-night phone calls and visits invariably meant somebody was in trouble. Or hurt. Or even dead.

Especially dead.

She kicked off her blanket and rose to her feet. Crossing the living room, she cast a wary eye at the wooden Louisville Slugger baseball bat leaning up against the wall behind the coat rack before putting her eye to the peephole. A familiar face smiled back at her.

'You in there, Dana? I saw your light on underneath the door and I thought I'd say hello. I haven't seen you in ages. I was beginning to worry.'

Dana let out a relieved breath and opened the door. Other than her black-and-white cat Oreo, who was now sleeping peacefully over on his soft bed next to the couch, the person on the other side of the door was her very best friend in the whole world.

'Eric!' she said happily as her across-the-hall neighbour breezed past her right shoulder and into her apartment. 'What are you doing still up?'

Eric turned around to face her and held up the last two Bud Lights of a six-pack by one of the empty plastic rings. The smell of Woods by Abercrombie & Fitch – his signature scent – filled Dana's nostrils.

'Couldn't sleep,' he said. 'Care for a nightcap?'

Dana briefly considered the proposition. *Very* briefly. Truth was, another drink didn't sound half bad right now, and she could use the company. She knew his offer of a

45

nightcap was just an excuse to check up on her, but right now his concern was welcome. No one cared about her as much as he did.

'Twist my rubber arm,' she said.

She'd first met Eric Carlton, a newspaper columnist at the *Plain Dealer*, when she'd moved into the apartment complex three years earlier. On the second day in her new home, a knock had sounded at her door. When Dana opened it, expecting to see the pizza-delivery guy she'd called an hour earlier or perhaps her new landlord wanting to tie up a few loose ends concerning the lease, she was puzzled to find Eric standing there instead.

He was a tall, ruggedly handsome man about fifteen years older than her, and the twin dimples fading in and out, along with his nervous smile, only accentuated his sculpted good looks. A shock of unruly brown hair had been falling softly over his forehead that day, and despite having just met the man for the first time in her life Dana found herself fighting off the urge to smooth it back for him. He'd been holding a plate of home-made brownies in his hands, shyly offering them out to her.

'I just moved in myself,' he'd said. 'I thought it might be kind of nice to have a friend in the building.'

It had been, as they say, the beginning of a beautiful relationship.

Dana looked at the beers and smiled. 'Crack those open and I'll go see if I've got anything in the kitchen for us to munch on.'

Eric chuckled, keeping things light. 'Don't hurt yourself in there on my account, Martha Stewart. I know you're world-famous for your culinary skills and all, but there's no need to whip up one of your signature feasts.'

Dana laughed – his easy banter was just what she needed right now. She went into the kitchen and opened the refrigerator door, peering in. Several more Coronas, a week-old container of Chinese takeout and half a block of Swiss cheese stared back at her. Other than that, though, it was a ghost town inside. She was amazed she didn't actually see tumbleweed blowing across the empty second shelf.

'Cheese and crackers OK?' she called out to Eric. 'I haven't got anything else.'

She heard him pop the tabs on the beers out in the living room. 'Sounds great. I'm starving. Haven't eaten a thing all day.'

Dana sliced the cheese up into reasonable facsimiles of squares with a long knife – whose blade hadn't seen the light of day in months – from the wooden block on her kitchen counter and in the pantry found some Wheat Thins that hadn't gone completely stale yet. Putting them on a plate, she returned to the living room and placed the food down on the coffee table before lowering the volume on the stereo with the remote control and taking a seat on the couch three feet away from Eric, who was now stroking a wildly purring Oreo curled up in his lap.

Dana reached over and scratched the cat behind his pointy white ears. 'Traitor. You act like I never give you any attention at all.'

Eric looked over at her and smiled. 'Hey, he just loves his daddy, that's all. Don't be so jealous all the time.'

Dana felt another twinge in her heart, once again wondering how different things might have been between them if Eric's sexuality hadn't been what it was; if they ever could've had a future together; what their kids would have looked like.

She shook the thought off, feeling selfish. From the very beginning Eric had been entirely upfront with her about his feelings for men so it was unfair of her to try to make him into something that he so obviously wasn't. Besides, some people might always have Paris but she and Eric would always have Oreo, and in the grand scheme of things that wasn't such a bad deal, after all.

Eric leaned forward and topped a Wheat Thin with a slice of Swiss cheese before popping the combination into his mouth. He searched her expression with his gaze. 'What's going on, Dana?' he asked gently. 'You look exhausted.'

Dana took a sip of her beer. 'I haven't been sleeping well lately,' she admitted. 'This case.'

Eric frowned. 'I heard about that murder on the east side today. Another dead little girl. It's disgusting. Seriously, Dana, I don't know how you do it.'

'Neither do I sometimes.'

Eric popped another cracker into his mouth, thoughtful now. 'This guy's really got to you, hasn't he? He's a real slick son of a bitch, huh? Do you want to talk about it?'

Dana knew she shouldn't *technically* be discussing cases with Eric, even in the most general sense, but ever since her partnership with Crawford Bell had broken up Eric had been her only outlet, the only person in her private life she felt comfortable confiding in. Besides, he was her only family now and she trusted him with her life. Sometimes the rule book just had to take a back seat to actually *living* – even for a stickler like her.

'Slick and obviously very well educated,' she said. 'Probably by guys like you.'

Eric grunted and took a long swallow of beer. As a member of the media, he knew that these days killers had their pick of any number of the different educational programmes out there to help them hone their craft. *Law & Order*; *Law & Order: Criminal Intent*; *Law & Order: SVU* – not to mention the ubiquitous show's many other offshoots. *CSI* – both the New York and Miami versions. *Dominick Dunne's Power, Privilege and Justice* on truTV. *Investigative Reports with Bill Kurtis* on A&E. Hell, they were all practically *instruction* manuals on how to commit murder and get away with it.

Don't want the bullet traced to a particular gun? Hell, just jam a screwdriver down the barrel to alter the grooves. Problem solved. Thanks, A&E.

Afraid your purchase of rope and a shovel at the local Ace Hardware might be traced back to you after you've strangled your wife and buried her in a shallow grave? Shit, just pay in cash and wear a disguise to hide your identity from the security cameras. Problem solved. Thanks, truTV.

Oh, and don't bother trying to clean up the crime scene after you've bludgeoned your mother to death and jammed her bloated body into an industrial-sized basement freezer, either. Haven't you ever heard of Luminol before? No matter what you do, the blood spatter's going to show up just as clear as day under a black light.

Dana tightened her lips. 'He's definitely better than most of the other killers I've come across in the past,' she said. 'Certainly smarter, at least. For the life of me, I just can't seem to figure him out.'

Eric nodded. 'Well, you're smart too. You'll get him. Just don't let it take you over, Dana. I know you. Anyway, I'm sure you'll catch a break soon.'

'That would be nice. I just hope it isn't in my neck.'

Eric winced and drained the last of his beer. 'Don't even

joke about it.' He rose to his feet and leaned down to plant a kiss on Dana's cheek. 'Well, it's late – I'm out of here, honey. Just wanted to say hello and have a quick beer, see you were OK. Get some sleep now – you look like you could use it.'

He glanced down at her book on the coffee table. 'And don't stay up reading that goddamn thing all night, OK? You need your beauty rest.'

Dana raised her eyebrows at him; glad he'd lightened the mood again. 'Is that a fact?'

Eric chuckled and kissed her again. 'Nah, you look beautiful already. *I'm* the one who needs my beauty sleep. These bags under my eyes aren't doing a thing for my social life, I'll tell you that much. Anyway, I'll talk to you tomorrow, all right? Sweet dreams, kiddo.'

When Eric had left her apartment, Dana read Kubler-Ross for another half-hour before finally snapping the book shut and tossing it back onto the coffee table. To hell with it. She'd reached stage five of her research now.

She *accepted* the fact that she still didn't have the faintest goddamn clue what made the Cleveland Slasher tick. She also accepted the fact that the beer just wasn't cutting it any more.

Not even close.

CHAPTER SEVEN

South Central Los Angeles – 12:43 a.m.

The world to which Mary Ellen Orton awoke forty minutes later wasn't the safe haven of her dreams. No longer was she lost in a champagne-soaked realm where she passed dizzying hours each night folded into the arms of the most handsome young men in the ballroom. The world to which she now awoke was *very* different.

When she finally understood that the figure's black outline wasn't simply a benign construct of her dreams, a violent spasm of fear abruptly slammed her heart out of rhythm. One hard beat was immediately followed by two stronger beats, repeating the discordant thumping until she was afraid it would simply *stop*. Her doctors had been advising her for years now to get a pacemaker implanted but she'd always refused the procedure – thought the whole idea rather silly, really. She certainly didn't want a ridiculous chunk of metal protruding from her brittle breastbone and making an absurd little bump in her thin floral dresses. People would *know*.

But now she wished she had listened to the doctors. How she wished she had just *listened* to them.

As her watery vision gradually cleared, she could see that the figure was simply standing over her bed, his huge arms hanging limply by his sides.

He was an extremely large man, much larger than Jerry. Much larger than even Ed had been, and Ed had been a rather big, strong man in his day. She couldn't quite make out his face in the darkness, but his deep voice was exceptionally calm when he finally spoke.

'Don't scream, Mary Ellen,' he warned softly. 'Don't even move, OK? Because if you make a noise – or even move, for that matter – I'm going to have to hurt you very, very badly. Do you understand what I'm saying to you?'

Stunned, Mary Ellen could only nod dumbly in response, part of her not sure if this was even *real* yet. A dozen questions raced through her mind before suddenly slamming into each other and shattering into an indecipherable jumble of useless letters.

Who was this man? How had he gotten into her apartment? Most importantly, what was he going to do *to her?*

She tried to speak but no words would come out. The fear had completely paralysed her vocal cords, robbing them of all their strength.

Heart pounding madly in her throat, she swallowed dryly and tried again. 'How do you know my name?' she finally breathed. 'Who *are* you?'

Amazingly the large man actually *smiled*. She knew this only because she could see his bright white teeth gleaming at her through the darkness. They were unnaturally phosphorescent, sharp, pointed – like a vampire's.

By way of introduction, he removed the cap from his head and bowed quickly to her with the exaggerated flair of an accomplished actor, moving with a speed that belied his considerable size. 'Why, don't you know me, Mary Ellen? My name is Richard Ramirez. I'm the Night Stalker.'

For a brief moment she was thoroughly confused.

Richard Ramirez. The Night Stalker. She remembered the name. The serial killer. But wasn't he in prison? Or *dead*?

The large man in her room dismissed the question on her face with a quick wave of his hand. Turning to his side, he carelessly flung his baseball cap like a black Frisbee over into the corner, where it landed softly on a large pile of dirty clothes. He shook his head as though he didn't approve. 'You really should clean this place up, you know. No offence, my dear, but it's pretty fucking disgusting.'

Mary Ellen didn't answer him, *couldn't* have answered him if she'd tried. Her badly labouring heart was now pumping so much blood that she was sure she'd used up a week's worth of beats in the past minute alone. She wondered hazily how many she had left, wondered if the pacemaker might have saved at least a *few* of them. After all, every little bit probably counted now.

Silently praying to God, she slid a trembling hand beneath Ed's pillow, feeling for the gun she knew wasn't there. Ed was gone, had been for more than a decade now. His gun, too.

'Looking for something, my dear?'

Mary Ellen shook her head weakly, badly tweaking a tendon in her neck and sending an electric jolt of pain shooting down her left arm. *A heart attack?*

If only she were so lucky.

'What do you want from me?' she whispered hoarsely. 'I don't have any money. Are you going to *kill* me?'

Through the darkness she saw him shake his head slowly again, looking almost disappointed with her question, disappointed with *her*. His look *shamed* her.

'Don't be ridiculous,' he grunted, the smile gone now. 'Of course I'm not going to kill you.'

But the words had barely left his mouth before he was suddenly lunging out for her throat in a black flash of movement. Recoiling in horror, Mary Ellen squeezed her eyes tightly shut, mortified to feel her badly swollen bladder burst in a warm, wet rush of urine that flooded her cotton underwear and completely soaked the threadbare sheets below. Somehow she managed to feel even *more* shame through her terror. She was embarrassing herself badly, she knew, and she had always prided herself on the ability to make a good first impression.

Unbelievably, she felt absolutely no pain at all as she was brutally being murdered. Not even a pinprick. *Odd.* Whenever she'd watched similar stories on *Cold Case Files*, she'd always thought it would hurt like hell.

Tentatively opening one eye into a tiny quivering slit, to her complete astonishment she saw that he was still standing over her bed, had only been reaching for the lamp on her bedside table, not her throat.

He clucked his tongue in disapproval. 'I *told* you I wasn't going to kill you, Mary Ellen. I'll tell you what, my dear – you're really going to have to try to be a bit more trusting if you expect us to get along here tonight. I haven't even made you swear your love for Satan yet and this is how you treat me?'

In the pale yellow light of the bedside lamp, Mary Ellen finally saw his eyes. Brown. Glittering. *Insane.*

A lifelong devout Catholic, in that instant she no longer believed in a God or a heaven. But hell was a completely different matter altogether. She had no trouble believing in that at this exact moment. She was there now, she knew.

With the devil.

The huge lump of fear clogging her throat was making it impossible to breathe. She desperately tried to swallow it away, but knew she might as well have been trying to swallow away a softball at this point.

Even the smog would be a welcome relief now, she thought hazily. *Big, hot, poisonous lungfuls of it.*

Anything was better than the nothingness she was choking on now.

Mary Ellen watched numbly as the large man removed a sharp knife from the leather sheath on his belt and slowly twisted the black handle back and forth in his palm so that the silver blade glinted in the soft glow of her bedroom lamp.

An impotent whimper escaped her cracked lips. 'You said you weren't going to kill me,' she sobbed.

Another disgusted look and Mary Ellen felt the hot shame rush into her cheeks again.

Was it possible to die of sheer embarrassment?

'Oh, I was telling the truth about that,' he grunted, his throaty voice suddenly charged with an unmistakable sexual energy. 'You see, my dear, it's not *me* who's going to kill you; it's Richard Ramirez who's going to do the deed. But first he's going to rape you. Don't take it personally. We certainly don't find you *sexy* or anything. It's all just part of the script.'

'Part of what script?'

Everything happened so fast from there that Mary Ellen didn't even have time to scream. Quick as a rattlesnake he struck out, launching his enormous body through the air and landing down hard on top of her.

She finally heard herself screaming as her fragile pelvis

exploded into a thousand jagged pieces beneath the crushing impact of his two-hundred-pound frame. Bright white stars of agony danced in front of her eyes and a sudden burst of vomit erupted from her mouth, completely drenching the front of her thin nightgown. In the very next instant his heavy fist crashed down hard into her brittle eye socket, caving it in on itself like an eggshell beneath his thick knuckles. More stars came, these ones purple and green. With preternatural speed he tore the thin sheet from her weak grasp, roughly forced her trembling, varicose-veined thighs apart with his powerful legs and drew back his well-muscled arm.

With terrifying fluidity the knife violated her again and again. That was when the shock set in.

Through the haze of mind-numbing terror, Mary Ellen somehow remembered the Life Alert. With the last ounce of energy she had left in her dying body – as the razor-sharp knife viciously shredded her most intimate parts – she frantically pressed the button for help just a moment before her world went completely black.

As she slowly floated off into the inky darkness of her eternal dreams, Mary Ellen Orton was dancing again, back in Ed's strong arms as they moved across the dance floor.

She'd always saved the last dance for him.

CHAPTER EIGHT

Fear and excitement gripped Nathan Stiedowe's heart when the sirens came wailing up outside several minutes later. Sputtering, he realised this wasn't just a fantasy any more. This was really happening and he had to execute the plan perfectly from here.

He'd been watching the headlines out in Cleveland with great interest for three months now and couldn't help wondering how they'd report this murder in the LA papers. Maybe he'd finally start getting the recognition he so richly deserved. Maybe he'd finally get a decent moniker, too.

About fucking time.

He leaped off the old woman's broken body and rushed to the bedroom window, flinging the curtain aside. The metal fasteners screeched across the rod and crashed in his ears like the screams of a thousand tortured souls.

An ambulance?

Medical techs frantically wheeling a gurney in front of them over the cracked sidewalk were rushing toward her door and loudly calling out her name. 'Mary Ellen? We're coming, sweetheart! Just hold on, ma'am!'

Nathan had to act fast. Heart slamming in his throat, senses on *fire* with the importance of the moment, he raced over into the corner of the room and scooped the AC/DC baseball cap off the pile of dirty clothes before dashing into the living room and tacking a plastic convenience-store bag onto the wall. Latest round of breadcrumbs dropped, he managed to pull himself up through the same window he'd entered an hour earlier just a split second before they burst inside.

Phase One complete.

The rental car would be abandoned – part of the plan and the beginning of Phase Two. The most *important* phase. If he did this correctly, the Night Stalker's unforgettable murder would leap through the years and land on the top of the front page again.

The story of Richard Ramirez's downfall flashed through his mind as he tried to control his hammering heart.

After traveling to San Francisco to kill the ridiculously named Peter Pan – a sixty-six-year-old Chinese man from Lake Merced – the Night Stalker had moved on to Mission Viejo for his next kills. When he was unsuccessful in his attempt to murder twenty-nine-year-old Bill Carns and his twenty-seven-year-old girlfriend Renata Gunther, the girl had caught a glimpse of his licence plate as he sped away.

Authorities quickly traced the number to a stolen car that Ramirez dumped a short time later. When they lifted his fingerprints from the vehicle, the Night Stalker's downward spiral began in earnest.

Ramirez was buying groceries at a family-owned convenience store in Los Angeles a week later when he noticed his picture on the front page of the newspaper. Several patrons – including the husband of one of his earliest victims – immediately recognised him and the chase was on from there. It didn't last long.

Nathan shook his head in disgust as he made his way as

calmly as he could over to the murmuring crowd that had gathered in the street around the flashing blue lights.

'What in the hell happened in there?' a pretty young Latina asked him.

Nathan took a deep breath and raised himself up to his full height. He glared down at her menacingly. The young woman's eyes widened in horror as her stare ran over the length of his body.

Do it, bitch. Do it now. Say the words I need you to say.

And she did.

'There's blood all over him!' the young woman screamed.

A stunned silence hung in the air before several large men in the crowd suddenly reacted, angrily coming for Nathan with murder in their eyes. But he was ready for the assholes, had been the entire time, every muscle in his body corkscrewed and ready for action, the painful memory of all those hill repeats still carved deep into his powerful thighs.

In the blink of an eye he exploded right past their outstretched hands and knifed his way down the alleyway at the side of the building. Reminding himself to control his breathing, he unbuckled the leather sheath from his belt and jammed it hard into his sock before tearing away the breakaway athletic pants to reveal the clean jogging pants underneath.

The hours of intense physical training paid off handsomely as he easily left the would-be heroes eating his dust. But just to be absolutely certain, he continued running through backyards and hopping over fences for the next twenty minutes, periodically lifting his stare to the sky to see if the LAPD had a chopper in the air. They didn't, of course. Incompetent fools.

When Nathan was finally out of breath, he stopped behind an abandoned old warehouse at the west end of town and lifted the cap off his head to mop at his heavily sweating brow with one muscular forearm.

His sides ached as he quickly stripped off the bloody shirt and tossed it to the ground. The grey undershirt he'd been wearing beneath was ringed with sweat but otherwise bore no evidence of the brutal murder he'd just committed.

No one had caught him. They hadn't even come close. A little goddamn *discipline* was all it had taken to get the job done right.

Panting as he leaned over and supported his weight on his trembling thighs, Nathan dropped the baseball cap to the ground. The fierce AC/DC logo glared up at him. After a moment, he smiled down at it.

Success.

Two hours later the taxicab dropped Nathan off at the cheap motel. The high was still with him as he walked back into his room. His body felt light, tingly, like flames were licking his skin.

As he settled in for the night, he rewarded himself for his flawless performance by slowly masturbating to the memory of Mary Ellen Orton's delicious terror. The others liked to take physical souvenirs from the scene – which was about the *stupidest* thing you could do in a situation like this – but all *he* needed were the graphic mental images he'd collected on the night.

The colours exploded in his mind in a rainbow of light. The whites of the old woman's terrified eyes. The purplish bruising from where he'd punched her hard in the face. The silver flash of his sharp knife. But none of the colours were as truly beautiful as the fluid that had sprayed forth from between the old woman's legs.

60

Blood red. His very favourite colour of them all.

His body gradually stiffened as the erotic images played in his mind. A moment later, he ejaculated hard all over his well-muscled stomach.

Nathan lay in bed for a long while after that, idly tracing the sticky semen across his ripped midsection with one long finger. Exhausted, *satisfied*, he finally rose to clean himself up. As the steaming shower water poured down over his body, he steeled himself to resume the hunt.

He was proud of himself for knowing *exactly* how to lure his target into his web. The thieving little bitch who had stolen his life wasn't the only expert on serial killers out there, after all, and starting with tonight's festivities his actions were sure to draw her to him like a fly drawn to honey. Once she pieced together all the little clues he'd been leaving for her over the past three months, he knew she wouldn't be able to resist.

Nathan sighed contentedly as he slowly drifted off into a dream-filled sleep with a satisfied smile playing across his full lips. He knew she was out there somewhere, just waiting for him.

Hell, he could almost hear the stupid little bitch *begging* him to come back into her life.

CHAPTER NINE

A splitting headache.

That was your reward for killing two beers and a bottle of Jim Beam by yourself.

It had taken most of the night to erase the gruesome images of Jacinda Holloway's mutilated corpse from her mind. But Dana had kept at it, finally drinking herself into enough of a stupor to pass out at four o'clock in the morning.

In her dream, the man with the sharp silver knife and strange brown eyes has come to visit her again. She is four years old and he is standing over her bed in the dead of night, just like he always does. Reaching down, he softly strokes her silky blonde hair as she sleeps.

Lost in that confusing middle-world somewhere between sleep and consciousness, Dana mumbles something to him, imagining it is her father, James, who is standing over her bed to protect her from the monsters in her dreams.

But the man in the room with her is not her father. The man in her room is someone different.

The very monster of her dreams come to life.

The jarring sound of the telephone jolted Dana awake. She groaned as her eyelids slowly fluttered open and she

62

realised her head was throbbing like a jackhammer. Jim Beam might have been just dandy to hop into bed with, but he sure as hell wasn't the kind of guy you wanted to wake up with the following morning.

Dana winced at the excruciating pain in her temples. Her drinking was really starting to get out of control now. She'd never been a complete teetotaller, of course, but neither had she drunk like this since her college days.

Bright shafts of early-morning sunlight streamed through the bedroom window and stabbed her brain through her eyeballs. The intense hammer-party going on in her skull right now was enough to make even the soft sound of the answering machine clicking on feel like a gun blast exploding in her tender ears.

Hello. You have reached Dana Whitestone. I am unable to take your call right now, but if you leave a detailed message I'll get back to you as soon as possible. Thank you, and have a nice day.

Beep!

The voice on the other end of the line slapped her in the face like a bucket of ice water. 'Dana, it's Gary Templeton. Just got word on Jacinda Holloway's autopsy. You're not going to believe this. Call me back as soon as you possibly can.'

Her heart kick-started by a dizzying rush of adrenalin, Dana removed the handset from its plastic cradle and quickly punched in Templeton's number.

He answered on the third ring. 'Templeton here.'

'Gary, it's Dana. What's up?'

Templeton blew out a slow breath. 'Just heard back from the coroner,' he said. 'There's no way of putting this nicely, so I'll just come out and say it. Apparently the broom handle was used to shove little plastic letters up into Jacinda Holloway's uterus. You know, the letters with the magnets on the back? The kind you put your kid's picture up on the refrigerator with?'

Dana sucked in a sharp breath and reached for a notebook sitting on her nightstand. 'What were the letters?' she asked, fully awake now.

Templeton quickly ticked them off. 'An *N*, an *L*, a *G*, a *B*, two *A*'s and an *I*.'

'Any idea what they mean?'

'Not a clue. Just heard back from the coroner about ten minutes ago and I haven't had time to process it yet. Probably spells out a word, I would imagine. Which one, I have no idea.'

'Were the letters all the same colour?'

Templeton seemed surprised by the question. 'No, as a matter of fact they weren't. Most were different. One for each colour of the rainbow. Two red ones. Why?'

'No matter.' Dana's mind cleared. 'Get court orders to exhume the other four bodies,' she said. 'I want complete autopsies on all of them, Gary. I don't care what you have to do. Pull strings, call in favours – just get it done as quickly as possible.'

'I'm on it.'

Dana thanked him and switched off. In her notebook, she began rearranging the letters. After ten minutes the only two combinations that made any sense to her were 'NAIL BAG' and 'BAG IN LA'.

Which was to say they didn't make the least goddamn bit of sense at all.

She'd resisted making the call many times since she'd moved back to Cleveland, wanting to prove she could go it alone, but perhaps now was the time to ask one of the sharpest minds in the FBI for help.

She picked up the phone again and punched in the number for Crawford Bell in Washington DC. She desperately needed whatever help she could get before another little girl died a gruesome death. And they'd been a good team once.

He picked up after five rings. 'Bell here.'

After a brief exchange of 'how are yous' Dana got straight to the point. Crawford wasn't one for small talk and this wasn't a social call. She filled him in as quickly as she could on what Templeton had just told her.

'They're significant, otherwise the killer wouldn't have left them like that,' Crawford said. 'Let me think.'

Dana heard him scribbling on a pad on his end.

'No, I'm not having any luck,' he said after a short pause. 'My brain isn't as sharp these days as it used to be. What do you think the letters mean?'

'No idea,' Dana admitted. 'I've tried everything. The only two things I can come up with are NAIL BAG and BAG IN LA. And what does that tell us? Zip.'

Crawford let out a shocked breath. 'Holy shit, Dana. It can't be a coincidence. Wait a minute.'

She heard him moving papers around as though he was looking for something. Then, 'Here it is. Look, I think you should come down here to DC,' he added unexpectedly.

Dana shook her head. What was he talking about? 'Absolutely not, Crawford. I'm in the middle of a case, with little if anything to go on. I really can't afford to take time out to go down there.'

'I know, but it would be easier to discuss the case face to face. Besides, there's someone here I think you *really* need to meet.'

'Crawford, I've told you – I don't have time—'

He cut her off. 'Dana, it's important. You should meet him.'

'Who's that, then?' she asked reluctantly. Crawford seemed serious so she might as well hear him out.

'Jeremy Brown,' Crawford replied. 'He works out of LA but flew in this morning to pick my brain about a murder out there last night. Just so happens that the killer tacked a plastic bag to the wall at the scene, Dana. Could be connected. Probably is.'

Now he had her full attention. Dana couldn't believe her ears. 'NAIL BAG and BAG IN LA,' she said. 'He was pointing us out to LA. It's the same guy.'

'That's what I'm thinking,' Crawford said. 'So can you come down to DC to meet Brown? I think you should.'

Dana winced again at the headache pounding away at her temples, and not just from her hangover. She thought for a moment as Crawford waited impatiently for her answer. Things had just gotten a whole lot more complicated, but could she really spare the time to go to DC? Templeton was good. He could cover for her. This could be a crucial lead or a blind alley but there was only one way to find out. And if Crawford felt she should go, she probably should – he wasn't in the habit of wasting people's time, least of all his own. It might be a slightly odd request, when she could easily speak to this Jeremy Brown on the phone, but she'd take the risk. She had to. She flipped her cellphone open and punched in the number for American Airlines. Although the feds had access to the Department of Justice's forty-million-dollar Gulfstream V, it sure as hell wasn't based in Cleveland. Like most of her colleagues, Dana had to use her own money to purchase tickets through one of the commercial airlines the government had contracts with and submit receipts for reimbursement later.

'Booking my ticket now,' she told Crawford. 'I'll be down there tonight.'

CHAPTER TEN

In Nathan's dream he is seven years old again.

It is 1961 in West Virginia, and he and Jamie Hufford are playing with Matchbox cars in her parents' sweltering barn.

Once a month their parents would get together for Bible study – *fellowship*, they called it – and the kids were allowed an hour to themselves. Neither were permitted toys of any kind, of course – the devil's playthings, their parents called them – but the last time they'd been together he and Jamie had found a plastic bag filled with rusted-out miniature Chevrolets, Jeeps and pickup trucks hidden in the woods along the edge of her rural property. They'd immediately stashed the bag in the barn and made a solemn vow never to tell another living soul about their sinful discovery.

The temperature in the barn could soar past a hundred degrees in the middle of August, like it was now, and the sweat would pour down their faces as they played. Old farming equipment and an antique drum used for storing heating oil littered the inside of the structure like enormous skeletons in a dinosaur graveyard.

Dusty rays of sunlight streamed down through the slats in the barn's roof as Nathan quickly wheeled a 1957 Chevy around an old wooden toolbox. 'You'll never catch me, coppers!' he shouted. 'All the money from the bank is mine!'

Jamie brushed her sweaty blonde hair out of her face and chased the Chevrolet with a boxy police car missing its rear-left wheel. She was an extremely thin girl with very bad teeth, and her sundress was dirty and tattered. As usual, no shoes covered her filthy feet. 'The good guys always catch the bad guys,' she giggled. 'We're taking you to jail, mister!'

The patrol car was catching up to the Chevy fast, so Nathan wheeled it around the toolbox twice more before blasting into overdrive and rising to his feet. His right foot slipped on something hidden beneath the hay.

'Caught you!' Jamie squealed, slamming the police cruiser hard into the Chevrolet in Nathan's hand to underscore her point. 'Now it's time for you go to jail, buddy!'

Nathan ignored her and swept his foot over the hay.

A book of matches.

'What is it?' Jamie asked, following his gaze down to the floor of the barn.

Nathan gritted his teeth. Why in the hell did girls always have to be so goddamn *stupid*? 'What do you think it is, dummy?' he snapped.

Jamie frowned. After a moment, her lower lip began to tremble and tears filled her eyes. 'Don't call me a dummy, Nathan. Don't call me a dummy or I'm telling on you.'

Nathan felt his stomach lurch. Jesus Christ, girls were so goddamn *sensitive* too. But when it came to his parents, getting told on was a fate worse than death, so he quickly switched gears.

'No, don't tell on me, Jamie,' he said. 'I'm really sorry. I didn't mean it. You're not a dummy. But seriously, don't you know what this is?'

The little girl rolled her enormous blue eyes at him. 'Of course I know what it is, dummy. It's a book of matches. And we better go tell that we found them or we'll be in big trouble for sure.'

Nathan sighed. Leave it to a girl to ruin what was obviously going to be a very good time. Stupid, sensitive and then stupid again – that was what girls were. No matter how long he lived, he knew he would never understand them. It was almost like they were from a different planet or something.

'We can't tell them about the matches because we didn't tell them about the cars,' he explained patiently. 'If we tell them about the matches they'll just know we have the cars and we'll get a whipping twice as bad.'

Jamie didn't look so sure. 'We'll get it three times as bad if they catch us,' she countered.

Nathan forced a smile and reached out a hand, placing it on her bare shoulder. 'They're not going to catch us, Jamie. I promise.'

He paused while the plan formed in his brain. 'I'll tell you what: let's see if the matches work first. If they work then we'll go tell that we found them. But if they don't they'll just be mad we bothered them in the first place.'

Jamie chewed on her lower lip while she thought it over. It *did* seem to make sense. 'OK,' she agreed finally. 'But how do we do know if they work or not?'

Nathan leaned down and plucked the matchbook off the floor. 'I've seen the preacher lighting the candles in church before. I'll try and do it the same way.'

He pulled out a match and scratched it against the rough

strip on the back cover. The head of the match disintegrated in little bits of red.

The second match didn't work either, but produced a sulphur smell that tickled Nathan's nostrils in a pleasant way.

'P.U.,' Jamie said, holding her nose.

The third match flared up briefly before burning out. Tendrils of smoke drifted up from the burned paper.

'Well?' Jamie asked impatiently. 'Do they work or not?'

Nathan tried to keep the irritation out of his voice. As much as she annoyed him, though, he couldn't risk getting told on. He hadn't had a whipping in a week now, and he wanted to keep it that way. 'I *think* they work,' he said, 'but I'm not sure yet. We'll have to light them all at the same time to find out for sure.'

Jamie nodded. Again, it *seemed* to make sense. 'What will we do when they're all lit up?'

'We'll jump our cars over them just like the motorcycle daredevils at the state fair.'

The little girl still looked uneasy, glancing around the barn to make sure no one was watching. 'OK. Just hurry up and do it already before we get caught.'

Nathan plucked out another match and slid it across the scratch-strip. The head of the match popped, flickered for a moment, then finally caught hold.

'Hurry,' Jamie urged.

Nathan kicked a space in the hay and dropped the matchbook on the floor. Leaning down, he carefully applied the burning match to the rest. The entire book immediately went up in flames.

'C'mon,' he said. 'We have to hurry.'

They knelt down on the floor of the barn and jumped

their cars over the burning matches for thirty seconds before Nathan's ears suddenly began to ring.

He looked over at Jamie and grinned. 'Hey, wanna play another game?'

The little girl didn't notice the swirling in his dark brown eyes. 'What game's that?'

'You go up into the loft with the police car and jump it down after the bank robber from there. It'll be just like Robert Mitchum in *Thunder Road*. You be the cops and I'll be Robert Mitchum.'

'Who's Robert Mitchum?'

'The actor in the movie.'

'What movie?'

'*Thunder Road*.'

'What's *Thunder Road*?'

Nathan sighed. 'Just go up into the loft, Jamie. It's gonna be a lot of fun, I promise.'

The little girl brushed her sweaty blonde hair out of her face with both hands and picked up the police car before heading toward the loft. She looked over her shoulder at him as she climbed the rickety ladder. 'OK, but this better be a *lot* of fun, Nathan. If it's not, then I'm definitely telling on you.'

Nathan nodded. 'OK, just go up into the loft already. It's going to be so much fun, I promise. Just wait, you'll see.'

The little girl ascended the ladder and looked down at him from above. She was afraid of heights, but Nathan had promised a good time, so she was willing to take a chance. 'Now what?' she asked.

Nathan waved a hand in the air. 'Hold on a minute, OK? I have to do something real quick before we can start.'

He walked over to the ladder and pulled it away from the

entrance to the loft before making his way back over to where she could see him.

'Now what?' Jamie repeated.

'Now we have some *real* fun,' Nathan said.

He was very careful not to burn his fingers as he picked the matchbook up by one corner and pressed it against the hay covering the floor of the barn. The hay smoked for a moment, then burst into bright orange flames.

'Hey!' Jamie shouted down from the loft. 'What are you doing down there? Is this part of the game?'

Nathan smiled up at her. 'Sure is, Jamie. Just stay up there a minute, OK? I have to go get something from outside, and then we can play *Thunder Road*.'

'What's *Thunder Road*?' Jamie whined.

But Nathan only smiled as he pulled the barn doors closed behind him. Inside, the fire began to spread. Thirty seconds later it reached the metal drum filled with heating oil.

The deafening explosion ripped both doors off the barn. A tractor wheel shot fifty feet into the air. The blue sky instantly turned black.

He quickly worked up an eyeful of tears as he ran toward the farmhouse to get their parents. He had to tell them that Jamie had insisted on playing with the matches even though he'd begged her not to. She just wouldn't *listen* to him, he'd say.

The whipping that night nearly flayed the skin off his backside, but it had been well worth it. If he lived another hundred years, Nathan didn't think he'd ever see *anybody* die hotter than little Jamie Hufford.

CHAPTER ELEVEN

Cleveland – Hopkins International Airport – 3:30 p.m.

Dana exited a yellow cab outside the busy terminal, flipped her cellphone open and punched in a number. A deep voice answered.

'Templeton.'

'Gary,' she said to the Cleveland cop. 'It's Dana Whitestone. Something's come up and I'm gonna have to go to DC, I'm afraid. I'm really sorry. You're in charge while I'm gone, OK? Can you keep me updated on any developments? I'll be on my cell.'

'What's going on?' He sounded temporarily panicked. 'We're in the middle of a case; we need you here. How long are you going to be gone for?'

Dana filled him in as quickly as she could on the possible connection to the murder out in LA. 'I'm not sure where all this is going to lead, but if there's a connection I'll probably head out to Los Angeles with this Jeremy Brown guy to investigate the scene if I can get the proper clearance. How's it coming along with the court orders for those other four autopsies?'

'Still working on it,' Templeton said, happier now that he understood the situation. 'Should hear something back any time now. I'll call you. Good luck.'

Dana stepped off the kerb just in time to avoid getting

run over by a beeping motorised baggage cart piloted by a bored-looking black man in his late fifties and wearing white earmuffs and a scraggly grey beard. 'Thanks, Gary,' she said, casting an irritated glance at the driver of the cart, who gave her a disinterested look in return. 'I really appreciate all your help.'

She switched off her call to Templeton. Once again she wondered if she was doing the right thing by heading off like this at Crawford's beck and call. Then she reminded herself of Crawford's phenomenal instinct for the tiny details that could crack a case wide open. If he thought she should go to DC then chances were he was right. Any possible clue, however small, that might lead them closer to this brutal killer had to be worth it, whatever the inconvenience to her or anyone else. She picked up the overnight bag at her feet and entered the bustling terminal. Inside, harried-looking mothers dragged small children behind them while businessmen in rumpled suits thumbed through slender copies of *Fortune* magazine. Bundled-up vacationers and college students wearing North Face backpacks hustled to their respective destinations with the heavy smell of Starbucks coffee hanging in the air.

When she'd been younger – never an especially happy time in her life following the untimely deaths of her parents – Dana had nonetheless always found airports hopelessly romantic. Without fail she'd fall in love at least three times in ten minutes, wondering where certain young men were off to in such a hurry. Were they on vacation? Off to attend a business seminar in Las Vegas? Rushing to be reunited with their estranged parents, whom they hadn't seen or spoken to in more than ten years? The possibilities were always endless, and they let Dana's imagination run wild, giving her mind a welcome break from the cold realities of her everyday life.

These days her everyday life seemed to consist of little more than work, work and still more work. A few months ago she'd joined a Thursday-night pottery class at the YMCA in the hopes of meeting some new people on a social level, but she'd found it hopelessly boring. She'd always enjoyed art in college, but shaping ashtrays out of clay just didn't appeal to her all that much. Not only did she not smoke, if she *had* smoked she could've easily picked up a ten-pack of cheap plastic ashtrays at Wal-Mart for a measly five bucks. What was the fucking point? Besides, the class had been filled with people just like her – lonely women rapidly approaching middle age who seemed more interested in finding a man to take them away from the drudgery of it all than in fashioning another useless trinket out of clay to clutter up the house.

It was forty-five minutes before Dana made it through the security line and another half-hour before she finally settled into her seat on the plane next to a middle-aged businessman wearing an immaculate blue suit and what smelled like at least two gallons of expensive cologne. Dana's eyes watered as she tried to identify the scent. No luck.

Ten minutes later the plane raced down the runway and lifted off into the air, shooting sharp little thrills through her stomach. She looked out the window and watched Cleveland disappear behind them in a fog of grey and white.

When they were flying at thirty thousand feet, Dana dug the morning edition of the *Plain Dealer* out of her overnight bag and read quickly through the grisly account of Jacinda Holloway's brutal murder again, wondering if the Cleveland Slasher was reading the same story at this exact moment, reliving his horrible crimes over and over again in his mind. No doubt the sick bastard was getting a charge out of the coverage he was receiving. If it were the last thing she ever did in this life, Dana would shove it all down his throat and make him choke on it when she finally caught the motherfucker.

And she *would* catch him. She had absolutely no doubt about that. She *always* caught them. From the child pornographer in southern Virginia to the gunrunners operating out of the Port of Miami to the meth-dealing motorcycle gang she'd helped bring down in Pennsylvania, she'd never *not* solved a case that she'd worked on, and she had absolutely no intention of ruining her perfect record over this murdering son of a bitch.

Above all others, though, it was killers that Dana wanted the most. Nothing more than sick animals whose only motive was to hurt the innocent. Even though they might not know it as they drifted off to sleep each night in their Strawberry Shortcake nightgowns, little girls all around Cleveland were counting on people like Dana to make sure the animals didn't hurt *them* too.

In addition to her current case, she'd worked on three other notable serial-killer cases during her thirteen-year career with the Bureau. She'd cut her teeth in DC as a junior agent working on the task force assigned to tracking down John Muhammad and Lee Boyd Malvo, the serial snipers who'd perpetrated the Beltway attacks along Interstate 95 in the Washington area in 2002, leaving ten people dead and three more seriously injured. That had been when she'd first met Crawford Bell. It had been a major turning point in her career, not to mention her life. For some reason he'd taken a special interest in her professional life, taking her under his wing and teaching her everything he knew about serial killers and how they operated.

'I just like your face,' he told her once when she asked him why. 'You remind me of my daughter.'

Dana had winced at that, knowing that Crawford had lost a wife and daughter to murder as a young man. That loss had prompted him to join the FBI, much like her own loss had driven *her* to join the Bureau. The three years of requisite full-time work experience in a criminal psychologist's office after college couldn't pass fast enough for Dana before she'd happily bolted for the FBI. After that, it was all killers, all the time.

When they'd finally caught up with Muhammad and Malvo, she and Crawford had worked closely on two other notable serial-killer cases during her time in DC – cases that the media inexplicably decided were unworthy of much attention. In her heart of hearts, Dana suspected she knew the reason for the lack of coverage, though. Probably because all the victims in both cases were black prostitutes, and if you didn't have fair skin, blonde hair and blue eyes – which was to say if you weren't *white* – you just didn't get all that much ink. That was the sad reality of a press corps constantly seeking the next big sensational story to increase readership and viewership, and hence charge higher rates for advertising. Money ruled the world.

Dana and Crawford's professional relationship had become extremely close while they'd been working those three investigations, and their personal relationship had become even closer. Probably a little too close, to tell the truth. There was nothing physical about it, of course, but

Dana eventually found herself relying on Crawford's expertise a little too much, unable but to wonder if it was stunting her own growth as an agent.

When Crawford had been pushed into a teaching role because of his age, Dana applied for and was granted a transfer to Cleveland. She'd wanted to spread her wings and fly on her own, and Cleveland was the place where she'd started out in this world. Maybe it would also be the place where she finally found some goddamn peace.

She'd felt bad for Crawford when he'd been taken out of the field, of course. After all, chasing killers was what had kept him going for thirty years after the brutal murders of his wife and daughter. Still, Dana was also secretly relieved finally to step out of his enormous shadow and make a name for herself.

She folded the newspaper back up with a sigh and tucked it into her bag before flicking through her notebook for the remainder of the flight. The businessman was preoccupied with his own work, but Dana was careful not to open the notebook too wide. She'd learned a valuable lesson when a young child had once asked her what she was reading, looking eagerly at the gruesome details scribbled across the page.

Now she revisited the details of Jacinda Holloway's brutal murder over and over again in her mind until she thought her head would explode. No matter how many times she went over the information, nothing was adding up. It was like one of those unsolvable maths equations that sadistic professors foisted upon their earnest students, telling them only at the end of the semester that there *was* no answer.

When her plane finally touched down at Ronald Reagan

International Airport two hours later, Dana caught a cab over to Quantico and headed straight for the indoor shooting range to blow off some steam. She wasn't due to meet Crawford until a bit later – she reckoned she might as well put the time to good use. During her time stationed in DC, the shooting range had been the place to which she'd always come while working on a particularly difficult case, and this current case was rapidly shaping up to be the hardest one of her entire career.

Twenty minutes later she was peering down the sight of her Glock-17 and squeezing off three shots in quick succession. The metallic ring of shell casings hitting the concrete floor echoed throughout the otherwise deserted shooting range for a moment, and then everything went silent once more. She paused and aimed the gun again. Three more shots rang out.

Taking off her standard-issue yellow-tinted Wiley X shooting glasses, Dana removed her hearing protection and pressed the button to activate the pulley system that would bring the paper target to her. Fifteen seconds later she was examining the tight pattern of bullet holes in the target's head and chest areas.

Dana closed her eyes and wiped a line of perspiration from her forehead, picturing a face at the top of the target. A face she didn't know at all and yet saw every day. Weird how your mind could make something you so desperately wanted to forget the only thing you could remember.

She snapped a fresh magazine into the Glock and clipped a fresh target into place while running through the case in her mind again. Everything from finding the first dead body in a garbage dumpster behind a grocery store in September to the discovery of Jacinda Holloway's mutilated corpse on the east side of Cleveland the previous night.

Each of the little girls had been sexually molested, but not in a *sexual* way. In each instance the vaginal tearing had been caused by a foreign object. No semen – no DNA *at all* – had been collected from any of the bodies.

The Cleveland Slasher was a very careful man; that much was clear. And unlike some of the other killers that Dana had come across in the past, he obviously had zero interest in getting caught.

The lack of DNA on the bodies didn't necessarily mean he wasn't getting a sexual charge out of the murders, though. Most serial killers got their pleasure out of the feeling of control they exerted over their victims, not from the sexual act itself.

Still, how was he not leaving *any* trace of himself behind at the scenes? It was almost impossible not to do so in this age of advanced forensics.

Unless, of course, you happened to know *exactly* what the authorities would be looking for. Of course, anyone could claim to be an expert these days with all the TV shows and books on the subject but this killer knew all the extra little details that only someone closer to an actual case could know. Either that or he was very smart indeed.

Dana's heartbeat quickened as a thought occurred to her. It was unlikely that anyone would be so audacious but she made a mental note to have background checks run on everybody who'd been involved in processing the crime scenes up to this point. She berated herself for not thinking of it earlier. If Crawford had taught her anything it was to not leave anything out. However fanciful or unlikely something might seem, sometimes that was where the truth could lie. She couldn't afford to ignore any thought or hunch, however random. Not when people's lives depended on her doing her job properly.

When the fresh target was in place fifty feet away, she quickly riddled it with bullets again. This time they all went to the head.

Ten minutes later Dana exited the shooting range and made her away across campus to the packed lecture hall. It was as if she'd never been away – everything was so familiar. Inside, close to a hundred students were listening to Crawford Bell explain the bizarre circumstances that had surrounded the case of a notorious serial killer known as 'Don Juan'.

It was the same lecture he gave to all students, of course, but Dana was always amazed at his ability to bring a fresh slant to each lecture he gave, the way he was always able to make things sound new and interesting again. No wonder the man was a *New York Times* best-selling author five times over. The guy was *good*. Captured the bad guys like Eliot Ness and then wrote about it like Truman Capote. A pretty potent combination, to say the least.

She watched him from the back of the hall. He hadn't changed in the months since she'd last seen him – physically, anyway – but there was something different about him. It was probably only visible to her because she knew him so well, or thought she did, but she detected a slightly distracted look in his eyes, his demeanour. And then it was gone. Perhaps she'd imagined it.

Crawford ended his lecture five minutes later and dismissed the class with a quick wave of his hand, which caused the simple gold wedding band on his left ring finger to flash in the bright overhead lights. Crawford might have been a widower for more than thirty years now, but the ring had never left his finger once. Dana's mentor and former partner might have been a lot of different things to a lot of different people, but *unfaithful* sure wasn't one of them.

He nodded at Dana as she crossed the wooden lecture-hall stage and made her way to his side, his manner indicating that he was almost surprised she'd actually come, which momentarily disarmed her. Then he turned and introduced her to the thin man with sandy brown hair and a boyish face sprinkled with freckles who was standing next to him.

'Special Agent Dana Whitestone, this is Special Agent Jeremy Brown.'

Dana and Brown shook hands.

Ever brusque, Crawford said, 'Now that we've all been properly introduced, Jeremy, perhaps you'll fill Dana in on what we've got going on?'

Brown cleared his throat. 'Yes, sir. Of course.' Turning to Dana, he said, 'Rather strange development in Los Angeles, Dana – if I may call you that.'

'Of course. No need for formalities here.'

'Great. Call me Jeremy.'

Brown spoke in a clipped professional tone as he ticked off the details. There was no time for idle chit-chat now. 'A seventy-nine-year-old woman was brutally murdered last night in South Central. She lived in a ground-floor apartment by herself. The victim's son lived in the apartment above her. The assailant entered through an open living-room window and raped her with a knife. The suspect left a vehicle behind at the scene – a rented 2004 Audi 3000 convertible. It's being processed now, but a preliminary check didn't yield anything. Was rented to a Darrell Wayne Baxter of Marin

County last Friday. Problem is, Darrell Wayne Baxter of Marin County died of a massive coronary two years ago. After the murder, our suspect successfully fled a small crowd attempting to give chase on foot. Ring any bells to you?'

'The Night Stalker,' Dana answered automatically as she felt the hair on the back of her neck rise. 'Fits perfectly. A copycat?'

Crawford was looking across the hall as if he was lost in thought. Then he loosened the perfect Windsor knot in the silk necktie at his throat and nodded. 'Exactly what I was thinking, Dana. Please go on, Jeremy.'

Brown turned back to Dana. 'Yes, sir. This is actually kind of weird, Dana, but there was also a plastic bag tacked to the woman's living-room wall. The kind they give you at a convenience store.'

Dana frowned. 'Crawford told me about that. Was there any lettering on the bag? What store's it from?'

Brown shook his head. 'Don't know. No lettering – just plain blue plastic. No way to trace it. At least, none that I know of. I heard about the letters inside the little girl in Cleveland. The anagrams you came up with would seem to connect the cases.'

'Yeah, but for what purpose?' Dana asked. 'Are we reading too much into it all? These clues really aren't clues at all. Kind of like the picture in Cleve—'

She stopped suddenly and turned to Crawford. 'I know what the larger photograph in Cleveland is,' she said quickly. 'Goddamn it, I know *exactly* what it is.'

Crawford looked at her, puzzled. 'What are you talking about?'

'Come with me,' Dana said. 'I've got something you guys need to see.'

84

She led Crawford and Brown out of the lecture hall and back across campus to a place where she'd spent hundreds of hours during her time as a student at the Academy.

The FBI library was located in a four-storey building in the centre of the dormitory complex, always the hub of activity at the Academy. Four reading rooms on the first floor offered comfortable chairs and tables for study or relaxation. The second floor contained the book collection and lounge chairs for readers. Internet stations were scattered throughout.

Dana, Crawford and Brown were seated in front of a computer terminal as roughly two dozen students stopped what they were doing and turned to stare at them, most of the stares fixed squarely on Crawford. It wasn't often that the King came down from on high to mix with the commoners, but Dana sincerely hoped none of them were taking counter-intelligence roles after graduation. Subtlety didn't exactly seem to be this particular group's forte.

A nervous-looking man approached and handed Crawford a glass of water. He frowned and immediately placed it down on the table next to the computer. 'Thank you,' he said.

Dana shook her head as the man scurried away. Stretching her fingers, she found the home row and quickly pecked 'Richard Ramirez Pentagram Photograph' into the search bar on 'Server in the Sky', a joint database that the FBI shared with senior British police officials which held photographs and vital statistics for millions of criminals and suspects.

The second picture was the one that Dana was after. 'There it is,' she said triumphantly, leaning back in her chair and running a hand through her hair while she double-clicked on the photograph.

Outfitted in a dark blue jumpsuit, Richard Ramirez was holding his left palm up to the camera lens to display the crudely drawn pentagram he'd sported during his trial. Scraggly black hair framed a ghost-white face featuring hollow cheeks sucked in below dark, soulless eyes. A half-smile covered his face, which surprisingly enough had been considered handsome enough for no fewer than half a dozen women to actually propose *marriage* to the Night Stalker at the height of his infamy. A pretty young woman named Doreen had eventually won the sadistic killer's black heart.

Dana dragged the thumbnail onto the desktop and selected the section featuring Ramirez's palm before blowing it up.

Crawford leaned forward in his seat and stared at the image on the screen. 'Well, I'll be goddamned,' he said. 'Perfect replica of the photograph in Cleveland. He was telling us where he was going to strike next.'

Dana nodded. 'Guess he thought the plastic letters inside Jacinda Holloway's uterus were a little too subtle for us to pick up on. Wanted to make damn sure we didn't miss his message.'

'So what does the convenience-store bag tell us?' Crawford asked. 'Where's he going to strike next?'

'No idea.'

'Try typing it into the search bar.'

'Typing what?'

'I don't know. Try "Plastic Bag Serial Killer."'

Dana did as she was instructed. Exactly point-eleven seconds later a hundred and thirteen thousand results popped up. She turned in her seat and gave her former partner a doleful look. 'I'll take the first fifty-six thousand or so if you guys'll take the rest.'

Crawford tossed her a look of his own before glancing down at his expensive watch. 'Hey, it was worth a shot.' He looked down at his watch again, then turned to Dana as if he had something he wanted to say to her specifically but couldn't find the words. Dana finally looked away first, embarrassed by his scrutiny. There was *definitely* something different about Crawford. She just couldn't say what.

Crawford took a sip of water, collected himself and said, 'So what's next? Where do you guys go from here?'

Dana fiddled with her necklace. 'I'd like to go out to LA with Jeremy here, if that's OK with him. I'd like to take a look at that crime scene.'

Brown nodded. 'Of course, Dana. I could use whatever help I can get.'

'We both could.' Dana turned back to Crawford. 'Could you clear it with Headquarters for me?'

'Not a problem.'

'Thanks. Could you also start compiling a profile for me? I know you're probably very busy but I'd really appreciate it. I thought I could handle this on my own. My mistake.'

Crawford smiled briefly. 'Don't be so hard on yourself, Dana. This is a tough case you're working on. Anyway, I'll start compiling the profile tonight. Should have something for you in the next couple of days.'

He looked down at his watch again before rising to his feet, which sent the two dozen gawking students running for their lives between the towering stacks of books. 'Now get out of here,' he said. 'You two have a plane to catch first thing in the morning and I've got somewhere I need to be.

I'll get the office to arrange the airline tickets and a couple of rooms for you over at the Radisson; so don't worry about that. Just go get some sleep.'

Forty-five minutes later – after agreeing to meet Brown outside the hotel entrance in the morning – Dana let herself into her room. She stayed up for two more hours researching even the most minor details of Richard Ramirez's horrific murders until she thought she'd go blind. She finally crawled into bed and pulled the comforter up over her body.

Her mind reeled from the events of the past couple of days – not to mention the horrific events of her past. As her tiredness finally overcame her, she wondered if the two had somehow become connected in her mind. Perhaps it wasn't surprising. After all, Dana knew of another little girl who'd once had a terrifying run-in with a killer. A little girl still trapped inside her mind who was screaming out desperately for justice.

Dana turned on her side and adjusted the pillow beneath her head. Her eyelids drooped. Slowly drifting back in time, she allowed herself to enjoy the one memory from her childhood that wasn't completely soaked in blood.

CHAPTER TWELVE

West Park section of Cleveland – 4 July 1976

Dusk darkened the summer sky as James Whitestone bar-becued hot dogs and hamburgers on a rusty outdoor grill. He flipped a burger expertly with a quick flick of his wrist and used the spatula to motion to the sandbox where Dana was playing quietly. He spelled out the word to his wife so that their only child wouldn't know what they were talking about. Although she was a precocious and highly intelligent little girl, Dana had yet to completely master the tricky art of spelling.

'Think we could let her hold a *S-P-A-R-K-L-E-R* when it gets all the way dark out?' he asked. 'She's been bugging me about it for weeks now.'

Sara Whitestone slid her sunglasses down the bridge of her slender nose and raised one perfectly groomed eyebrow in her husband's direction. 'Yeah, right, James. *You*'re the one who's been bugging me about it for weeks now and you know it.'

Her husband grinned at her. He looked absolutely ridiculous in his *Kiss the Chef* apron, which was par for the course for him. James Whitestone was easily the world's biggest dork – but then again that was *precisely* what Sara loved so much about him.

'C'mon, honey,' he whined. 'Whaddya say? It'll be a lot of fun. Don't pretend it won't.'

Sara let out a soft sigh, knowing she'd lost the argument already. Dana was the apple of her daddy's eye, and he never denied her anything that wasn't unsafe for her. Probably the result of his growing up as the youngest of five sons of a strict Presbyterian minister, a stern man who would have been happy if playtime had been classified as the Eighth Deadly Sin. 'Fine, you big goofball.' Sara finally relented. 'But you're the one taking her to the emergency room when her hair catches fire.'

Her husband's lopsided grin exploded into a full-blown smile as he easily covered the fifteen feet between the grill and the lawn chair where she was sitting in three long, graceful strides. He leaned down and planted a kiss on the top of her head. 'That anything like when my mom told me not to come running to her when I broke my leg?'

Sara laughed and punched him on one tree-trunk thigh. 'Damn straight it is. Moms always know what we're talking about. It's hard-wired into our psychology.'

James groaned theatrically as he straightened back up, as though the strain of leaning down to kiss his wife had been enough to throw his back out of alignment.

Sara Whitestone was a remarkably small woman; a trait that Dana would inherit as she herself grew into woman-hood. Standing a shade under five feet tall, Sara tipped the scales at just below a hundred pounds, though those she went up against in court as a litigating attorney for the law firm of Smith, Frey and Bogner never seemed to mention anything about her size. Her diminutive stature simply didn't register with them when she was in front of a jury, more often than not whipping their tails and looking for all the world exactly like what she was – an intellectual giant with a brilliant legal mind. Whenever people asked her if it was nice always being the smartest person in the room, she'd smile politely and reply, 'Well, no. Actually, it's hell.'

Sara pouted and punched her husband on the leg again, harder this time. 'Hey, be nice to me, you oversized gorilla. Be nice to me or no dessert for you tonight.'

James smiled and dropped down to his knees in front of her. His weight dented the soft grass as he wrapped his strong arms around her slender body and leaned forward to press his face into her breasts, which were braless and straining against a tattered Abba-concert T-shirt. 'Just exactly what kind of dessert are we talking about here, Mrs Whitestone?' he breathed into her chest.

Sara laughed and pushed his face away. 'Nip it, lover boy. Nip it right in the bud. There's a time and place for everything, and this is certainly neither the time nor the place for this little conversation. If you're a good boy, though, maybe we'll revisit this subject later on tonight when our little angel is in bed sleeping. Play your cards right and anything's possible, I suppose.'

Favouring her with a comically lecherous wink, James rose to his feet and returned to the grill by way of the sandbox, stopping just long enough to ask Dana what heinous and unforgivable crime her Holly Hobby doll had committed to warrant the extreme punishment of being buried up to her neck in sand. Sara smiled at them as she watched them talk before turning her attention back to the legal brief she'd brought home from work.

Fifteen minutes later James announced that the food was ready and that Dana needed to go into the house to wash before they could eat.

'Why do I have to?' the little girl asked, turning her enormous blue eyes up to meet his.

'Well, you have to because your hands are all dirty from playing in the sandbox, silly goose.'

Dana stood up with a dramatic sigh. Tiny granules of sand cascaded down from her Barbie T-shirt as she wiped her hands across the butt of her previously clean white shorts and held them up for her father to inspect. 'There, that should do it. All clean now. See, Daddy?'

James threw his head back and roared with laughter. It was a deep, joyful sound. 'Sorry, kiddo. Not good enough.'

He paused and grinned down at his daughter. 'Now, I could be all wrong about this, but I'm pretty sure it's just about time for *this* plane to take off.'

And with that he ran over and swept her small body up into his strong arms, swinging her out wildly to his side in a horizontal position five feet above the ground. Dana's eyes lit up brighter than the runway lights at Hopkins airport as he held her suspended in the air. They had played this game many times before and it was one of her all-time favourites.

Winking at Sara again, James began humming loudly to imitate the rumbling of a plane's engines. The sound came from deep within his chest and Dana could feel the vibrations as they tickled her body. 'The pilots are ready for take-off in the cockpit!' James boomed. 'Are the passengers ready?'

'Ready!' Dana giggled. 'All the passengers are ready for take-off, Daddy!'

Engines rumbling joyfully, the impromptu summertime flight quickly taxied down the runway of the backyard and into the house, where it banked sharply to the right in the foyer before finally touching down at the kitchen sink to complete its vital hand-washing mission with a fresh bar of Ivory soap.

When father and daughter had returned and they were all seated around the wooden picnic table in the middle of their backyard, the young family began eating and fell into an easy conversation centring on Dana's trio of imaginary friends: Lula, Pano and Mr Sunday.

'And just what is Mr Sunday up to on this fine Fourth of July?' Sara asked, dabbing with a paper napkin at a smear of mustard that had found its way onto her daughter's left cheek.

'He's working today. No fireworks for him. And, boy, is he ever sad about that.'

'That's too bad.' James empathised. 'Seems pretty darn unfair he has to work when everybody else is out there having a good time. What line of work is he in, anyway, sweetheart?'

'He's a filthy prostitute,' Dana mumbled through a mouthful of half-chewed hot dog.

A shocked look flashed across Sara's delicately pretty face. '*What* did you say?'

'I said Mr Sunday's a filthy prostitute and he's gotta work today,' Dana repeated nonchalantly, her attention now squarely focused on the tiny army ant steadily marching its way across the table and toward her plate.

James arched an inquisitive eyebrow at his wife before turning back to his daughter. 'Where on *earth* did you learn a word like that, honey?'

'From that movie you were watching last night, Daddy. You know, the one with all the filthy prostitutes in it. Did you forget about it already?'

Sara shot her husband a look that could have frozen water. 'That's it, James. That is *it*. No more late-night television for you until this little girl's been in bed and sawing logs for at least an hour. You ever hear the saying about little pitchers having big ears? Well, there you go. There's your proof right there, buster.'

'But, Mom!' Dana whined.

'But, Mom!' James echoed in the same tone.

Sara held up a hand to silence them. 'Don't *But, Mom* me, you two. That's final. I mean it, James. Only PBS until she's in bed and lost in dream world, you hear me? The only words she needs to be learning are the ones they teach her on *Sesame Street* and *The Electric Company*.'

Turning back to Dana and frowning, she added, 'And I don't *ever* want to hear that word out of your mouth again, little lady. It's a bad word and if I ever hear it again you're getting the soap. You didn't like it very much the last time, remember?'

Dana rolled her eyes and took a long drink of her Kool-Aid before smacking her red-stained lips once. 'Fine, Mommy. I heard you the first time, you know.'

It took everything Sara had to hold back the laugh she felt coming on. In some ways her daughter seemed so advanced for her young age that she often had to remind herself that Dana wasn't even five years old yet. 'I only said it once, Little Miss Smarty-Pants.'

'I know you did, and that's the same time I heard you say it.'

'Hard to argue with that logic,' James chimed in helpfully.

Sara shot him another look. 'You stay out of this, James. Stay out of it or you can consider the dessert menu off-limits to you tonight, if you get my drift.'

James turned back to his daughter with a grin and held up his large hands, shrugging his broad shoulders in good-natured defeat. 'Hard to argue with *that* logic, too. Sorry, kiddo, but Mom's definitely got the trump card on this one. Daddy's not the smartest guy in the whole world but he sure as hell knows when he's been beat. Only PBS on that television from now on.'

By the time they'd finished eating, cleared the table and brought the leftovers inside to the kitchen, the sun had set fully and the moonless sky above had sufficiently darkened for the Whitestone family festivities to begin at last. Off in the distance they could hear the booming of the fireworks downtown as they streaked deep into the night to the accompaniment of the Cleveland Orchestra.

With an air of ceremony that made both Sara and Dana giggle, James switched off the back porch light and lit a sparkler from a box of ten with a cheap plastic lighter before solemnly handing it over to his daughter. Taking his wife's hand in his own, they watched Dana gleefully run through the yard waving it around in figure-eight patterns. Little sparks of fire jumped off the stick in all directions, illuminating both a small circle of the night and the unadulterated joy on their only child's smiling face.

'I'm a fairy princess!' Dana squealed with delight. 'I'm a fairy princess and this here's my magic wand!'

Sara smiled and slipped an arm around her husband's waist, gently rubbing the small of his back. 'You know what?' she said softly. 'This is as good as it gets. I really think it's moments like this we've worked so hard for all these years.'

A single tear formed silently in the corner of her right eye, wavered there a moment as though unsure what to do next, then slowly spilled out onto her smooth cheek.

'You know what?' James answered, pulling his wife closer and gently kissing the tear away. 'I think you're absolutely right.'

Sara Whitestone's slender shoulders started to shake as she began to cry harder, once again asking herself how she could continue keeping such a huge secret from this man who so obviously loved her more than he loved life itself.

But James Whitestone just held his wife tighter and kissed her again.

Even softer this time.

CHAPTER THIRTEEN

The Blanton Inn – Los Angeles – 7:12 a.m.

On the morning following Mary Ellen Orton's vicious murder, Nathan Stiedowe bought a copy of the *Los Angeles Times* in the motel lobby and brought it back up to his room before searching for the account of his previous night's escapades.

He scanned the front page quickly. The lead story was about Obama's timetable for pulling US troops out of Afghanistan. The right-hand two columns were devoted to an article about H1N1 vaccinations, a story that jumped to A3. The centrepiece feature, complete with a four-column colour photograph above the fold, showcased an area depicting Brownie troops' efforts to collect canned goods for the upcoming Thanksgiving holiday. A story about the rising cost of school lunches was stripped across the bottom of the page.

Nothing about him. *Fucking idiots wouldn't know a good story if it bit their goddamn noses off.*

He didn't make the front of the local section, either. Finally, he found the story buried on the bottom of page B5, cleverly positioned right next to an ad for a funeral home. *Hardy-har-har. Copy editors and their hilarious fucking jokes.*

The short account was accompanied by a minuscule twenty-point headline. Light-faced, of course.

97

WOMAN MURDERED OVERNIGHT IN SOUTH CENTRAL

Nathan quickly read through the reporter's woefully amateurish work. Probably a cub still wet behind the ears considering the overnight crime-beat shift he'd pulled. After a moment, he thought he understood the reason why. The idiot hadn't even gotten the victim's name right, calling her 'Mary *Ann* Orton' instead of 'Mary Ellen'.

Nathan clenched his teeth. When he'd been a crime reporter this shit wouldn't have flown. Not by a long shot. The managing editor would have kicked his ass up and down the newsroom while the other reporters busted a gut laughing at him with the *Schadenfreude* so inextricably linked with those engaged in the journalism profession. Nobody ever wanted to get called out on sloppy work, and if somebody else was in trouble it only meant their own jobs were safe enough for the time being in an industry that was rapidly dying with each passing day. But come on. With the Internet and today's 24/7 news cycle on cable television, the *least* you could do in print was get the victim's goddamn *name* right.

He balled the paper up and hurled it across the room in disgust before taking a deep breath and forcing himself to calm down. *Fuck it.* The important part was that he'd meticulously recreated Richard Ramirez's unforgettable crime, and now the time had come to take his bloody red pen to the second infamous serial killer on his hit list.

He thought he remembered reading somewhere before that Dennis Rader – the infamous BTK who'd gotten his nickname by binding and torturing his victims before finally killing them in and around Wichita, Kansas – had always enjoyed steak and eggs for his morning repast. Sadly, Nathan was a vegetarian, so that simply wasn't going to work. After all, there were certain principles even *he* refused to compromise.

No matter. A little improvisation was always good for the artist's soul, right?

Goddamn right it was.

Recreating Dennis Rader's infamous quadruple slaying of the Otero family back in 1974 was certainly going to be *fun*, but first Nathan had to make sure all the details were absolutely perfect. That was crucial, after all – the main crux of his sacred mission – and to do it would require a quick trip to the library.

He went into the bathroom and took a moment to really *study* his reflection in the grimy mirror. He was an exceptionally good-looking man, of this fact he was well aware. He was very tall, nearly six foot four. He had strong, straight white teeth, compelling brown eyes and a chiselled physique meticulously sculpted from countless hours spent lifting weights in a dark basement gym with nothing more than his loud grunts and the sound of heavy iron plates clanging together to keep him company. Coupled with the rigorous running routine he'd religiously performed since his days in the military, he was in the very best shape of his life now. And a good thing too. He'd need to be in absolute peak physical condition to pull this next job off without a hitch.

Today just so happened to be his fifty-seventh birthday, but when people guessed his age they often thought he was much younger. Just a few nights ago, for example, hadn't the attractive blonde co-ed he'd met at the bar and later taken back to the motel for a rough session in the sack said he looked at least fifteen years younger?

He hadn't felt the need to correct her at the time. No, what he'd *really* felt like doing as the musky scent of sex clung to their bodies like a second skin was *killing* her. Killing her dead. And not very softly, at that.

The fresh sweat was still sparkling on her flat stomach like diamond-kissed ripples of sunshine on the ocean – her hard pink nipples still standing proudly erect on her surgically enhanced breasts – and all Nathan could think about was how much he *hated* the little whore.

Like most women he'd come to know in such an intimate fashion – and make no mistake about it, boys, there were *scores* of them out there – this bleached-blonde slut with the fake tits only reminded him of the bitch who'd stolen his life. And simply because of that irritating detail, every last fibre of his being screamed out for him to wrap his remarkably strong hands around her pretty little throat and squeeze and squeeze with all his might until the light flickered out of her clear blue eyes for ever and she was quite dead.

Surely that wasn't asking too much, was it? It was, after all, his *birthday*.

As difficult as it had been to resist the overwhelming urge, the next morning he was infinitely grateful that he'd summoned the inner strength to let the little slut go un-harmed. There was much more important work out there left to accomplish, and it would have been a sign of great weakness and an unforgivable lack of self-control if he'd given in to his dark desires at that precise moment.

To prepare for his upcoming study session, Nathan cranked up Irish concert-pianist Ashley Ball's version of Ernesto Lecuona's 'Aragon' on the bedside stereo and took a long, leisurely shower before dressing in a crisp white dress shirt, perfectly creased slacks and a stylishly understated silk necktie. He completed this rather dashing ensemble with a lightweight, flawlessly tailored Armani sport coat and a pair of seven-hundred-dollar Bruno Magli shoes, the same brand made infamous by OJ Simpson and chosen for precisely that reason. The Juice had nothing to do with his sacred mission, of course – a mission that would ultimately culminate in the death of the greedy little life-stealer he was after – but there was no law against having a little bit of fun along the way, now was there? Besides, he had expensive tastes and enough money to indulge them whenever he damn well pleased, which wasn't to say the financial security hadn't come at a terrible cost.

Knowing full well that his expensive wardrobe made him look dangerously out of place at the cheap motel, Nathan's next order of business was finally to check out, stopping just long enough to favour the plump middle-aged desk clerk with one of his perfectly dazzling smiles before he left.

Down in the parking lot of the motel three minutes later, he slipped behind the wheel of the latest exquisite rental car that had been dropped off earlier in the day – a mint-condition cherry-red Porsche Boxster this time – and began the short drive over to the nearest satellite branch of the Los Angeles Public Library.

Fifteen minutes later he was inside the building and making a beeline toward the extensive True Crime section in back. With a clear sense of purpose, he carefully selected a thick volume from the somewhat dusty shelf and found a quiet corner table overlooking the bright sunlit courtyard before opening the book, sighing contentedly. He began to read.

Thankfully the material was not a disappointment – it

drew him into the magical world of murder at once. The morbid tales possessed Nathan's imagination with much the same feeling as that of a new and unfamiliar lover beneath his strong body as he quickly devoured one deliciously depraved page after another.

As was usual when he studied, the time raced by. When he finally raised his striking brown eyes to the large round clock on the far wall, he was surprised to find that he'd been in his seat for nearly five hours. It was now almost six o'clock in the evening.

It was time to move on. Nathan was a man on the hunt *and* a man being hunted, and that was a lot for *anybody* to deal with.

Back in the leather-appointed Porsche five minutes later, he pulled out his alligator-skin Kenneth Cole wallet and checked his driver's licence again. Nathan had many aliases – each one impeccable and backed up by clean Motor Vehicle Bureau records in five different states – but to remain under one identity for too long would simply be foolish, would only make him an easier target for the greedy little bitch who'd stolen his life, and he planned on *winning* this dangerous game that they were now playing.

Still, he wasn't overly concerned about his identity at this exact moment. Even if nobody else out there knew it yet, Nathan Stiedowe knew *exactly* who he was. Knew exactly who he was and *exactly* what he was capable of doing.

Besides, there were always more identities to turn to whenever he needed them – always plenty of harmless, bleating sheep ready to be culled from the flock.

CHAPTER FOURTEEN

Los Angeles International Airport – 9:30 a.m.

Dana's head was still spinning from information overload by the time her and Brown's flight finally touched down at LAX thirteen hours later.

Her research last night in her hotel room into the details of Richard Ramirez's horrific crimes – and the similarities between Mary Ellen Orton's murder and the Night Stalker's first kill – had been astounding. She'd wanted to discuss it with Brown during the trip out to LA but he'd fallen asleep on the plane so she'd have to bring him up to speed later. He was obviously as exhausted and overworked as she was – Dana just wished she could fall asleep so easily. Her mind was too full to switch off.

She'd taken quick mental breaks on the plane to steal furtive glances at Brown as he slept. No wedding ring – and he wasn't all that hard to look at, either. A smooth, unlined face and tousled brown hair. A nice build and a beautiful smile. He was the first man in a while who'd attracted her interest and she took note. If she ever got around to actually *having* a social life outside the train wreck that was Match.com, she didn't think she'd have any trouble pencilling him in on her dance card. But butterfly kisses and little candy hearts would just have to wait. Right now she had a killer to catch and so far she'd been doing a piss-poor job of it – at least, by her own standards.

She'd be damned if she was going to let death win this time. Not again. Not this time. Not on her watch. She wasn't a helpless child any more, a kid who just sat back and let bad things happen to herself and the people around her. She needed to be one hundred per cent focused on catching this sick bastard.

But there were a lot of big names and plenty of lofty expectations for Dana to live up to; that was for sure. It was her case, the biggest since she'd gone solo, and she couldn't afford to get distracted by anything. She only hoped she was doing the right thing by moving the investigation out to Los Angeles now and not simply flying three thousand miles away while the Cleveland Slasher blissfully went unimpeded about his work of murdering another innocent little girl back in Ohio.

Dana thought again about how insistent Crawford had been that she should fly down to Quantico. She was so used to doing his bidding that she hadn't really questioned it after her initial misgivings. And several times he'd seemed on the brink of telling her something but had then become preoccupied. No matter. If he had something to say he knew where to find her, and it had proved useful, hadn't it?

An hour after their flight landed, she and Brown were in the crime lab of the LA FBI field office downtown. The sickly-sweet smell of formaldehyde was heavy in the air as Dana pulled on a pair of thin rubber gloves and unzipped the oversized evidence bag containing the bloody black clothes that the killer had slipped out of while fleeing the angry mob. Forensic pathologist Dr Melissa Guthrie was in the room with them.

'Have these already been typed for blood?' Dana asked. Although Brown was effectively in charge of this particular murder, it was Dana's case overall; she would take the lead.

'Sure have,' Guthrie answered. She was a very pretty woman in her early forties, but she had way too much brainpower to give her appearance much attention. Her glasses were thick and oversized for her delicate face and her stringy blonde hair snaked crazily down the front of her white lab coat before tangling itself in a hopeless mess in the silver stethoscope hanging around her neck. 'Only blood on those clothes belongs to Mary Ellen Orton. He didn't leave us a trace of his own DNA.'

No surprise there. It looked like it *was* their guy.

Dana turned the pants inside out. After a moment of careful examination she wasn't very surprised to find the irregular stitching inside. 'Got a scalpel?' she asked Guthrie, handing the pants over. 'Let's cut these stitches open and see what we've got here.'

The forensic pathologist took the pants and produced the sharp instrument from a sterile metal tray before carefully slicing the stitches away. Dana's breath caught in her throat when a small sheet of paper fluttered to the floor.

Guthrie leaned down to pick it up with a pair of tweezers before unfolding the note and reading the handwritten message inside out loud:

'"Big deal. Death always went with the territory. I'll see you at Disneyland."'

Guthrie shook her head in confusion. '"I'll see you at Disneyland"? What's that all about?'

Dana blew out a quick breath that fluttered her bangs. She knew *exactly* what it meant. She could practically write an essay on it. 'It's what Richard Ramirez said while he was being led out of court on 20 September 1989. He got nineteen separate death sentences for his trouble. From what we can tell, this guy here was pretending to be the Night Stalker. I think this was probably a copycat of a murder involving a victim named Jennie Vincow. He was just play-acting.'

But even as she ran through her theory of the killer's motivation to Melissa Guthrie, something was still bothering the hell out of Dana, a nagging little impression at the back of her mind that wouldn't quite leave her alone. But what was it?

She shook her head to clear the feeling away and turned to Brown. 'What kind of set-up do you guys have around here? Sketch artists, handwriting analysts, blood-spatter experts – that kind of stuff.'

'We've got a pretty good group of guys who cover all those areas,' Brown said. 'Some of them are among the best in the country. Jim McGreevy's working on the composite drawing and Jeff Simmons is doing the blood work. I'll get Fred Spangler to analyse the note.'

'Thanks. And what about the witness in the crowd chasing the suspect on the night of the murder? The young Latina. Could we set up an appointment with her too? I'm sure your guys did a thorough job – I'd just like to talk to her myself, in case . . .'

'No problem,' Brown replied, already keying into his cell.

Dana thanked him again and turned back to Guthrie. 'If you could please get this note analysed for prints, fibres and DNA as quickly as possible before the handwriting guy takes a look, I'd really appreciate it. There probably isn't anything, but it's worth a shot.'

When Brown and Guthrie had left the room, Dana sat down on a plastic chair and tried to collect her thoughts. It felt good to be swinging into action like this. Could she allow herself to hope that they might finally be making progress? That they might at last be getting closer to the Cleveland Slasher?

Unbidden, the thought of another killer flashed into her mind: the killer she *really* wanted. The killer who was the main reason why she'd joined the FBI in the first place.

The monster who'd murdered both her parents in cold blood when she'd been only four years old.

CHAPTER FIFTEEN

Nathan sat in the Porsche on Timber Drive in the nicest area of Ventura, California, listening to Ashley Ball's rendition of Lecuona's 'Malaguena'. He was about an hour north of Los Angeles. He lit up a cigarette and inhaled deeply. The fancy car didn't draw much attention here, so that was good. It just took its place quietly among all the Jags and Beemers and Corvettes scooting about. Hell, it wasn't even the nicest car on the block. *That* distinction went to the yellow Lamborghini parked in the driveway of the biggest house on the street, a faux-colonial rising up higher than its neighbours and creating the distinct impression that it was looking down its nose at them.

He lifted the binoculars to his eyes and focused on the window of the master bedroom on the second floor. The curtains were open and the stunning blonde standing there was completely naked, in full view of the entire street. Still, Nathan was the only one looking.

He'd found Brenda McCarty through the Lonely Hearts Club website, the Internet dating site that would become his hunting ground from here on. His wireless Internet card gave him the flexibility he needed, allowing him to log on whenever he damn well pleased, so it was a natural fit.

Even though Brenda McCarty would be a red herring if they ever connected her to him, Nathan wasn't especially concerned with what the authorities might think right now.

Fuck them. He was in charge here, the storyteller writing the goddamn script, and it was time for a little bit of fun. Hell, he'd *earned* that much.

Sensing a peeping Tom in the neighbourhood, the woman turned in his direction. Her double-D breasts didn't move like natural breasts. As a matter of fact, they didn't move at all. They'd been fashioned out of the finest silicone that money could buy.

Still, she was one sexy bitch for fifty-eight, no doubt about that. When she spotted Nathan, her green eyes widened briefly in surprise. Then she smiled and crooked her finger in his direction.

Nathan smiled back and turned off the Porsche's ignition before stubbing out his cigarette in the ashtray. Brenda McCarty's husband was a successful stockbroker who cared absolutely nothing about his wife's indiscretions, so he wasn't especially worried about an angry husband coming home and catching them in the act. She just liked to play at being kinky, or so she wrote in her e-mails – thus the role-play of him spying on her from the street and supposedly getting caught.

Nathan sighed. Whatever turned her on. Everybody had their own little kinks. Hell, he knew that better than most.

He got out of the Porsche and crossed Timber Drive, pausing to let a school bus to cross the street. A young Hispanic girl smiled a toothless grin at him from one of the back windows, and Nathan smiled back.

The front door would be unlocked. He knew this because the entire scenario had been discussed in excruciating detail via e-mail, right down to the scripted lines he would utter. Or, rather, the scripted lines that Brenda McCarty *thought* he would utter.

His ears rang as he navigated the stone walkway lined with blood-red roses. Three houses down on his left a dog barked.

A moment later he was inside the marble-tiled foyer, where a crystal chandelier sparkled over his head. So far, so good.

An elaborate double staircase led up to the second floor. Nathan took the set of stairs to the right and made his way down the hall. He paused outside the French doors at the end of the hall and took a deep breath before he pushed them open.

Brenda McCarty was lying on her back on a huge four-poster bed. Her head was thrown back and her tan thighs were parted. A low buzzing sound filled the room. Nathan looked between her legs and saw that she was pleasuring herself with a blue vibrator.

Kinky, kinky, kinky. He liked her already.

She looked up at him and feigned shock. 'Who the fuck are you?' she stammered, yanking the comforter up to cover her naked body. 'Get the fuck out of my house!'

Nathan smiled at her. 'Sorry, bitch. Can't do that. I'm here to rape you.'

Brenda McCarty paused. Then she smiled back and lowered the covers, revealing her naked body once again. 'Well, what the hell are you waiting for, then? It's just little old me in this big old bed and I obviously can't do a goddamn thing to stop you.'

Nathan's smile brightened. 'Oh, I know that, Brenda. Not you – and not anybody else, either.'

He produced a switchblade from the back pocket of his pants and flipped it open. 'Now, what do you say we have some *real* fun?'

The woman's bright green eyes widened again, partly from apprehension and partly from the thrill of just how *good* it felt to be so *bad*. 'Go easy with that thing,' she said warily. 'Don't forget we're just playing a game here.'

Nathan took a step forward. 'Oh, believe me, Brenda, I'm going to go *real* easy with this thing. Hell, I'm not even going to torture you like Dennis Rader did to his victims. I'm simply going to kill you, that's all. Easy breezy – no fuss, no muss. This here is just *practice* for me.'

Brenda McCarty's fear was suddenly very real now. 'What the fuck are you talking about? We didn't agree to any of these lines. Say what you're supposed to say or get the fuck out of my house. I don't need this shit.'

Nathan sprang forward and clamped a hand over her mouth to muffle her screams. 'Neither do I, Brenda.'

When he slid the sharp knife deep into her carotid artery, the fleshy tube opened up like a burst water main and sprayed a fine mist of bright red blood all over the room.

Nathan wasn't at all surprised to see that Brenda McCarty bled like a stuck pig. After all, that was exactly what she was.

Or, at least, what she *had* been.

CHAPTER SIXTEEN

Dana called Gary Templeton in Cleveland and brought him up to speed on the latest developments out in LA. Everything from the note stitched into the killer's pants to the possible connection to the Night Stalker's first murder. Templeton was her eyes and ears out in Cleveland; it was absolutely essential that he knew everything she did. And God forbid the killer returned to his first hunting ground while she was out in LA.

'Keep working the angles in Cleveland,' Dana told him. 'I don't want to miss anything else. Don't leave a single rock unturned, OK? How's it coming along with the court orders for those four autopsies?'

Templeton let out a breath. 'I persuaded a judge to push all four through at once,' he said. 'As we speak, Alice Maxwell, Trina Bonderman, Kaitlin Jackson and Michelle Thompson are under the knives of four different MEs. Shouldn't be long now before we know what we're looking for.'

Dana's stomach flipped with the idea that they might finally be making some real progress on this case, not just belatedly reacting to the Cleveland Slasher's moves when it was already too late to do any good. The implications of what the autopsies might uncover could be huge. She just hoped she wasn't pinning her hopes on what could turn out to be another dead end. The killer had outsmarted them enough already.

'Thanks, Gary,' she said. 'Let me know as soon as you hear anything, OK?'

'Will do, Dana.'

Dana thanked him again and switched off. A moment later, Brown entered the room. 'I've got an appointment set up with the witness at the Mary Ellen Orton scene,' he said. 'Where do you want to start?'

Dana took a deep breath and brought Brown up to speed on the Cleveland case. She'd given him a brief overview earlier but now she spelled out all the facts in excruciating detail. 'Let's start at the beginning,' she told Brown. 'I did some interesting research last night on the Night Stalker and how that case might relate to Mary Ellen Orton's murder.'

She held up the sheaf of papers that she'd printed off from the database the previous night. 'Let's compare the Night Stalker's original murder with the Mary Ellen Orton case and see what else we come up with. I could use your input. And who knows? We might get lucky and catch lightning in a bottle.'

Brown cracked his knuckles. 'Sounds like a plan to me. Shoot.'

'Good. Let's get to work.'

On a large white dry-erase board, Dana quickly sketched out a profile of Richard Ramirez's known activities on the night he'd killed Jennie Vincow. Beneath each, she noted the similarities and disparities involved:

Night Stalker victim's name: Jennie Vincow
Current victim's name: Mary Ellen Orton

Age of Night Stalker victim: 79
Age of current victim: 79

City of Night Stalker attack: Los Angeles
City of current suspect's attack: Same

Date of Night Stalker attack: 28 June 1984
Date of current suspect's attack: 12 Nov. 2010

Night Stalker's method of entry: Ground-floor window
Current suspect's method of entry: Same

Night Stalker's known crimes: Murder, rape (necrophilia)
Current suspect's known crimes: Murder; rape and sodomy
via knife

Incidental coincidences?
Night Stalker was chased down and caught by an angry
mob after a composite sketch of him was released to the
media. Current suspect outran crowd; witness working
with sketch artist to develop composite now. Both were
dressed all in black and wearing AC/DC baseball caps.
Richard Ramirez eventually left his hat behind at a
subsequent crime scene.

Dana took a step back and she and Brown both looked at
the board. It was good to be working with him like this.
She'd forgotten how much she'd enjoyed that side of things
when she'd been working with Crawford.

'Looks spot on,' Brown said after a moment, studying her notes. 'The age thing isn't exactly subtle to me, and everything else looks pretty goddamn close, too. This guy really did his homework.'

Dana shook her head in frustration. 'Yeah, but how is he managing not to leave a single trace of himself behind at the crime scenes? I'm thinking maybe he might know the same things we do when it comes to processing the scenes.'

Brown looked surprised, then thoughtful. 'Are you saying this could be the work of someone out in the field? Really?'

Dana shrugged. 'I don't know. I've been thinking – he leaves no trace, he . . . It's a horrible idea, but I just think we should at least consider the possibility. I've got Gary Templeton running background checks on everyone involved with investigating the murder scenes out in Cleveland. You never know. Could you do the same thing here in Los Angeles?'

Brown was silent for a moment and then said, 'Sure. You're right. It's worth checking. We have to look at every angle with this killer. It does feel as if he might have inside knowledge.' He paused. 'And what about the other stuff? Any word from Quantico on the plastic-bag connection yet?'

Dana shook her head. She'd placed a research request with the Child Abduction and Serial Murder Resources Center in Quantico yesterday asking them to cross-reference serial killers who'd used plastic bags in the commission of their crimes, but she still hadn't heard back from them. Might be up to a week before she did, they'd said.

'I'm afraid we're going to have to wait a little bit longer on that one,' she told Brown. 'For now, let's go over and talk to the witness we've got. The young Latina. Maybe the initial interviewer missed something in all the excitement.'

'Sounds good,' Brown said. 'Let's go.'

Just then, Dana's cellphone rang in her pocket. She held a finger up to Brown and motioned for him to wait while she fumbled it out.

'Hello?'

'Dana, it's Gary Templeton. The autopsies are done.'

A flutter of hope tickled Dana's chest. "Did they find anything?'

Brown looked at her expectantly.

Templeton's voice was amped-up. 'They sure did. There was a single plastic letter inside each girl's uterus. Just like the letters they found inside Jacinda Holloway.'

Dana's ears rang. Her hands shook as she flipped open her notebook to jot the letters down. 'What were the letters?' she asked.

Templeton took a deep breath. 'Starting with Alice Maxwell and ending with Michelle Thompson, in chronological order the letters were *D*, *A*, *N* and *A*.

'They spelled out your name, Dana.'

PART II

CHANNELLING DENNIS RADER

CHAPTER SEVENTEEN

The audio recording of Dennis Rader's 2005 confession filled the car as Nathan streaked down the Pacific Coast Highway at ninety miles an hour. Judge Gregory Waller was interviewing the infamous BTK in open court.

'In regards to Count 1, please tell me in your own words what you did on the fifteenth day of January 1974, in Sedgwick County, Kansas, that makes you believe you are guilty of murder in the first degree.'

'Well, on 15 January 1974, I maliciously—'

'All right, Mr Rader, I need to find out more information. On that particular day, on the fifteenth day of January 1974, can you tell me where you went to kill Joseph Otero?'

'Um . . . I think it was 1834 Edgemoor.'

'All right, can you tell me approximately what time of day you went there?'

'Somewhere between seven and seven-thirty.'

'At this particular location, did you know these people?'

'No, that was part of what . . . I guess what you call my fantasy. These people were selected.'

'So you were engaged in some kind of fantasy during this period of time?'

'Yes, sir.'

'Now, when you use the term fantasy, is this something you were doing for your personal pleasure?'

'Sexual fantasy, sir.'

'I see. So you went to this residence – and what occurred then?'

'I had did some thinking on what I was going to do to either Mrs Otero or Josephine and basically broke into the house, or didn't break into the house . . . but when they came out of the house I came in and confronted the family and then we went from there.'

'Had you planned this beforehand?'

'To some degree, yes. After I got in the house I lost control. It was, you know, in the back of my mind. I had some ideas of what I was going to do. I basically panicked that first day, so . . .'

'Beforehand, did you know who was there in the house?'

'I thought Mrs Otero and the two kids, the two younger kids, were in the house. I didn't realise Mr Otero was going to be there.'

'How did you get into the house?'

'I came through the back door. I cut the phone lines. I waited at the back door. I had reservations about even going or just walking away, but pretty soon the door opened and I was in.'

'So the door opened for you, or . . .'

'I think one of the kids, I think Junior, the younger Joseph, opened the door, 'cause he let the dog out, 'cause the dog was in the house at that time.'

'Now when you went into the house, what happened then?'

'Well, I confronted the family . . . pulled a pistol, confronted Mr Otero and asked him to, you know, that I was there, that basically I wanted . . . to get the car . . . hungry, food. I wanted . . . asked them to lie down in the living room . . . and at that time I realised that was not a good idea. So I finally, the dog was a real problem, so I asked Mr Otero if he could get the dog out. He had one of the kids put it out. I took them back to the bedroom.'

'You took who back to the bedroom?'

'The family . . . the four members. At that time I tied them up.'

'While still holding them at gunpoint?'

'In between tying, I guess.'

'After you tied them up what happened?'

'Well, they started complaining about being tied up and I reloosened the bonds, tried to make Mr Otero as comfortable as I could. Apparently he had a cracked rib from a car accident so I had him put a pillow down for his head. I think he had a parka or a coat underneath him. He talked to me about giving me a car. I guess he didn't have very much money. Then I realised that, you know, I didn't have a mask on or anything, that they could ID me, so I made a decision to go ahead and put 'em down, I guess, or strangle them.'

'All right, what did you do to Joseph Otero?'

'Joseph Otero?'

'J. Joseph Otero Sr, Mr Otero, the father.'

'I put a plastic bag over his head and then some cords and tightened it.'

'This was in the bedroom?'

'Yes, sir.'

'Did he in fact suffocate and die as a result of this?'

'Not right away. No, sir, he didn't.'

'What happened?'

'After that I did Mrs Otero. I had never strangled anyone before so I really didn't know how much pressure you have to put on a person or how long it would take . . .'

'Was she also tied up there in the bedroom?'

'Yes, both their hands and feet were tied up. She was on the bed.'

'Where were the children?'

'Josephine was on the bed and Junior was on the floor at this time.'

'We are talking first of all about Joseph Otero. So you put the bag over his head and tied it and he did not die right away. Can you tell me what happened in regards to Joseph Otero?'

'He moved over real quick-like and I think tore a hole in the bag. I could tell that he was having some problems there, but at that time the whole family just went panicked on me so I worked pretty quick.'

'You worked pretty quick. What did you do?'

'Well, I mean I strangled Mrs Otero . . . she went out, passed out, and I thought she was dead. I strangled Josephine and she passed out. I thought she was dead. And then I went over and put a bag on Junior's head, and then if I remember right, Mrs Otero came back . . . she came back and . . .'

'Sir, let me ask you about Joseph Otero Sr. He tore a hole in the bag. What did you do with him then?'

'I put another bag, either that . . . I recollect, I think I put either a cloth or a T-shirt or something over his head and then another bag and then tightened it up.'

'Did he subsequently die?'

'Well, yes, I mean I was . . . didn't stay there and watch him. I was moving around the room.'

'So you indicated that you strangled Mrs Otero after you had done this, is that correct?'

'I went back and strangled her again. It finally killed her at that time.'

'So this is in regards to Count 2. You first of all put the bag over Joseph Otero's head and he tore a hole in the bag, then you went ahead . . . did you strangle Mrs Otero then?'

'First of all, Mr Otero was strangled . . . a bag put over his head and strangled him. Then I thought he was going down. Then I went over and strangled Mrs Otero, and I thought she was down. Then I strangled Josephine and she was down, and then I went over to Junior and put the bag on his head. After that Mrs Otero woke back up and, you know, she was pretty upset with what's going on, and at that point in time I strangled her . . . the death strangle at that time.'

'With your hands?'

'No, with a cord, with a rope. Then I think at that point in time I redid Mr Otero and put the bag over his head, and then Junior . . . oh, before that she asked me to save her son so I actually had taken the bag off. I was really upset at that point in time. So basically Mr Otero was down, Mrs Otero was down, then I went ahead and took Junior. I put another bag over his head and took him into the other bedroom.'

'What did you do then?'

'Put a bag over his head, put a cloth over his head, a T-shirt and bag so he couldn't tear a hole in it. He subsequently died from that. I went back up, Josephine had woke back up.'

'What did you do then?'

'I took her to the basement and hung her.'

'You hung her in the basement?'

'Yes, sir.'

'Did you do anything else at that time?'

'Yes, I had some sexual fantasies, but that was after she was hung.'

'All right. What did you do then?'

'I went through the house, kinda cleaned it up. It's called the right-hand rule. You go from room to room to clean things up. I think I took Mr Otero's watch. I guess I took a radio. I had forgot about that but apparently took a radio.'

'Why did you take these things?'

'I don't know . . . I have no idea.'

'What happened then?'

'I got the keys to the car . . . in fact I had the keys, I think, earlier before that, a way of getting out of the house, and cleaned the house a little bit, made sure everything was packed up and left through the front door, then went over to their car and drove over to Dillons and left the car there. I eventually walked back to my car.'

'All right, sir, from what you have just said I take it that the facts you told me apply to all of Counts 1, 2, 3 and 4 – is that correct?'

'Yes, sir.'

Nathan smiled as the tape clicked off and the strains of Ashley Ball's version of Lecuona's 'En Tres Por Cuatro' came on over the car stereo. With very few exceptions, he'd soon be following the exact script he'd just heard to a T.

CHAPTER EIGHTEEN

Dana flipped the cellphone off and felt all the blood drain from her cheeks. Dizziness clouded her brain. She found it hard to breathe. Jeremy Brown stepped forward quickly as she swayed back and forth on her heels in the centre of the conference room.

'Whoa,' he said, taking her by the shoulders and leading her gently to a chair. 'Easy, now. Let me get you some water.'

Dana's head swam as Brown went over to the water cooler in the corner and drew her a drink from the blue tap. A moment later he handed her a little conical paper cup. Dana threw her head back and drained the entire thing in one quick pull. The cold water numbed the back of her throat and cleared the fog in her brain.

Brown's face creased with concern. 'Want some more?'

Dana shook her head. 'No, thank you. I'm better now. I was just feeling a little dizzy there for a minute, that's all.'

Brown took the empty cup from her hand and crumpled it up before tossing it into a garbage can. 'Bad phone call, I take it. Is everything OK?'

'Not really.'

'Anything I can do to help?'

For a moment Dana considered telling him all about the terrible night when she'd been four years old. No matter how hard she tried, she just couldn't shake the growing feeling that the man who'd murdered her parents more than three decades earlier was somehow connected to the current murders more intimately than just by calling her out. That he had come back to finish off what he'd started with her all those years ago. Still, she had no concrete evidence for these feelings and the case was already complicated enough without clouding it further with suspicions that she couldn't prove. And she wasn't sure she could trust her judgement any more. Besides, getting called out by a killer certainly wasn't anything new in the history of law enforcement. Crawford could have told her that, and he was the only one in the FBI who knew about her past.

John Muhammad, the Washington-area serial sniper they'd chased, had left the authorities a 'Death' tarot card near a school where he'd apparently lain in wait. On the card, he'd written, 'Dear Police, I am God.' The Zodiac Killer regularly signed off on his correspondence to newspapers with the symbol of the zodiac – a cross superimposed on a circle. Ted Kaczynski, the infamous 'Unabomber', had demanded that his rambling, 35,000-word manifesto should be published in the newspapers or he would kill again. The best profilers in the FBI, including Dana's former partner Crawford Bell, believed it was the killers' way of exerting power and control over society. They got off on the notoriety they received, even if *they* were the only ones who knew their true identities. So instead of telling Brown about her troubled past, Dana took a deep breath and filled him in on what Templeton had just told her.

'Jesus Christ,' Brown said when she'd finished. 'Why would your name be spelled out, Dana? What do you think it means?'

'No idea,' Dana said, a little too quickly. She gazed down at the floor, composing herself and hoping he'd think she was still feeling a little dizzy.

Brown narrowed his eyes. 'You absolutely sure about that?'

Dana looked up at him, surprised. Her cheeks flushed hot, and then all the blood suddenly drained away again. She wasn't used to having her integrity called into question, even when she knew she was lying. 'Excuse me?'

Brown held his hands up in the air with his palms facing her in a placating manner. 'Take it easy, Dana. I didn't mean to offend you. It just feels like maybe you're holding something back from me, that's all.'

'Well, I'm not.'

Brown pursed his lips. 'Fair enough. But if we're going to work together we really need to trust each other, OK? It's the only way we're ever going to get anything done.'

Dana could only nod.

After an awkward pause, Brown looked down at his watch. 'I'll tell you what. Let's take a ten-minute break to catch our breath and collect our thoughts, then we'll head over to meet up with the witness. I'm gonna go grab a quick cup of coffee. You want anything?'

Dana shook her head. 'No, thank you. I'm fine.'

When Brown left the room Dana leaned forward in her chair and rested her head in her hands, knowing that the LA agent was absolutely right. She *was* holding something back, and she would have reacted the exact same way had she been in his position. After all, if you didn't have trust with your partner you didn't have a goddamn thing.

But the truth was that she couldn't help thinking her suspicions were right. All her life she'd feared her parents' killer would come back to find her, but she'd tried desperately not to let her imagination get the better of her, had tried to move on. And still he haunted her. Much as she didn't want to admit it, deep down she *knew* what those letters meant, and now she also knew why each of the victims in Cleveland had been innocent little girls. The monster from her dreams was sending her a very clear message, reminding her of the fact that there was still unfinished business left between them. But why was he coming back for her *now*? What had happened to wake up his rage after all these years?

Dana stood up on shaking legs. She really needed some fresh air. She also needed a new life. The one she was living right now wasn't fit for a dog. A million questions raced through her mind at once, but she didn't have answers for any of them. Still, she knew she'd better find at least *some* of those answers pretty damn quick. People's lives depended on it.

Including, apparently, her own.

CHAPTER NINETEEN

Nathan's thumb found the wheel on the high-powered Nikon binoculars and he brought the image into sharp focus before he allowed himself a small smile.

Excellent. Dana Whitestone was indeed on his trail out on the West Coast now – exactly where he *wanted* her to be. It meant she must've finally received the message he'd been sending her piecemeal over the past three months.

About fucking time.

She was older now, of course, but still looked great. Only the faintest traces of laugh lines had begun to form around the corners of her beautiful mouth and pale blue eyes, and even at thirty-eight she looked a hell of a lot better than most women ten years her junior.

As she left the downtown LA FBI field office and raised her face to the sun with her eyes closed, Nathan wondered idly what made her think she was so goddamn *special.* If she thought she was the only one out here who knew how to play this deadly little game, she was sadly mistaken about that. And now he supposed it was up to him to make that fact painfully clear to her.

He'd been following Dana's career from a distance and with great interest from the very start. And sometimes from not even all that much of a distance at all. Hell, he'd been in the fucking *auditorium* the day she'd received her diploma from the FBI Training Academy following seventeen gruelling weeks of training. Nobody had been happier – or *prouder* – than Nathan when she'd marched across the stage that day and into her new life as a full-fledged agent with the Federal Bureau of Investigation.

She'd stumbled a few times early on in her career, of course, like they all did, but her move to Cleveland had clearly done her a world of good. She'd finally left the safety of the nest in Quantico and spread her wings to fly on her own, which meant she was ready to take him on as an equal.

Again, about fucking time. After all, if this wasn't to be a fair fight, what the hell use was there in even having a fight at all? He could easily have snapped her neck or gutted her like a fish any time he'd wanted to over the years, of course – the ultimate goal when everything was said and done – but now he was extremely thankful he'd waited. It would only make the final *coup de grâce* all that much more delicious.

Nathan lit up a menthol cigarette, his second of the day, and snapped the silver Zippo shut before carefully pulling the Porsche out into traffic with the sounds of Ashley Ball playing Lecuona's 'Yo Te Quiero Siempre' filling the car. He took a long, satisfying drag on the cigarette and exhaled the wonderful smoke out through his nostrils in a smooth blue stream. Time to review the material he'd learned during his latest study session.

First there were Paul Bernardo and Karla Homolka. What a delightfully heartless pair they had been!

The Ken and Barbie of murder were an attractive blond Canadian couple possessed of a sexually driven bloodlust – he a rapist and insatiable sexual sadist, she his more-than-willing partner in crime. All told, Bernardo and Homolka were suspected of forty-three sex attacks and a long string of killings. Their tragic fall from grace could be traced directly to the day she'd cut a deal with their prosecutors as a result of which he'd received a life sentence.

Moral of the story? Never work with a partner.

That wouldn't be a problem for Nathan. He wasn't married any more – much to his infinite dismay – and his black heart was quite unavailable for the stealing by any other woman than the one who'd been so cruelly ripped from his life all those years ago.

The second case he'd studied had concerned Anatoly Onoprienko, a Ukrainian serial killer who'd stalked the countryside murdering at random. Nathan had committed the entire *Eastern Economist* newspaper article to memory, an exquisite gift that he'd sharpened to a razor's edge since childhood. In his mind's eye, he could actually *see* the words printed on the page:

ONOPRIENKO SENTENCED FOR MURDER SPREE
ZHYTOMYR – The Zhytomyr Regional Court on 1 April passed sentence on Anatoly Onoprienko, who murdered 52 people, handing down the expected death sentence. Mr Onoprienko, a 39-year-old former sailor, will remain in solitary confinement at a Zhytomyr prison while President Leonid Kuchma considers his appeal. It is unlikely Mr Onoprienko will face execution in the foreseeable future due to Ukraine's current moratorium on capital punishment.

Moral of the story? Always live alone – as had been proven when Onoprienko had been turned in by the cousin he'd been living with at the time.

Not a problem for Nathan, either. The settlement from the wrongful-death lawsuit had left him with money to burn, so it wasn't as though he needed to scrape up the rent money each month. Besides, he'd lived alone since that awful night so many years ago and he was fairly accustomed to it by now.

Was accustomed to it, mind you, but certainly not *happy* about it.

He wiped a tear away from his eye and fought off the sudden feeling of melancholy that he felt settling over him. He stubbed out the cigarette in the Porsche's ashtray, shifted the sports car into fourth gear and pressed down hard on the accelerator. The Porsche's engine purred like a satisfied tiger underneath the hood.

Nathan shook his head. What the hell was there to be sad about, anyway? He was already better than these other killers and he knew it. He was already better than them, and he was only getting better with each passing day. Cold comfort as it was, at least it was *something*.

And maybe a quick little trip to Wichita, Kansas, would help take care of the rest.

CHAPTER TWENTY

Dana wheeled an FBI loaner car onto Edison Street in the Pico-Union section of Los Angeles twenty minutes later and pulled the vehicle over to the side of the road. She switched off the ignition and turned in her seat to face Brown.

'Sit tight for a minute, OK?' she said. 'I think I should probably handle this one on my own.'

Brown glanced out the window at the decrepit neighbourhood. 'Not a good idea, Dana. You got called out by name, you know you're not supposed to do any investigating outside the office by yourself.'

Dana detected a note of genuine concern for her in his voice and found she appreciated it. It felt good to have someone looking out for her. She liked him – in fact, if she let herself go there she'd have to admit she liked him a lot – and she got the feeling it was mutual.

'I know,' she said, 'but she might open up to me more if I go alone.'

Brown looked as if he wasn't going to let it go, then shrugged. 'How about a compromise? I'll go with you but I promise I'll keep in the background – a bodyguard sort of thing.' Then, to lighten the mood, he added, 'And you're right. You might be able to strike up a womanly bond with her. Genetically speaking, that's something I've never been especially good at.'

Dana laughed. She knew his easygoing manner belied a steely resolve when he needed it. She enjoyed working with him. 'Good point,' she said. 'Let's go.'

They climbed out of the car and Dana took a look around. Pico-Union was a dull, grey place – the part of town they never glamorised in the movies and one that felt even more forlorn and forgotten when you saw the massive piles of uncollected garbage rotting away on every street corner.

Not only was the woman they'd come to see today one whom the copycat killer had approached outside Mary Ellen Orton's apartment on the night of her vicious murder, Luz Moreno also happened to be a member of *Mara Salvatrucha* – MS-13 – one of the deadliest street gangs in the world.

It had been started in Los Angeles by Salvadorean immigrants tired of being pushed around by the more entrenched Mexican gangs. *Mara* literally meant 'gang' in Spanish. As for *Salvatrucha*, there was some debate about that. Some said it meant 'Salvadorean army ants' while others maintained it referred to the group of Salvadorean peasant guerrillas who'd made up most of the gang's initial membership in the early 1980s. The '13' was generally considered a tip of the cap to another ruthless LA street gang, *El Emes*, or 'the Ms' – the thirteenth letter of the alphabet. Whatever translation you chose to use, however, it usually meant only one thing to those who dared to cross them.

Muerte. Death.

Dana glanced at Brown, who nodded, and then she

walked toward the street corner where Luz Moreno had told Brown she'd be when they'd talked over the phone an hour earlier. Four or five of Moreno's heavily tattooed fellow gang members stood on alert sentry duty just out of earshot thirty feet away.

Moreno was shorter even than Dana, maybe five-three. Maybe nineteen. Definitely gorgeous. A distinctly Latina face was framed by full, thick hair piled up high on top of her head above a pair of enormous silver hoop earrings. Chocolate-brown eyes gleamed over a broad, flat nose pierced with a tiny diamond. She was wearing a pair of tight black jeans, unlaced Timberlands and an Enyce coat five times too big for her petite frame.

Dana shifted her gaze to the ornate script tattoo on Moreno's neck. *Orgullo Salvadoreno*. Salvadorean Pride.

'You from El Salvador?'

Moreno didn't answer, just as she didn't bother responding to Dana's outstretched hand.

'OK, then – I guess we'll just skip that part.'

Over the past couple of days the Indian summer had shattered like a fumbled dinner plate, dropping the temperature to a chilly if more seasonable sixty degrees, so Moreno shuffled her booted feet against the pavement and shoved her hands deep into her puffy coat pockets against the cold. 'What the hell do you want, lady? It's fuckin' *freezin'* out here and I ain't got all goddamn day. The wrong homies see me talkin' to you and I end up like Brenda Paz. No fuckin' thank you.'

Dana searched her memory until she remembered the name. Brenda Paz was the MS-13 member who'd been found murdered along the banks of the Shenandoah River in northern Virginia in the summer of 2003 – the victim of her fellow gang bangers, who'd taken exception to the fact she'd been sharing information about *Mara Salvatrucha* with the feds.

Brenda Paz had been all of seventeen years old at the time of her brutal murder, just a couple of years younger than Luz Moreno. Brenda Paz had been stabbed more than a dozen times. Brenda Paz had also been four months pregnant.

Blood in, blood out. You live for your mother, you live for your God, you die for your gang.

Dana pulled her collar up against the cold wind that was sweeping the street like an icy broom and fought off a sudden shiver. She couldn't remember Los Angeles ever being *this* cold before, even at this time of year.

'I need you to tell me what you remember about the man you saw in South Central that night, Luz,' she said. 'Anything. Everything. Start at the beginning.'

Moreno screwed her pretty face up in irritation. 'Goddamn it, lady, you gonna get me killed over some stupid shit like that? I already told them fuckers everything I know. Already helped them make their stupid little drawing. Read the fuckin' police report, why don't you?'

Dana stared at her evenly. 'I did, Luz. Now like I said, start at the beginning.'

The young Latina tried holding Dana's blazing stare for a moment, but quickly realised it was a battle she was going to lose. Crawford Bell wasn't the only one in the FBI who could stare somebody down.

Sighing, Moreno shook her head and said, 'OK, here's how it goes – and this is the last goddamn time I want to say it. I was visiting a friend of mine over there when I heard the sirens going off. I went outside to see what the fuck was up and that's when the creepy motherfucker bowed up on

136

me. He stood there until I saw the blood all over him and I screamed. Then he hauled his ass the fuck outta there. There ain't nothin' else to tell, lady. That's the whole goddamn story.'

'What do you mean, he "bowed up" on you?'

Moreno shook her head, an action Dana took as disgust for her ignorance of street slang. 'I mean the motherfucker raised up on me and tried to stare me down, that's what the fuck I mean. Got all up in my face.'

'Did he say anything to you? Anything at all?'

Moreno considered the question for a moment before snapping her gum and stealing a quick peek over her shoulder at the esses. 'Nah,' she said finally. 'He just stood there looking down at me all crazy and shit. It was definitely fucked up, though.'

'How do you mean?'

Moreno eyed Dana for another long moment before sweeping her head around to check the position of her homeboys again. They hadn't moved, but neither had they taken their eyes off them. The natives were definitely starting to get restless. It was good to know Brown was watching *her* back, Dana thought.

Moreno leaned in close – close enough for Dana to catch an unmistakable whiff of Tommy Girl floating on the air. 'He didn't *say* nothin', but it was almost like he was waiting on me to say something to him, you know what I mean?'

The young Latina shook her head, sending her huge silver earrings swaying back and forth. 'All I know is it was royally fucked up and I hope to God I never see his creepy ass again. And that's the truth.'

Dana nodded. She knew the feeling. 'Anything else you remember from that night, Luz? Anything at all?'

For once, Moreno didn't hesitate with her answer. 'His eyes,' she said quickly. 'I remember his eyes.'

'What about them?'

The girl's lower lip began to tremble, and for the first time Dana could see that she was just a frightened little child underneath all her tough bluster. Dana didn't blame her in the least. It was a rough world that Luz Moreno had to live in.

'*Los ojos de Diablo,*' she whispered.

'Translation?'

'It means his eyes were all fucked up, bitch. It means he had the eyes of Satan.'

CHAPTER TWENTY-ONE

Dana brushed her way past the pack of underage, wannabe gang bangers walking down the sidewalk in their matching uniforms of FUBU clothes and returned to the loaner car. FUBU stood for 'For Us, By Us,' which meant that whites weren't welcome to participate. Judging by the hostile glares she received from the aggressive-looking group of young black and Latino boys, she figured that was pretty much the motto for the entire neighbourhood.

Wordlessly, she and Brown got in the car and Dana hit the power door-locks before pulling on her seat belt and cranking the engine to life. Tracy Chapman's 'Fast Car' came on over the stereo.

'Nice song,' Brown said. 'Pretty damn appropriate, considering the circumstances.'

'How much you figure real estate goes for around here? I'm thinking a nice little place for the summers,' Dana said, keeping things light and trying to keep her frustration and fear in check. Mainly frustration. Moreno hadn't told her anything new.

Brown rolled his eyes at her. 'Let's just take our fast car and get the hell out of here. I'm moving. This place gives me the creeps.' He turned serious then. 'So what did Luz Moreno have to say? Looked like things were getting serious there for a moment.'

Dana filled him in as they drove back to the LA field office.

'So we're looking for Satan, huh?' Brown asked.

'Either him or one of his minions.'

'Charming. I'll make sure I start bringing my crucifix along from now on.'

He paused and cracked the passenger-side window to let some fresh air into the car, then glanced down at his watch. 'You ready to move on? We've got a full day of fun activities in front of us.'

'So what's next on the list?' Dana said.

'Well, first we'll meet with the handwriting expert back at the office. Hopefully he'll be able to help us break down the note stitched into the killer's pants. After that we'll go see the sketch artist Luz Moreno worked with the day after the murder. To top things off, we'll meet up with the blood-spatter expert over at Mary Ellen Orton's apartment in South Central.'

'Sounds like fun. Let the games begin.'

Twenty minutes later they were back in the field office conference room downtown discussing possible motives for the killer. Maybe this time they'd make a real breakthrough.

'He obviously hates women,' Brown said. 'No surprise there because they usually do. A revenge complex, perhaps? Maybe he had a horrible mother or a wife who dumped him? Like they always say, there's a very thin line between love and hate.'

Dana was on the verge of coming clean with Brown when a soft rap sounded at the door. A moment later a large unkempt man in his early sixties entered the room holding a sheaf of papers in his right hand.

'Hey, Fred,' Brown said. 'Thanks for coming.'

The handwriting expert smiled a full smile of brown

teeth at Dana while Brown introduced them. Brown pulled back a seat at the conference table for him and he and Dana took seats opposite.

'What have you got for us, Mr Spangler?' Dana asked, taking over.

Spangler lowered his overweight frame into a plastic chair and spread photocopies of the Disneyland note out on the table in front of them. 'Well, near as I can tell, it looks like a classic case of OCD.'

Dana studied the papers. 'What makes you say that?'

Spangler leaned forward and traced the letters on the note with a ballpoint pen. 'See here how each occurrence of every letter is exactly identical? That's actually very unusual. Most people tend to write in *approximately* the same manner, but this guy is off the charts for consistency.'

He produced a small magnifying glass from the breast pocket of his rumpled suit and ran it over the note. 'See here how all the Ds have exactly the same hump, and how each of the Es curls down in exactly the same fashion? It's like that throughout the entire note.'

'Don't most people do that?' Brown asked. 'I know my handwriting's always been pretty consistent.'

Spangler shook his head, sending his impressive jowls quivering into motion. 'That may be the case, Jeremy, but you most certainly don't do it with this precision.' He rifled through his sheaf of papers and slid a transparency over the note. 'I've copied down the letters in question. As you can see here, there's not even the *slightest* deviation in any of them. It's almost like he was using a typewriter.'

'But he was using a normal ballpoint pen, right?' Dana asked.

Spangler nodded. 'A Scripto Blue No. 4, to be exact.

141

Anyway, that's what makes this so goddamn unusual. He did this by hand – but he also managed to do it with the precision of a machine.'

Dana looked up at him over the papers. 'What else does the handwriting tell us?' This wasn't really telling them anything they didn't know or suspect already, but Spangler might just hold an ace up his sleeve.

Spangler leaned forward again, excited now. 'Glad you asked. As you can see here, his writing also has a lot of pressure to it. That's what makes it appear so dark. The heavier the pressure, the more emotional energy the writer possesses. Also, the lack of a slant is very important to note. People whose handwriting slants to the right are more likely to keep their cool under pressure than those who don't exhibit any slant at all. People who possess very little emotional energy use light pressure and a leftward slant. They generally prefer to avoid confrontation. That's definitely not the case here.'

'So what's your verdict, then?' Brown asked.

Spangler looked up at him. 'My verdict is that this guy doesn't like disorder, Jeremy. In *anything*. My verdict is he craves perfection, even on a subconscious level.'

'A pretty lofty goal,' Dana said.

Spangler gathered his papers together into a loose pile and, with a groan, rose to his feet. 'Lofty, yes, but I'd say this guy is pretty close to perfect already.'

CHAPTER TWENTY-TWO

Ten minutes after Spangler left the conference room, Dana and Brown made their way down the hall to Jim McGreevy's office where they found him hunched over a large drafting table in the middle of the room, the fresh pencil in his left hand poised and ready for action.

At fifty-four and jokingly referred to as 'Rembrandt' by his less artistic co-workers, McGreevy was generally considered the best composite-sketch artist in the country. People everywhere knew his work, if not his name. His two most famous examples – or, more accurately, *infamous* examples – could be found in the ubiquitous composite he'd done of the Unabomber in 1996 and the widely distributed sketch he'd made of the phantom black man that Susan Smith claimed had abducted her two young sons out in South Carolina shortly after she'd drowned them in a man-made lake in 1994.

McGreevy looked up when Dana knocked on the door. 'Special Agent Whitestone,' he said, rising from his chair and extending his right hand. 'I've been expecting you. Please come in.'

Dana shook hands with McGreevy, who then turned and smiled at Brown. 'How you doing, Jeremy?'

Brown sighed. 'I'll be doing a hell of a lot better if you

can tell us something we can actually use, Jim. I feel like we're running around in circles here.'

Dana interjected, 'We were told that Luz Moreno came by to see you the other day, Mr. McGreevy.'

McGreevy nodded. 'Yes, as a matter of fact she did. Quite the little wildcat, that one.'

Dana smiled. 'Tell me about it. I just got done talking to her myself an hour ago. Anyway, did anything productive come of the meeting?'

McGreevy nodded again and turned to unlock the large silver filing cabinet next to his desk. Reaching in, he extracted a folder and took out an eight-by-ten sheet of paper. 'Ah yes, the composite of the Night Stalker copycat. Have a look for yourself.'

Dana took the sheet of paper from his right hand and looked down at it, suddenly feeling like she'd just been slapped.

The eyes jumped off the paper at her like a rapist in the night. Dark, simmering, unbalanced. *Los ojos de Diablo.* Luz Moreno was absolutely right. He *did* have the eyes of Satan.

He also had the eyes of someone else Dana knew from her past.

Almost almond-shaped with impossibly long eyelashes, the eyes were the exact same eyes that had visited her dreams every night for the past thirty-four years. A chill went through her, right to the bone.

Other than the eyes, though, the rest of the composite drawing was hardly remarkable. No other distinctive features you couldn't find in half the male population of the United States. Still, the eyes were enough to make Dana's heart thud in her chest.

Brown looked at the drawing. 'Charming-looking fellow.'

McGreevy chuckled. 'Homicidal maniacs usually are. I'll tell you what – his eyes remind me of good old Charlie Manson's. You know, how they looked in that picture on the cover of *Life* magazine? But young Miss Moreno insisted that's what they looked like. Other than that, though, she wasn't able to provide very much detail, I'm afraid. Actually happens quite a bit, to tell you the truth. The eyes are the only things anyone can ever seem to remember.'

Dana nodded. She knew the feeling. She remembered the eyes of the monster who had murdered her parents as well as she knew her own, but she wouldn't have been able to pick the rest of his face out of a line-up if her life depended on it. 'When's this going to be released to the media?' she asked, trying to disguise the undercurrent of fear rippling through her voice. She could no longer ignore the now very real possibility the killer was *her* killer. It had been just a feeling before, a very strong feeling, but a hunch that she could push aside as her overactive imagination working overtime. Now too many things were coming together for her to be able to dismiss her feeling as paranoia. She'd have to tell Brown about her past, and soon.

'It's already out there.' McGreevy broke through her thoughts.

Dana was happy to hear at least this bit of good news. 'Great. It's one of the best leads we've got so far—'

'One of the *only* leads we've got so far,' Brown cut in.

Dana turned to him and smiled thinly, fear still rippling through her body. She took a deep breath and steadied herself. 'Exactly. So what do you say we get back out there and try to drum up a few more before this jerk has the chance to kill again?'

'Lead the way,' Brown said.

They thanked McGreevy for his help and made their way back outside to the loaner car. As they drove over to Mary Ellen Orton's apartment, they discussed the composite drawing that the sketch artist had prepared. Even though the focus was mainly on the eyes, hopefully somebody out there would recognise the rest of the face, no matter how bland the rendering, and they'd take another step toward tracking this killer down. Still, Dana knew she couldn't rely on that. She and Brown had to start making some serious inroads through good old-fashioned police work.

Ten minutes later Dana slid the car into an open space on Drexel Street in South Central and she and Brown got out. It was their last appointment of the day. Dana just hoped this would give them something new. Each expert was painting a very ugly picture, but had they given them enough to actually catch the sick son of a bitch?

FBI blood-spatter specialist Jeff Simmons got out of his own vehicle fifty feet away and waved them over. He was wearing a snug pair of Levis, old work boots and a tight white T-shirt with a slogan on it that said 'Talk Nerdy To Me'.

Simmons smiled at them as they approached, showing straight white teeth. 'Pleasure, guys,' he said. To Dana, he added, 'Special Agent Whitestone, nice to meet you. Been hearing some really awesome things about you.'

'Same here,' Dana lied. 'Your reputation precedes you.'

Simmons laughed and adjusted the canvas bag on his shoulder. 'That's what I was afraid of. Anyway, come on in and I'll give you guys the grand tour.'

Thirty seconds later he lifted the yellow police tape stretched across the front door and led them into Mary

146

Ellen Orton's apartment. Dana stepped inside and was immediately surprised by just how *tiny* it was. Not much bigger than a studio apartment, if that. There was a small living room with a couple of pieces of mismatched furniture, including a rickety TV table with a pair of metal knitting needles lying across the top. To her right there was an even smaller kitchen. The musty smell of an old person's home pervaded the entirety of the tight space, tickling Dana's nostrils and making her want to sneeze.

A short walk that took all of five seconds led them to the only bedroom. In the middle of the hopelessly small space it looked as though a plastic Heinz ketchup bottle had exploded on the single bed shoved against the far wall.

Dana fought a wave of revulsion as Simmons passed out thin latex gloves for them to pull on. 'What does the blood tell us?' she asked.

Simmons dropped his canvas bag to the floor and pulled the blackout curtains closed. He flicked on a flashlight and ran the light over Mary Ellen Orton's sheets. Dana blinked as her eyes adjusted to the new lighting.

'There are three basic types of blood spatter,' Simmons said, his frat-boy tone giving way to a decidedly more professional demeanour now. 'Low, medium and high velocity. I'll give you a quick rundown on each. Where do you want to start?'

'How about we start at the beginning?' Brown said.

Simmons nodded. 'Good idea. The first thing to remember is that blood acts a lot like spilled water. Low-velocity spatter usually happens from drippage and comes from a force of impact of five feet per second or less. The size of the droplets is only a couple of centimetres. Say somebody was stabbed and they stumbled around the room bleeding. Low-velocity spatter happens in cases like that. It's not from the initial injury, but more of a secondary circumstance.'

'And medium-velocity?' Dana asked.

Simmons waved the hand he was using to hold the flashlight, casting eerie dancing shadows on the ceiling. 'Medium-velocity spatter comes from a force of impact between five and a hundred feet per second. Usually comes from blunt-force trauma, but a stabbing can cause it, too. Usually happens when someone is beaten to death with a baseball bat or a fist or something like that, though. We call it "projected blood". It leaves a very distinctive pattern. Think of it this way: it's like somebody shot blood through one of those Super Soaker water guns. Same basic result.'

Brown looked at the bloody sheets covering Mary Ellen Orton's bed. 'Pleasant thought,' he said. 'So that brings us to high-velocity spatter.'

Simmons nodded and refocused the flashlight on the sheets. 'Exactly. High-velocity spatter travels more than a hundred feet per second, resulting in a fine spray. The droplets measure less than a millimetre in diameter, and that kind of spatter usually comes from gunshot wounds.'

Dana studied the sheets. 'That looks like fine spray to me. Wouldn't that mean high-velocity spatter? But the killer didn't use a gun. He used a knife.'

Simmons nodded. 'You're right. But gunshot wounds usually cause spatter in the front *and* back. Obviously we're not dealing with that here because there's no spatter in the back, only in the front. So when we add the blood indications to our knowledge that the old woman was mutilated with a knife, it's a pretty simple equation to figure out. And if you look closely you'll see a void, which makes a knife our most likely suspect. This shit was up close and personal.'

Brown and Dana exchanged a look. 'A void?' Brown said.

Simmons shook his head. 'Sorry about that.' He ran the flashlight over a clean area on the sheets and focused the light in the middle. 'A void occurs when the blood spatter is stopped by something, an interrupting object. In this case we've got a void roughly the size of a man's torso. That explains the blood you guys found on the killer's clothing. He blocked the spray with his body.'

'Very considerate of him,' Brown said.

Simmons laughed and flicked the flashlight off before reopening the curtains. 'Yeah. No doubt this guy was second runner-up in a Miss Congeniality contest somewhere down the line.'

Dana squinted her eyes against the bright LA sunshine streaming into the room. 'Your conclusion?'

Simmons pulled his gloves off with a loud plastic snapping noise. 'My conclusion is that we're dealing with one powerful son of a bitch here, Special Agent Whitestone. Much stronger than your average guy. Or at least a hell of a lot angrier.'

Dana and Brown left Mary Ellen Orton's apartment and stepped outside. The schizophrenic Los Angeles weather had heated up once again, so Brown took off his coat and Dana did the same. They hadn't really gotten anywhere with any of the experts, but Dana was glad they'd given it a shot. It beat the alternative.

They were halfway to the car when her cellphone rang in her purse. She stopped walking and dug it out. A female voice sounded in her ear.

'Agent Whitestone, this is Maggie Flynn at the Child Abduction and Serial Murder Investigative Resources Center in Quantico. We've come up with a likely probability regarding serial killers who used plastic bags in the commission of their crimes.'

Dana's heart leaped up into her throat. 'Go on.'

'Dennis Rader,' Flynn said. 'The BTK Killer. Killed ten people out in Wichita, Kansas, starting in 1974. Didn't get caught until 2005.'

Dana thanked the woman and flipped her cellphone off, trying to control the hot jolt of adrenalin suddenly coursing through her veins.

Brown folded his coat over his arm. 'What was that all about?'

Dana's hands shook as she looked up at him and relayed what Flynn had just told her.

'Holy shit,' Brown said, his eyes widening. 'So are you going to book the plane tickets, or do you want me to do it?'

CHAPTER TWENTY-THREE

On the flight out to Wichita the next morning Dana finally filled Brown in about how the plastic letters in Cleveland might tie in with her own past, keeping her voice low to make sure no one overheard them discussing the case.

His deep brown eyes flashed with anger as he put his tray table up and turned in his seat to face her. 'Jesus Christ, Dana. You're just telling me this *now*?'

Dana's ears burned. She didn't blame him for being upset with her for withholding the information, but it wasn't as if *no one* in the FBI knew about it. Still, that didn't mean he couldn't show a little sympathy for what she'd been through. She doubted *he*'d ever been called out by name by a serial killer. Then she berated herself. This wasn't a 'pity-me' party.

Almost as if he sensed what she was thinking, Brown took the sharp edge out of his voice. 'I'm sorry that happened to you, Dana. I can't imagine how hard that must have been.'

'Still is.'

Now it was Brown's turn to feel embarrassed. 'Of course. I guess I'm no whiz in the social-graces department, am I? Add that to the long list of other things I'm no good at.'

An awkward moment of silence passed between them before he cleared his throat. 'So did you go live with your relatives after it happened or what? You were an only child, right?'

Dana nodded. 'Yeah, but there were no relatives for me to go stay with, so I sort of got shuttled around to various foster homes after that. I guess I wasn't very easy to deal with. Nobody ever seemed to want to keep me for very long.'

Brown looked uneasy. 'I don't know what to say, Dana. I'm very sorry. I just wish you'd told me sooner. It makes the case a whole lot more complicated, that's for sure.'

She waved a hand in the air. 'I know, and I'm sorry too. But I'm all grown-up now and we have a killer to catch.'

Brown nodded. 'So now that we know what the plastic bag at Mary Ellen Orton's apartment probably meant, what else do we know about Dennis Rader?'

As quickly as she could, Dana recounted BTK's first murders – horrific affairs that had claimed the lives of four members of the Otero family. Then she went on to describe the other murders that had followed.

'Rader was eventually caught when he mailed a round of taunts to Wichita Police on an ordinary floppy disk under the mistaken impression that it couldn't be used to track him down,' she said. 'But when the authorities traced the metadata on the disk they saw that a man calling himself "Dennis" had created it. He'd also left behind a link to a local Lutheran church where he served as a deacon. In the end, a simple Internet search was all it took to bring him down.'

Brown shook his head. 'Not very smart of him.'

'Yeah, but I'd say the guy we're after now is smart

enough for both of them. That's the problem. We're not dealing with an idiot here. He's starting to make Hannibal Lecter look like an amateur.'

Brown stared into her eyes. 'So, do you think it might be the same man who murdered your parents?'

Without warning, tears sprang into the corners of Dana's eyes. She closed them quickly so that Brown couldn't see the pain hidden there. 'I don't know.'

Brown reached out a hand and touched her arm lightly. 'It's OK to feel scared, Dana. Anybody in their right mind would feel the exact same way in your situation. Hell, I feel scared too.'

Dana opened her eyes and looked at him. She straightened up. The killer from her past wasn't going to ruin the rest of her life like he'd ruined her childhood. 'It's not that I'm scared *of* him. It's that I'm scared of what I'm going to do *to* him when we finally catch the motherfucker.'

It was almost noon before their flight finally touched down in Wichita. They found a cab outside the terminal and rode in silence over to the Sedgwick County Sheriff's Office. Dana felt like a football player in the locker room right before the big game. She took several deep breaths and put her game face on. For the first time in months she felt like she was finally taking some real steps to close the gap between herself and the killer.

Half an hour later she and Brown flashed their badges and were buzzed into the building that housed Sheriff Don Jackson's office. A pretty woman in her early sixties wearing a fashionable purple blouse and stylishly cut short silver hair was seated behind a massive desk in the reception area. She looked up and smiled at them when they came in.

'I'm Janie Briggs,' the woman said. 'The sheriff's receptionist. I take it you're the folks from the FBI who called earlier?'

Dana nodded, and Janie Briggs turned in her seat. She motioned to the mahogany door on her left. 'Please go right in. Sheriff Jackson is expecting you.'

A moment later Dana knocked on the door and pushed it open. Don Jackson was sitting behind his desk sharpening a fishing hook. He put it down on the desk in front of him and rose to his feet as they came in, pushing a wide-brimmed hat back on his head and smiling brightly. He looked like he'd stepped right out of central casting, every inch the do-good middle-America county cop in the latest Hollywood movie.

'Special Agent Whitestone, Special Agent Brown. Welcome. It's a pleasure to have you here.'

Jackson gestured to a pair of chairs on the other side of his desk. Dana was reminded of the fact that the position of sheriff was an elected one, which most likely explained Jackson's obvious political acumen. Someone from the top would have had to clear this with him. 'Please have a seat,' Jackson said. 'Would you care for a drink? Coffee? Tea? Water?'

Dana shook her head, and Brown did the same.

'No, thank you, Sheriff,' she said. 'We're fine. Thank you for having us, though. I know you must be a busy man so I'll get straight to the point. We have reason to believe that our killer is going to strike again, right here in Wichita. In fact, it's more than a hunch. He *is* going to strike again – here. We don't have a single moment to lose.'

Jackson frowned and leaned back, his stomach protruding over his belt. He sat forward again, his hands on his desk. 'Can't say I like the sound of that. What exactly do you need from me?'

'How many deputies do you have on your force?' Dana asked.

'Three hundred and fifty. Give or take.'

'How many are on duty right now?' Brown asked.

Jackson leaned back in his chair again. 'Well, now, we work in three shifts so that means about a hundred and twenty or so are working right now.'

Dana nodded. 'When did the last shift get off?'

Jackson glanced down at his watch. 'About an hour ago.'

'That counts them out,' Dana said. 'How long would it take you to get the rested shift out on the streets?'

Jackson pursed his lips; he was looking worried now. 'Everybody's on a beeper, so I could probably have them out there within the hour, but I really don't have money in the budget for all that overtime, Special Agent Whitestone. I'm on a shoestring already as it is.'

Brown waved a hand in the air and rose to his feet. Dana did the same. 'Just get them out there, Sheriff,' he said. 'The government will cover any cost overruns.'

Jackson nodded. He'd obviously made a decision. They were serious about this. They needed all the manpower he had at his disposal. 'OK, I'll get on it right away. Is there anything else you need?'

Dana held Jackson's gaze as they left the room. 'As a matter of fact, yes. If your officers find themselves in any danger – any danger at all – tell them to shoot first and ask questions later.'

CHAPTER TWENTY-FOUR

18 Overlook Drive – Wichita, Kansas – 1:30 p.m.

Bind. Torture. Kill.

That had been Dennis Rader's plan way back in 1974, and that was Nathan Stiedowe's plan today.

His latest target wasn't the thieving bitch who'd stolen his life, but rather just another bored suburban housewife and mother on the lookout for some extramarital hanky-panky. Unfortunately for this philandering housewife, however, responding to his ad on the Lonely Hearts Club website would net her a hell of a lot more than just a little afternoon delight while hubby was away at work. Before the day was over she'd never again look at her cosy little street as if it was the hillbilly equivalent of Wisteria Lane.

The sounds of Ashley Ball playing Lecuona's 'Gitanerias' filled the car as Nathan swung his latest beauty – a silver 2005 BMW 350*i* equipped with power *everything* this time – onto Overlook Drive in Wichita, Kansas, and let out a deep breath.

He parked half a mile down the street from the Aiken house and leaned over to retrieve his briefcase from the passenger seat. No need to bother with the ski mask, obviously; a disguise wasn't called for this time either. Once again it was *important* that they should see his face. A copy of the *Los Angeles Times* lay across the back seat.

He'd finally made the front page – or at least his *likeness* had. Not that the composite sketch was much of a likeness at all. As always, the amateurs had produced hopelessly amateurish work, but that wasn't surprising. Hell, they were making things almost *too* easy on him.

Nathan was still whistling the melody of 'Gitanerias' when he turned up their driveway five minutes later and made his way around to the back of the residence before pulling back the leather glove on his left hand and checking his expensive watch.

One thirty-seven p.m. *High fucking time for history to rewrite itself.*

He set the briefcase down next to the back door and extracted a pair of wire cutters. As he began systematically snipping the phone lines he tried to conjure up a sexual fantasy but it was difficult. Janice Aiken's profile picture showed only a porky couch potato who most likely spent the majority of her time watching *Oprah* while popping an endless series of bonbons into her big fat mouth. Still, even if love wasn't in the cards for today, Nathan knew that updating Dennis Rader's unforgettable crime would go a long way toward helping him accomplish his *own* sacred mission, and the importance of that could never be underestimated. He and Dana Whitestone still had a lot of unfinished business left to attend to and he wouldn't rest until that business was finally complete.

But first a little more fun. The thieving little bitch was going to just *love* this.

He'd just finished cutting the wires and was in the process of clicking the briefcase shut when the back screen door suddenly banged open.

She was a girl of about sixteen, the hard nipples on her

pert breasts straining against a ridiculously tight white Snoopy T-shirt. She smiled at him quizzically, showing a mouthful of silver braces. 'Whoa! You scared the shit out of me, mister!'

She laughed the nervous laugh of a teenager, unsure of herself despite her budding beauty. Smiling, Nathan felt a stirring in his jeans.

The girl was blushing noticeably as she tapped her chest rapidly to indicate he'd nearly given her a heart attack. 'What the hell are you doing back here anyway? Is there something I can help you with?'

Rednecks. Why were they always so goddamn *trusting*?

Nathan quickly turned up the wattage on his smile as he straightened back up. 'Sorry about that, miss – didn't mean to startle you. My name is Travis Seldon and I'm actually here to see your mom. Seems there's been some trouble with the phone lines in the area lately and since I'm the district supervisor they sent me out here to check things out.'

Smiling wider – instantly at ease – Marlene Aiken opened the screen door all the way and stepped aside to let him in. 'Well, come on in then. You want something to drink?'

'No, thanks, dear. But thanks for asking.'

As soon as he stepped inside the doorway of their warm little house, Nathan's heart almost exploded in his chest when the huge black Labrador came barrelling around the corner at him like a runaway freight train, barking furiously as its hard nails clicked and slid across the tiled surface of the kitchen floor. Skidding to a halt three feet away, the massive Lab bowed its muscular back and bared its sharp yellow fangs. A low, menacing growl issued from deep within its thick throat.

Marlene Aiken reached down and grabbed the dog by its worn leather collar. 'Settle down, Rocky!' she admonished harshly, at the same time raising her big blue eyes back up to Nathan and smiling sheepishly. 'Don't worry about him, mister, he's just a big ol' baby, this one. I'm serious – he's all bark and no bite.'

More than he could say for himself. Still, dogs were always bad news. They had that uncanny ability to *sense* things.

Nathan forced a quick laugh. 'All the same, could you maybe put him outside while I'm here? He really is a beautiful dog – used to have one like him myself when I was a kid, as a matter of fact – but I have these terrible allergies, you see.'

Marlene Aiken was still smiling as she tugged at Rocky's collar. 'Can't put him out because he'll just run away, but I'll put him in my bedroom and let my mom know you're here. Make yourself at home.'

Even as he fought his irritation at the altered script, Nathan nonetheless felt another, more powerful stirring in his jeans as he watched her walk away, the sight of her tight little ass shifting back and forth in her tiny yellow shorts driving him wild with lust. Why the hell did fresh meat always have to be so goddamn *erotic*?

Halfway through the fantasy where he had the little slut bent over the living-room couch while he drilled her from behind, a man in his early fifties walked into the kitchen, smiling broadly as he extended his right hand. 'Hey there, I'm Scott Aiken. You're from the phone company?'

Without hesitating, without even *thinking*, Nathan dropped his briefcase to the floor with a dull thud, took one quick step forward and drove his right fist hard into the exposed area beneath the man's outstretched hand, audibly cracking several of Scott Aiken's ribs. A quick progression of surprised, pained and disbelieving looks jockeyed for position on his weather-beaten face as his groan of pain filled the homey little kitchen decorated with a variety of ridiculous knick-knacks.

'Nice to meet you, Scott,' Nathan said calmly. 'Tell me, sir, do you have *any* idea what a stupid whore your wife is?'

CHAPTER TWENTY-FIVE

Dana and Brown borrowed an unmarked car from the lot at the Sedgwick County Sheriff's Office. Dana didn't want to waste time here waiting for a rental company to deliver them a car. That kind of delay could mean the difference between life and death. So they agreed to keep the arrangement quiet and adjusted the scanner to the closed frequency that Jackson had told them about. A descrambling device inside the scanner ensured that only law enforcement would be privy to any communications, so there'd be no need to worry about the press getting wind of what they were up to. Thank God for small favours. They didn't want anything getting in the way this time.

'Where exactly are we going?' Brown asked her.

'We're just going to drive around and keep our eyes peeled,' Dana said. 'Four more eyes on the street can't hurt.'

Brown nodded and opened a window a crack. 'Makes sense.'

Though it was almost the middle of November now, it was unseasonably warm in Kansas so there wasn't any snow on the ground yet, which was a bad thing. Snow usually picked up a fair amount of trace evidence, including footprints. Dana closed her eyes. Why should the weather be different from anything else? Up to this point, *everything* had seemed to be working against them.

'Forgive me for bringing this up again,' Brown said, 'but I think your parents would have been very proud of you, Dana. You do know that, right?'

Dana opened her eyes again. 'Yeah, I guess on some level I do. But I still miss them every single day.'

'Ever think about getting married?' Brown asked. 'Having a family of your own?'

Dana laughed. 'Nah, I don't think I'm cut out for it. Don't have the personality for it.'

Brown produced a hard *pfft* sound with his lips. 'What are you talking about? You're a wonderful woman, Dana, and I'm sure you'd make a wonderful mom, too. Don't sell yourself short. The rest of the world will do that for you. And if I've learned anything about you since we started working together, it's that the rest of the world would be making one hell of a big mistake . . .' He blushed, aware that he might have overstepped the mark.

Dana's own cheeks flushed. Not knowing how to respond, she deflected the line of questioning with one of her own. 'What about you?' she asked.

There was an awkward pause as Dana pulled the car onto a sleepy little lane about ten miles away from the Sheriff's Office. 'Listen, Dana,' Brown said after a while. 'My timing's lousy, I know, and I'm really sorry if this is out of line, and please just say so if it is, but I was thinking that maybe we could go out for bite to eat once this is all over.'

Dana tried to hide the smile on her face as she gently pressed her foot down on the accelerator and eased the car down the street.

'We'll see, Jeremy,' she said. 'Maybe we could.'

CHAPTER TWENTY-SIX

Janice Aiken walked in from the bedroom where she'd been watching one of her movies on the Lifetime Network and was shocked to find the man from the phone company holding a huge black pistol to her husband's head.

Obviously in great pain, Scott was clutching at his side and groaning, but he still tried to smile at her. Despite their many marital difficulties and the fact that twenty years of marriage had cooled down most of the passion they'd once shared in the bedroom, Scott was still a *good* man.

'Don't be afraid, baby,' he told her. 'This man just needs the car and he needs some money. If we don't give him any trouble he's going to leave us alone. Everything's going to be all right if we just keep our cool and don't do anything stupid.'

He turned to Nathan. 'Isn't that right, sir?'

Nathan smiled. 'Right as a summer rain, my friend. You're all going to be just fine. You have my word on that.'

A moment later Marlene Aiken came into the kitchen to find out what all the commotion was about. Her jaw nearly hit the floor as she stared at them in disbelief. 'What the *fuck*, you stupid asshole?' she snapped, breaking the words off with her teeth like peanut brittle. 'Get the fuck away from my dad!'

Scott took a deep breath, wincing at the pain in his ribs. 'Marlene, just shut up, OK, honey? We're all going to be real cool and listen to what this man says.'

In the girl's bedroom down the hall Rocky was going *berserk*, barking angrily at the top of his healthy lungs and repeatedly throwing his massive body against the thin door. As the door rattled fiercely against the jamb with each powerful blow, Nathan wondered idly how much longer it would hold.

He shook the thought from his head and turned to Janice. 'Better shut that dog up or it's going to end up with a bullet in its head. I hate dogs, anyway, you know. Disgusting creatures. They eat their own shit.'

The pitiful little sound that came out of her made all the small hairs on the back of his neck stand up.

'What do you want from us?' she sobbed. 'We didn't *do* anything to you.'

Despite everything else going on at the moment, Janice Aiken felt her cheeks flush with embarrassment at the sound of her own voice. God, how she wished she could be stronger, more like the heroines on the Lifetime Network, who would no doubt grab a kitchen knife from the nearest drawer and fearlessly attack the man threatening her family. But Janice knew her place in life. Growing up as the fat girl everywhere she went, she'd *always* known her place.

He was handsome, too. She was disgusted with herself for thinking it, but it was true. His dark brown eyes were menacing but full of life, and his hands looked very strong – the kind of hands she imagined running over her body while she soaked in her bubble bath each night, often allowing her own hands to slip beneath the surface of the water to relieve the constant ache throbbing between her thighs.

She watched numbly as the man in her kitchen leaned down to retrieve his shiny black briefcase from the floor. He straightened back up and slowly looked at each of them one by one. 'OK, everybody, time for the next act. Let's all head back to the master bedroom.'

Scott Aiken took a step forward, but the girls didn't move a muscle. 'Do as he says,' Scott said sharply, repeating the order more harshly when they didn't comply immediately.

As the terrified family headed in single file down the hall, Rocky nearly broke down Marlene's bedroom door as they passed. But the jamb still held.

Once inside the master bedroom, Nathan looked over at the TV with disgust – some obnoxious drivel starring Lindsay Wagner, who was sporting two of the fakest-looking black eyes he'd ever seen in his life. 'Turn that crap off,' he said to Janice. 'It'll rot your fucking brain.'

With shaking hands she clicked the remote, rendering the house silent save for Rocky's relentless barking.

Nathan set his briefcase down on the floor and tossed two lengths of cord over to Janice before motioning to Scott. 'Tie him up – feet and hands. Try anything funny and I'll shove this gun right up your daughter's tight little pussy and pull the trigger. Don't test me on this. I'm really not in the mood for any games right now.'

Janice hesitated, but Scott smiled at her. 'Just do it, honey. It's going to be OK, I promise. This man has given me his word.'

When his wife had finished securing his wrists and ankles, Scott looked at Nathan again. 'Would it be all right if I lie down on the bed? My ribs are killing me. You've got one hell of a punch there, partner.'

Nathan smiled, surprised to find himself actually *liking*

Scott Aiken despite the odd circumstances they found themselves in. The man was a co-star in his nifty little play without even knowing it, and a damn talented one at that. 'Be my guest, Scott,' he said warmly. 'You've been such a hospitable host I think you've earned it.'

Turning to Marlene, Nathan said, 'Put a pillow under his head. Make your daddy as comfortable as possible, baby girl.'

The young girl glared at him, her silver braces flashing in the bright sunlight streaming through the bedroom window, but did as she was told. When her father was in a prone position on her parents' bed she turned back to Nathan with her small hands planted defiantly on her slender hips. 'Now what, dickhead?'

Nathan chuckled. *Teenagers.* Why did they always think they were going to live for ever?

He tossed two more lengths of cord at her bare feet and motioned to Janice. 'Take those and tie your mom up, too.'

'No way. No fucking way.'

God, she was sexy.

'Marlene!' Scott snapped. 'Just do it, honey. Don't talk back any more.'

Reluctantly, the young girl finally did as she was instructed. But if looks could have killed, then Nathan Stiedowe would have been dead on the floor.

CHAPTER TWENTY-SEVEN

Dana and Brown were almost at the end of the sleepy little lane when the scanner crackled out a report over the closed frequency.

'Possible domestic – 18 Overlook Drive,' the disembodied voice of the dispatcher said. 'Several calls from neighbours of a dog barking and people screaming.'

Dana's heart somersaulted in her chest. 'Punch the address into the GPS,' she told Brown.

Her partner did as instructed. After what seemed an interminable wait while the global-positioning satellite processed the directions, a female voice with a slight British accent finally spoke.

'Turn around and go to the end of the street. Turn left after four hundred yards.'

Dana whipped the car around and slammed her foot down hard on the accelerator. The engine whined to life underneath the hood. 'How far?' she asked Brown.

Brown studied the readout on the GPS. 'Twelve point one miles. Ten minutes if we hurry and avoid traffic.'

Dana activated the power window on the driver's side of the car and slapped a powerful magnetic siren onto the roof. 'Buckle up,' she told him. 'We're going to make it in five.'

CHAPTER TWENTY-EIGHT

The little girl had spunk. Nathan liked that. Not to mention those hot little tits and that sweet little ass of hers. Still, even though he would have loved to fuck her right there in front of her parents, he just didn't have time for simple fun and games at the moment. It really was a pity.

When Janice had been secured and was lying next to her husband on the bed, Nathan took two more lengths of cord from the briefcase and quickly tied Marlene up in the same fashion. He reached back into the briefcase and took out a pair of sharp scissors before slowly backing her up against the bedroom wall, looking over his shoulder at her parents as he deliberately ran his hands over their daughter's delicious little pubescent breasts. He smiled when the girl's nipples hardened involuntarily beneath his touch.

Scott Aiken groaned – the sound a mixture of pain and rage while tears of abject horror pooled in his eyes – but he didn't say a word. The fool was still trying to play it cool. But when Nathan used the scissors to cut away their daughter's Snoopy T-shirt, finally exposing those delectable little buds, Janice Aiken's ear-splitting scream caused an enraged Rocky to redouble his frantic efforts to break free of his prison in the girl's bedroom down the hall.

Nathan turned to her and slowly shook his head. 'Bad

move, Janice. You know what you just did? You just cost your daughter one of these pretty little nipples, that's what the fuck you just did.'

In a flash he had Marlene's throat pinned hard against the wall with his left elbow. Reaching down, he pinched the puckered areola of her left breast between his right thumb and index finger and pulled at it like a piece of bubble gum until it was nothing more than an elongated piece of stippled pink flesh.

Marlene Aiken's big blue eyes widened in horror as Nathan Stiedowe calmly snipped her left nipple off.

When he let go of her throat, her horrified scream of pain was deafening, and Nathan watched in amazement as the bright red blood gushed from her severed nipple and down over her belly-button-ringed navel, staining her tight yellow shorts and splashing down onto her legs. Her mother's screams followed an instant later; screams of murderous rage and disbelief. Howling with impotent fury at the sound of his masters' suffering, Rocky crashed against the girl's bedroom door again.

Nathan would have to work more quickly now. Within thirty seconds he had a strip of silver duct tape slapped over both of the females' mouths, finally shutting the screeching bitches up.

He tossed the bloody scissors back into the briefcase and took out a plastic convenience-store bag before taking a step toward Scott Aiken.

'No, please, God, no!' Scott moaned, frantically jerking his head away.

But a moment later the bag was on and Nathan was tightening it around Scott's neck with the final length of cord. Scott's gaping mouth desperately sucked away at the blue plastic as he tried in vain to draw a breath into his tortured lungs, the horrified expression on his face alternately visible and then invisible again through the thin translucent material.

Her husband slowly suffocating to death in front of her eyes, Janice Aiken was next. Fully erect now, Nathan leaned over Scott's flailing body and wrapped his powerful hands around her double-chinned throat, squeezing with all his might until he felt her jugular vein collapse beneath the enormous pressure. She was dead within a minute.

Marlene Aiken was last. *Dessert.*

Tears of horror streamed down her pretty face and streaked her mascara in thick rivers of dirty water as Nathan calmly wrapped his strong hands around her slender throat and began to squeeze. The light scent of her fruity perfume floated up into his nostrils and made him feel dizzy.

'No time to fuck today, honey,' he moaned into her ear. 'Believe me, sweetheart, I'm just as disappointed about it as you are.'

Marlene Aiken's big blue eyes fluttered as she lost consciousness.

'As a matter of fact, I'm probably *more* disappointed about it than you are.'

Just then, the gunshot sound of splintering wood down the hall heralded Rocky's sudden arrival, causing Nathan to turn his head just in time to see the huge dog come barrelling into the master bedroom at full speed. Almost as if the scene were unfolding in slow motion, the animal launched its muscular body through the air, its sharp fangs like yellow daggers pointed at Nathan's throat.

Acting on instinct alone, Nathan dropped Marlene's dead body to the floor and whipped a pistol from his waistband in one fluid motion, squeezing the trigger and finally silencing the yapping mutt in mid-air with a single headshot between its eyes.

As Rocky lay convulsing on the bedroom floor three feet away, Nathan moved forward and drew back a powerful leg, kicking the dog in the head as hard as he could. Neck badly broken, the Labrador suddenly ceased its thrashing.

On his way out of the house, Nathan heard Marlene's pink cellphone vibrating on the kitchen table but didn't bother answering it. Instead, he simply paper-clipped the pornographic photograph of a naked transsexual to the floppy disk he'd created and tossed it onto the kitchen counter next to the sink.

A bead of sweat slipped down the back of Nathan's neck as he grabbed the keys to the Aikens' Infiniti G35 from a hook on the wall and quickly left through the front door. Thirty seconds later he was inside their car and making the short drive over to the nearest Wal-Mart SuperCenter. They were all over the place in Kansas. Big fucking surprise.

He abandoned the car on the west end of the crowded parking lot and took his time walking the two miles back to his own vehicle, thoroughly pleased with his performance.

A mile away from the crime scene, an unmarked car suddenly flew past him with its sirens wailing. Nathan put his head down and spat on the sidewalk when it had passed, the pure *contempt* he felt for Dennis Rader and his pathetic fucking victims setting his teeth on edge.

CHAPTER TWENTY-NINE

Dana and Brown screamed up Overlook Drive five minutes later and came to a screeching halt in front of a small well-kept house with Thanksgiving decorations taped to the front door. Seven patrol cars were already parked in haphazard angles on the street out front, their blue and red lights flashing.

A young uniformed cop approached as they left the vehicle, his face white. 'Nobody inside,' he told them in a halting voice. 'At least, no one alive. Three dead bodies and a dead dog.'

Dana's mind raced. She couldn't believe that they'd missed him, but he couldn't be far away. He wouldn't have had time. 'Get a dragnet set up in a ten-mile radius,' she ordered.

The young cop looked sick. 'Who are we looking for?'

Dana resisted the urge to scream at him. 'Just detain anyone who even looks suspicious. Ten-mile radius. Get on it now.'

The officer scampered away. A moment later, having contacted LA and ordered McGreevy's artist's sketch sent countrywide, Dana and Brown walked through the front door of the house. In the living room Dana stopped a lieutenant who appeared to be in charge. 'You absolutely sure this place has been cleared?' she asked.

The lieutenant nodded. 'Yes, ma'am. Searched it top to bottom myself. Nobody here except the vics.'

Dana stretched her neck. 'Get everybody out of here right now. I don't want the crime scene compromised.'

'Yes, ma'am.'

When the last of the deputies finally cleared out, Dana and Brown pulled on their PPE and carefully rechecked every room for themselves. Three victims in the master bedroom – two females and one male. The male victim had a plastic bag tied tightly over his face. The younger female victim was naked from the waist up and soaked in blood. Dana almost threw up when she saw that the girl's left nipple had been sliced off.

'Jesus Christ,' she breathed.

In the kitchen they found a photograph of a naked transsexual paper-clipped to a computer disk and sitting on the counter next to the sink.

'Ten to one there's nothing in the metadata,' Brown said. 'What's the picture about?'

Dana's mind whirred. Her brain was still trying to tell her something through the hot rush of adrenalin, but it was almost as if the words were coming through in a different language.

Then, suddenly, they clicked into place one by one. 'I'll tell you what I think in a minute,' she told Brown. 'For now, just run the metadata and see what's on that disk.'

Brown nodded and left the kitchen, passing Don Jackson as the sheriff was walking in.

'We must have just missed the motherfucker,' Jackson growled. 'This couldn't have happened more than ten minutes ago. The family car is gone.'

Dana looked up at him. 'Find out what make it is and get an APB out on that vehicle. Then get on the phone and have them shut the airport down. I think I know where he's going next, and it's too far for him to drive. We don't have time to wait for FBI Headquarters to make the request, and I think he's going to try to fly out of here.'

Jackson frowned. 'We'd need FAA approval for something like that. Might take some time.'

Dana glared at him. 'Time is something we really don't have right now, Sheriff Jackson. Just get it done as quickly as possible. Please.'

For a moment Jackson looked as though he might protest further, but then he thought better of it. 'Yes, ma'am. I'll see what I can do.'

Dana left the kitchen and pulled off her mask. She stepped out of the house and flipped her cellphone open. Outside, two ambulances and three TV news trucks had joined the phalanx of cruisers out front. So much for keeping things quiet.

A pretty young blonde reporter closely followed by a cameraman wearing a backwards baseball cap immediately stepped forward and shoved a microphone in her face. 'Megan Carter, Channel 4 News. What happened in there, ma'am?'

Dana ignored the question and turned to a uniformed cop twenty feet away. 'Get a police line around this house and the two houses on either side. Don't let anyone through without the proper credentials.'

To the reporter, she said, 'Call me later. I'll try to give you something in an hour or two, but right now I'm busy. I'm sure you understand. Get my number from Sheriff Jackson's office.'

When the reporter and other members of the press had been safely escorted a hundred yards away, Dana punched Crawford Bell's cell number into her phone and brought him up to speed on the latest developments. He'd asked her specifically to call him the moment she had news – good or bad.

Crawford let out a shocked breath. 'How many killed?'

'Three.'

'A family?'

'Yeah. Murdered just like the Oteros.'

'Any more weird clues at the scene?'

Dana shielded her eyes against the late-afternoon sun. 'Yeah. There was a picture of a he-she attached to a floppy disk.'

'A he-she?'

'Yeah, you know. A tranny. A girly-boy. A chick with a dick.'

'Yeah, Dana, I get it. What was on the disk?'

'Don't know yet. Brown's processing it now.'

'How long will it take?'

'Ten minutes maybe.'

Crawford paused. 'BTK was eventually tracked down through a floppy disk, wasn't he?'

'Yeah.'

'That's what I thought. So at least you're getting closer. What are your thoughts on the photograph of the transsexual?'

Dana paused to fix the idea in her mind before sharing it with Crawford. 'You remember that videotape of Richard Speck? The one taken when he was in prison? The one that turned out to be Bill Kurtis's big break? Kurtis was only local until he broke that story.'

'You mean the videotape where Speck was smoking drugs with his boyfriend in their jail cell? The one where he had breasts from taking all those female hormones?'

'Exactly,' Dana said. 'After they locked him up, Richard Speck became a tranny. He did it to protect himself on the inside after he murdered a houseful of nurses in Chicago in 1966. That's where I think this guy's going to strike next. Or at least where he's going to *try* to strike next. Have you finished the profile yet?'

Crawford coughed. 'No. I've been dealing with some other things. I promise to get it to you soon.'

Irritation flared in Dana's chest. *Soon* didn't cut it in this situation. Not when people were dying. She steadied herself and quickly told Crawford about her attempt to have the airport shut down.

'Good idea,' Crawford said when she'd finished. 'Let me know how things shake out. I want to know *everything*. No holding out on me, Dana. Not now that it's getting personal.'

'Will do.'

Dana switched off her cellphone, wondering momentarily what he'd meant by that last line. Don Jackson approached, shaking his head. 'FAA refuses to shut the airport down. I've got the terminal flooded with deputies right now, but that's the best I can do.'

Dana hissed under her breath. 'Goddamn it.' Then calmed herself and said, 'Thanks, Sheriff. I know you're doing the best you can. We dropped this shit-storm into your lap at the last minute and it wasn't fair of us.'

Jackson looked relieved. 'What else can I do to help?'

'Just sit tight for now,' Dana told him. 'I'll let you know if and when I need something else, so be prepared to act fast.'

Jackson nodded. 'Yes, ma'am.'

Dana closed her eyes as Jackson moved away. If it had been a terrorist threat – even a *perceived* one – the FAA would have tripped over its own feet shutting the goddamn airport down. But they wouldn't do it for a very real serial killer? It was complete and total bullshit.

She was lost in her thoughts when Brown's voice jolted her back. He frowned and handed her a sheet of paper. 'This was on the metadata,' he said.

Dana took the sheet of paper and looked down at it. Big block letters spelled out another message from the killer:

FOOL ME ONCE, SHAME ON YOU. FOOL ME TWICE, SHAME ON *ME*. HAPPY HUNTING, ASSHOLES. I'LL SEE YOU AGAIN REAL SOON. TELL ME, DANA – HAVE YOU FIGURED OUT *WHERE* YET?

PART III

UPDATING RICHARD SPECK

CHAPTER THIRTY

Nathan took the off-ramp ten miles south of the airport and pulled into a busy corner gas station to fill the tank of the BMW and buy a cup of black coffee, confident in the knowledge that the authorities would be looking for the Oteros' Infiniti. *Fucking idiots.*

The sharp smell of fuel burned his nostrils as he unhooked the nozzle and thought about his sacred mission again. There were still many prizes to be had along the way, of course, but the biggest prize of all would be the chance to finally get even with Dana Whitestone, the thieving little bitch who'd so carelessly stolen his life all those years ago. That would be the sweetest gift of all.

He'd *relish* that one.

When the automatic pump clicked off to indicate the tank was full, Nathan went inside and peeled off a hundred-dollar bill from the thick stack that he kept secured with a sterling money clip in the front pocket of his trousers. Handing it over to the obese male clerk with the bad teeth and the drooping breasts of a very old woman, he dropped his gaze to the floor and shifted impatiently while he waited for the idiot to count out the change.

After several interminable moments, he finally looked up again.

Jesus Christ! The moron's lips were moving as he counted out the bills!

Just when Nathan was sure he'd be forced to lean over the counter and strangle the life out of the inept clerk for so foolishly wasting his time, the sound of the small gold bell above the door jangled cheerily behind him, causing him to turn his head just in time to see a pair of busty blonde nurses from Wichita General strutting in on their long tan legs and brilliantly white shoes.

And just like that, there it was. The unmistakable confirmation he'd been waiting for.

Nathan's ears rang as he watched the nurses fill their large styrofoam cups with steaming double lattes. No way in *hell* was this a coincidence. These two were safe enough, at least for tonight, but he knew of someone else who wouldn't be quite so lucky.

Finally receiving his change from the Darwin Award-winning clerk, he hustled back to the BMW and logged on to his wireless MacBook Pro connection before accessing his membership at the Lonely Hearts Club and calling up the nursing student's profile. His throat tightened as he read through it again with renewed interest.

He glanced at the note posted above her picture; saw that she'd be at the library tomorrow night before meeting up with some of her friends for a study session later on.

Absolutely fucking *perfect*. Especially with her friends along for the ride.

In the driver's seat of the BMW Nathan felt his heart thrill with the possibilities. An electric charge ripped through his muscles as he put the car in gear and pulled out into traffic with the sounds of Ashley Ball playing Lecuona's 'Vals De Las Sombras' on the stereo.

Goddamn, it felt good!

He was finally ready to spread his wings and fly like an eagle again, finally ready to recreate Richard Speck's unforgettably sadistic crime once and for all.

With one very notable update, of course.

Next stop: Chicago.

CHAPTER THIRTY-ONE

Dana filled Brown in on the possible Richard Speck connection and asked him to arrange for details around all the major hospitals in Chicago.

'It's a shot in the dark, but we might just get lucky,' she said. 'Richard Speck's victims were nurses, so I'm thinking that's who our man will go after next.'

Brown looked at his watch. 'When do you want to head out to the Windy City? It's beginning to look like we missed him here.'

Dana paused. There was still work to be done processing the murder scene here in Wichita, and she wanted to make sure that the work got done the proper way. Only one solution. Brown probably wouldn't like it – not now that he seemed to think he was personally in charge of her safety.

She took a deep breath. 'I want you to stay out here for the next day or two and work the scene for me,' she told him.

She saw him about to protest and cut him off. 'I need you here. It's important. I'll head out to Chicago by myself tomorrow and start things there. First I'm stopping off at home in Cleveland to pick up my notebooks and take care of a few other things. I need to touch base with Templeton properly, for a start.'

'Are you sure that's a good idea, Dana? Going out to Chicago on your own? I don't think I like the idea of you going out there with no backup. We could leave Sheriff Jackson in charge here. Seems like a pretty capable guy to me.'

Dana shook her head, touched by Brown's concern but firm in her resolve. 'No, I want you to do it. Jackson's all right, but he won't know what he's looking for. You will.'

'And what exactly *am* I looking for?'

'You'll know it when you see it,' Dana said. 'I have complete faith in you.'

'Thanks for the vote of confidence.'

'Don't mention it.'

Brown blew out a breath. 'Well, OK, then, I guess. You're the boss.'

Dana laughed and punched him lightly on the shoulder. 'Damn straight, buster, and don't you ever forget it.'

Brown clicked his heels together and snapped off a stiff mock salute. 'Yes, *ma'am*.'

CHAPTER THIRTY-TWO

Once upon a time life had been very different for Nathan Stiedowe.

In the beginning things had been pretty rough – there was certainly no denying that. He *knew* that his parents were horribly abusive religious nutcases, sick people through and through. It was just that simple, not to mention a singularly odd thing for such a young child to understand.

His father was an overbearing prick who got off on dispensing Bible verses along with the stinging swats administered with a switch across Nathan's bare backside for even the *slightest* infractions. A pilfered apple from the pantry, for example, would find young Nathan with his britches down around his ankles, barefoot in several inches of snow as he hugged the huge oak tree that stood bordering the woods of their secluded property. Over the years, Nathan would grow to *hate* that tree.

His father's loud voice, a pompous mixture of sadism and self-righteousness, would boom out after every stinging lash of the switch. Apparently there must have been a terrible dearth of apples around the country at the time.

'The thief cometh not but for to steal and to kill and to destroy!' his father would proselytise. 'Book of John, chapter 10, verse 10. Learn it, boy.'

The switch bit deep into Nathan's flesh, raising a nasty-looking welt.

'A false balance is an abomination to the Lord, but a just weight is His delight! Proverbs, chapter 11, verse 1. Make these your words to live by.'

Again with the goddamn switch.

'In thee have they taken gifts to shed blood; thou hast taken usury and increase, and thou hast greedily gained of thy neighbours by extortion and hast forgotten Me, sayeth the Lord God! Behold, therefore I have smote Mine hand at thy dishonest gain which thou hast made and at thy blood which hath been in the midst of thee. Ezekiel, chapter 22, verses 12 and 13.'

As the angry red welts popped up on his backside, the tears rolling down Nathan's cheeks would sometimes freeze in the frigid winter air, but his father never showed any mercy. It just wasn't in the old man's nature. Seemed he was more of an Old Testament type of guy.

'Tell me, son,' his father would eventually ask, breathing heavily from the exertion as vapours of cold breath issued from his mouth. 'Do you understand why I am punishing you?'

'Yes, father,' Nathan would manage to choke out, desperately fighting to keep his voice even. The old man *hated* displays of weakness, would attack it like a rabid dog that had glimpsed a flash of blood on a child's throat. 'I understand.'

'Are you *sure* you understand, boy? A word to the wise here – think very carefully before answering me.'

Heart in his throat, Nathan would reply, 'Yes, sir. Stealing is wrong. I understand that.'

It was the wrong answer.

'You lying little son of a bitch!'

His father's enraged voice echoed throughout the deep woods all around them, startling a family of rabbits from its winter burrow. 'For men shall be lovers of their own selves, covetous, boasters, proud, blasphemers, disobedient to their parents, unthankful and unholy! Two Timothy, chapter 3, verse 2. Never boast of knowledge you do not possess, you foul bastard.'

If Nathan ever cried out during these regular beatings, things only got worse from there. His father would take a mere whimper as though it were an impudent slap across the old man's face – that was something he'd learned almost from the very beginning.

After one especially vicious blow during a lashing administered for forgetting some lines of a Bible verse he'd been expected to memorise, Nathan had instinctively yelped out in pain. Turning around, he immediately realised his mistake when he saw his father's big, ugly face mottled with fury.

The switch continued in rapid succession from there.

'Do not cry the false tears of hypocrisy, son! These are not genuine tears of repentance! You weep only because the Lord your God will not deliver you from your just punishment, not because of your sins!'

The old man shook his head in disgust. 'You are simply *evil*, boy – an evil stalk sprung from an evil seed planted in a foreign field.'

That was dear old Dad.

His mother hadn't been much better. An obese woman who didn't bathe on an especially *regular* basis, Nathan always suspected she secretly *liked* to see her son punished. And the sour-milk smell always wafting from her armpits eventually turned his stomach to the point where he couldn't stand even to be around her any more. To this very day the mere *memory* of her smell was enough to make his gorge rise.

Thankfully, though, his mother largely ignored him for the most part. Still, he wasn't sure if that hurt even worse than the abuse his father heaped upon him. But in the end his mother was mostly content to spend her days eating everything in sight – even the precious goddamn apples – while paging through one of her well-worn Bibles with her chubby fingers. As near as Nathan could figure the sin of gluttony wasn't a section with which she seemed especially familiar, but he'd never dared mention such an observation.

There had never been any hugs or kisses when he'd been a child, and he'd always had to tend to his own wounds after the beatings, which wasn't very easy since they were mostly on his backside and the backs of his thighs, where the teachers at school and the parishioners at church couldn't see them.

Amazingly, his parents seemed to get along just *fine* with one another. Nathan was always amazed and disgusted to hear their iron bed creaking late at night beneath his mother's massive bulk, always wondering to himself how his father could bring himself to lie with such a foul woman. Then again, the old man wasn't much of a prize himself.

As a child, Nathan's chores had been many, but instead of trying to avoid them, as most children were wont to do, he quickly learned to lose himself in them. The chores were a safe haven for him, a temporary relief from the hellish existence of his daily life.

A floor in their rickety old log cabin, for example, was

truly *scrubbed* when the task was assigned to him. And if he were ordered to organise the pantry, he'd carefully wash the dust off all the jars of preserves before neatly stacking them. Each label pointed outward and was perfectly aligned, the foods alphabetised and arranged for the most convenient access.

As he grew older, Nathan's obsession with cleanliness eventually sharpened to the point where a mere *speck* of dirt beneath his fingernail was enough to send him scurrying for their outdoor shower to frantically scour his entire body from head to toe with the harsh lye soap, even in sub-zero winter temperatures.

Eventually, everything in his life – at least everything he had control over – had to be perfect.

Perfect and *clean*.

CHAPTER THIRTY-THREE

Four hours after leaving the horrific murder scene at the Otero house, Dana slipped beneath the covers at the downtown Wichita Hyatt. She'd just closed her eyes when the phone on her bedside table rang.

She fumbled in the darkness to pick it up and placed the receiver to her ear. 'Hello? This is Special Agent Whitestone.'

There was a crackle of static, the trace of a garbled voice.

'Hello?' she repeated, sticking a finger in her right ear to cut down on the background noise. 'Who *is* this?'

The line finally cleared. 'Hello, Dana.'

Dana sat up straighter in bed. 'Who in the fuck is this?'

The voice on the other end of the line was deep and robotic, computer-altered by a speech-masking device. 'In good time, my dear. All in good time. But you *do* know who this is, don't you? I'd hate to think you've forgotten about me already.'

Dana's heart thudded in her ears. Tears pooled in her eyes. In a fraction of a second she was reduced to being four years old again. The adult Dana fought for control. She fumbled open her cellphone and attempted to text Brown – who was staying in the same hotel – to get him to set up a trace on the phone line, but she was too shaken up. The killer had caught her unprepared, just like always.

She tried to keep the fear out of her voice, her hands

trembling as she held the phone to her ear. 'Why are you doing this? Talk to me and maybe we can figure a way out of this trouble you're in. Nobody else has to die if we work together.' It was important to keep him on the line for as long as possible.

A robotic chuckle filled Dana's ear. 'Come, now, Dana. You know that's not going to happen. Besides, I'm not the one who's in any trouble. *You* are.'

Much as Dana didn't want to talk to him for a moment longer, she had to keep hearing his chilling words. She willed herself to stay calm.

'Fine, then just come after me,' she said. 'Leave everybody else out of it.'

'Can't do that.'

'Why not?'

'Patience, Dana. Patience, my dear. You'll find out why not soon enough.'

There was a click as the connection was cut. 'Hello?' Dana shouted into the phone. 'Hello? Are you still there?'

Nothing. Only silence.

Dana dropped the receiver and jumped out of bed. She had to move fast. She was pulling on a pair of jeans when the phone on her bedside table suddenly rang again, almost giving her a heart attack. She raced across the room and picked it up. 'Hello?' she screamed. 'Are you there? Just talk to me, goddamn it!'

The static crackled again. Then a puzzled voice came on. 'What the fuck are you talking about, Dana? Is everything OK?'

Dana's heart slammed against her ribs. 'Jesus Christ, Crawford. Where the hell are you, a wind tunnel? I have to clear this line. The killer just called me here at the hotel. Call me back on my cell.'

'Did you set up a trace?'

'Just clear the line, Crawford!'

The phone clicked dead. Dana's cellphone rang ten seconds later.

'What the hell's going on?' Crawford asked. 'Did you set up a trace?'

'I'm calling Brown and meeting him in the lobby now.'

'Call me back when you've got it done.'

Dana hung up with Crawford and punched in the number for Brown's cellphone. She related the details as quickly as she could.

'Christ, Dana,' Brown said when she'd finished. 'I'll make some calls and get some people over here to trace the call. I'll meet you in the lobby in ten minutes.'

Twenty minutes later the lobby was teeming with FBI phone techs from the Wichita office. A tall thin woman named Sandy Lecroix had two cellphones to her ear and a third line plugged into a conference call with AT&T. Lecroix fiddled with wires and pecked information into her laptop. After half an hour, she turned to Dana and sighed.

'It wasn't easy, but I managed to trace it,' she said.

'Where did the call come from?' Dana asked.

Lecroix flipped her laptop closed and handed Dana a sheet of paper. 'It was set up on a relay system. The landline originated in Cleveland, but it was shuttled through Los Angeles.'

'What does that mean?'

Lecroix rubbed her neck. 'It means whoever made the call did it from a cellphone. The cell called the landline in Cleveland, which in turn called a landline in Los Angeles, which in turn called the number of your hotel room.'

'Can we trace the cell number?' Brown asked.

Lecroix shook her head. 'I'm afraid not. The number's been masked. Probably originated outside the country. The best I can do is tell you what cell tower the call connected to first. As far as I can tell, whoever made the call is still here in Wichita.'

Dana's mind raced. That *couldn't* be true. She knew in her gut that the killer had already moved on. He was playing them – *again*. To Lecroix, she said, 'Couldn't the cellphone have been activated by another cellphone? Couldn't he have left a dummy phone here in Wichita that he called from somewhere else?'

Lecroix pursed her lips. 'Well, that's certainly a possibility, I suppose. Theoretically, there could be an infinite number of relays involved.'

Dana looked down at the sheet of paper that Lecroix had just handed her. Her heart almost stopped. 'Is this number the one from Cleveland? This (216) 288-9686?'

'Yeah. Are you OK, Special Agent Whitestone? You look sick.'

Dana fought the urge to throw up. 'I'm fine,' she lied.

The truth was, however, that Dana *wasn't* fine. Not by a long shot. The number on the paper was the same number as her home phone as a child. Her parents had insisted she memorise it when she was three years old, along with their address, in case Dana ever got separated from them. Despite the precautions taken, the ultimate separation had occurred less than a year later. No amount of calling the number of her youth would ever get her parents back.

Dana thanked Lecroix and called Crawford back in DC. At the risk of inviting an investigation by the Office of Professional Responsibility, the FBI's version of internal affairs, she kept the information about her childhood phone number to herself. She was thankful she had when she heard what Crawford had to say next.

'I'm getting a lot of pressure from the Director to withdraw my support from keeping you on the case, Dana. I'm fighting Bill Krugman with everything I've got, but I don't know how much longer I can hold him off.'

Dana shook her head. If they found out about the phone number it would be the straw that broke the camel's back. *Fuck the goddamn rule book*. Crawford was right. This shit *was* personal now. 'We're making some real progress here, Crawford,' she said. 'I promise. I just need a little more time. Please do what you can.'

'I'll do my best, but you have to hurry. And just remember, Dana – it's *both* our asses on the line now. Don't make me regret this.'

CHAPTER THIRTY-FOUR

Growing up poor in West Virginia was difficult even in the best of times, but the gods had eventually smiled down on Nathan and provided him with a key to another place where he felt safe.

A library card.

As a boy he'd been absolutely delighted to discover the wonderful world of books. The first compilation of true-crime murder stories had initially horrified him, but then a strong, nameless urge had taken him over.

He had to read it again.

And then again.

He read it until his eyes were bloodshot and bleary. He read it until the library closed. He checked the book out and read it some more at home. He read the stories so many times that the murderous cast of characters eventually became such an integral part of his psyche that they began to visit him every night in his dreams.

For the first time in his life, Nathan Stiedowe had finally found some *friends.*

With the help of the wonderful books he managed to survive his abusive childhood long enough to enlist in the Navy at the age of eighteen. Assigned as a radioman to the USS *William H. Standley* in Norfolk, Virginia – a guidedmissile cruiser that was haze-grey and under way eighty per cent of the time – he'd avoided Vietnam and visited such places as Paris, Sweden, Greece and Egypt along the way. They were nice places – much nicer than West Virginia, certainly – but even in those faraway foreign ports he could still sense his father's rage reaching across the miles for his throat. Distance was no salve.

When Nathan's enlistment was finally up four years later, he returned home reluctantly for a short while until he could figure out what to do next, mostly because he simply had nowhere else to go. That was when his life changed for ever.

His parents were off at church that fateful Sunday morning when he'd stumbled across a box of documents while searching for his discharge papers to include with a college application that he was sending out – the GI Bill would cover the cost. What he found instead took his breath away.

Adoption papers.

It took a month of ignoring the voices in his head before Nathan finally broke down and heard them out. As always the ringing sounded in his ears.

They have to pay. For the beatings. For the abuse. For the childhood you should *have had. Make them pay.*

Yes, Nathan finally agreed. *I will make them pay.*

Soon enough, everyone would have to pay.

Especially *her*.

CHAPTER THIRTY-FIVE

Dana said goodbye to Brown outside the terminal at Wichita Mid-Continent Airport the next morning. An awkward silence passed between them during which she felt as if maybe she should give him a hug or something. But in the end they'd parted ways with a simple handshake.

'Take care of yourself, Dana,' Brown told her. 'Call me if you need anything.'

An hour later Dana settled into her seat in the economy section of Continental Flight 353 non-stop from Wichita to Cleveland Hopkins and watched the Kansas skyline slowly fade away into the distance.

At least now she had even more of a reason for heading out to Cleveland. And not just to pick up her notebooks. Her early ones had everything she'd ever written about her parents' case; she wanted – *needed* – them with her now. And the truth was that she felt herself getting a little too close to the edge. She needed the comfort of familiar surroundings, a little time out, however brief. She didn't want to admit it but the case was finally getting to her. She knew why, of course, but she couldn't give up now. They were so close. She could feel it. She needed to be back at the top of her game. She *had* to catch this killer. He had taken those she'd loved best in the whole world. When she was only an innocent little girl he'd ripped her world apart. Now he'd killed innocent little girls like her, a defenceless old woman and a happy family. He had to pay.

Checking out the house in Cleveland that the previous night's phone call had been shuttled through would legitimise the trip and give Dana a chance to catch her breath. Still, a cold dread coursed through her veins at the prospect. It was the house of her youth. She had no idea how she was going to keep *that* a secret – or for how long – but she knew she had to try.

The home had been purchased through a number of intermediaries, which made finding the true owner virtually impossible. It would have taken months just to track down all the paperwork, and they didn't have that kind of time. That fact would work both for and against Dana. It would help keep her on the case, which was certainly a good thing, but it also meant she probably wouldn't find the Cleveland Slasher holed up there, either. Sadly, he just wasn't that stupid. Sadistic and sick? Hell, yes. Stupid? Fuck, no.

Dana shuddered. The obvious care with which the killer had plotted his every move chilled her blood. Still, even though he was clearly the best killer she'd ever come across she just had to hope that she was a better hunter.

After the events of the previous night, Dana had resisted the urge to crack open the bottle of Absolut in her hotel room only by the slimmest of margins. But without the assistance of the alcohol she had found it impossible to fall asleep, so now she was utterly exhausted. Exhausted all the way down to the bone.

To hell with it. She could always sleep when she was dead. And at the rate this case was going, that outcome might come a hell of a lot sooner than she'd ever planned.

Dana plucked a magazine from the elastic holder on the seat back in front of her and leafed through the pages of *People* with little interest for several minutes before she realised she was having trouble concentrating on the words in front of her. The watery word jumble was swimming together on the page and not making the least goddamn bit of sense to her. She had too much on her mind at the moment, too many things to think about; too many unanswered questions.

Chief among them: how was she going to *catch* this killer finally? They were getting closer to him all the time now – she could *feel* that much – but he was still managing to stay one step ahead of them at all times.

The *People* article was talking about how another lottery winner had squandered away his instant fortune over the course of a couple years, but who could feel sorry for people like that? Once again it was painfully evident that the saying about a fool and his money soon being parted had some real teeth to it.

Some time after the plane had lifted off and was cruising along at an altitude of thirty thousand feet a pretty flight attendant sashayed down the aisle pushing a drinks cart in front of her. She stopped at Dana's seat and smiled at her.

'Care for a drink, ma'am?'

'Vodka, rocks,' Dana heard herself saying. Then, 'Better make it a double.'

Dana knew that she shouldn't be drinking, even just a little bit, at this crucial point in the case. But if the alcohol helped her to steady her nerves and think more clearly, what the hell harm was there in having a drink every now and then? She just had to watch herself, that was all. *Drink in moderation. Don't overdo it.*

The flight attendant poured the drink into a flimsy plastic cup and tonged in three crescent-moon slivers of ice before handing it over. Dana threw her head back and took it down in one quick swallow.

The strong drink burned like hell as it slid down her throat, but at least the jolting sensation reminded her that she was still an inhabitant of the real world, not some ghostly apparition floating through the nightmare existence she'd found herself in since flying out to LA a few days earlier.

Coupled with the mental weariness weighing on her mind, the alcohol caught up with Dana twenty minutes later and pulled her down into the confines of an uneasy sleep. When she awoke two hours later, she lifted her arms over her head and desperately tried to stretch the kink out of her slender neck. Economy class was worse than a straitjacket.

A moment later the captain keyed the intercom and announced they were beginning their final descent into Cleveland Hopkins.

Dana rubbed at her tired eyes and tried to shake off the remnants of the recurring nightmare she'd been having almost every night since she was four years old. The dream was every bit as much a part of her now as her short blonde hair, pale blue eyes and the small brown mole perched just above the right side of her mouth.

In her dream, the man with the strange brown eyes is standing directly over her bed and holding a huge knife in his enormous hand. Drops of bright-red blood slide down the silver blade and cling to the sharp tip for the briefest of moments before gravity causes them to fall like rust-coloured water from a leaking faucet. One by one the droplets fall in slow motion before plopping onto her face and sizzling away into vapour with a nasty hiss.

Five minutes after the captain's announcement the plane landed with a bump, taxied down the runway and came to a complete stop. When the seat-belt sign was switched off, the passengers stood up, collected their things and filed out toward the exit.

When it was Dana's turn to disembark she smiled a goodbye at the flight attendant who was posted by the door and robotically thanking everyone for flying Continental.

The flight attendant smiled back. Up close, the woman's meticulously made-up face looked drawn and tired, with fine crow's feet etched deep into the corners of her soft brown eyes. 'Have a nice day, ma'am,' the woman said.

Dana reached out a hand and lightly touched the other woman's shoulder. 'You, too, ma'am. You too.'

CHAPTER THIRTY-SIX

Books had truly saved Nathan's life.

His enduring love of words soon translated into a journalism degree from Anderson Community College, and after graduation he'd finally left home for good to start work as a newspaper reporter across the river in Shockley, Ohio. His parents didn't act as if they cared very much when he left, but he wasn't terribly surprised by their lack of emotion. In his heart of hearts he knew that they were as happy to be getting rid of him as he was to be rid of them.

'Walk the path of righteousness, son,' his father told him that day, a Winchester rifle bent into the crook of his left arm. 'Walk the path of righteousness or the devil will certainly get you. Make no mistake about it, boy: you've already been marked. You've been marked just as surely as Cain himself was marked.'

Nathan hadn't answered the old man, hadn't bothered even turning around. He knew he was walking away from the devil already. Whether or not he'd walk the path of righteousness after taking those first few steps off his parents' property had still remained to be seen at that point.

To his great relief he finally found his place in the world when he got to Ohio. He was overjoyed to discover that he possessed a certain aptitude for the writing position to which he'd been assigned, not to mention an enviable talent for prising information out of even the most reluctant sources. He regularly scooped his competition at the newspaper in the neighbouring city on their shared crime beat, and he took a great deal of pride in that.

True, things hadn't *always* gone smoothly.

Nathan was working at his desk one hot summer afternoon when the police scanner in the middle of the newsroom crackled out a report of a murder at a local motel, a disgusting hovel notorious for the drug-related slayings that seemed to take place there just about every other week. When the scanner went silent, his managing editor had looked around the newsroom for a moment before his gaze finally landed on Nathan. 'Get on it now. Don't bother coming back if you get scooped.'

He'd arrived at the scene fifteen minutes later to find the parking lot buzzing with police and ambulances and various bystanders, most of them the drug-addicted denizens of the seedy motel itself. He'd talked to all of them, of course, which ended up yielding no usable information. As usual, the asshole cops weren't cooperating with him at all.

One drunken resident, a grizzled man in his late fifties who smelled as if he hadn't taken a bath in a year, offered to supply Nathan with the inside story – *the real story*, the man whispered in his boozy voice – in exchange for a twelve-pack of beer. Full of a cub reporter's desperate belief in journalistic ethics at the time, Nathan had thanked him politely and declined.

The murder had taken place on the second floor of the two-storey motel, but the stairs leading up to the room were blocked off with yellow police tape so that avenue was a no-go.

Half an hour after he'd arrived a large elderly black woman

accompanied by three or four of her friends pulled up in a beat-up Cadillac. Cautiously approaching them with his notebook in hand, Nathan had identified himself as a reporter. 'Can you tell me what happened in there, ma'am?' he'd asked.

The black woman looked up at him incredulously. Perhaps she was not used to talking to a white person, Nathan thought.

'I'm his mama,' the woman said, but the sound of her thick, fat-person's voice made it very difficult to understand her.

'Excuse me?'

'I said I'm his mama,' the woman repeated.

Finally understanding this, Nathan's heart immediately leaped with visions of a front-page banner headline. *The victim's mother.* The perfect source.

Nathan's pulse raced as he quickly pulled a pencil from behind his right ear and poised it over his notepad. 'Can you tell me how it happened, ma'am?'

The woman continued staring at him. 'What in the hell are you *talking* about, motherfucker?'

Suddenly realising that he was probably coming across as coarse and insensitive, Nathan did a quick rethink and tried again. 'I'm very sorry about your loss,' he said as gently as possible.

What happened next shocked him right down to his very *soul*. First the old woman's face collapsed. The next thing he knew, she was falling to the pavement and shrieking out in grief. 'My baby! My baby! Oh my God! Oh my sweet Jesus! They killed my baby! They killed my baby!'

It wasn't until after her friends had helped her to her feet and back to the car that Nathan discovered she'd been called to the scene on the simple *possibility* that it had been her son who'd been murdered. As things turned out, that *had* been the case, but Nathan had inadvertently been the one to inform her of this, which had certainly been neither his function nor his intention.

As he walked slowly away from her, stunned beyond belief, one of the asshole cops grinned at him. 'Got any more questions there, Scoop?'

By the time Nathan finally regained enough of his composure to resume his sniffing around, the coroner informed him that the victim had had his *head cut off* for infringing on a rival drug dealer's territory.

'Typical shit,' the coroner said off the record. 'Promise me you'll never stay in a place like this, son. This kind of shit always happens in dumps like this.'

Nathan promised that he wouldn't.

As fate would have it, the photographer assigned to cover the scene with him that day had captured the entire embarrassing incident reel by reel. Returning to the newsroom an hour later, Nathan was caught completely off guard by the loud, derisive cheer from his fellow journalists that suddenly went up.

Mortified, he saw the stop-action scenes pinned frame by frame across the large bulletin board in the centre of the room:

Nathan approaching the woman, notebook in hand.

The look of confusion on the old woman's face.

Nathan's declaration of condolence.

The woman's face collapsing; the can of Dr Pepper flying from her hand and staining Nathan's clean white dress shirt as she fell to the ground.

Nathan leaning down to help the woman to her feet, the look of chagrin clearly evident on his face.

The very last frame showed the grieving mother being led away by her friends, turning around to look over her shoulder at Nathan Stiedowe – the man who'd just informed her that her only son had been murdered.

He knew the image would remain etched in his mind for ever. At one point, the incident had bothered him to the point of interrupting his sleep.

It didn't bother him so much any more.

Following those initial growing pains, Nathan had steadily risen to become one of the top reporters in the city – a big fish in a very small pond, admittedly. But it didn't take long to figure out that the editors who bossed him around weren't there because of any sort of journalistic talent they possessed.

No, as was the case in most of the smaller newsrooms across the country you rose through the ranks simply by sticking around long enough in a place that paid like shit, treated you like shit and cranked out reams of shit stories on a daily basis until they *had* to promote you. And in the wide world of journalism, Nathan soon discovered that you couldn't swing a stick in a full circle without hitting some asshole who had absolutely no business telling you what to do.

When the *Plain Dealer* recruited him a year later he'd happily jumped ship and moved to Cleveland. The bitter lifers in Shockley didn't even bother saying goodbye to him as he walked out the door on his last day, but he didn't mind. Their punishment was their simple station in life. They were stuck. He wasn't. He had talent. They didn't. They resented that, and he resented them. It was a match made in hell.

At the *PD*, things really began falling into place for Nathan. Things were more *professional* there, the people in charge actually seeming to know what the hell they were talking about for the most part. In addition to quickly making a name for himself in the western suburbs of Cuyahoga County, it wasn't long before he met Kelly, a pretty little intern from Walsh University.

He'd first noticed the young redhead as she was neatly arranging her desk on a cool spring day. She was obviously the kind of girl who couldn't stand clutter – the kind who had to rise from her chair and pluck a stray piece of paper off the floor if it happened to fall in the line of her peripheral vision – and that drew him to her as insistently as a moth drawn to a flame.

Three months of dating followed before he proposed to her in the kitchen of his small apartment. 'The Rainbow Connection' – her favourite song – was playing on the living-room stereo as he got down on one knee. A year later Jennifer was born. She was the prettiest baby Nathan had ever seen.

Things had been good then. Things had been *perfect*, actually.

But that was before he'd come home late from work one night to find himself lost in the worst nightmare of his entire life.

CHAPTER THIRTY-SEVEN

Out in the bustling terminal at Hopkins, Dana powered on her cellphone and saw that she had a missed call from Crawford. She found a quiet table tucked away in the corner fifty yards from the main concourse and called him back on his own cell.

'Bell here,' he said.

'Crawford, it's Dana. What's up?'

Crawford blew out a slow breath. 'Not sure if you're going to like this, Dana. You got a minute?'

Cold dread spread through her limbs like icy fingers fluttering over a dead body. 'Yeah. What's up?'

Crawford cleared his throat. 'Well, I've got some good news and I've got some bad news. Which do you want first?'

'The good news. I really think I need it right now.'

Crawford laughed. 'I figured you'd say that. Anyway, the good news is that I talked Bill Krugman into letting you stay on the case. At least for now. He was a hundred per cent against it but I managed to sway him.'

'How'd you do that?'

Crawford paused. 'Well, that's what I'm *hoping* you don't think the bad news is. Krugman wants me to join you on the investigation, officially. Help out if I can. You have a problem with that?'

Dana considered the question. *Did* she have a problem with it? A few months ago she'd have jumped at the chance, even though she was doing just fine on her own. But now things felt different between her and Crawford. She'd noticed a certain aloofness in him. Perhaps she'd imagined it but she didn't think so. Still, he was one of the very best agents the FBI had. And she had to face it, she needed all the help she could get. Besides, she got the impression she didn't have any choice in the matter. And they'd been a good team once. They could be again.

'Don't be ridiculous,' she told Crawford now. 'Of course I want your help. Speaking of your help, what's the word on the profile? It would be a huge boost if I knew something concrete about this guy's psychology. I feel like I'm shooting in the dark at this point.'

Crawford was silent. Dana could hear him breathing on the other end of the phone. She waited. Eventually he spoke. 'There's something I need to tell you, Dana. I haven't been able to compile a profile yet. I've been dealing with some other things.'

Dana couldn't believe her ears. She tried to keep the irritation out of her voice. 'Like what, Crawford? We're chasing a serial killer here. Don't you think that should be Priority Number One?'

'Yeah, I know,' Crawford said, his voice breaking. He coughed and continued. 'I haven't been feeling all that well lately. After you left for Los Angeles I went to the doctor to find out what the hell's wrong with me. They did a CAT scan and an MRI and a bunch of other tests.' He paused, then after a short hesitation began again. 'Look, Dana, I'm sorry to tell you on the phone like this but it turns out I have terminal brain cancer. They're giving me six months to live.'

Dana almost dropped the phone in shock. Hot tears flooded into her eyes. 'Oh my God, Crawford. I'm so sorry.'

'Yeah, me too. But what the hell can you do, right? When it's your time, it's just your time. Anyway, I really think working on this case will be good for me. Sort of help me keep my mind off the other stuff going on, you know what I mean?'

Dana didn't know what to say. He sounded oddly detached, matter-of-fact, but perhaps that was the only way he could deal with a death sentence like this. She was no medical expert, but she'd heard that brain cancer could sometimes wreak havoc on people's minds, making them unable to think clearly. If that was the case here, she didn't want Crawford to further endanger his health by getting mixed up in all this. She didn't even want to think about what losing him was going to mean to her. He'd been like a father to her all these years. 'Is Bill Krugman signing off on this?' she asked, just about keeping her emotions in check. Now was not the time for her to break down. Crawford would need her to be strong. He'd expect her to be.

'Actually, I haven't told him yet. And I'm not going to. You're the only one who knows at this point, Dana. I want to keep it that way. You can't tell anyone.'

A single tear spilled out of Dana's right eye and down her cheek. She had her own secrets to keep, and she sure as hell wasn't going to rat out her mentor and former partner after what he'd just told her, not after everything he'd done for her over the years. Once again, the rule book could just go out the window at this point.

'I won't tell anyone,' she promised. 'So, where do you want to start?'

'I was thinking maybe I could fly up to Cleveland and

help you check out the house where the phone call came from,' Crawford said. 'I could be there in a couple of hours, if that's OK with you.'

Dana paused. She'd wanted to check out the house for herself first, knowing how emotionally hard it would be on her. If Crawford were there with her, she knew he'd sense that something was wrong and call her out on it. Sick or not, Crawford had the ability to see through her like he would through a sheet of glass. At the moment he hadn't connected the number with the address – he'd know exactly what house it was when he saw that. He knew the contents of that file almost as intimately as she did. But what in the hell could she say at this point? Her hands were tied. She'd just have to get there first and explain later.

'That'll be fine,' she told Crawford. 'I was planning on heading home first for a little bit before I go over there, anyway.' She glanced down at her watch. 'It's eleven a.m. now. Could you meet me there around three-thirty?' That should buy her enough time, she reckoned.

'Of course. I'll see you then. Text me the address. And Dana?'

'Yeah?'

'Thanks, partner. I really need this.'

Dana flipped the cellphone off and closed her eyes. Just what else was the man upstairs going to throw at her next? She was hanging by a thread as it was. And now the man who'd been there for her, who'd encouraged her when she'd nearly given up, had just told her he had six months to live.

Could it *get* any worse?

CHAPTER THIRTY-EIGHT

It was the night of his and Kelly's second anniversary when Nathan finally returned home from work just as the clock's hands were nearing eleven p.m. He glanced down at his watch and desperately hoped that Kelly wouldn't be too upset with his tardiness on their special day.

To guard against this possibility he held a large bouquet of fresh calla lilies – her favourite flowers – in one hand while he fished in his coat pocket for his apartment key with the other. He slid the silver key into the lock and was surprised to find the door simply pushed open.

Nathan let out an irritated breath. How many goddamn times did he have to warn Kelly about locking their door at night? That living downtown wasn't always the safest place to be? Although perfect in just about every other respect, actually *following through* on things had never been one of his lovely wife's greatest qualities.

He walked into their modest apartment, surprised and a bit hurt to find that she hadn't waited up for him. Then again, Jennifer was teething now, so that milestone probably wore away at his wife's frazzled nerves every bit as much as it did at their sweet baby's tender little gums.

He called out tentatively anyway, not wanting to wake Jennifer in case she'd just fallen asleep. 'Kelly? Honey? I'm home.'

There was no answer; not a sound in the entire apartment save for the rhythmic ticking of the mantel clock. Nathan's heart thrummed painfully in his chest as he tossed the flowers onto the kitchen table and quickly hurried through the darkness to the open doorway of their bedroom.

He peered in and let out a grateful sigh of relief when he saw his wife and beautiful little baby girl curled up in bed together.

They were fast asleep.

Smiling down at them, Nathan couldn't resist flipping on the light for a better look at the two loves of his life.

CHAPTER THIRTY-NINE

Dana had packed light – just the one carry-on bag – so she didn't have to stop by to visit the baggage-claim area. Instead, she fought her way through the crowded terminal and took her place waiting in line for the string of yellow cabs outside. When it was her turn, she climbed inside an ancient vehicle that smelled like at least fifty cartons' worth of stale cigarette smoke and wrinkled her nose up against the odour as she gave the driver directions to her modest apartment complex in Lakewood, a suburb on the western outskirts of Cleveland.

Half an hour later the driver pulled up to the kerb in front of her building. Dana fumbled in her purse for a fifty to pay him with before she hastily hopped out.

She breathed in several deep lungfuls of fresh air as she made her way to the front doors, infinitely happy to finally be out of the stinky cab. But her brain felt hardboiled as she punched the button in the elevator for the fourth floor in the nine-storey complex. In her heart of hearts, Dana knew that she should probably be heading out to Chicago immediately, but she felt that she should be the one to check out the house where the call had come from – the home of her childhood. Maybe it wasn't at the top of the investigating team's to-do list, but they had to pick up on any and every possible link. And something was drawing her back. She *had* to go back. Besides, Brown had arranged for details around all the major hospitals in Chicago, where Dana suspected the Cleveland Slasher – she still thought of him as that, original monikers tended to stick – might strike next in order to recreate the crimes of serial killer Richard Speck. It wasn't as if they weren't following all the proper procedures. Plus, Crawford himself hadn't said anything to question the course of action. Instead, he was coming out to Cleveland to assist Dana in working the investigation. Crawford was the best agent she'd ever known, and he would have immediately questioned the trip to Cleveland if he had thought it was a wild-goose chase.

Dana fought back more tears. Poor Crawford. What would she do without him in her life? He'd single-handedly turned her into the woman she was today, taking a nervous young agent who hadn't known her ass from her elbow and selflessly shaping her into one of the top agents in the Bureau, at least according to Dana's file folder back at FBI Headquarters.

There was always hope, of course. Dana had read about cases where supposedly terminal cancers had gone into sudden and mysterious remission. She only prayed her former partner was lucky enough to be one of them. Hell, he *deserved* that much after everything he'd been through. Losing his wife and daughter to murder hadn't turned him into a helpless mess like it would have done to so many lesser men. Instead, he'd focused his energies on making the world a better place, which was a lot more than most people could have said in his situation.

When the elevator doors opened, Dana stepped out and walked down the hall to apartment D13, accidentally

216

scratching the delicate glass face of her mother's watch against the concrete wall in the process.

'Goddamn it,' she hissed under her breath.

She came to the outside of the apartment door and took a deep breath. This was not her apartment – hers was D12, directly across the hall – but it was time for a little good old-fashioned TLC. God knew she needed it right now. She could pick up her notebooks later.

Dana rested her head against the cold surface of the apartment door and knocked. A deep mellifluous voice sounded from inside almost at once.

'Come on in! It's unlocked!'

Dana turned the knob and stepped inside. There, in an expensively upholstered wing-backed chair, sat Eric Carlton, an unlit briarwood pipe on the end table by his side and a dog-eared copy of *Memoirs of a Geisha* in his hands. Oreo was curled up in a furry ball in his lap, purring contentedly.

'Well, now, if this ain't the picture of domestic bliss, I don't know what is,' Dana said, almost overcome by the normality of the tableau before her. 'Reminds me of a Norman Rockwell painting. Either that or Norman Bates. To tell you the truth, I haven't quite made my up mind yet when it comes to you two characters.'

Eric laughed and rose to his feet as Dana entered the stylishly decorated apartment. Art deco furniture was tastefully arranged around the room, with original oil paintings of Cleveland's skyline spaced evenly on the walls.

'Dana!' he said happily. He placed Oreo down on the floor and took a step in her direction to give her a hug. 'It's about time you got home. We've missed you.'

'I've missed you guys, too,' Dana said, a catch in her

voice. She hugged him back before leaning down to scratch Oreo behind his pointy ears, tears threatening again. In return, the cat rubbed his fat body against her legs and purred like a generator.

Eric picked up on the emotion in her voice at once. 'What's wrong, honey?' he asked softly. 'Here, sit down. I'll get us some coffee and then you can tell me all about it.'

He took her firmly by the shoulders and led her to the dining-room table before disappearing into the kitchen and returning a moment later with two steaming mugs. 'Now, tell me what's going on.'

So Dana took a deep breath and filled him in on all the latest developments, leaving out the part about Crawford's diagnosis and her planned upcoming trip to the house of her childhood. That would only make Eric worry more than he already did.

He frowned. 'So you've got to go out to Chicago now?' he asked incredulously. 'Dana – do you really have to? When is this shit ever going to end?'

'It's going to end when we finally catch this guy.'

Eric pressed his lips together. He'd always respected what she did, even when things got tough – but that didn't stop him from caring. 'Well, that makes sense, I suppose. Still, I'm worried about you. You don't seem yourself.'

Dana smiled at him. 'I'm just frustrated, is all. I've got a million great questions but not a single goddamn answer to any of them.'

Eric shifted in his chair. 'And you really think Crawford Bell's going to help out all that much answering those questions, Dana? I don't know.' Eric had never liked Crawford. He'd only met him once, at a party, and they'd gotten into a bullheaded argument about healthcare, of all things. 'Seems to me he's coming into this pretty late in the day,' Eric continued. 'You've already told me he still hasn't given you a profile, and something about him rubs me the wrong way.'

Dana waved his concern away with a sweep of her hand. 'And here I was thinking another man couldn't possibly rub you the wrong way. Guess I was wrong, huh?'

Eric didn't laugh at her feeble attempt at a joke. 'Just watch your ass around him, would you?'

Dana laughed. 'If you weren't so goddamn gay maybe I'd leave that job up to you, Rock Hudson.'

Eric finally cracked a smile. 'In another lifetime, Dana. In another lifetime.'

'Just my luck. All the good ones are either taken or gay.'

Eric leaned back in his chair and looked like the cat that swallowed the canary. A devious smile played across his full lips. 'Or taken *and* gay, dear. Don't forget about that possibility.'

Dana widened her eyes in surprise. 'Find yourself a boyfriend now, did you? Why didn't you tell me?'

'You've been away, remember?' he said. 'Anyway, up to this point it's only been over the computer but it's looking pretty promising so far.'

Dana rose to her feet and tousled his hair. Seeing Eric had done her a little bit of good at least, as she knew it would. Shame she couldn't just stay here for ever. 'Good for you, you old dog, you. But that guy better treat you right or he'll have to answer to me.'

She leaned down and wrapped her arms around his neck from behind. 'Sweetie, could you please watch Oreo while I'm in Chicago? I promise I'll make it up to you when I get back.'

Eric reached up and pulled her arms closer around his body. 'You know I could never say no to the mother of my only son. Now get the hell out of here and go do whatever the hell it is you've got to do, Special Agent Whitestone. But just be *careful* out there, for Christ's sake, would you? Oreo and I worry about you, you know. We'll be waiting for you here with bated breath until you get back home.'

Dana kissed him on the cheek. 'Thanks, buddy. You're a prince. I'll stop by and say goodbye before I leave for the airport tonight, OK?'

Eric rose to his feet and shooed her out of the apartment with both hands. 'Sounds great, but I'm no prince and we both know it. Now *scoot*.'

CHAPTER FORTY

When the light went on in their bedroom Nathan saw red *everywhere*.

Kelly was naked, legs spread, her throat slashed. She'd probably been raped. Little Jennifer was cradled in her mother's arms, her sweet face blue; the pillow that had been used to smother her to death had been tossed carelessly to one side.

In an instant, Nathan's entire world collapsed. He looked numbly around the room and saw the bloody handprints covering the walls. The Kermit the Frog piggy bank in which they'd been carefully squirrelling money away for Jennifer's college education was smashed open and empty. There had been about a thousand dollars inside.

Five hundred dollars apiece for the lives of his wife and daughter.

Looking down at their destroyed bodies in horror, the silly little lullaby that Nathan had composed for Jennifer started playing in his mind. He sang it to her every night and it had always made her smile up at him and laugh. He'd *loved* those moments.

Jenny-Benny, you are the love of my life. Jenny-Benny, you are so pretty, you are so nice.

The song in his head stopped playing as abruptly as the

needle scratching off a record at a junior high-school dance when the familiar ringing sounded in his ears. But Nathan passed out cold before the connection could be made.

When his world finally swam back into focus an hour and a half later he felt strangely calm, knowing *exactly* what he had to do.

First he stripped completely naked and went into the kitchen. Returning a moment later with a packet of sponges and a bucket filled with steaming-hot water, he gently washed the blood off his dead wife and daughter. He carefully placed their bodies side by side on the floor and stripped the bloody sheets off the bed before shoving them into a large black garbage bag.

Next he remade the bed with fresh sheets and reclothed his beloved girls in clean attire. Placing them back in the bed, he fluffed the pillows up beneath their heads and pulled the comforter over their bodies to keep them warm. Jennifer went back in Kelly's arms, her sweet blue face snugly cradled up against her mother's soft breast.

In a trance, Nathan methodically scrubbed the bloody handprints off the wall. Then he vacuumed. Then he dusted. Retrieving the calla lilies from the kitchen table, he placed them in a vase on the bedside table and arranged them as carefully as a master florist before taking a long hot shower and finally crawling into bed with Kelly and Jennifer.

Exhausted, he wrapped his arms around his dead wife and daughter and quietly cried himself to sleep.

When the police arrived several hours later, Nathan was arrested on the spot and roughly tossed into a downtown cell for an overnight stay. But even with all the compulsive acts that had destroyed so much of the evidence, the *real* killer had left more than enough clues behind for the cops to catch up with him less than a week later.

As the story slowly unfolded in the media, Nathan was *stunned* to discover that the murders of his wife and daughter had been nothing more than thrill kills, inexpertly pulled off by the son of a wealthy Cleveland real-estate developer just for kicks.

He sat there in court every day just watching the man who'd so brutally butchered his young family. He would have gladly killed the bastard with his own bare hands had he been given half the chance, of course, but even through his overwhelming grief and despair at the loss of his beloved girls he couldn't help feeling *dismayed* at the ham-handed manner in which the idiot had committed the murders. Kelly and Jennifer had deserved more.

At the very least they had deserved *professional* deaths.

The criminal trial resulted in the expected death sentence for young Prentice McIntyre when a jury of his peers took less than a week to decide unanimously that he wasn't fit to walk the Earth with them any more. The civil trial that followed two years later made Nathan five million dollars richer, but he'd continued showing up for work every day for the next year anyway. From that terrible and bloody night forward, however, every waking moment of his life was consumed with his desire to extract revenge from the world that had fucked him up so badly in so many different ways since the very day he'd been born.

And now he had the money to pull it off.

The money and the perfect plan.

Nathan finally quit his job at the *Plain Dealer* thirteen months later and used his media connections to audit a profiling class at the FBI Training Academy in Quantico,

Virginia. He took to the course like a duck to water, of course. If anything was right up his alley, it was this.

He was *so* good, in fact, that it wasn't very long before he decided he could probably teach the class himself.

Hell, Nathan knew so much on the subject that he could probably write a goddamn *book*.

CHAPTER FORTY-ONE

Dana crossed the hall and let herself into her own apartment. She'd put on a brave face for Eric but more than twenty-four hours had passed since she'd last slept, not counting the short nap on the plane, and it was really starting to catch up with her. Exhausted as she was, though, sleep really wasn't an option right now. Not when she had a long-overdue date with the demons of her past.

She shuddered and glanced down at her watch. Almost two o'clock already, and Crawford had agreed to meet her over at the house in West Park at three-thirty after stopping off to pick up a search warrant from a judge downtown. If she left now that would give her just enough time to make sure that she got all the crying out first. With any luck she could fix her make-up and pull herself together before Crawford arrived and had the chance to realise she'd been there before. That was if he didn't remember before then why the address rang a bell and had something to say about it. She was slightly surprised he hadn't phoned to bawl her out already. Probably, understandably, because he had other, more important things on his mind.

Dana shook her head and went into the bathroom to freshen up. Her career was on the line here if anybody got wind of the fact that she was suppressing information her superiors had every right to know. All her hard work over the years and the sterling reputation she'd built up as a person who always played by the rules would go right down the toilet. But what choice did she have? If she told them about the connection to her past they'd yank her ass off the case so fast her head would spin, and that really wasn't an option. Not at this point. If that meant the end of her career, so be it. She'd worked at K-Mart throughout her high school and college days, and she could probably catch on back there if she really needed to. Hell, it might not be the most glamorous job in the world, but innocent people didn't usually die at K-Mart so there was something to be said for that.

Dana locked her apartment's front door behind her and made her way down the hall to the elevator. Down in the parking lot of the apartment complex two minutes later, she hopped inside the Protégé and began the short drive over to West Park.

Her pulse quickened when she pulled onto Eastlawn Street fifteen minutes later. Most of the houses on the street looked exactly the same, with the odd different paint job here and there. The exact same maple trees lined the exact same perfectly manicured tree lawns, blowing gently in what appeared to be exactly the same breeze.

Dana got out of the car before she could change her mind and stood in front of the house of her childhood. The single-storey ranch-style home was still painted white, with black shutters adorning the windows. A metal sign in the front yard declared that Chem-Lawn had been there recently. Even though it was November now, the chemicals made sure the grass stayed a deep, lush green – unlike the lawn next door, where the grass had slowly withered and died before fading away into a limp lifeless brown.

Dana marshalled her courage and marched up to the front door before looking down at her watch again. *Fuck the search warrant.* She was going in without it. She'd clean up the mess with Crawford later on if it came to that. That was the least of her worries.

She jimmied the lock on the door and pushed it open. Stale, unmoving air filled her nostrils. The living room was empty save for a small desk with an old rotary phone sitting on top. Exact same model as the one from her childhood.

Dana sucked in a sharp breath and looked around. Her mind immediately slammed back to 1976. She could almost *hear* the sound of her mother's laughter as she chuckled at another one of her father's silly jokes. She walked into the kitchen and remembered the faint pencil lines that had been drawn on the wall next to the refrigerator marking her slow growth in height over the years. They'd been long ago painted over now.

Hot tears filled her eyes as she went back into the living room. Down the hall to the right was her bedroom. She started in that direction, but the sudden sound of a telephone ringing almost made her jump right out of her skin.

Dana's heart slammed in her chest as she stared at the old rotary phone on the desk. Several seconds passed before she realised that the ringing was coming from her own cellphone. She dug it out of her pocket with shaking hands and flipped it open. Crawford's voice filled her ear.

'Slight change of plan, Dana,' he told her without a preamble. 'I'm in Cleveland now but I won't be coming out to West Park. I managed to get an appointment with Dr Anthony Justice over at the Cleveland Clinic. He's the best brain-cancer specialist in the country and I had to pull a lot of strings to get the appointment so I really don't want to miss it. Could you manage without me for another day or two?'

Dana shook her head hard to clear the cobwebs away while the ghosts of her past gleefully danced in the living room all around her. Her beautiful mother. Her handsome father. The sadistic killer who'd murdered them both. 'Of course,' she told Crawford, desperately trying to keep her voice even. 'I'll be fine. I'm headed out to Chicago in a couple of hours, though. You can meet up with me there when you're done in Ohio.'

'Where are you now?' he asked.

'At the house in West Park. I couldn't wait.'

'Find anything interesting?'

Dana looked over at the rotary phone and tried to ignore the apparition of her parents' killer laughing at her. 'Not really.' Crawford obviously hadn't made the connection yet and perhaps it was just as well that he wasn't coming over. She found herself torn between relief that he wasn't about to walk into her past and surprise that he would miss out on something potentially key to their case. But of course he'd want to see the specialist. She couldn't possibly understand how he was feeling right now – and so she couldn't possibly judge him. She just wondered why he hadn't told her before that he was trying to get an appointment.

Crawford coughed and said, 'Well, soon as I get this damn appointment over with I'll be at your full disposal.'

Dana brought the conversation to a speedy conclusion and switched off the phone. Her skin crawled, being in this place, and she needed to get out. *Now.*

She practically ran through the living room to escape, the ghost of her parents' killer hot on her heels.

Finally reaching her car ten seconds later, she let out a deep breath. Coming here by herself had definitely been a very bad idea, to say the least.

She slammed the Protégé into drive and peeled out. She didn't bother looking back, fearing the house of her childhood would be laughing at her, too. She'd walked straight into the emotional trap the killer had set for her.

Twenty minutes later she was back inside her apartment in Lakewood. She went into the kitchen and grabbed a quarter-bottle of Jack Daniel's by the neck off the counter and unscrewed the cap. She lifted the bottle to her mouth and winced as she drained the remainder of the contents in four quick swallows. Then she headed straight for her bedroom and fell into bed. Exhaustion flooded over her. A moment later, her eyelids drooped.

Six hours later Dana awoke with a start and stared at the clock on her bedside table.

'Goddamn it!' she yelled, hauling herself out of bed. What was wrong with her? How could she fall asleep *now*? She couldn't miss her flight – she had to get to Chicago on time.

She rushed into the bathroom and slipped out of her clothes, letting them fall to the floor in a pile at her feet before stepping inside the shower and turning the hot water up full blast. She had to wash the filth of her memories out her hair, out of her nostrils, out of her skin.

Without warning, a low gurgling noise sounded deep in the pit of her stomach. A split second later a rainbow of vomit exploded from her mouth and covered her naked body. The Jack Daniel's, coupled with exhaustion and a whole lot of other shit she was carrying around with her.

Gagging with dry heaves now, Dana twisted the shower

off – it made a metallic squeak – and stepped out onto the tiled floor. She stumbled to the sink and brushed her teeth for five solid minutes. She gargled for another two before finally using a clean white towel to wipe the steam away from the mirror. Still nauseous and shaking, she gripped the sides of the sink and peered at her reflection.

'You look terrible,' she told herself. 'You really look like shit, sister.'

She towel-dried her hair and quickly dressed in a pair of hip-hugger jeans and an oversized green turtleneck before strapping her Glock into the holster around her waist and checking the mirror again.

Much better.

She glanced down at her watch. Only thirty minutes until take-off. She'd really have to hustle.

Tossing a couple of changes of clothing, her notebooks and some toiletries into a second overnight bag, Dana bolted down the fire-escape stairs toward the parking lot. No time to wait for the elevator, and Eric and Oreo would just have to miss out on their goodbye kiss tonight.

Down in the parking lot two minutes later, she switched off the car alarm with the keychain control and slid behind the wheel of her silver Mazda Protégé before cranking the engine to life.

Five minutes later she was on Interstate 90, headed back to Hopkins for her second plane trip of the day. Ten minutes after that she was hurrying her way through the crowded terminal again. As she was signing for her ticket, a voice came over the intercom to announce that her flight was now in its final boarding phase.

Dana looked down at her watch again and let out a deep breath. She'd cut it pretty close, but she'd made it.

CHAPTER FORTY-TWO

Nathan's flight from Wichita passed entirely without incident, serving its intended purpose of transportation while he whetted his enormous appetite for murder with a dog-eared paperback copy of Vincent Bugliosi's *Helter Skelter* balanced on his knee. He'd easily sidestepped the Sedgwick County Sheriff's Office deputies at the airport, but that came as no surprise. He'd waited a full day to leave and the officers had grown bored with the hunt, just like he'd known they would. Like everything else, *that* step had been planned right down to the tiniest detail. And even if that photo had ever made it out of Cleveland there was no way that anyone would have recognised *him* from it.

He leaned back in his first-class seat, wishing like hell he'd brought his scrapbook along for reading material. Inside, Dana Whitestone's entire career had been intricately chronicled through newspaper clippings and photographs. Still, there was no way in hell that he would've been stupid enough to bring incriminating evidence along with him, so he'd just have to rely on his exquisite memory to amuse himself on the ride.

As the plane streaked deep into the cold black night, he imagined the voice in his head filling the delightful role of

Charles Manson in Bugliosi's book. He, of course, would play the part of Tex Watson.

The man who got things done.

Nathan smiled. Obtaining the plane ticket hadn't posed the slightest problem. Nobody had given him any trouble along the way, not so much as a sidelong glance. His fake driver's licence had worked perfectly both times he'd been compelled to produce it, and that didn't surprise him in the least. Years of meticulous planning simply awaited careful translation into perfect execution now. Everything the voice had foretold was coming to pass – everything was proceeding *exactly* according to schedule – and he had every confidence in the world that events would continue to unfold in the precise manner prescribed.

Three hours after his plane touched down at O'Hare, he pulled up to the guard shack protecting the western entrance of Loyola University in downtown Chicago and pressed the button to activate the power window in the rented blue Acura. The black-tinted window slid down with a mechanical whine and he smiled up at the frail old codger manning the booth, saw the half-empty bottle of vodka wedged into one corner, only half-hidden by a leather book bag.

'Welcome to Loyola University, sir,' the guard said. 'May I help you?'

Nathan slid his prescription-free glasses down the bridge of his nose. 'Yes, sir. I'm certainly hoping you can be of some assistance. I'm here to see a friend of mine.'

The old guard smiled brightly. 'Name?'

'Ted Jansen.'

'I meant your friend's name, sir.'

Nathan's cheeks flushed as he quickly turned up the wattage on his own smile. 'Of course, sorry about that.' He told the guard the girl's name.

The old man squinted down at his clipboard – probably a visitor's log – then back at Nathan. 'Right-o, sir, here it is. Do you have an authorised visitor's pass?'

Nathan handed him the pass he'd paid a student down the street twenty bucks for – beer money, no doubt – and the security guard waved him through with a cheery 'Have a great night, sir!'

As the gate slowly creaked up and Nathan eased the Acura carefully over an irritating series of huge yellow speed bumps, he reached out a hand and punched a button on the tape player. A moment later the narrator's perfectly pitched voice filled the car.

'Jeremy Bryan Jones,' the man intoned. 'Jeremy Bryan Jones was a smooth-talking, extremely handsome psychopath who raped and murdered more than two dozen women, bragging that he could "talk the panties off a nun". '

Arriving at the library three minutes later, Nathan parked the car in an open space and hurried inside. The tape was enough for the time being, but what he really needed right now were his precious *books*.

Five minutes of poking around the shelves finally produced what he was after. Brand-new hardback copy of Truman Capote's *In Cold Blood* firmly in hand, he staked out an empty table near the Medical Sciences section and opened the book, sighing contentedly.

Twenty minutes into his tale about the unfortunate Clutter family, who'd so foolishly decided to call their remote Kansas farmhouse home, the young woman from the Lonely Hearts Club settled into a chair two tables away, looking even *more* beautiful than she did in her profile pictures, if that were possible.

She looked up and smiled shyly at Nathan when she noticed him staring. Anticipation slammed in his chest as he smiled back.

She was absolutely fucking *perfect*.

Lowering his eyes, he flipped a page in his book and began getting into character mentally, infinitely happy that the time had finally come to recreate Richard Speck's deliciously unforgettable crime once and for all.

2010-style.

CHAPTER FORTY-THREE

Ahn 'Annie' Howser felt ridiculous as she smiled at the tall man two tables away. He was handsome enough, sure, but he must have been at least twice her age. Maybe even three times, considering how young she was.

At nineteen, the Vietnamese girl was three years younger than even her best friends at Loyola. But having skipped the tenth and eleventh grades in high school when standardised testing revealed her IQ to be in excess of 170, she now found herself in the same graduating class as Lindsey McCormick and Liza Alloway. And thank God for that.

Outwardly, the three girls seemed to have little in common. A casual observer passing them on the street might have even remarked to a companion that they were among the *unlikeliest* trios he'd ever encountered. Actually venturing such a comment, however, would have been roughly akin to mentioning that the summer skies of Montana often seemed quite blue.

Lindsey was the cheerleader of the group – bright, pretty, peppy and cheerful. A straight-A student and everybody's best friend. Liza was the tomboy of the bunch – rough-and-tumble, loud and boisterous from her days of growing up on a cattle ranch out in Deer Trail, Wyoming. The kind of girl who was never afraid to speak her mind about *anything*.

A shy, quiet girl by nature herself, Ahn had forged a slow

friendship with the American girls after they'd bumped into her – quite literally as it had turned out – in between the towering reference stacks at the campus library.

They'd all been in search of the same single copy of a nursing techniques guide that day, a book that the school – for whatever arcane reason – would only allow to be utilised under the disapproving glare of the reference librarian, a woman infamous on campus for always strangling her brittle silver hair in a mercilessly tight bun with never the slightest concession to season or occasion.

Four hours of intense studying followed. The trio of budding nurses carefully examined heart rates and blood pressure; thoughtfully discussed ocular inspections and platelet counts; and delicately attempted to unravel the intricate mysteries of blood-cell variations – all while trying to ignore the pointedly disgusted looks coming from Loyola's very own answer to Nurse Ratched.

When they'd finally had enough of both the books and the looks, the girls decided to unwind by grabbing a quick beer at Sparky's Place, a local watering hole popular on campus for its notoriously lax policy on checking IDs.

At the bar a single beer magically turned into three and three into five before their little group finally managed to drag themselves down off their stools and drunkenly hail a cab back to campus.

They'd had an absolute *blast* that night, and their relationships had subsequently developed to the point where Ahn now considered the American girls to be the sisters she'd never had. Lindsey and Liza felt the same way about the Vietnamese girl, anglicising her name to 'Annie' when she'd timidly asked them for a nickname that would help her feel more American.

Ahn smiled to herself. No, she guessed skipping those grades in high school hadn't turned out so badly, after all. But that was the past and this was the present – and right now she had to go meet up with her sisters. They were expecting her.

CHAPTER FORTY-FOUR

Twenty minutes passed before Nathan peeked up at the girl over the cover of his book again.

There she was, just as lovely as ever.

His skin prickled. He'd waited a long time for this night to arrive – *too* long, really – and now that it was finally here he was itching to take the next step.

His thoughts briefly went to Kelly and Jennifer, missing them so badly that he thought he would break down and start crying right there in the middle of the library.

I love you, girls. Daddy will be home soon.

Nathan smiled with the knowledge that Dana Whitestone would be the one to send him on his way to their joyful reunion. And – as was befitting their special relationship – he'd take her along for the ride, of course. It was only fair, after all. She'd stolen his life and now he'd steal her life in return.

Over the years he'd lived in his mind the night that now lay ahead a million times over, the terror of the dead nurses springing to life each time he closed his eyes. Now all that remained was the careful execution of the script.

Another ten minutes passed before the young woman rose from her seat and collected her things. She smiled a polite goodbye at him, and Nathan returned the favour before waiting a full sixty seconds by the smooth sweep of the hand of his Rolex watch and following her outside at a discreet distance. Looking up into the night sky, he saw that it was very dark.

Already in character, it was time to change into his uniform now. After all, it was of vital importance to recognise those who had come before him, now wasn't it? To remember those who had paved the way.

To thumb his nose at them.

As he followed the girl back to her dorm, Nathan drifted back in time to one of his earliest study sessions as a young boy, remembering the story of the man he would soon become.

Born 6 December 1941 in Kirkwood, Illinois, Richard Franklin Speck at the age of nineteen visited a tattoo parlor and had BORN TO RAISE HELL inked into his arm. At twenty-four, he broke into a townhouse at 2319 East 100th Street in the Jeffrey Manor neighbourhood of Chicago and systematically butchered eight student nurses from South Chicago Community Hospital. On 5 December 1991 – exactly one day shy of his fiftieth birthday – he died of a massive heart attack at Silver Cross Hospital in Joliet after complaining of chest pains.

Nathan sighed. No matter. In this case, death was only a temporary thing. Thanks to him, tonight Richard Speck would finally be reborn in all his glory to finish off what he'd started more than forty years ago.

After following the girl back to her dorm at a safe distance, Nathan hustled back to the Acura on foot to get dressed in his work clothes. Once he was properly attired, he shoved the ski mask deep into the side pocket of his heavy black coat and slid behind the Acura's leather-wrapped steering wheel before cranking the engine to life.

As he drove back across campus, the narrator's deep voice once more filled the car.

Finally reaching the parking lot of the girl's dorm three minutes later, Nathan parked the car in an open space and swung his booted feet out onto the snow-covered pavement. He removed his coat and affixed the temporary tattoo to his left biceps. Again, it was the *details* that mattered most here. In addition to everything else they had in common, he and Richard Speck now shared the same ink.

He almost laughed out loud at the thought. *Brothers-in-arms.*

A moment later the girl simply walked right out the back door. Head down, she began cutting quickly across the campus quad.

Nathan's mouth dropped wide open. She'd passed within twenty yards of him and hadn't noticed he was there, hadn't even bothered to look up.

Silly fucking rabbit.

To be sporting, he gave her a five-minute head start before he got out of the car. On his way through the parking lot he swiped a parking citation from beneath the windshield wiper of a beat-up Chrysler Sebring and shoved it into the side pocket of his black jeans. Just another breadcrumb for Dana Whitestone to follow.

As he silently tracked the Asian girl along the deserted pathway, Nathan gave thanks to the dark gods for his exceptionally sharp eyesight. She was just fifty yards ahead of him now, and he was closing fast.

A moment later he'd halved the distance, then halved it again.

At ten yards he was jolted by the sudden noise of a

vehicle on the cart path behind him. Heart slamming in his throat, he leaped quickly behind a stand of landscaped bushes and watched in complete astonishment as the security guards came driving around the bend in their ridiculously modified golf cart.

With every ounce of energy left in his body, Nathan fought the overpowering urge to leap from the bushes with a blood-curdling scream and strangle the life out of them with his bare hands. He took several deep breaths and forced himself to calm down. His emotions were running far too hot, and that was always a dangerous sign. Angry men made stupid mistakes, and he had much bigger fish to fry at the moment – even if the nasty little gook *had* just wriggled off his hook. So he simply gritted his teeth and watched helplessly while the dark night slowly swallowed the Asian girl alive.

CHAPTER FORTY-FIVE

The bitter winter wind sliced hard through Ahn's coat as she walked across campus to join her friends for their planned study group, swirling up around her thin legs a maelstrom of dead leaves and debris that looked and acted just like a miniature tornado. Each gust, more powerful and painful than the last, only reminded her that Loyola was largely deserted now, most of the students and staff having long since headed home to the spend the Thanksgiving holiday with their loved ones. Though it made her feel silly and self-conscious to do so, she nonetheless made the sign of the cross against the faceless evil she felt hovering all around her in the chill night air. Ahn wasn't quite sure *what* she believed on the spiritual side of things, but she did know that she didn't want to think she was all alone in this world with no one to watch over her. *That* thought was too horrible even to comprehend.

She heaved a grateful sigh of relief when she finally came to the outside of Lindsey's dormitory building ten minutes later. Quickly ascending the metal stairs on the outside of the building two at a time, her heart nearly exploded in her chest when a heavy footstep sounded on the landing directly behind her.

She spun around frantically, her eyes desperately searching

the night for the source of the noise, but found only the darkness and howling wind in pursuit. She wrestled nervously with another powerful gust of wind in her effort to open the heavy steel door on the second floor.

Finally winning the battle, she stepped inside and paused to shake off the cold before taking several deep breaths and quickly making her way down the hall to Lindsey's door.

Despite her overwhelming anxiety, a slow smile spread across Ahn's pretty face as she came to the outside of Lindsey's room. From inside, she clearly heard the familiar sound of Liza Alloway swearing up a blue streak about something or other. More likely than not the swearing was connected to the complicated list of trauma procedures they were expected to memorise for their finals. Although Ahn never swore herself, she couldn't blame her friend for doing so in this instance. It was tough stuff to get a handle on – 'a real bitch,' as Liza might say.

She lifted a delicate hand and knocked lightly on the door. It opened almost at once.

'Annie, baby!' Liza boomed, blocking out most of the narrow doorway with her huge body. 'Where ya been, girl? Get your tight little ass in here, bitch! We've got us some studying to do!'

The buxom redhead draped a heavy arm around Ahn's slender shoulders and drew her into the warmth of the room and the tight circle of their friendship. Once inside, Ahn immediately felt the unease that had dogged her on the walk over drift away like smoke from the end of a burning cigarette.

She was safe now. She was with her sisters.

They cracked their books and studied in earnest for a solid hour before Lindsey snapped hers shut abruptly and tossed it aside. 'I'm starving,' she announced. 'Let's go raid the vending machines on the fourth floor for some quick brain food.'

'I hear that,' Liza said, her bright green eyes lighting up like emeralds at the prospect of some hard-earned sustenance. 'I'm so fuckin' hungry I could eat a goddamn horse.'

She stopped, horrified. 'Well, not Tinkerbell, my Appaloosa, of course, but you know what I mean. Let's go, bitches.'

Ahn and Lindsey exchanged a quick private smile, knowing full well that Liza would wind up consuming the lion's share of the bounty, which was perfectly OK with them.

Giggling happily, the girls dug through their purses and came up with several dollars in change between them before heading out the door and bounding up the stairwell toward the vending machines on the fourth floor.

CHAPTER FORTY-SIX

From his concealed post in the bushes, Nathan finally regained visual contact with the Asian girl just as she was ascending the metal staircase of an old red-brick dormitory building about a hundred yards away.

He watched as she opened a door on the second floor and stepped inside.

Five minutes later he was opening the very same door. He paused outside each of the rooms, but heard nothing but silence coming from any of them.

Except for one. Room 232.

Excellent. The Asian girl did indeed have friends – she hadn't been making it all up.

A full hour passed but Nathan didn't mind. He was an exceptionally patient man, had learned patience very well as a child. He'd already waited *years* for this night to arrive finally, and waiting a little bit longer now certainly wasn't going to kill him.

But it might very well kill *them*.

He ducked into the laundry room across the hall when he heard the girls' plan through the thin plywood door. They were headed up to the fourth floor for some quick brain food. Good for them.

It would be their last supper.

CHAPTER FORTY-SEVEN

The only thing Ahn Howser can think is this: *It's not real.*

Her eyes can clearly see what's happening – it's happening right there in front of her face, after all – but her flash-frozen brain is having trouble comprehending the ungodly images they are conveying to her.

She, Lindsey and Liza have just returned from the fourth floor, arms laden with bags of potato chips, snack cakes and Diet Cokes. Ahn has come into the room first, followed by Liza. Lindsey is bringing up the rear.

Dumping the packages from her arms onto the beat-up couch, Ahn turns around to say something to Liza, but the words die in her throat when she sees him standing there.

He is a tall, menacing figure dressed entirely in black. Black jeans. Black turtleneck sweater. Black Navy-issue pea coat with tiny black anchors etched into its shiny black buttons. A black ski mask covers his face.

In his right hand, the man is holding a long knife. Its shining blade glints a wicked silver in the fluorescence of the overhead light. Bright red drops of arterial blood drip from its sharp edge.

Ahn lets her horrified eyes slowly drift downward and sees that Lindsey is sprawled on the floor just inside the doorway, one arm flung wildly above her head. An angry-looking slash pulses on the right side of her neck.

Her jugular, Ahn thinks stupidly. *He cut her jugular.*

The gold necklace and crucifix that Lindsey had been wearing just a moment before have been cleaved neatly in two. She seems to stare at the braided strands of ruined jewellery for a moment before her eyes suddenly flutter and roll to a complete, fixed stop in the back of her head.

Everything is going in slow motion now, like an old horror film with bad special effects, as Liza strikes out at the man and rakes his throat just beneath the bottom of his ski mask with the long, perfectly manicured fingernails of her right hand. A pair of bright red lines appears at his black-stubbled throat at once. Twin scarlet streaks of blood spill through his wounds and slip down the surface of his neck.

But he barely flinches under the assault.

Instead his reaction is as swift as it is terrifying as he calmly whips the knife through the air in a preternaturally quick backhanded motion.

Liza Alloway is nearly decapitated by the blow.

It is a startlingly graceful movement, almost beautiful to watch. Liza's green eyes briefly widen in surprise as she clutches at her throat. Rivers of blood spill through her fingers. Then her knees buckle and she collapses to the floor three feet away from Lindsey.

When the man then turns his attention to Ahn, she watches his pink lips slowly curve upward into the shape of a smile. Glittering wetly through the holes in the ski mask, his eyes are the most demonic shade of brown she has ever seen, ringed with almost imperceptible striations of yellow and green.

How strange. His eyes are so strange.

'Get under the bed.'

His voice is clear and strong as he speaks to Ahn, but comprehension is very slow to set in with her. He is staring at her so intently with his evil eyes, she is so utterly lost in his gaze at this exact moment, that her vision has completely overridden all her other senses. It is impossible to make sense of the words he is saying.

He opens his mouth and speaks again, but this time his voice only sounds like a record being played at the wrong speed.

When he repeats the order a third time, the chilling understanding finally dawns on her.

'Get under the bed.'

His voice is incredibly calm as he speaks to her. It is deep and gravelly and more than a little bit scary under the circumstances, but otherwise seems devoid of any discernible human emotion.

Once his terrible instructions have been finally processed by her shocked mind, Ahn's body instantly freezes. The fear and enormity of her situation have turned off a switch in her brain. She knows this much: he wants her to move. But she also knows she is thoroughly unable to comply with this order. She is having so much trouble even drawing breath into her badly constricted lungs that there is no way in hell she will ever be able to move.

When she doesn't immediately do as instructed, the large man takes a step in her direction, covering a quarter of the distance between them, but her feet feel as though they are nailed to the floor.

Another step.

No good – her legs still won't work. Signals from her brain are getting crossed up; going haywire; zigging when they should be zagging; sabotaging her when what they *should* damn well be doing is concentrating on saving her life.

Another step.

Every fibre of her being is screaming out for her to move now. *Just move, goddamn it!* But her legs – *her useless fucking legs!* – are still refusing to listen. One more step and he'll be upon her.

When he takes that step, the man raises the bloody knife directly over his head. As the knife goes up, his eyes glaze over so completely that for a moment Ahn thinks he surely isn't even *human*. Lost in his stare, dumbstruck by his peculiar eyes, her mind barely registers the fact that his arm is coming down on her now in a lightning-fast stabbing motion.

Moving now! Dear Jesus, I'm moving now!

OhthankGodinheaven. Thank you, God. Thank you, Jesus. Thank you, God.

The knife whistles through the air over her head, missing her throat by inches as she lands on her belly and scurries under the bed, just another cockroach exposed to a bright overhead light. But she is all the way under the bed, just like he told her.

Though she has finally followed his instructions, though she is still *alive*, the voice in Ahn's head is still refusing to leave her alone. Now it is screaming out a new set of instructions for her to follow, but she is having trouble making sense of these as well.

What, exactly, is it that she needs to do?

Breathe, goddamn it! Breathe or you'll die, you fucking idiot!

But for several long moments Ahn *can't* breathe. She is too terrified. She tries several times to inhale but might as well be trying to draw breath through a plastic bag that has been tied tightly over her face. Vaguely aware that she is growing dizzy from the lack of oxygen, the first black fringes of unconsciousness creep into the corners of her huge almond-shaped eyes.

There!

A single breath finally forces its way into her tortured lungs. It is the only thing that keeps her from passing out. But maybe it would be better if she *did* pass out. Just pass out right now and slip under the warm, dark blanket of sleep. Surely even he can't get to her there.

Can he?

Get a hold of yourself! Mustn't think like that now. She must stay conscious, stay alert so she can keep watching him. She can't take her eyes off him for even an instant, for taking her eyes off him will surely mean death.

Another cool rush of air into her lungs braces her. That's better. She's under the bed and she's breathing again, just like he told her. Most importantly, she is still *alive*.

When he then stares down at her under the bed – the cobra freezing its terrified prey in its hypnotic gaze – Ahn cannot possibly resist the siren call of those horrible eyes and once again raises her own stare to meet his, nothing more than a timorous supplicant trembling before his vast power. There is no escape. She is going to die looking into those maddening brown eyes.

Like a hard punch to the stomach, she feels it physically when he releases her abruptly from the prison of his stare. If a mere look from him is enough to completely shut off her airflow and other vital functions, how much worse will it be when he is done with her friends and finally comes for her?

Moving to Liza, the man viciously kicks her in the ribs with one of his enormous booted feet. An involuntary grunt escapes Liza's mouth as the brutally expelled air rides up from her lungs and over her severed vocal cords.

Stepping over Liza, the man is moving more quickly now. He kneels down next to Lindsey, and Ahn watches in horror as his gloved hands wrap around her hacked and bloody throat. A moment later, the horrible gurgling sounds that had been coming from Lindsey as she choked to death on her own blood fall silent.

Poor, sweet, beautiful Lindsey: valedictorian, prom queen and everyone's best friend.

Lindsey Mae McCormick is dead.

The man moves back to Liza and kneels beside her body, strangling the remaining breath from her lungs as well before once again rising to his feet.

That's when he pauses.

If you haven't been looking for it, it would be very easy to miss. But Ahn is so transfixed by the sight of him, noticing even the most minor muscle twitches around his terrible brown eyes, that *she* sees it.

For the briefest of moments he has stopped in his tracks, looking almost . . . *sick*.

Swaying on his enormous booted heels in the middle of the room, he then takes a deep breath that expands his massive chest almost to the point of bursting and speaks the words that cause the blood in Ahn's veins to run ice-cold.

'Richard Franklin Speck never wavered in his moment of truth, therefore neither will *I* waver in my moment of truth. And my moment of truth is upon me now.'

These strange words seem to stabilise him, and the man is once again very sure of himself, in complete control of his movements as he steps over the lifeless bodies of Ahn's friends on his way to the wall by the door. There he opens a large black briefcase that has been propped against a chair. He takes out a clean white towel and wraps it around the bloody knife before placing it inside. Next he takes out a large, sharp boning knife, studying it for a moment before shaking his head and putting it back. He is the cautious surgeon carefully choosing his instruments, and he has selected the pair of handheld pruning shears instead.

Before Ahn has time to wonder what he'll do with his odd assortment of tools, she finds out. Timidly peeking out from beneath the bed skirt – a frightened fawn cowering away from a pack of drunken hunters in the woods – she realises that her nightmare has only just begun. The large man picks Liza's limp right hand off the floor, the one with which she had managed to scratch him.

One by one he calmly chops off each of her fingers.

The sound is nauseating as metal bites into flesh. It is the sound of bone-dry twigs snapping underfoot on a brisk walk through the woods on a crisp fall day. When he grunts softly with the effort, the bones in Liza's fingers break. Sheared cleanly off, they fall to the floor with dull little thumps that will forever echo in Ahn's traumatised mind.

This is not really happening.

She is not really here in this room. She is not really here in this room and this man has not really killed her friends. She is in a bad dream and she desperately needs to wake up.

But deep inside her heart, in that dark, secret place within all of us where the only person you *can't* hide from is yourself, Ahn knows she will never wake up from this terrible nightmare. She will never wake up from it because she isn't sleeping, isn't dreaming this up in her fevered mind. She is wide awake and what is happening now is very, very real. It is the realest thing that has ever happened to her and it is happening right here, right now and right in front of her very eyes.

This man really *has* killed her friends, really *is* mutilating them, and there isn't a goddamn thing she can do to stop him. She is too weak, too scared to fight him. If a mere *look* from him is enough to paralyse her lungs with such an all-consuming fear she can't even *breathe*, how in the hell can she ever possibly be expected to *stop* him?

He will kill her too, she knows. He will kill her just as soon as he is finished with her friends.

She doesn't know why, but the thought that suddenly occurs to her makes perfect sense, as if *anything* could make any kind of sense right now – perfect or otherwise.

Reaching around to the back pocket of her jeans, Ahn withdraws a small plastic object the size of a credit card and holds it in trembling hands in front of her face as though it is a talisman meant to ward off a demon sent from Hell to steal her very soul. And she has no doubt this man is a demon. She has never been more certain of anything in her life.

When he finishes his gruesome work with Liza, the large man calmly picks her severed fingers off the floor and drops them one by one into a large Ziploc sandwich bag. Placing the bag back into the briefcase, he snaps it shut, locking the macabre contents inside with a loud click.

Turning to Liza, he kicks her again, audibly cracking several of her ribs this time. But even as he delivers this powerful blow, Ahn is surprised to see no real malice in his strange and terrible and demonic brown eyes as he does so.

Towering over Liza, his fingers find the scratches at his

throat. 'Sorry about that,' he says, though he surely must realise he is apologizing to a corpse. 'I have to take your chubby little fingers with me, honey. You see, I learned a very important lesson from Timothy Spencer. You might know him better as the Southside Strangler. I'll bet you didn't know he was the first serial killer convicted through DNA evidence, did you? Yep, it's true. He raped and murdered five little girls, which was very good, but he also slipped up by leaving his DNA behind, which was very, very bad. I'm not going to make that same mistake here. I'm *smarter* than that.'

He pauses and runs his sparkling reptilian eyes over the length of Liza's broken body. 'Damn, girl, you're not much of a scholar, but you're one hell of a sexy little wildcat, you know that? You and I could have been something really special, but you had to go and fuck things up before we got the chance to find out, didn't you? Now look where it's got you.'

And that is all Ahn needs to hear. She has finally seen and heard enough. The man in the room with her is clearly insane, and she knows lunatics are completely incapable of regulating their own actions. This one simple and incontrovertible fact makes him exponentially more dangerous than all the other malevolence in the world combined.

Violent, uncontrollable shivers rack her as she presses her tiny body up against the cold concrete wall under the bed – as far away from him, as far away from the *demon*, as she can possibly get. The bones in her skeleton rattle like loose window panes in a passing train as she waits for the unimaginably horrifying feeling of his blood-smeared gloved hand on the back of her neck. He will pull her out from under the bed now, she knows – just another terrified rabbit chosen for the slaughter. He will pull her out from under the bed and to her certain, horrible death.

Several agonising moments pass as Ahn listens to him breathe. The rhythmic tide of his heavy breath is the only sound in the room now, dark waves of evil crashing loudly against the shores of insanity. His breathing sounds excited.

Retching, she realises he is *enjoying* himself.

There is a pause as he holds this last breath longer than the others. Then, unbelievably, she hears the sound of his footsteps as he turns and walks slowly to the door.

He seems to pause there for several endless moments, as though he is trying to decide whether he should turn around and kill her after all, before she finally hears the door shut behind him with a soft *click*.

Only silence now. Ahn strains her ears for the sound of his terrible breath.

Nothing.

He is gone. The demon has spared her.

But *why*?

The reason isn't important. He is gone and that is all that matters now.

She waits beneath the bed for five more minutes just to be absolutely certain, carefully timing it on her wristwatch. When the time finally passes several lifetimes later, she once again strains her ears for the sound of his maniacal breathing.

Still nothing. The only sound in the room now is coming from the annoyingly incessant hum of the fluorescent light above. With every last fibre of her being, Ahn wishes the goddamn humming would just stop! If she doesn't get out now the sound will surely drive her mad.

An intense combination of fear and shock and adrenalin convulses her tiny body as she peeks out from beneath the bed skirt, determined not to look at the gruesome sight of her murdered friends – her murdered *sisters* – before walking through the room and to a telephone from which she can call the police. But in the exact instant her head appears she looks up in horror to see his heavy black boot coming down on her face.

The back of her skull is driven into the floor with the sheer blunt force of a sledgehammer slamming into a cinder block. The fragile bones in her face have little choice but to shatter away into a thousand tiny pieces at the crushing impact. Somehow, he has stationed himself right next to the bed, right next to *her*, without ever having made the slightest sound. He has tricked her.

The demon has tricked her.

Ahn Howser does not have time to worry further that her gaze will fall unintentionally upon the grisly scene in which Lindsey McCormick and Liza Alloway have played out their final acts, for this night will serve as her curtain call as well. Just as it is that there are angels who walk the Earth, so it follows there must be demons as well. The delicate bones in her face have splintered as easily as an eggshell beneath his heavy foot, and the waffled sole of his huge black boot is the last thing she will ever see in this life.

A moment later, her world fades away blissfully into eternal darkness.

CHAPTER FORTY-EIGHT

Nathan grabs the Asian girl beneath her slender arms and drags her petite body roughly from beneath the bed like a rag doll before giving her the same treatment with the knife that he's given her friends. Though the little gook is already quite dead, he wants to be fair to the others, so he removes the switchblade from his back pocket and slices her wind-pipe with a quick flick of his powerful wrist.

It is easy work, he thinks. Easy and not in the least bit unpleasant.

No one has heard the commotion in the room. The campus is a ghost town for the Thanksgiving holiday break, and Nathan has planned these murders to take place at precisely this time for exactly that reason. When you have *years* to plan a mission, you can afford the luxury of getting every last detail right. And that's exactly what he's done. Now all he has to do is avoid the goddamn security guards on his way out and he'll be home free.

His gloved hands now very slick with the beautiful blood he has spilled here tonight, they slip a little as he wraps them around the Asian girl's impossibly thin neck. Finally finding purchase in her throat, it pleases him greatly to hear the birdlike bones snap as he viciously squeezes the re-maining air from her dead lungs.

He leans down and gently lifts her destroyed face to his own, pressing his lips to hers with great tenderness. He lingers there for several long moments, tasting the blood on his lips, on his tongue, in his mouth.

He has waited so very long for this moment! He has waited long but it has been well worth the wait.

Regretfully breaking the kiss, he brushes the back of a gloved hand across the girl's mouth to remove any trace of saliva that he may have left there. He is a very careful man. He has to be. He requires everything to be perfect. Everything. Perfect and clean. Anything less is unacceptable.

From the briefcase come a hammer and a nail. From the pocket of his black jeans comes the parking ticket he swiped off the Chrysler Sebring. Five swift and accurate blows affix the citation squarely to the centre of the Asian girl's fragile breastbone.

Breadcrumb hammered home, he moves back to the others and favours their corpses with his blood-kiss as well before once again rising to his feet.

'Thank you,' he says, his voice cracking with such great emotion that he thinks he will surely cry.

Their wonderful gift is now part of something far more important than anything they could ever have hoped to accomplish on their own. They are connected in eternity now, the whole of their beings much greater than the simple sum of their parts.

They will all go down in history together.

Bowing to them with a graceful flourish, he bends deeply at the waist in a courtly manner, the brilliant actor acknowledging his breathless and appreciative audience.

And so it is that Nathan Stiedowe is solemn as he walks out of the dormitory room and down the empty hallway, finally allowing the tears of gratitude freely to sting his eyes like a million tiny needles.

Shoving open the heavy outer door with ease, he descends the metal staircase and slowly disappears across campus, a solitary figure fading away into the inky darkness of the cold night.

Looking up into the night sky, he sees that it has begun to snow. This makes him smile. A new season is upon them.

It is the season of the eagle.

PART IV

REPRISING DAVID BERKOWITZ

CHAPTER FORTY-NINE

Dana found a cab outside the terminal at O'Hare and reached into the front pocket of her jeans before handing the driver the address she'd hurriedly scribbled down on a Post-It note. It was almost midnight by the time they finally pulled up to the entrance of Chicago Police Headquarters on a busy downtown street bustling with traffic.

Dana rubbed at her temples and stifled a loud yawn. Chicago was her fifth major city in the space of little less than a week, and they were all beginning to look oddly the same to her weary eyes.

A squat man with a powerful build and the boxy scrunched-up face of a bulldog met her as she ascended the cement steps in front of the building. 'Special Agent Whitestone?' he asked in a deep voice tinged with an unmistakable southern drawl.

'That's me.'

He smiled. 'I'm Detective Constantine Konstantopolous, but you can just call me CK. Everybody else does. We've been trying to call you for an hour now.'

Dana felt in her pocket for her cellphone, suddenly realising that she hadn't remembered to turn it back on when her plane touched down. 'What's going on?' she asked.

The Chicago cop's face darkened. 'The killer slipped right through our fingers.'

Dana was so shocked for a moment that she couldn't even breathe. 'Not again,' she said, her voice barely above a whisper.

The cop shook his head in disgust. 'He stayed away from the hospitals, but three nursing students were found murdered an hour ago in a dorm room at Loyola University. The killer hammered a parking ticket into one of their chests.'

Dana's stomach lurched. For a brief moment she was afraid she was going to throw up again. She'd been on the plane when the killer had struck this time. Not only were three more people dead, Dana had stopped off at home in Cleveland to play chicken at the house of her childhood instead of heading directly out to Chicago. No way in *hell* they were going to let her stay on the case now. Still, her brain automatically snapped into action, processing the parking-ticket clue – the mental equivalent of a whiplash reflex.

David Berkowitz. Wait until she told Crawford.

The notorious serial killer known as the 'Son of Sam' had terrorised New York City in the 1970s. He'd finally been caught when somebody had decided to check out the parking citations handed out on the night of one of his murders. Not exactly a subtle connection there.

To CK, she said, 'What else do you have?'

The Chicago cop pulled open the door to the station house and held it for her as she stepped inside. 'Well, there's also a chance there may be a link to some unsolved murders out in Wyoming. We've got the ex-boyfriend of one of the victims in custody now – found him hiding in a dumpster on campus shortly after the discovery of the bodies.'

Dana's heart flipped despite the dread of knowing just how badly she'd messed up by not immediately coming out to Chicago. *They had a suspect in custody? Their* killer?

CK filled her in on the rest as they walked down a bustling corridor past petty thieves and painted-up prostitutes handcuffed to O-rings on holding benches.

'Campus was pretty empty because of the holiday break, so no witnesses. Nobody we've talked to so far saw or heard anything. Pretty grisly scene, knife was used. Finger marks around the throats of all three victims, but no prints to run through Interpol. Coroner says it's tough to figure out what actually killed the girls – the knife or the strangling – but she figures either method could have turned the trick on its own.'

CK paused and ran his stubby fingers through his thinning black hair. 'Oh, and get this. The ex-girlfriend of our suspect also had all the fingers on her right hand chopped off with some kind of heavy-duty scissors or something.'

Dana winced.

'Yeah. Not pretty. Anyway, his clothes were all crusted in dried blood. Said it's hog-slaughtering season back home on the ranch in Wyoming and he just didn't bother changing before heading out to Loyola. The clothes are at the lab now, just waiting for the test results to come back. Should be tomorrow, Thursday at the latest. Like I said before, turns out he's the ex-boyfriend of one of the murdered girls. His name is Trent Bollinger.'

CK nodded at the desk sergeant and took in a lungful of air before resuming his narrative. 'We called up to Wyoming to check him out and when they heard about what's going on around here they told us they've had a spate of similar murders up there. *Spate* – helluva nice word, huh? But that's exactly what they said. A *spate*.'

CK shook his head and continued. 'Anyway, we've got Bollinger in lock-up now, but he's not talking. Says we're a bunch of assholes and we can just go fuck ourselves seven ways to Sunday. Doesn't want a lawyer, either. Claims we're trying to pin a murder rap on him and he's not saying anything to anybody from now on. To tell you the truth, we were kind of hoping you could use your female powers of persuasion to change all that.'

Dana turned to him as they came to a stop in front of the holding cells. 'I'll see what I can do, CK, but I'd really prefer to take a look at the murder scene before I talk to Bollinger. Is there any way someone could take me over there for a look around?'

The Chicago cop didn't miss a beat. 'How would I do, ma'am?'

Dana nodded. 'Thank you, sir. You'll do just fine.'

CHAPTER FIFTY

CK led Dana through a labyrinth of halls in the sprawling metro police station and out to the parking lot where the unmarked cars were kept. They got inside a battered 1986 Toyota Corolla with peeling brown paint and a heavily dented front fender and talked on the short ride over to Loyola. Dana found CK's inconsequential everyday chatter reassuring. She needed it right now to block out the turmoil of emotion she was feeling, let alone the incessant negative chatter going on in her own head.

'Married, three kids here,' he was telling her over the static of the police radio. 'I swear to God, my Becky's an angel for putting up with a mug like this one. Luckily the kids all got their good looks from her. How about you? Married? Boyfriend? Any kids?'

Dana shook her head. 'Nope. Not married, no boyfriend. No kids, either, unless you wanna count Oreo, of course.'

'Who's Oreo?'

So she told him all about the day she'd found her furry little friend at the animal shelter near her home.

Oreo was one of about thirty kittens she'd stopped to pet in their cages. After scratching him behind his pointy ears for a moment, she'd started to move on to the next cage when Oreo had stuck his little paw through the bars and snagged the arm of her sweater. Looking directly into her pale blue eyes with his greenish-yellow ones, he'd let out a soft, heartbreaking meow – as though to ask her where the hell she thought she was going. Wasn't *he* good enough for her? The kitten had stolen her heart in that very moment and they'd been together ever since.

CK whistled appreciatively. 'Sounds like a real ladies' man you've got there.'

'He's neutered, CK. Doesn't have much interest in females any more, I'm afraid.'

He winced. 'Ouch. Tough break, but better him than me, I suppose.'

Ten minutes of easy conversation later they drove up to the guard shack on the east end of campus and CK flashed his badge before wheeling the car in. He manoeuvred through a few mostly deserted streets before coming to a stop outside an old red-brick dormitory building just as a light snow began to fall. Emergency medical technicians were loading rubber body bags into the backs of three different ambulances. No fewer than fifteen cruisers lit up the night sky with their blue-and-red flashers, casting weird dancing shadows on the facades of the surrounding buildings. It was time to get serious.

CK turned in his seat to face Dana. 'This is it,' he said. 'They cancelled classes for next week. Called all the students up and told them their Thanksgiving vacations had just been extended. That means we've pretty much got the place to ourselves.'

'Fantastic.' At least that was something.

They got out of the car and CK led her through the police line and up a metal staircase on the outside of the building.

He opened a heavy outer steel door on the second floor that segued into a long narrow hallway. They stopped in front of Room 232. More yellow police tape was stretched across the threshold. At least a dozen crime-scene technicians were processing the room inside.

'I'll just wait outside for you while you go in and take a look around,' CK said.

'Thanks.'

Dana ducked under the police tape and into the room, taking a quick inventory as a noisy fluorescent light bathed the room in a pale yellow. What it illuminated took her breath away.

Dark splotches of maroon covered the carpet in three distinct areas. The spatters of blood on the surrounding furniture and walls made it look as if someone had taken a brush with bright red paint dripping from its bristles and wildly flung it in random directions from the centre of the room.

High-velocity spatter again, Dana noticed. Still, it didn't take a world-class forensics expert to see that a terrific bloodbath had taken place here.

'Sweet Jesus,' she breathed. It was worse than she'd expected. *Much* worse, actually. She felt a swell of anger. Was there nothing he wasn't prepared to do? And for what?

A man wearing full protective gear approached and asked, 'Special Agent Whitestone?'

Dana nodded.

The man handed her a clear Ziploc bag with a student-identification card inside.

'This was under the bed between the mattress and the latticework of the supporting springs,' he said. 'Thought you'd probably want to see it.'

Dana took the bag and looked down at it. The card inside showed the smiling face of a delicately pretty, extremely young-looking Asian girl. The name on the card was Ahn Howser, the murder victim who'd been found – throat slashed, skull crushed and parking ticket hammered into her chest – lying right next to the bed.

And that was when everything became clear in Dana's brain. All the nagging little thoughts in the back of her mind that had been bothering her since she'd first started investigating the copycat murders finally made perfect sense to her.

She felt nauseous as she left the room and found CK on the metal staircase outside, smoking a cigarette in the cold night air. He took a long, final drag on his Camel and flipped the butt over the railing as she stepped out onto the landing. 'Any luck?' he asked. 'You look like you've just seen a ghost.'

'I think I just might have,' Dana said. 'I'll tell you about it in the car.'

On the ride back to headquarters she filled him in on the discovery of Ahn Howser's ID card.

'What do you think it means?' CK asked when she'd finished. 'Why was her ID card under the bed?'

Dana took a deep breath. 'How long have you lived in Chicago, CK? What do you know about Richard Speck?'

The Chicago cop frowned, deepening the already impressive network of wrinkles lacing his forehead. 'Been here about three years,' he said. 'Transferred up from Tennessee. I'm the original redneck Greek. Anyway, as far as Richard Speck goes, the only thing I know about him is what they told me in the briefing. That he killed a bunch of nurses in a boarding house sometime back in the 1960s. Why do you ask?'

Dana cracked a window to let some fresh air into the car. Cold winter air through her coat sleeves shot goose bumps shivering up her arms. 'Richard Speck was eventually convicted based on the testimony of a nurse who was in that boarding house that night – a young Filipina woman by the name of Corazon Amurao,' she said. 'Amurao managed to slide under a bunk bed and hide from him there while he killed the others. Apparently Speck forgot about her before he left. In all the confusion he must've simply lost count.'

The Chicago cop knitted his thick eyebrows. 'What the hell does that have to do with anything?'

Speaking more rapidly now, afraid that if she slowed down even for an instant she'd lose the courage of her convictions, Dana continued. 'If Trent Bollinger really *is* our guy, then we've got a hell of a lot bigger problem on our hands than I initially thought,' she said. 'He's not just a simple copycat. He's doing more than that. He's recreating every single aspect of the crimes, right down to the positioning of the victims. I think he *ordered* the Asian girl under the bed. In fact, I'm almost sure of it. Somehow, as horrible as it must have been, Ahn Howser maintained the presence of mind to leave us a clue.'

'Why would he order her under the bed?' CK asked. 'It doesn't make any sense.'

Dana held up the Ziploc bag with the identification card inside. 'But it *does* make sense,' she said. 'It makes all the sense in the world, at least to him. She was under the bed but she wasn't forgotten this time. So if Bollinger really *is* our guy he's not just copying the crimes, he's practically *photocopying* the goddamn things. The only people who would know the kinds of details he knows, and make this

271

kind of link between these specific serial killers, are students who studied under Crawford Bell.'

'Who's Crawford Bell?'

Dana shook her head and quickly filled CK in on her former partner's background. She paused to cement the idea in her mind while her brain raced to come up with an alternative explanation. There weren't any. Not a single one. But *who*?

'There are five main subjects of Crawford's introductory class for students at the FBI Training Academy,' she said. 'Richard Ramirez, Dennis Rader, Richard Speck, David Berkowitz and John Wayne Gacy. I honestly can't believe I'm just remembering this now. It's what's been bugging the shit out of me all this time. Anyway, Ramirez, Rader and Speck have all been recreated now. The parking ticket hammered into Ahn Howser's chest means David Berkowitz is probably next. I think we're dealing with a former FBI agent here.'

CK narrowed his dark brown eyes. 'Or a *current* one,' he said. 'Hell, maybe it's Crawford Bell himself,' he joked.

Dana's ears rang at the sound of his words. She wanted to dismiss the idea outright. CK had been joking after all, but suddenly a nagging doubt started to work its way into her mind. Now that she thought about it, was it such a wild idea? Crawford had failed to come up with a profile. He'd been behaving oddly recently. Maybe, after a lifetime immersed in the bloodiest murders America had ever seen, his tumour had pushed him over the edge, into the dark. He was the only one who knew her parents' case inside out, she'd told him details no one else could possibly know, details that weren't even in the files. Details this killer seemed to know. He had taught, written articles, even a book about the notorious serial killers *this* killer seemed to be copying. Was it a coincidence? Or had the sickness in his brain – the sickness his bosses didn't even *know* about – twisted his mind that crucial step *too* far? Even Crawford would admit he was obsessed by those killers; had he become so obsessed that he'd decided to recreate their crime scenes? To prove he was somehow better than the best? Or was it a grisly homage of some sort? Had studying them so closely for so long turned him into a monster too? Or had he always been a monster, just biding his time . . .?

Dana shook herself. He was her friend, her mentor, he cared about her, and he was dying. He couldn't be the killer, could he? She'd have to pull files on every student who'd ever attended his course – it had to be one of them.

'It can't be Crawford,' she said, even as the terrifying doubt remained. He'd taught her everything she knew; he couldn't be using that against her now, surely? 'It can't be him. At least, not physically. He can't be at two places at the same time, and I've been in constant contact with him the entire time.'

'I was only joking,' CK said when he registered the look on her face. 'You think he's directing someone? You think he's directing Trent Bollinger?'

Dana closed her eyes. 'I just don't know.' Surely she had finally gone mad. Nothing made sense any more.

CK scrunched up his boxy face. 'Well, let's get out of here and go see what Bollinger's got to say about all this. Let's go see how much *he* knows about the history of serial killers and the details of their crimes.'

Dana reached out a hand and lightly touched CK's muscular forearm. At least CK didn't think she'd lost her mind. Not yet, anyway. 'Thanks, CK. I really needed that.'

In the unnatural green light of the Toyota's dashboard panel, she thought she saw the Chicago cop's craggy face suffuse with colour.

'Any time. Now let's go nail Trent Bollinger to a cross already.'

Dana smiled thinly at him. 'Best offer I've had all week.'

CHAPTER FIFTY-ONE

Trent Matthew Bollinger was seated on a metal folding chair with his back against the wall in the cramped space of Interview Room Three at downtown Chicago Police Headquarters.

He had the massive muscular build of an experienced weightlifter, and since the bloody clothes he'd been wearing earlier that night were off being tested at the lab he was sitting there now in the bright orange jumpsuit that the city of Chicago had so generously loaned him. The jumpsuit strained hard against his chest and shoulders like an overstuffed sausage skin threatening to split at the seams in a microwave turned up full blast.

Dana and CK watched from behind a two-way mirror as Bollinger took a drag on a Marlboro Menthol Light despite the handcuffs hampering the free movement of his wrists. He inhaled deeply on the cigarette and leaned his head back, releasing a long, smooth stream of greyish-blue smoke into the air. The smoke swirled around the room in roiling patterns for several moments before finally settling into a general haze three feet above his head.

Bollinger's eyes were badly bloodshot, but Dana wasn't at all surprised to see this. After all, jail didn't exactly offer the four-star ambience of the Radisson.

It wasn't even the Holiday Inn.

Tired or not, though, Bollinger's puffy eyes did little to hide his extreme good looks. He was at least twenty years older than Liza Alloway but you wouldn't have known it just by looking at him.

His longish brown hair had obviously been finger-combed recently but still managed to stick up in several directions in an oddly endearing manner, making him look a lot more like an oversized little boy than a deranged killer who'd brutally murdered three college girls just a few hours before, stopping just long enough to chop off all the fingers on his ex-girlfriend's right hand before he left.

'Doesn't look like much of a killer to me,' CK said after a moment. 'More like George Clooney's twin brother. Liza Alloway must've had one hell of a personality.'

'What makes you say that?'

The Chicago cop looked embarrassed. 'Well . . .'

'Hey, not every girl can look like Cindy Crawford,' Dana said. 'Besides, some serial killers don't look the part. Just look at Ted Bundy. Who would've thought a handsome devil like that was such a monster underneath it all?'

'Good point. So you ready for this or what?'

Dana took a deep breath. 'Ready as I'll ever be, I guess. Wish me luck.'

'Go get him, tiger.'

Dana stepped into the hall and motioned to the desk sergeant, who nodded in acknowledgement before pressing a button on the control panel hidden beneath his desk. A loud buzzing sound accompanied the electronic click of the disengaging lock as Dana stepped inside the interview room. She cleared her throat loudly when Bollinger didn't acknowledge her presence immediately. The entire space stank of cigarettes.

When Bollinger finally looked up, he did so only briefly before lowering his haggard brown eyes once again and releasing a disgusted sigh. Trails of smoke issued from his mouth and nostrils when he spoke.

'Who the fuck are you? Some kind of psychologist or something like that?'

'Something like that.' Was he really a cold-blooded killer – on his own or controlled by a criminal mastermind? He didn't look the part, but as she'd said to CK you couldn't always judge a killer by his appearance. She'd learned that practically at Crawford's knee. But she didn't want to think about Crawford now.

Bollinger looked up and gave her the once-over. 'Look, lady, like I've already told these guys a million goddamn times, I'm not copping to no murder rap. I didn't kill Liza or her stupid little friends, so if you think I'm just gonna sign my life away for the first nice piece of ass they send in here, you can just think again. Ain't gonna happen.'

Dana took a step forward and held her hands up with her palms facing him in a placating manner. 'Whoa. Slow down there a minute. Let's not get off on the wrong foot here.'

She removed the FBI badge from the back pocket of her blue jeans and slid it across the table to him. 'My name is Special Agent Dana Whitestone. You can call me Dana if you want. I'm going to call you Trent, so it's only fair I extend the same courtesy to you.' *Keep it nice and polite.*

Bollinger leaned his head back and blew a perfect smoke ring. 'Whatever. What the fuck do you want?'

Dana ignored his arrogance. 'I just want to talk to you, Trent. That's all. I'm not asking you to confess anything. Scout's honour.'

He picked up her badge and studied it for a moment.

When he looked up again and his stare locked onto hers for the first time, Dana's stomach dropped.

'You sure you're FBI, sweetheart?'

His voice jolted her back. 'What?'

He repeated himself slowly, enunciating each word as though he were talking to a four-year-old.

Dana shook her head to clear it, ashamed to feel the fear beating so hard in her chest. She took a deep breath and tried to calm her shaking hands. No use. For a moment there she'd thought she was looking into *those* eyes.

'Yeah, I'm sure I'm FBI,' she said. 'I've got a big old gun here and everything. What makes you ask?'

Bollinger's smile crinkled up the tiny crow's feet in the corners of his glittering brown eyes, revealing a set of remarkably sharp white teeth. 'Pretty little girl like you might get herself killed running around playing cops and robbers, that's all.'

Dana pulled back a chair at the table and took a seat opposite Bollinger, hoping that her shaking hands weren't too obvious to him. She opened his case file and quickly scanned the top page, trying to ignore the feeling of his eyes homing in on her breasts. 'Let's get down to business, Trent,' she said. 'Says here you work on a ranch out in Deer Trail, Wyoming. Ranching, huh? That sounds like a pretty dangerous job itself.'

Bollinger sat up straighter in his chair and squared his huge shoulders. 'Shit, bitch, it *can* be dangerous, but not if you know what you're doing and don't go off being stupid about the whole thing. I'm real strong, but I'm not your average meathead. I'm real smart, too.'

He paused and laughed at her. 'Smarter than you assholes, at least.'

Strong and smart enough to overpower and kill three innocent college girls because one of them committed the unforgivable sin of dumping you, asshole? Dana wondered. *Or are you just a mindless puppet getting your strings pulled by someone else, someone like Crawford Bell?*

But this was good. He was already starting to open up to her, and she wanted to keep him talking. If she continued playing to his pride and didn't push him too hard right away, there was always a chance for a break in this case that was only getting more bizarre with each passing minute.

'That right?' Dana asked. 'You a pretty smart guy, Trent?'

'Fuckin' A, sweetheart.'

Sensing her opening, Dana abruptly switched gears. 'Why were you hiding in the dumpster, Trent? Sounds like a pretty clear-cut case of going off and being stupid about the whole thing to me. Not a very smart thing to do at all.'

Amazingly, Bollinger's face actually *reddened* at the question. Odd for such a cocky guy.

'It was a stupid-ass mistake,' he said. 'I wanted to see Liza, *had* to see Liza, really, but them goddamn rent-a-cops told me they'd make sure I'd go to jail if they ever caught me on campus again.'

He held up his handcuffs and jangled them in her direction. 'Guess they wasn't lying, was they?'

Dana acknowledged the irony with a nod of her head. 'Guess not. Where you were before you got to Loyola, Trent? You haven't made any side trips to California or Kansas lately, have you? Ever been to Cleveland?'

He leaned back in his chair and pulled on his nose in disgust. 'California or Kansas? *Cleveland?* What in the fuck are you talking about, lady? Hardly fucking likely since I was driving two straight nights through from Wyoming.'

Dana slammed her hand down hard on the table. 'Quit lying to me!'

Bollinger stared at her in shock. 'Excuse me?'

Dana clenched her teeth and leaned forward across the table. 'I told you to quit lying to me, Bollinger. I know you're too stupid to pull off these murders yourself, but you'd better tell me who you're working for or I'm going to take my gun out right here and split your skull wide open.'

Dana studied the rage in his eyes. Definitely the kind of guy who could kill someone if he got angry enough. And definitely stupid enough to fall for the solo 'bad-cop' routine she was pulling on him right now.

'I'm done dicking around with you, Trent. Just tell me who you're working for and I'll make all the bad things go away for you. Deal?'

Bollinger looked like a helpless rabbit caught in a hunter's snare, the cockiness completely gone from his eyes now. 'Seriously, lady,' he said in a voice several octaves above the one he'd been using before. 'I ain't working for nobody and I don't know what the fuck you're talking about. Honestly. I ain't been nowhere else because I been driving here for two straight days. Soon as I stepped on campus I seen all these cruisers and ambulances and shit all over the place. I have warrants back home – stupid, petty shit, mostly. The dumpster was the first place I seen where I could hide. That's all there is to it. That's the whole story, I promise.'

Dana flipped through his file again and felt her heart sink in her chest. The preliminary coroner's report said the college girls had been killed sometime between eight-thirty and eleven p.m. Chicago PD received the call from a night janitor reporting the murders shortly past eleven, and they'd found Bollinger hiding in the trash receptacle fifteen minutes later. If he was telling the truth about arriving just in time to stumble upon the chaotic scene of the responding units – which was by no means a given, of course – he wouldn't have even been on campus at the latest possible time of the murders.

He wouldn't have had time to kill the girls. And it was unlikely he'd killed anyone else.

She tried to keep her voice even as she stared at him across the table. 'I'm going to ask you a very important question now, Trent. Answer it truthfully and you'll clear up a whole pile of shit for both of us.'

He looked at her with pleading eyes. 'Go on.'

'How many miles does your pickup truck get per gallon?'

'You talkin' city or highway?'

CHAPTER FIFTY-TWO

Dana flipped off her cellphone and returned to the observation room where CK had been watching but not listening to the interview.

She tossed Bollinger's file onto the table in disgust. 'You might as well let him go,' she said. 'He didn't do it.'

CK looked up at her. 'Don't you think it might be a good idea to at least wait for the clothes to come back from the lab before we let this guy go?'

Dana nodded and chewed on her lower lip. 'Yeah, I suppose you're going to have to, but the tests are going to come back negative.' She paused and tucked a loose strand of blonde hair behind her right ear. 'Well, they'll come back positive for blood all right, but he was telling the truth, CK. It's hogs' blood on those clothes.'

The Chicago cop wasn't buying it. Not for a dollar and not for any other price in the world, either. He held up one massive hand and quickly ticked off the evidence on his thick fingers.

'How in the hell could you possibly know that? Let's see here: we find the guy covered in blood and hiding in a dumpster on the night of the murders. One of the victims is his ex. He drove two thousand miles to see her and she just so happens to wind up dead on the very same night. I don't know. Sounds like a pretty strong case to me, even if it's only circumstantial so far.'

Dana didn't disagree. It *did* sound like a pretty strong case. As a matter of fact, the DA was probably drooling over the chance to prosecute such a headline-grabber at this very moment. But she had information that they didn't.

'I made some calls to American Express headquarters and charmed them into opening their files up to me,' she said. 'I just got off the phone with a regional account manager.'

'You're worried about your credit-card balance at a time like this?'

Dana ignored the remark and flipped open her notebook. 'According to American Express, Trent Matthew Bollinger was filling the tank of his pickup truck in Lorain, Illinois, at ten-thirty p.m. tonight. He filled up at a Marathon station and paid with his credit card. Lorain is an hour west of here, CK. If the coroner got it even *remotely* close in her preliminary report, Bollinger couldn't have committed the murders. He didn't have time.'

'You need a subpoena or else that evidence is going to be tainted, you know.'

'Yeah, I know. But I don't have time to wait for the courts right now. Not when the killer's still out there, planning his next move.'

The Chicago cop was silent long enough then for Dana to suddenly become aware of the large round clock loudly ticking on the far wall.

'Motherfucker,' he finally muttered, watching his carefully crafted circumstantial case drift away into the dark Chicago night. 'Wouldn't you know it.'

Dana reached out a hand and touched his shoulder. 'I'm sorry, CK. Bollinger's definitely a nasty piece of work, but he's not a killer. At least, not the one we're looking for, anyway.'

CK waved the apology away. 'Hell, don't apologise to me. You probably just saved me a shitload of work on the wrong guy. Still, I think I'm going to need three aspirin tonight to deal with this fucking headache. Probably four.'

He paused and looked up at her. 'Looks like you've got one yourself.'

Dana sighed. 'I'm fine. It's just that I haven't been getting very much sleep lately and I think it's finally starting to catch up with me.'

CK nodded and rose to his feet, tucking Bollinger's file under his left arm. 'Well, do you have a place where you can crash? We've got an extra bedroom over at our place if you want. Believe me, Becky would be thrilled with the company. Seriously, Dana, we'd love to have you.'

Dana smiled, genuinely touched by the offer. 'No, thanks. I appreciate it, but I've got a room over at the Hilton and that bed is calling out my name.'

'Want a lift over there, then? It'll save you the cab fare, at least.'

Dana nodded. 'That would be great. If I see one more taxicab or airplane today, I'm afraid I'll probably end up killing somebody myself.'

CK laughed and twirled his car keys around one thick finger. 'In that case we'd better get you the hell out of here before your face winds up all over the eleven o'clock news.'

On the tail end of his shift anyway, CK filed his report with the desk sergeant, updating the man on Bollinger's credit-card purchase in Lorain and instructing the sergeant to call him at home as soon as word on the bloody clothes came back from the lab.

They walked in silence through the long, winding halls in the sprawling metropolitan police station and to the parking lot where his personal vehicle was parked. Getting inside a white Ford minivan positively *littered* with toys, CK reached over and removed a stuffed Pikachu from the passenger seat before tossing it into the back where it made a high-pitched squeak on impact. He turned in his seat and smiled dolefully at her.

'Pokemon this, Pokemon that. Soon as something new comes out, guess who's got to buy it for them? Thank God for overtime, that's all I've got to say.'

When CK had dropped her off at the Hilton twenty minutes later, Dana checked in at the front desk and struggled to keep her eyes open while she rode the elevator up to the fourteenth floor. It was a losing battle the entire way. She should probably contact Brown and Templeton; fill them in. And Crawford – although what she'd say to him God alone knew. She was too tired to think straight.

Finally letting herself into her room, she immediately collapsed onto the queen-sized bed nearest the door. Before she could gather the strength to change into her nightclothes, brush her teeth and wash her face, her body suddenly shut down hard, crashing her mind into a violent, dream-filled sleep.

CHAPTER FIFTY-THREE

There truly was no place like home.

Nathan pulled the bright floral curtains across a window that looked out nowhere, finally putting the finishing touches on his ultimate masterpiece.

It was here that the ending of the story would be written, and not a moment too soon, either. He was itching to begin the most thrilling journey any human being could ever hope to experience, and he needed Dana Whitestone to send him on his way.

He sat down in a comfortable leather chair over in the corner and used a solid gold cutter to snip the tip off a fresh Cuban cigar he'd been saving for the occasion. He waved the flame of his silver Zippo over the tobacco and squinted his eyes against the fragrant smoke that curled up into his face.

Nathan leaned his head back and took a long, hard pull on the cigar before blowing five perfect smoke rings.

Everything was almost perfect now. Just a few more details to attend to – just a few more loose ends to tie up – and all the pieces would finally be in place.

The twenty acres of remote woodland in Cuyahoga County was the first major purchase he'd made with the money he'd received from the wrongful-death settlement.

He could have purchased anything in the world he'd pleased at that point, of course, but he'd chosen this. It was the only thing that would do, really.

Over the years, he'd carved the bunker out of the earth with his bare hands, a shovel and pickaxe his only tools. It was backbreaking work and extremely slow going for the most part – especially in the wintertime when the ground was frozen solid – but Nathan had kept at it like a madman, diligently working away until this day had finally arrived.

Nathan looked around the room he'd put together from memory. A frilly single bed was covered with a Big Bird comforter and flanked by two small night tables. Tiny dresses hung in an earthen closet carved into the north wall. A small generator under a large wooden wardrobe powered a Wonder Woman night light plugged into a socket next to a comfortable blue beanbag. On a tripod-mounted magnetic easel three feet away, his name had been spelled out in colourful plastic letters.

Sitting there on that comfortable leather chair underneath the frozen ground twenty miles west of Cleveland, Nathan Stiedowe took another hard pull on his cigar and let himself drift slowly back in time.

CHAPTER FIFTY-FOUR

It was truly amazing, the information one could obtain with simple press credentials. Doors locked down tighter than Fort Knox for the general public swung open as though with a magic key for journalists. Everyone was so goddamn *terrified* of bad press.

It had taken Nathan less than a month after the murders of his wife and daughter to track his mother down. It had been ridiculously easy with his adoption papers in hand. Twenty minutes spent digging through the neatly organised files produced the information he was after.

His *real* name.

The name of his *real* mother.

Standing alone between the stacks of metal filing cabinets as dusty sunlight filtered in through the grimy windows, Nathan held the thin sheet of paper in his trembling hands and stared down at his birth certificate for a very long time.

Fifty bucks to a private investigator had provided him with the rest. His mother's address in the West Park section of Cleveland was less than a ten-minute drive away from his apartment, and the short bio the PI had come up with let him know that Sara Whitestone was a lawyer now – and a highly respected one at that. Good for her. Married for six years to an electrical engineer – they'd had a baby daughter together a few years back. Apparently she'd decided to keep this one.

The thieving little bitch who had stolen his life.

He'd hoped initially to reconnect with his mother, maybe even start all over again. But as he watched them celebrate the Fourth of July from behind a stand of neatly landscaped bushes on the edge of their suburban property, Nathan knew he might as well have been dead to her.

Unfortunately for slutty little Sara, there would be no reunion today after all.

Only revenge.

CHAPTER FIFTY-FIVE

Before Nathan went after their happy little family – what should have been *his* happy little family – his hands were shaking so violently that he could barely hold the gun. These murders would change his life for ever.

It had been ridiculously easy to get in. He had walked right through the unlocked front door and quietly stationed himself in the little girl's closet while she and her parents celebrated the Fourth of July in their backyard; completely oblivious to just how little time they had left on this Earth.

Their mother loved his little sister very much, that much was clear. Nathan's own miserable childhood had been nothing like that. Instead of the hugs and kisses and laughter she was now experiencing, *he* had been treated only to beatings, torture and abuse. Watching their happy lives unfold in front of his eyes had ripped the scabs off his very painful wounds and now they'd have to pay for it.

Especially *her*.

It was simple, really. He'd release his own terrible pain simply by transferring it onto this happy little family, what should have been *his* happy little family. It was only fair, after all. He'd already suffered in a prison of pain by himself for far too long.

He is standing between the frilly dresses and tiny sweaters in the little girl's closet now, where he can hear her squeals of delight coming in through the open bedroom window. It is very dark inside the closet, but he can see clearly nonetheless.

Moving his hand around to the back of his jeans, he feels the .22-calibre pistol tucked snugly into the waistband. The cold steel is a comfort but will only be used as a last resort. The long butcher's knife he has taken from the wooden block on their kitchen counter is the *true* key that will unlock the horrible pain of his past.

When they finally come back into the house half an hour later, completely unaware of his presence, the sounds of the television coming from the living room cause all the little hairs on the back of his neck to stand up.

Don't they care about *him*? Don't they care about his *pain*?

No, he decides finally. *They don't.*

It is something they will soon regret.

CHAPTER FIFTY-SIX

In her dream, Dana is four years old again.

It is the Fourth of July and she and her parents have just come back into the house after having enjoyed a wonderfully exciting holiday picnic in their backyard.

Still all wound-up from being allowed to play Fairy Princess with a magic-wand sparkler, there is another hour of frantic play before the first signs of sleep begin to creep into the corners of her enormous blue eyes.

She finally curls up in her father's lap as he sits on the living-room couch watching the evening news on their cabinet-style television. As usual, her mother is at the kitchen table reviewing a large pile of legal briefs that she has brought home from work, periodically jotting down notes on the yellow legal pad at her side.

As Dan Rather signs off for the night, Dana stretches her arms over her head and lets out a loud yawn.

'Getting sleepy, honey bear?' James Whitestone asked, lightly scratching his daughter's back over her Barbie T-shirt.

Dana nodded and yawned again. 'Mmhmm. I think I'm ready for bed now, Daddy.'

Hearing this declaration, Sara stood up, crossed into the living room and plucked Dana from her father's lap. 'Well then, let's go brush your teeth and get you ready for bed, sleepyhead. Then I'll tuck you in and read you a bedtime story. How does that sound?'

'Sounds good, 'cept why do I gotta brush my teeth again? I brushed them this morning, remember? They're still pretty clean.'

Sara laughed and rapidly kissed the soft hollow of her daughter's neck. 'You have to brush them again, silly, so that the Cavity Creeps don't invade Toothopolis while you're sleeping tonight.'

Dana squirmed in her mother's arms. 'OK, OK, already! Just stop that – you're tickling me, Mommy!'

When they'd finished up in the bathroom, they got Dana dressed in her pyjamas and into bed. Sara pulled back the Big Bird covers and gently tucked them in around her daughter's small body. 'What shall we read tonight, princess?' she asked.

Dana screwed up her face in concentration. Important decision here. 'Hmm. How about we just do the story of Dana and the Three Friends again instead of reading from a book?'

Sara smiled. It was their own personal version of *Goldilocks and the Three Bears*. Over time and with Dana's considered input, the story changed slightly with each telling.

Switching off the overhead light left only the soft yellow glow of Dana's bedside lamp. Sara cleared her throat dramatically and began this night's version of the tale.

'Once upon a time there lived a delightful group of three friends, and their names were Mrs Lula, Mr Sunday and their precious baby – the wonderfully cute and adorable little Pano. They all lived together in a cosy little cottage in the forest and they enjoyed their peaceful lives there very much.'

'Nope,' Dana corrected. 'That's not right. They live in a

293

gingerbread house in the forest now, Mommy. They moved last week.'

Sara laughed and tickled her daughter's belly. 'Okay, smarty-pants, they moved last week. I think I can live with that. Anyway, the Three Friends all lived together in a cosy gingerbread house in the forest and they enjoyed their peaceful lives there very much.'

The story progressed from there with the Three Friends deciding to take a walk in the forest to give their chocolate-cake breakfasts time to cool down. When they'd finally made it back home, Dana suggested they get James to do the voices.

'He does them best,' she said.

James was summoned and took a seat next to his wife on the bed. Sara continued the story, leading him into his lines.

'The Three Friends had just returned home,' she prompted. 'Pano could hardly wait to eat!'

'What's this?' James asked in his Mr Sunday voice. 'Somebody has been nibbling on my cake!' Switching to his feminine Mrs Lula voice, he said, 'And somebody has been nibbling on my cake, too!' Finally, Pano's high-pitched and deeply wounded voice. 'And somebody's been nibbling on my cake too, and they've eaten it all up!'

'Uh-oh,' the real Dana cut in. 'Somebody's in a shitload of trouble.'

Sara slumped her shoulders, much too tired to correct her daughter's language again. She glanced over at her husband and gave him a meaningful look before continuing. 'Looking around the room, Mr Sunday noticed the chairs,' she said.

'Somebody has been sitting in my chair,' James growled as Mr Sunday. 'And somebody has been sitting in my chair as well!' he offered in his Mrs Lula voice.

'But it was Pano who was the most upset, the tears coming from his eyes.'

'Somebody has been sitting in my chair, too, and they broke it all to pieces!' James thundered. 'This is complete and total bullshit!'

'*James Allen Whitestone!*' Sara cried out. 'It's no wonder she talks like a trucker!'

James tried to choke out an apology but couldn't do it through the waves of laughter racking his body. After several long moments he finally took a deep breath and wiped at his misty eyes. 'Let me try that again,' he said. 'Somebody has been sitting in my chair and they broke it all to pieces.'

Sara paused and looked at him expectantly. She knew he wouldn't be able to resist.

'They broke my favourite chair, the inconsiderate little bastards,' James muttered under his breath.

Dana giggled happily, but Sara just ignored him. 'Don't listen to him, Dana. Don't listen to a single thing he says. I don't know why they ever let him out of the Bad Boys' Home in the first place. I'm calling them first thing in the morning so they can come pick him up.'

She stared at her husband for several measured beats before turning back to her daughter. 'Now, where was I before we were so rudely interrupted?'

'The Three Friends had just found out their chairs were all busted up,' Dana answered helpfully.

'Oh, yes. That's right. Thank you, honey. The Three Friends did not know what they would find next, so they dashed upstairs lickety-split. Mr Sunday was the first to look into the bedroom.'

Sara paused and looked over at her husband, who obediently took his place back in the story.

'Somebody has been sleeping in my bed!' James bellowed as Mr Sunday. Switching to his Mrs Lula voice, he added, 'And somebody has been sleeping in my bed, too!'

'Pano rubbed his eyes in disbelief.'

'And somebody has been sleeping in my bed, and there she is now!' James cried out.

Dana's big blue eyes went saucer-wide as she peeked out from beneath the covers.

'Suddenly,' Sara said, her voice taking on a sense of urgency now, 'Dana opened her eyes and shrieked at the sight of the Three Friends glaring down at her. But the friends never had a chance to do anything to her, for Dana jumped out of bed, ran down the stairs and was out of the house in the blink of an eye.

'Needless to say, the Three Friends never saw Dana near their cosy little gingerbread house in the forest ever again. And as for little Dana, well, let's just say that she became a lot more careful in her future adventures.

'The End,' Sara pronounced.

'Mommy?' Dana asked quietly, slowly rubbing at her eyes with a tiny balled-up fist.

'Yes, honey?'

'Maybe tomorrow the Three Friends can call Dana up on the phone and ask her to come over to watch TV with them. That way they could be the Four Friends from now on.'

She paused and looked up at her mother. The innocence in her big blue eyes nearly broke Sara Whitestone's heart. 'Don't worry, Mommy. We'll only watch PBS, I promise.'

Sara smiled. 'I think that would be just fine, but it's time for bed now, my little princess.'

She leaned forward and kissed her daughter softly on the

forehead. 'Sweet dreams, my darling little baby girl. I love you with all my heart.'

Somehow Dana managed to mumble her reply just a moment before promptly falling asleep.

'I love you too, Mommy.'

CHAPTER FIFTY-SEVEN

He'd planned on killing them as soon as they'd all entered the little girl's bedroom. But he stopped suddenly when the ridiculous bedtime story began. *Let the mice have their fun.*

He almost laughed out loud at the thought.

Three blind mice.

When their moronic tale finally concluded, his mother thoughtfully closed the door behind them, leaving him alone with his sister for the first time in their lives.

Nathan paused a moment to consider his situation. He wasn't a bona fide killer yet – not as an adult, at least – but he knew he'd be just that before the night was over.

How do you like them apples, Dad? And you always said I'd never amount to anything.

But everything had to be perfect. Perfect and *clean*.

Quietly opening the closet door, he is very careful not to make even the slightest sound as he makes his way to her bedside. The soft glow of the Wonder Woman night light illuminates her sleeping face in the darkness. She really is lovely. So soft. So pretty. So innocent.

All in all, a delicious little morsel of a mouse.

Lifting the butcher's knife over his head, he is ready to plunge it deep into her tender throat when a troubling thought suddenly occurs to him. What if he really did it – really *killed* the little girl – and the pain was still there?

He amends his plans quickly and decides to kill his mother and her husband first. If that doesn't make him feel any better he can always return for his sister later on.

Reaching down, he softly strokes her silky blonde hair as she sleeps. 'I'll be back for you in just a minute, sis. That much you can count on.'

The little girl only mumbles dreamily in response.

Out in the hallway he is surprised to hear the soft sounds of lovemaking coming from the master bedroom. The plan comes to him in an instant.

He is little more than a dark shadow as he moves past their open bedroom door and slips into the bathroom. Stepping inside the tub, he pulls the shower curtain closed to hide his presence. From his concealed post he hears them climax simultaneously, their soft moans an obvious attempt to avoid disturbing the sleeping child and quite a difference to the sounds of whale-mounting *he*'d been subjected to as a kid.

Moments later – as he'd known would happen – someone enters the bathroom. The overhead light goes on and he hears the hollow sound of plastic connecting with porcelain as the toilet seat goes up.

It is the husband, James.

In a trance, he thumbs off the safety on his gun and noses the shower curtain aside. He assumes a shooter's stance and his finger twitches once, setting off a tremendous bang. Chunks of brain matter and skull slide down the wall above the toilet in a fascinating rainbow of grey and white and red.

James Whitestone is dead before he hits the floor.

A concerned voice sounds outside the door a moment later. 'James, honey? Are you okay? What was that noise? Did you fall?'

It is his mother, sexy little Sara.

'I'm fine,' he coughs. 'I'll be out in just a minute.'

Unbelievably, the dumb bitch buys it. 'Jesus Christ. You scared the shit out of me, babe. I thought you broke your neck in there or something. Hurry up and come back to bed already.'

He smiles as he listens to the sound of her footsteps receding down the hall. Stepping over the dead body of her husband, he re-enters the dark hallway.

The master bedroom is no more than fifteen feet away. He pauses a moment to let his eyes adjust to the darkness, then swiftly covers the distance.

His mother is in bed lying on her side, wearing only a flimsy off-white negligee. Her pretty head is propped up coquettishly on one hand.

'You just gonna stay out there all night, or are you gonna come keep me company in this big old bed, lover boy?'

Smiling, he crosses the threshold. She bolts upright in horror when she realises he is not her husband. A tiny squeak escapes her lips, but the mouse is too stunned to scream immediately.

'Good evening, Sara,' he says calmly. 'It's a pleasure to meet you again at last.'

When she finally screams, it is a loud, ear-splitting wail that startles him. This is not good, not part of the script. If she screams, someone will hear her and come to try to stop him. They will try to cage the eagle and he simply cannot have that.

Racing across the room, he clamps a large hand over her mouth. 'Shut the fuck up, bitch,' he hisses, spraying hot saliva all over his mother's smooth cheek. 'One more sound and I'll chop your precious goddamn daughter up into so many pieces they won't be able to put her back together again for the funeral.'

His mother squirms wildly in his strong grasp, an impotent little field mouse struggling to escape the eagle's powerful talons. He smiles and leans down into her face. From this distance, he can actually *smell* her fear – a scent not unlike urine mixed with battery acid. 'Tell me something,' he says. 'Do you even know who I *am*?'

And in that precise moment Sara Whitestone *does* know.

'Jeremiah,' she whispers.

He almost breaks a finger slapping her across the face. 'That's not my name any more, slut. You made damn sure of that a long time ago, and now I'm going to kill you for it. But tell me something first, Mom. How could you do it, anyway?

'How could you give your own fucking *baby* away?'

CHAPTER FIFTY-EIGHT

As a sophomore at Trinity Catholic Academy in Eastlake, Ohio, during the 1950s, Sara Beth Quigley drew a lot of attention.

For one, she was generally considered the smartest person in the entire school. Not just the smartest *girl*, mind you, but the smartest *person* – teachers included.

She'd already aced the PSATs twice, won a national science fair as a freshman for her study of mutating genes in Lake Erie carp, and was a confident and eloquent public speaker at an age when the majority of her female contemporaries suffered from such low self-esteem that a single blemish might very well cause them to call in sick for the day.

Receiving straight As every quarter, there were even rumours that the teachers just pencilled them in for her on the first day of class. These rumours were patently untrue, of course. Sara Quigley had *earned* every mark she'd ever received and, what was more, was the furthest thing from a grade-grubber on the planet.

Like just about everybody else who'd ever come into contact with her, the nuns at the school absolutely *adored* Sara, and with very good reason. She was an extremely sweet and pious young girl, the kind who volunteered to clean the church every Saturday afternoon. Many of the Sisters were even quietly encouraging her to look into joining the convent after graduation and Sara was actually giving it serious consideration. After all, a life completely devoted to God was certainly a life well worth living. Besides, there was a long and respected tradition of religious service in her family and she wouldn't have minded being a part of that one little bit.

But Sara Quigley wasn't all just brains and good deeds. Far from it. She was also a remarkably beautiful girl. Extremely petite, with long shiny blonde hair and enormous twinkling blue eyes, her early-developing body and peaches-and-cream complexion drove her classmates completely crazy – for very different reasons, of course.

The girls all ate their hearts out with jealousy every time she passed them in the hall, and the boys did what boys do in the privacy of their own homes after school each day in an effort to deal with the overwhelming lust that she inspired in them.

Behind her back, the girls would sometimes call her a *slut*, and the boys would laughingly refer to her as a *dick-tease*, but everybody knew that neither label was true in the least. As a matter of fact, Sara had been kissed just once in her entire life, and it hadn't been an especially pleasant experience at that.

Bobby Andrews, a hulking junior and the swaggering bully who was the captain of the varsity football team, had forced his slimy tongue down her throat at a school dance a few weeks previously. While it was happening, Sara was terrified she would throw up directly into his liquor-coated mouth before she finally managed to push his huge body off her.

To say the least, Bobby Andrews had not been pleased with her reaction.

*

It was a sunny spring day a few weeks before the prom as Sara strolled down the wide, locker-lined hallways with her best friend, Nicole Applebaum. Both girls wore long skirts, virginal white blouses and saddle shoes with bobby socks. They moved down the hall with their school books clasped against their chests.

'So who are you going with, anyway?' Nicole asked. She was a very pretty girl with glittering hazel eyes and short dark hair cut into a bob. 'I hear Bobby Andrews is going around telling people you're going with him. Please tell me that's not true.'

Sara looked sideways at her best friend and crinkled up her nose. 'Please, Nikki, give me a little bit of credit over here. I wouldn't go to the prom with that boy if he were the last available option left on Earth.'

She leaned over and said in a conspiratorial whisper, 'Actually, I was kind of hoping *Ben* would ask me.'

Nicole rolled her eyes. 'Well, he wouldn't be *my* first choice, but speak of the devil,' she said as the topic of their conversation rounded the corner by the gym and headed their way. 'I'm out of here, honey. Write me a note and tell me how it went, you bad little girl, you!'

Nicole Applebaum ducked into her biology class and Sara felt her heart skip a beat in her chest. Benjamin Martin was a tall, slender, almost *painfully* shy boy who she'd been surprised to find herself falling for when they'd been paired up together in a creative-writing class. His sensitive language touched her heart in a way she'd never known before, and she knew a lot of people were missing out on his gentle soul by misreading the cover of the book. He certainly didn't talk very much but, if the way he blushed whenever she spoke to him was any indication, she knew he probably felt the same way about her.

He put his head down and quickly began passing her in the hall before she called out cheerily to him. 'Hey, Ben! How are you doing today?'

The auburn-haired boy stopped dead in his tracks, unable to bring himself to look her in the eye. When he finally managed to speak, his voice was little more than the soft whisper of satin against skin. 'Hey there, Sara.'

His shyness was so damn cute that Sara surprised herself by what she blurted out next.

What the hell. You only live once.

'Ah, Ben? I know it's pretty short notice, but I was kind of wondering if you'd like to go to the prom with me.'

Though it was unheard of for a girl to ask a boy out in those days – pretty much an unwritten rule, as it were – Sara didn't especially care. Besides, it was a *stupid* rule, anyway.

To her complete horror, Ben Martin's face first blanched, then turned so red she was afraid that he would *pass out*. His lips were moving but no sounds were coming out. His mouth had morphed into a silent, trembling O.

Sara reached out a hand and touched his arm lightly. 'Well, what do you say, silly? Come on, it'll be a blast.'

Ben shuffled his brown-loafered feet and stared down hard at the floor as though he might somehow find the answer to her question written there. 'I'd love to,' he said finally. 'To tell you the truth, I've been trying to get up the courage to ask you the same thing for the past week.'

Sara's heart skipped another beat in her chest. 'Great! It's all taken care of, then. I'll tell you what. I have to clean the church tomorrow afternoon, but why don't you stop by around two so that we can devise our plan of attack?'

As fate would have it, Bobby Andrews happened to be

walking by at that precise moment. Shouldering Ben hard against the lockers, he wheeled around to glare at the smaller boy. 'Out of my way, asshole!' he growled.

'Hey! Watch where you're going, you big jerk!' Sara called after him as he strolled away arrogantly. 'Why don't you pick on someone your own size for once in your life?'

She turned back to Ben and frowned. 'Are you OK?'

Benjamin Martin's face reddened again, but it wasn't from embarrassment this time. To Sara's great delight, she saw something of a *backbone* hiding underneath all that sensitivity. 'Somebody ought to teach that guy a lesson one of these days,' he muttered.

Sara waved a hand in the air. 'Ah, don't worry about him. He's just a big jerk who's so full of himself it isn't even funny. Anyway, forget about him. So what do you say? You, me, two o'clock at the church tomorrow afternoon?'

Looking her squarely in the eye for the first time in his life, Benjamin Martin smiled. He had *beautiful* teeth.

'I'll be there, Sara.'

CHAPTER FIFTY-NINE

Sara was on her hands and knees the next afternoon, scrubbing the marble floor in front of the altar at St Anthony's Catholic Church. She was just reaching into a steaming bucket of soapy water when she heard the back doors of the church suddenly bang open.

She smiled to herself. Ben hadn't chickened out.

Hearing his shy footsteps approaching cautiously from behind, by the time he was directly behind her she'd already mentally picked out her prom dress and corsage, his tuxedo, her engagement and wedding rings, her wedding dress and the names of their first three children. Two boys and one girl – Penelope Abigail for the girl.

In the next instant his powerful hand was on the back of her neck, squeezing painfully as he lifted her off her feet and slammed her hard across the altar. Rough hands ripped her shorts and lacy white panties down around her ankles. Trembling in shock and terror, Sara stared up into the eyes of Jesus Christ hanging on the cross.

When her attacker pierced her hymen with an audible pop a moment later it sent bright red blood sliding down her pale white thighs.

'You think you can pass me up?' Bobby Andrews hissed into her ear. 'For that fuckin' faggot Ben Martin?'

He pulled her hair back and drove himself into her even harder. 'I don't fuckin' think so, you goddamn whore.'

When he came inside her a moment later it was all hot and wet and sticky. Sara retched painfully and threw up all over the altar, but Bobby Andrews just laughed at her.

'Tell anybody about this and you're one dead bitch,' he grunted as he carelessly buckled his jeans back up. 'You hear me, you little slut? *Dead.*'

When he left by a side door twenty seconds later, Sara sat down on the steps of the altar and cried uncontrollably for the next hour. Finally leaving the church on badly shaking legs – the bucket of soapy water now spilled all over the floor – she asked God what she could possibly have done to deserve such a horrible fate.

Outside, in the harsh glare of the springtime sun, Benjamin Martin was lying in the bushes alongside the building. He was badly beaten and bloody, and the look of shame in his eyes was almost more than Sara could bear.

'Ben . . .' she began. But he was up and bolting down the street before she could finish.

Sara could barely walk home under her own power. It felt as though a white-hot lance had been thrust up hard between her soft thighs, and the blood was beginning to seep into her underwear now, staining the crotch of her virginal white shorts. Worse, people on the street were actually starting to *notice*.

She told no one what had happened, of course. You simply didn't do such a thing in those days. Besides, nobody would have believed her, anyway.

Sara Beth Quigley didn't go to the prom that year – she would never return to Trinity Catholic Academy again, as a matter of fact. Over the summer, her parents shipped her off to stay with 'an aunt' in Colorado until she could deliver the illegitimate baby boy at an orphanage run by Catholic missionaries.

On the day her son entered the world, following a nightmarish twelve-hour delivery, they let her hold him for only a moment before gently prising him from her arms.

'It's better this way,' one of the nuns told her, brushing a lock of sweaty blonde hair out of Sara's blurry eyes. 'He'll have a better life this way.'

The baby wailed for her as they left the room, and Sara felt her heart break into a million tiny pieces as she watched her son being taken away from her for ever.

'I love you, Jeremiah,' she whispered.

The nun turned around in the doorway and smiled at her. 'I'm sure he loves you too, honey. But this is God's will.'

CHAPTER SIXTY

'Fucking lying bitch!'

Nathan crushed his mother's shoulders beneath his knees with all his weight and stared hard into her eyes.

He took a deep breath and forced himself to calm down. 'That's a real touching story, Mom. Really it is. Still, I'm afraid it's not quite good enough. Time to pay the piper, cunt. But first I think I'll give you a little taste of what it was like for *me* growing up. How does that sound?'

Roughly, he flipped Sara onto her stomach and yanked her satin panties down around her knees. He slapped her hard on her bare buttocks, a stinging blow that turned her backside red.

'"For this you know – no fornicator, unclean person nor covetous man who is an idolater has any inheritance in the kingdom of Christ and God!" Ephesians, chapter 5, verse 5.'

He slapped her again, harder this time.

'"Let the people turn from their wicked deeds! Let them banish from their minds the very thought of doing wrong! Let them turn to the Lord that He may have mercy on them! Yes, turn to our God, for He will abundantly pardon!" Book of Isaiah, chapter 55, verse 7.'

Nathan flipped Sara back over and pinned her shoulders beneath his knees again. He ran the knife lightly over her throat, leaving a superficial but very painful cut in its wake. He moaned softly. Even in the darkness, he could just make out the beautiful contrast between the bright red blood and the pale white skin of her throat.

Just then, her panicked blue eyes suddenly widened in horror at the sight of something over his left shoulder. Turning around, Nathan followed his mother's gaze to the doorway and saw his little sister standing there in her pyjamas. She was holding a teddy bear in one tiny hand and shifting from one foot to the other as though she had to go to the bathroom.

'Mommy, what's happening?' the third mouse asked, her small voice quiet and shy. 'You're scaring me. Who's that man on top of you? Where's my daddy?'

When their gazes locked for the first time in their lives, Nathan's little sister froze in his stare. He never took his eyes off her as he whipped the sharp blade across Sara Whitestone's slender neck again, this time cutting all the way to the bone.

Jolted out of her stupor, the little girl screamed so loudly that it nearly drowned out the watery gurgling sounds their mother was making as she choked to death on her own blood.

Nathan sprang off the bed and went after her. Her enormous blue eyes widened in terror as he yanked the sharp knife over his head. Wet droplets of their mother's blood slid down the blade and plopped onto her tiny up-turned face.

That was when the front door slammed open with a violent bang.

'Sara? James? What the hell's going on in here? It's Ralph Wilson from next door. Nancy and I heard screaming and called the police. Is everything all right?'

Fear and anger seizing his heart, Nathan bolted past the now-catatonic little girl. From the corner of his eye, he saw a dark circle of urine slowly spread across the front of her pyjama bottoms.

His heart pounded madly in his throat as he dashed into her bedroom and pulled himself up through the open window. Tears of absolute *rage* spilled from his dark brown eyes as he darted quickly across the yard and disappeared into the darkness. He'd been scared, and he'd fucked up.

He had left his little sister alive.

CHAPTER SIXTY-ONE

Liquorice. She'd smelled liquorice on his breath.

The man with the sharp knife was standing over her bed again when the jarring ring of the hotel telephone jolted Dana awake less than an hour later.

She fumbled for it in the darkness, nearly dropping the receiver in the process.

'Hello?' she mumbled groggily.

The voice on the other end of the line was intense and unmistakable. 'Dana, it's Crawford. I need you to meet me in Cleveland right away. Jeremy Brown's already here. There's a charter waiting for you at O'Hare. You need to be on it.'

Dana shook the sleep violently from her brain. Crawford. What was he calling her for? 'What's going on, Crawford?'

She heard him blow out a slow breath. 'The killer has made contact, Dana. He's made contact and he's killed again.'

CHAPTER SIXTY-TWO

Nathan clicked on www.ariseandshine.org and frowned.

When he'd interviewed David Berkowitz – the notorious Son of Sam – in the early 1980s while doing research for one of his books, the man had still been an unrepentant whack-job mumbling about 'Father Sam', a neighbour whose barking dog Berkowitz claimed had demanded that he should kill young women all around New York City. Now he was just another fucking idiot who'd found Jesus Christ.

The website of the notorious serial killer featured a photograph on the home page that showed a smiling face topped off by neatly trimmed fringes of salt-and-pepper hair. Soft-looking hands were clasped in front of his body in a non-threatening manner. Worst of all, he was now calling himself 'The Son of Hope'.

Nathan rolled his eyes and navigated the cursor over a link titled 'David's Apology':

> *As I have communicated many times throughout the years, I am deeply sorry for the pain, suffering and sorrow I have brought upon the victims of my crimes. I grieve for those who are wounded, and for the family members of those who lost a loved one because of my selfish actions. I regret what I've done and I'm haunted by it.*

Not a day goes by when I do not think about the suffering I have brought to so many. Likewise I cannot even comprehend all the grief and pain that they live with now. And these individuals have every right to be angry with me, too.

Nevertheless, I apologise for the crimes I committed. My continual prayer is that, as much as possible, these hurting individuals can go on with their lives.

In addition, I am not writing this apology for pity or sympathy. I simply believe that such an apology is the right thing to do. And, by the grace of God, I hope to do my very best to make amends whenever and wherever possible, both to society and to my victims. – David Berkowitz, 2007

Nathan yawned and closed the lid of his MacBook Pro. False repentance was so goddamn *boring*. Besides, he preferred to remember the Son of Sam when he'd still been a *real* man. And, thanks to him, David Berkowitz would be just that again very soon.

At least for a little while.

CHAPTER SIXTY-THREE

Dana touched down at Hopkins two hours later and retrieved the Protégé from long-term parking before slamming down hard on the accelerator and racing down Interstate 90 to the east side of Cleveland. Her nerves were hanging by their final thread. Apart from everything else going on, she was about to come face to face with the man that she seriously suspected might be their killer, a sadistic, corrupt, cold-blooded murderer. A man she had cared about – hell, still did. Did he have a brain tumour or was that a lie too? But would he really use her like that, and be right there at the latest crime scene? Whatever happened she had to remain calm. She couldn't show her hand, not yet. And part of her still didn't want to believe it might be true, though it looked more and more likely to be so. She didn't even want to think about her parents and that he might have killed them, then guided her in her career. Was it to lead her to this point? It couldn't be. And he had kind eyes, didn't he, not the eyes of a killer?

The press descended on Dana's car as soon as she pulled into an empty space outside the Section-8 apartment complex. She pushed her car door open hard against the knees of a cameraman and stepped out. Bright television lights and the flashes of a dozen rapidly shuttering cameras blinded her immediately. The questions rained down on her from all directions.

'Special Agent Whitestone, how old were the victims this time?'

'What is the FBI doing to stop the Cleveland Slasher?'

'Ma'am, when is a full-fledged task force going to be assigned to this case?'

Dana put her head down and fought her way through the crowd to the police tape. Several uniformed cops stepped forward to hold the press back.

Inside the building, she took the elevator up to the seventh floor. Three doors down from the Jacinda Holloway murder scene, Crawford Bell and Jeremy Brown were directing dozens of crime-scene technicians as they scoured an apartment that still smelled faintly of cinnamon rolls. Dread coursed through Dana's entire system. She wasn't sure she could do this.

'Dana,' Crawford said. 'They're in the back bedroom.'

Dana nodded a hello to Brown – at least she was pleased to see *him* there – then turned back to Crawford, unable to control the queasiness in her stomach at the sight of him. Still, suspicions were one thing and cold hard facts were something different altogether. Besides, if Crawford *was* involved in these murders, how could she possibly broach with him the subject that the re-creations were following his introductory class killer for killer? And who *else* could she broach the subject with? CK knew what she was thinking, but he was still back in Chicago working the Richard Speck deaths, so he couldn't help her. She might be able to discuss her suspicions with Jeremy Brown but, despite how closely they'd worked together out in Los Angeles and Wichita, she still didn't know him all that well. For now she'd just have to keep playing things cool. She had no choice. Still, she couldn't help but wonder if the cancer in Crawford's brain had turned him into a killer.

'What's going on?' she asked.

'Go have a look for yourself,' Crawford said.

Dana walked across the living room and down a short hallway. Sergeant Gary Templeton was posted outside an open bedroom door. He lowered his tear-filled eyes when he saw her. 'We missed him again,' he said. 'He came right back to the same fucking apartment complex and we missed him again.'

Dana stepped past him into the bedroom. The young woman she'd interviewed just days earlier was naked and lying on the bed, her legs parted and her throat slashed. She'd probably been raped. In her arms she cradled her baby, the little girl's sweet blue face snugly cradled up against her mother's soft breast.

Dana threw up all over the carpet.

'Whoa!' Templeton said, taking her by the elbow and leading her roughly out of the bedroom. 'You'll compromise the crime scene.'

Dana tore her elbow from his grasp and wheeled around to glare at him. 'There's nothing here!' she screamed. 'There's never anything at any of the goddamn scenes!'

Brown stepped quickly between them. He took Dana back out into the hallway of the apartment complex while Crawford talked to Templeton.

A moment later her mentor and former partner joined them out in the hall.

'Go home and get some sleep, Dana,' he said. 'You're not doing anybody any good in this state. Pull yourself together.'

She stared up at him in disbelief. Bile crept up her throat. 'But, Crawford . . .'

He shook his head and cut her off before she could continue. '*Now*, Dana. That's a goddamn order. Get out of here.'

CHAPTER SIXTY-FOUR

By the time Dana finally made it back to her apartment complex in Lakewood it was nearly four a.m. She couldn't think straight. All she wanted to do was get inside. She'd left Crawford there – but could she really have accused him outright? Even Jeremy would have laughed in her face. She was a fool, she'd blown it, she'd lost control, nearly contaminated a crime scene.

She pulled into the parking lot and her heart jumped into her throat when she saw the press that had set up camp there. A dozen of them immediately crowded around her driver's side door as she eased the car into an empty space.

'Special Agent Whitestone, are the copycat murders related to the slayings of the little girls?' a tall man in the middle of the pack shouted. 'When are you going to catch this guy? Our viewers want answers!'

Dana stepped out of the car and blinked her eyes against the bright television lights. She put her head down and fought her way to the front doors, bumping her shoulders against the mass of humanity on both sides while yet more questions rained down on her.

Thirty seconds later the aggressive audience was still shouting questions at her as she slipped her key-card through the magnetic reader on the front doors and stepped inside. Outside, the reporters turned immediately to face their respective cameras in order to toss the insatiable beast known as 24/7 journalism another hunk of bloody red meat.

Dana closed her eyes while she rode the elevator up to the fourth floor. She stepped out of the elevator and glanced down the hall to make sure that no particularly enterprising members of the press had made it inside. So far, so good.

Quietly, she let herself into Eric's place and retrieved Oreo from his living-room couch. The back-and-forth with the cat would just happen all over again in the morning, but she really needed Oreo as a security blanket tonight.

Returning to her own apartment with Oreo in tow, she stepped inside her bedroom and quickly changed into her pyjamas before slipping between the covers and pulling the comforter all the way up over her head.

For a brief moment she was hazily aware of being afraid that she wouldn't be able to fall asleep. The next thing she knew, the alarm clock was wailing loudly in her ear and Oreo was curled up around her neck like a furry, purring scarf.

Dana squinted her eyes over at the small digital alarm clock on her bedside table. Almost eight a.m.

She groaned and hit the snooze button but came awake again with a start a moment later when the events of the previous night came flooding back into her mind. She dragged herself out of bed with another groan and walked over to the bedroom window, looking down into the parking lot. She breathed a sigh of relief. *No press out there yet, thank God.*

She made her way into the kitchen with Oreo trailing at her heels and poured some dry cat food into his bowl before pouring a large glass of vodka for herself and sitting down at the kitchen table. She guzzled the clear liquid down in four quick swallows while Oreo crunched loudly on his food five feet away.

Ten minutes later the phone jangled on the wall.

She picked it up. 'Hello?'

'Dana, it's Jeremy Brown. Get any sleep?'

'Not nearly enough.'

'Well, I'm afraid it's going to have to do for now. I'm over at your office now. Can you meet me here in, say, an hour?'

'Of course. What's up?'

Brown let out a slow breath. 'I've got something I need to talk to you about. It's Crawford Bell.'

CHAPTER SIXTY-FIVE

Nathan felt very calm as he polished the .44-calibre hand-gun in the weak morning light struggling through the grimy windows of his rented apartment. He knew that he had nothing to fear. Smarter and better prepared than those who would try to stop him, he was steadily evolving into the mighty eagle. Soon he would be perfect.

Perfect and worthy of redemption.

Having drawn his sister back home, tonight he would shoot two deliciously young girls who had long dark hair. Once that was done, David Berkowitz's crimes would finally be updated to his satisfaction.

Nathan smiled to himself. As always, he was in complete control of everything. The authorities were simply his marionettes – his *dummies* – and he was the puppet-master pulling their strings.

He'd altered his profile on the Lonely Hearts Club website to attract this latest group, of course – switching his photo to that of a good-looking kid who could have passed for an Abercrombie & Fitch model – and he'd peppered his profile with enough of the idiotic jargon they all used these days to ensure that the young girls had responded in waves from there.

LOL. BRB. C U L8R. It was enough to make him want to scream.

Shooting the girls in the head would not be as satisfying as using the knife, but Nathan knew he had to follow the path set by the one who'd come before him, so he would resist the urge to slice them up into human fillets with his sharp blade.

He'd stayed up all night designing his run-down apartment to the exact specifications obtained from an Internet website. Every detail was precise; everything was in place. There was no yapping dog next door, no conveniently named neighbour, but he would use his imagination to fill in the gaps. His imagination was very good.

A parking ticket would not stop him this time.

CHAPTER SIXTY-SIX

Dana got into the Protégé an hour later and quickly drove over to the FBI field office located on Lakeside Avenue in downtown Cleveland.

She closed her eyes and leaned her forehead against the cold surface of the elevator wall next to the bank of buttons while riding up to the tenth floor. When the doors opened she stepped out and made her way down the hall on rubbery legs.

Jeremy Brown was seated behind the cluttered desk in her office.

'Dana,' he said, rising to his feet. 'Come on over here. I've got something you need to see.'

Dana frowned at him and took the sheet of paper he was holding out. 'What is this?' she asked.

'Just read it.'

Dana settled down into a leather chair beneath the fronds of an artificial palm tree. Her breath caught in her throat at the sight of the precise handwriting. Same handwriting as the Disneyland note.

Dear Special Agent Whitestone,

I am deeply hurt by your calling me a wemon hater. I am not. But I am a monster. I am the 'Son of Sam'. I am a little 'brat'.

When Father Sam gets drunk he gets mean. He beats his family. Sometimes he ties me up in the back of the house. Other times he locks me in the garage. Sam loves to drink blood.

'Go out and kill,' commands Father Sam.

Behind our house some rest. Mostly young – raped and slaughtered – their blood drained – just bones now.

Papa Sam keeps me locked in the attic too. I can't get out but I look out the attic window and watch the world go by.

I feel like an outsider. I am on a different wave length then everybody else – programmed too kill.

However, to stop me you must kill me. Attention all police: Shoot me first – shoot to kill or else. Keep out of my way or you will die!

Papa Sam is old now. He needs some blood to preserve his youth. He has had too many heart attacks. Too many heart attacks. 'Ugh, me hoot, it urts sonny boy.'

I miss my pretty princess most of all. She's resting in our ladies house but I'll see her soon.

I am the 'Monster' – 'Beelzebub' – the 'Chubby Behemouth'.

I love to hunt. Prowling the streets looking for fair game – tasty meat. The wemon of Cleveland are z prettyist of all. I must be the water they drink. I live for the hunt – my life. Blood for papa.

Ms Whitestone, ma'am, I don't want to kill any more. No ma'am, no more but I must, 'Honour Thy Father'.

I want to make love to the world. I love people. I don't belong on earth. Return me to yahoos.

To the people of Cleveland, I love you. And I want to wish all of you a happy Thanksgiving. May God bless you in this life and in the next and for now I say goodbye and good night.

Police: Let me haunt you with these words;
I'll be back! I'll be back!
To be interrpreted as – Bang, Bang, Bang, Bang, Bang –
Ugh!!

Yours in murder
Mr Monster
(P.S. – Have a look at the *Chicago Sun-Times* Friday
morning. I think you'll find it an interesting read.)

Dana looked up at Brown over the top of the sheet of
paper and shook her head in confusion. She had to force the
words around the painful lump that had formed in her
throat at the sight of her own name in the letter. 'Where did
this come from? New York City?'

Brown shook his head. 'Nope. It was at the crime scene
last night, Dana. Crawford said he didn't want you to see it.
Said it would only make things harder on you.'

Dana could hardly breathe. 'Where is he now?'

Brown shrugged. 'No idea. It's weird. After you'd
gone he went from barking orders to suddenly saying he
had some other things to take care of and then he left. We
haven't been able to get hold of him since.' He paused and
looked at her. 'You're not the only one who graduated
from the Academy. I've been thinking . . .'

She stared up at him. 'What?'

Brown looked uneasy. 'Well, you'll probably think I'm
crazy. I mean, you know him better than I do – and – well,
it's probably a long shot. But you know when you said a while
back that it could be someone who was close to a crime scene?'

Dana nodded, not daring to speak, not wanting to put
words into his mouth.

'Well,' he continued, 'it got me thinking on another angle – about how well the killer picks his copycats. So then, when I got back to my hotel room, I started thinking about what I know about Crawford Bell. I remembered taking his course at the Academy. Richard Ramirez, Dennis Rader, Richard Speck, David Berkowitz and John Wayne Gacy are the main subjects of that course, aren't they? Dennis Rader is the only addition since we graduated.'

Dana's heart pounded in her chest. 'Go on.'

Brown sat back down behind her desk and cracked his knuckles. 'Seem a little coincidental to you?'

Dana shook her head. 'No. I've been thinking the same, Jeremy, but it could be a student of his . . .'

'It could, but would a student – say, like you and me – remember every little tiny detail enough to replicate them exactly?'

'You're right, and he's the only one who knows every little detail of my parents' murders – apart from me, that is.'

As Jeremy voiced his own suspicions, the possibility that Crawford was their killer became horribly real. Dana respected Jeremy and knew that he thought things through carefully. If they had both reached the same conclusion, didn't that point to the terrible truth?

'So what do we do?' she said after a beat.

'Don't know yet.'

'Neither do I.'

She paused before asking the question that she already had a pretty good idea of the answer to. 'What else did he leave behind this time?'

'A red clown's nose,' Brown said. 'Need a refresher course on what that probably means?'

'No. So he's going to copy John Wayne Gacy next? But

he hasn't done anything for David Berkowitz yet.'

Brown leaned back in Dana's chair and rolled his head on his shoulders. 'That's the problem. The letter is a play on David Berkowitz's letter to Captain Joseph Borelli of the New York City Police Department. Practically word for word from the original. The obvious substitutions here are your name and the reference to Thanksgiving instead of Easter. Do we know anybody who's a scholar on that kind of stuff?'

Dana tried to keep the frustration out of her voice. 'Did you find out what's so interesting about tomorrow's edition of the *Sun-Times*?'

'No. Crawford said the managing editor told him he'd have to wait for the big reveal right along with the rest of the country.'

Dana was incredulous. 'He could *subpoena* him, for Christ's sake.'

Brown nodded. 'I know, but Crawford said the paper would already be out by the time a subpoena made it all the way through the courts. Freedom of the press and all that shit. Said our hands were tied on this one.'

Dana shook her head in disgust. In his entire career, Crawford Bell had never backed down to anyone, not even to the President of the United States. Now he was turning tail on a simple newspaperman? What was it that he didn't want them to see? And where was he now? Off claiming his next victim?

Her stomach churned. 'So where should we go from here?' Should they put a trace on Crawford? It was one thing for her and Jeremy to imagine the worst, but could they convince someone like Krugman? Did they have any real, tangible evidence to link him to the actual crime scenes?

Brown shook his head. 'Don't know. Ahn Howser's father said his daughter spent a lot of time online, so I'm looking for any possible links between all the victims. Other than that, I have no idea.'

Dana held Brown's gaze and told him about Crawford's tumour. She didn't owe her mentor any loyalty any more. She didn't owe him anything any more. Not after what he'd done.

Brown took the news in his stride, looking weary. He seemed much too tired to be surprised by anything at this point, not even by a bombshell like the one that Dana had just unleashed on him. 'You're going to have to tell Krugman, you know,' he said.

'Yeah, I know.'

CHAPTER SIXTY-SEVEN

Dana left the office and called Crawford's cellphone. Maybe he could explain everything away. It was a long shot, but she had to give him that chance.

He wasn't answering.

'Goddamn it, Crawford,' she hissed under her breath. 'Where *are* you?'

She ducked inside the Starbucks half a block away from her office and ordered a large black coffee before settling down at an empty table. It was no good. If he killed again and she hadn't said anything – well . . . And if they found him and she was wrong no one would be happier than her. She dug her cellphone out of her pocket and punched in a number. She couldn't keep her suspicions a secret any longer.

She needed help from the top on this one.

A deep voice answered after six rings. 'Bill Krugman.'

Dana took a deep breath and sat up straighter in her seat. 'Sir, I need to talk to you about Crawford Bell.'

The FBI Director shouted something at someone in his office before coming back on the line. 'Do you know where he is? He's been out of contact since last night. I've been trying to reach him.'

'No,' Dana said. 'I have no idea where he is. That's the problem.'

'Why do you say that?'

Dana filled the Director in on her and Jeremy's suspicions as quickly as she could. Everything from the copycat murders following Crawford's introductory course to his failure to compile a profile to Crawford's revelation that he had a brain tumour that would probably soon cost him his life.

'Jesus fucking Christ,' Krugman said. 'Hang tight, Agent Whitestone. I'll be up there in a couple of hours. If you're right about this – and I sure as hell hope you're not – it's a disaster . . . Either way, this case has just blown wide open.'

Dana flipped her cellphone closed. At least Krugman seemed to take her suspicions seriously. And for him to come all the way up to Cleveland meant he must've been getting some real heat from the White House about the murders. Even though it was unheard of for a Director to become personally involved in a case that he could easily monitor from DC when an arrest didn't appear imminent, the President himself must have weighed in on the matter and directed Krugman to Ohio.

Dana sighed. What was his motto again?

Oh yeah. Keep hope *alive*.

CHAPTER SIXTY-EIGHT

On the north wall of his apartment Nathan had scrawled a message in black magic marker:

AS LONG AS DANA WHITESTONE IS IN THE WORLD, THERE WILL NEVER BE ANY PEACE, BUT THERE WILL BE PLENTY OF MURDERS.

He liked the look of his writing. It looked strange, demented.
It looked . . . *perfect*.
How he so desperately longed to be perfect!
In the bedroom he'd kicked a hole into the wall. An arrow pointed inside the space. Beside it he had written another message:

HI, MY NAME IS MR WILLIAMS AND I LIVE IN THIS HOLE. I HAVE SEVERAL CHILDREN I'M TURNING INTO KILLERS. WAIT TILL THEY GROW UP.

The rest of the day was spent relaxing and reading from *The Silence of the Lambs*. Nathan admired Hannibal Lecter very much and wished he could assume the maniac psychiatrist's identity for these next kills. But he knew he must restrict his activities to the real world so he simply sighed and turned another page.

The weather outside was very cold. At exactly eight o'clock he dressed in his heavy black clothes, causing his forehead to break out into a profuse sweat. After placing the gun in the side pocket of his coat, he stepped out into the chill night air.

The white Pontiac Sunfire had been stolen from a used-car lot in Strongsville. It would be days before its disappearance was noticed. Tonight he would abandon it in an east-side ghetto and steal another vehicle for his getaway.

Nathan knew the streets around Cleveland very well. They were *his* streets. A left turn onto Wooster was followed by a right onto Center Ridge. Half a mile later he pulled into the crowded parking lot of the Westgate Shopping Mall in Rocky River, Ohio.

This was where he would find them: the keys to finally recreating the Son of Sam's deliciously heinous crime.

He parked neither extremely close to nor extremely far from the mall's entrance. From this vantage point he had an excellent view of the happy Christmas shoppers milling about and bleating at each other like a flock of mindless sheep as they blithely went about the pitiful routines of their pathetic little lives.

Nathan shook his head in disgust, irritated at the inconsistencies in the script. The original Son of Sam had committed his murders in the sweltering heat of the summer of 1977 – back in the days when the chicks had been a hell of a lot tougher – but sometimes you just had to adapt to survive.

Still, very much like David Berkowitz – 'The Wicked King Wicker' – Nathan desperately wished that he could kill them all. And slowly, at that.

But he knew better than to stray further from the script at this late stage of the game, so he simply turned off the car's engine, logged onto his MacBook Pro and waited in total silence for his prey.

CHAPTER SIXTY-NINE

Despite his earlier promise of getting up to Cleveland in a couple of hours, Bill Krugman didn't land at Hopkins until nearly eight p.m. that night. He hustled down the steps of the DOJ's Gulfstream V and met Dana and Brown on the tarmac.

'Sorry,' he said. 'I got caught up in a debriefing session with the President. He's really breathing down my neck on this one. I talked to some of the others. I even went over to Crawford's house – no show. He's not answering his phone. Looks like you could be right, Dana. Anyway, I've got an APB out for him with the local police and all the Ohio field offices. We need to resolve this *fast*. My job is on the line with this one. *All* our jobs are.'

Dana nodded as the cold winter wind howled across the tarmac. For a moment she wondered if something might have happened to Crawford, but his tumour suddenly didn't seem relevant any more. He had betrayed her.

She doubted they'd ever find him. He'd obviously planned these copycat murders for years, and nobody in the world knew more about FBI search procedures than him. Hell, he'd literally written the goddamn *handbook* on the subject.

'So where do we go from here?' Dana asked.

Krugman glanced down at his watch. 'We'll start at daybreak,' he said. 'Right now we all need to go and get rested up. There's nothing more we can do tonight. We've got a big day ahead of us tomorrow.'

Dana frowned. 'Can't we start now?' she asked. 'Can't we just—'

Krugman cut her off before she could continue. 'Wasn't a request, Special Agent Whitestone. This isn't your case any more. It's mine. If you've got a problem with that, let me know now.'

Dana shook her head and dropped her gaze to the tarmac. 'No, sir, that's fine. I'll see you in the morning.'

CHAPTER SEVENTY

Fifteen miles west of Hopkins International Airport, Marcia Reynolds and her best friend Amy Wohlers were sitting together in the food court at the Westgate Shopping Mall munching on cinnamon sticky buns.

'That's a totally cool purse you got at the Gap,' Marcia said. 'Your mom's totally gonna freak out when she opens it. Seriously, Aim, she's gonna love it.'

From their stylish clothes to their carefully plucked eyebrows, the girls were mirror images of each other. Both of them were tall and thin, and both had a coltish pubescent beauty. Each wore long auburn hair dyed at the same salon to make them look even *more* alike than nature had intended. They got a kick out of it when people asked them if they were sisters, always replying that they were fraternal twins.

'You really think so?' Amy asked. She removed the sleek black handbag from the shopping bag and inspected it again. 'I don't know. You don't think it's, like, too *young* for her, do you? She's already thirty-nine, you know.'

'No way,' Marcia assured her. 'Besides, that's totally the style now. Everybody's going for the young look these days. It started, like, out in California or something, and now it's here. Trust me, Aim, she's gonna die when

338

she sees it. It's totally rad.'

Amy felt better about the purchase immediately. Of everyone she knew nobody had better fashion sense than Marcia. She could trust her, knew her best friend wouldn't steer her wrong. If Marcia said the purse was cool, then the purse was cool. End of subject.

The girls were both seventeen now, juniors at Magnificat High School and co-captains of the school's cheerleading squad. Though the school was an all-girls institution – or perhaps *because* of that fact – they were even more boy-crazy than their co-educational-school counterparts, finding nothing more enjoyable than dolling themselves up for a night of hunk-hunting at the mall, a ritual they'd performed at least twice a week since the sixth grade.

A young man wearing a pair of faded blue jeans and a tight white T-shirt that showcased the hard muscles in his upper arms strutted past their table.

'Whoa!' Marcia said when he'd passed. 'Did you get a load of that? Total hottie, but totally conceited too.'

'Definitely an asshole,' Amy agreed. 'I'll take that sales guy from the Gap any day.' She sighed dramatically. 'I swear to God, Marcia. I've probably spent a thousand bucks in there over the past three months and he still hasn't even looked at me twice yet.'

'He will, Aim,' Marcia soothed. 'He totally wants you, I know he does.'

'Well, then I wish somebody would tell *him* that. Shit, I'm gonna be, like, twenty, before he even asks me out at this rate.'

Just then, Marcia's BlackBerry beeped in her purse. She held up a finger to Amy and motioned for her to wait. 'Hold on a minute, Aim. Incoming message.'

She dug out the device and rolled her eyes at the message blinking on the screen.

HEY BABY, WANNA FUCK?

Marcia quickly pecked out her response.

GO FUCK *YOURSELF*, ASSHOLE!

'What the fuck was that all about?' Amy asked as Marcia shoved the BlackBerry back into her purse.

'Nothing – just some perv from the dating site asking me if I wanted to get it on.'

Amy screwed up her pretty face in irritation. 'What is it with all these jackwads online? I get that kind of shit all the time.'

'Who knows, and who cares? They probably just get off on it.'

Amy smiled across the table at her best friend. 'Come on, bitch, tell the truth. You know you get off on it too.'

Marcia Reynolds's perfectly lipsticked mouth dropped wide open in the kind of shocked and disbelieving look that could only be pulled off with any measure of credibility by a teenaged girl. 'Fuck you, you fucking slut! *You*'re the fucking perv!'

They both laughed until they cried.

Fixing their make-up and finishing off their cinnamon buns a moment later, they stuffed the wrappers into an overflowing trash receptacle and decided to take a final stroll through the mall before they had to leave. Amy had a strict curfew of nine o'clock, and it was going on eight-thirty already.

'Come on,' Marcia said, slipping her arm through Amy's. 'Let's walk past the Gap one more time before we go. You keep looking straight ahead when we get there and I'll look back to see if he checks you out.'

They made their way past Radio Shack, Bath & Body Works and Waldenbooks before passing the clothing store where the object of Amy's affection was busily folding sweaters on a display table.

'Oh my God!' Marcia squealed, grabbing Amy by the elbow and hustling her forward. 'He totally checked you out, Aim! He was, like, *undressing* you with his eyes!'

'Shut up!'

'I'm dead fucking serious. I *told* you he wants you. Next time we go in there you *have* to talk to him.'

'You really think so?'

'I *know* so. But when he's, like, your boyfriend and shit, you'd better not be dissin' me to hang out with him all the goddamn time.'

Amy Wohlers laughed happily. 'Well, maybe he's got a hot friend or something. That way we could all double date.'

The girls discussed their game plan to hook Amy up with the hottie from the Gap as they walked out of the mall and into the crowded parking lot. Marcia had been given a red Ford Mustang convertible for her sixteenth birthday, and they got inside the car. Eminem's 'Crack A Bottle' blasted from the cranked-up stereo system as they drove.

'I think Eminem's totally hot,' Marcia shouted over the deafening music. 'I'd fuck him any day.'

Amy rolled her eyes. Both girls were still virgins, so it was funny to hear Marcia talk like she was so sophisticated when it came to sex. 'You're way too good for him, Mar,' she shouted back. 'He's a woman-hater. Don't you hear all that shit he says about Kim in his lyrics? And he hates gays, too, you know.'

Marcia considered this for a moment before snapping her gum and shrugging her shoulders. 'Well, he's totally hot and he's totally rich. Besides, I'm not Kim and I'm not gay, so I'd fuck him anyway.'

Amy paused, then burst out laughing. 'I would, too. That dude is totally fucking hot!'

They were still giggling as they drove past the post office and pulled up to the kerb in front of Amy's house on Jamestown Avenue a few minutes later.

Marcia downshifted to park and turned the music down before turning in her seat to face her best friend. 'What are you wearing tomorrow?'

'I think I'm gonna wear those new jeans and that black sweater I bought last week.'

'Going goth on me now?'

'Nah, just going for the mysterious look.'

'Good – I'll wear black too, then.'

Amy opened the passenger door and stepped out. She leaned back in and grabbed her purse from the floorboard. 'Call me as soon as you get home, OK? I want to make sure you're safe.'

As she leaned her reed-thin body back out of the car, the first slug caught Amy Wohlers just above her left ear, spraying her brains all over the Mustang's passenger-side window. The second bullet ripped through her throat before slamming into the dashboard.

The second girl was too stunned to scream. The headlights briefly illuminated the terrifying figure that Nathan cut in his black clothing as he calmly walked around the car to the driver's side.

'Good evening,' he said, though he knew she couldn't possibly hear him through the rolled-up window. 'And good night to you, as well.'

Adjusting the white convenience-store bag over the .44-calibre handgun – *a condom*, David Berkowitz had called it – he lifted his arm and pulled the trigger twice.

The first bullet shattered the glass before entering Marcia Reynolds's heart and killing her instantly.

The second shot penetrated her skull dead centre between her expertly shaped brown eyebrows.

Nathan dropped his hand to his side and quickly walked away, disappearing into the night. *Four down, one to go.*

And then things would *really* start to get interesting.

CHAPTER SEVENTY-ONE

The ringing of the telephone on Dana's bedside table woke her early the next morning. It was Jeremy Brown.

'I sent a cruiser over to your apartment with a copy of the *Chicago Sun-Times* about an hour ago,' he said. 'Should be outside your door now. Give it a read and we'll see you over here in an hour or so.'

Dana hung up and dragged herself out of bed. She left the bedroom and walked though the living room before opening the front door. The newspaper was lying on her welcome mat.

She picked it up and sat down at the kitchen table before reading the six-column forty-point headline stripped across the top of the front page.

SERIAL KILLER LINK IN LOYOLA MURDERS?
By Chelsea Garret
Sun-Times Staff Writer

CHICAGO – On Nov. 23, a night janitor discovered the murdered bodies of three female nursing students in a dormitory room at Loyola University.

The victims, Lindsey McCormick, 22, of Seattle; Liza Alloway, 22, of Deer Trail, Wyo.; and Ahn Howser, 19, of

San Diego, were all strangled. Each also had her throat cut.

According to police reports, all the fingers on Alloway's right hand had been chopped off. An autopsy later revealed she also had four broken ribs.

Chicago Police apprehended a suspect on the night of the murders, but later released him when Special Agent Dana Whitestone of the FBI was flown in to investigate.

For the past week, Whitestone, working again with renowned FBI profiler and former partner Crawford Bell, has been investigating the highly publicised 'Night Stalker' murder of Mary Ellen Orton in Los Angeles and the 'BTK' killings of the Aiken family in Wichita, Kan. Previously, Whitestone had been assigned to the 'Cleveland Slasher' case, in which five little girls were brutally murdered over the course of three months.

Late last night, an envelope containing a bloody swatch of clothing arrived at the downtown offices of the *Chicago Sun-Times.* An anonymous police source confirmed the swatch is from a sweatshirt worn by McCormick on the night of the murders.

As of press time, neither Bell nor Whitestone could be reached for comment. The lead investigator in the Loyola slayings, Det. Constantine Konstantopolous of the Chicago Police Department, declined comment on the grounds the investigation is ongoing.

The article ended with contact information for the reporter, Chelsea Garret. Next to Dana's standard FBI ID photo, a short sidebar accompanied the main story. Dana took a deep breath and forced herself to read it. She'd always known it was only a matter of time before they dredged up her past.

WHO IS DANA WHITESTONE?

As a small child, Special Agent Dana Whitestone witnessed the brutal murders of her parents in their Ohio home. No suspect was ever apprehended for the crimes. She was adopted at the age of five by Stephen and Linda Grabowski of Painesville, Ohio. Tragically, the Grabowskis died in an automobile accident less than a year later. Whitestone was then placed in a succession of foster homes until her eighteenth birthday.

Whitestone graduated with a degree in criminal psychology from Cleveland State University in 1994, then applied for and was accepted into the FBI Training Academy in Quantico, Virginia.

Commissioned as a special agent in 1997, Whitestone is unmarried and currently lives in the Cleveland area.

Dana put the paper down on the table and suddenly felt very dizzy. Pushing back her chair and quickly standing up only made things worse.

She should have been used to the press by now, but the shock of seeing her name, Crawford's, all the crimes, then her picture and life story on the front page of a 700,000-circulation daily newspaper hit her like a mule kick to the stomach. It was too much to take.

Before she could stop them from coming, random scenes from her childhood started flashing through her mind. It was a movie montage stuck on fast-forward.

Her mother's voice calling out to her. Her father's strong hands reaching down to pick her up. The silver flash of a knife. The horrible squeal of tyres on a rain-slicked road.

The very last thing Dana remembered thinking was that she really needed a drink. She needed to block out all the pain, confusion, lies, betrayal and hurt. Then she blacked out so completely that she didn't even feel her head smacking the sharp edge of the kitchen table on her way to collapsing on the linoleum-covered floor.

CHAPTER SEVENTY-TWO

Nathan sat in his rental car outside his sister's apartment complex in Lakewood and listened to the narrator run down a list of America's most notorious serial killers. If there were any justice in the world, the very next edition of this audiobook would feature his name at the top of the list.

He leaned forward and turned the volume up.

Everything was absolutely perfect now. Through the miracle of technology he had his murderous friends by his side, and his geography couldn't be any better.

He was thoroughly engrossed in the tape when he was suddenly jolted back to his surroundings by the sound of an ambulance siren wailing. His jaw dropped when the vehicle came to a screeching stop in front of the main doors of the apartment complex. Three EMTs flung the doors open and rushed inside.

Nathan's heart slammed in his chest. What the fuck was *this* all about?

Five minutes later he watched his sister being wheeled out on a gurney.

Nathan clenched his teeth so hard that he nearly chipped a tooth. Slipping the car into gear, he followed the ambulance as closely as he could without getting into an accident. Thankfully, the hospital was less than a mile away.

So help me God, he thought as he pulled into the busy parking lot five minutes later. *If she's already dead there's going to be hell to pay.*

This one was *his*.

CHAPTER SEVENTY-THREE

Dana groaned as her world swam back into focus and she became aware of three grave faces clustered around her bed and staring down at her. She felt ridiculous, like Dorothy waking up from her infamous tornado-induced coma in *The Wizard of Oz*.

It was Bill Krugman, the Wizard himself, who spoke first. 'Agent Whitestone, how are you feeling?'

Dana winced at the rawness in her throat. 'Not so hot,' she mumbled.

Krugman nodded. 'I don't imagine you do.'

Dana closed her eyes. When she opened them again, she found herself looking up into Jeremy's warm brown eyes. The Tin Man if ever she'd seen one.

'Remember me?' he asked, with a gentle smile.

'Where the hell am I?' Dana asked.

'Fairview General Hospital,' Brown said. 'When you didn't show up at the office, we got worried and called your friend here.'

Eric moved forward next, an identical look of concern clouding his handsome features. Who was he? The Scarecrow? Or the Cowardly Lion?

Definitely the Scarecrow.

He placed a hand on the side of her face. 'I found you

passed out in your apartment, honey.'

Dana shook the cobwebs out of her brain. 'I feel like I've been run over by a freight train. How long have I been out of it?'

'About three hours now,' Krugman said.

He lifted his left wrist and checked his watch. 'In any event, I'm glad you're OK. You just take it easy for today. Agent Brown and I are going downtown to get back to work. I'm staying at The Wyndham on Euclid Avenue. If you need anything, call the front desk. If I don't hear from you by tomorrow morning I'll assume you've recovered enough to join us.' At least he hadn't pulled her from the case.

With their expressions, Krugman and Brown both sent Dana their own individual messages of concern as they left the hospital room. When they'd gone, Eric pulled a chair over to the side of Dana's bed and ran his thumb gently over the top of her hand, being very careful not to disturb the intravenous tube.

'How are you feeling, buddy?'

As she looked up into Eric's eyes, all the tragic events in Dana's life caught up with her. For once, she decided to just let them all go.

The tears came in a hot torrent for two solid minutes.

When they had subsided, Eric sat back in his chair and rubbed at his own misty eyes. 'Talk to me, Dana,' he said. 'It's obvious that something serious is going on with you.'

Dana pushed herself up straighter in bed. 'I'm *scared*, Eric. That's what's going on with me. I'm so fucking scared I can't even think straight.'

Just then, a soft knock sounded at the door and a middle-aged physician with a large strawberry birthmark in the centre of his forehead entered the room.

'Hello, Dana, I'm Dr Rami,' the man said in a deep voice marinated in a thick Indian accent. He glanced down at the medical chart hanging by a length of plastic at the foot of her bed. 'How are you feeling?'

Dana wiped at her eyes. 'Not that great, doc,' she answered honestly. 'But I really need to get back to work, so it doesn't matter how I feel right now. When can I get out of this place?'

Rami frowned and looked at Eric. 'This is a very serious thing that has happened to you, Miss Whitestone. May I speak with you in private for a moment?'

Eric rose to his feet to leave but Dana raised a hand to stop him. 'That won't be necessary. Eric's eventually going to hear what you say, anyway, so you might as well just say it in front of him.'

Rami nodded and flipped a page on her chart. 'Stress-induced blackouts are a very serious condition, Miss Whitestone. Not to mention I found alcohol in your system this morning. I'd like to keep you in overnight for observation. As a precautionary measure.'

Dana shook her head. 'Can't do it, doc,' she said. 'I really need to get out of here.'

Rami frowned and pushed his horn-rimmed glasses up on the bridge of his nose. 'Very well, then,' he said, seeing the look of determination and defiance on her face. 'I can't stop you. I'll discharge you today if it's absolutely necessary, but only if your friend here promises to keep a close eye on you and calls me if you start feeling ill again.'

'That won't be a problem, doctor,' Eric assured him.

Rami held Dana's gaze as he left the room. 'I'm very serious about this, Miss Whitestone. Please don't take this condition lightly.'

Five minutes later a squat nurse with the prettiest smile Dana had ever seen breezed into the room. She unfastened the tube from Dana's hand and rubbed an alcohol swab over the redness. She winked at Dana when she saw Eric standing over by the window. 'You may not be feeling so hot, honey, but I'd say you're a lucky girl all the same. Sure wish I was going home with a hunk like that.'

She lowered the bedrail and helped Dana to her feet before she brought Dana's clothes into the bathroom so she could change for the trip home.

The nurse winked at her again when Dana had finished dressing. 'I'll send an orderly in with a wheelchair in a minute, honey. But just remember, if you ever need any help with this one – any help at all – I'm available any time. Day or night. Don't be afraid to take me up on that offer, either.'

Dana smiled. 'I'll keep that in mind.'

As promised, a tall, muscular orderly with wavy brown hair arrived a few moments later and helped Dana settle into a wheelchair. He turned to Eric, smiling. 'You can wheel her out if you want. Just make sure you stop off at the front desk and sign out before you leave, OK?'

'Not a problem,' Eric said.

When the orderly had left the room, Dana turned to Eric. 'Ready to go, you big hunk? We'd better get you out of here before you get kidnapped. I'm pretty sure that nurse who was in here has her heart set on you, and she doesn't strike me as the kind of woman who takes no for an answer.'

'That's nice, Dana, but to tell you the truth I was more attracted to the orderly.'

'I figured as much.'

When Eric Carlton smiled at her, for the first time in months Dana felt like everything was going to be all right. As long as she had Eric in her life, everything else would sort itself out. She was sure of it.

'Sit tight for a minute,' he said. 'I have to make a quick pit stop before we go.'

Dana smiled up at him from her wheelchair.

CHAPTER SEVENTY-FOUR

The anger burned in Nathan's chest as he left the hospital room.

He ducked into the bathroom and splashed some cold water on his face in an effort to calm down, but it was no use.

Staring deep into the reflection of his glittering brown eyes in the spotless mirror above the sink, he decided it was reparation time.

CHAPTER SEVENTY-FIVE

At precisely seven o'clock that evening Eric served dinner, clucking around Dana like a mother hen. It seemed utterly surreal to be suddenly transplanted into a domestic idyll in the middle of a murder hunt, but with Krugman refusing to let Dana anywhere near the case until after the twenty-four-hour rest that the doctor had ordered she didn't have much choice. And it probably was *exactly* what she needed right now. A nice, normal meal with someone who would do anything for her – before real life kicked in again.

As they sat down to a delicious meal of duck *à l'orange*, crisp green beans and baby carrots, Eric reached across the table and covered Dana's hand with his. His eyes misted over.

'I'm so worried about you, Dana,' he said with an audible hitch in his voice. 'I don't know what I'd do if I ever lost you. I *need* you, for Christ's sake. I was so scared when I found you passed out this morning. I couldn't help but wonder what I'd do if you never woke up again.'

A painful lump formed in Dana's throat. 'I'm sorry, Eric.'

He took his hand away and let out a deep breath. 'I think you should quit the case.'

Dana shook her head. 'You know I can't do that. Too many people are counting on me.'

'Counting on you so much that you get ill. You heard what the doctor said.'

When Dana didn't respond, Eric went on. 'Is there anything I can do to help at all? I feel so goddamn useless.'

Dana held back the sobs that she felt coming on. 'You're already doing everything you can for me,' she said. 'You're being my friend, and that's what I really need right now.'

Eric smiled gently. 'You mean your *best* friend.'

Dana laughed, tears smarting in her eyes. 'Of course that's what I mean, you goofball. You're the best friend I've ever had in my life.'

Now Eric had tears in *his* eyes. This was turning into a sob-fest, but Dana didn't care. She knew how serious her collapse had been: it was a warning sign – a big one – that something had to change. But right now she just wanted to hide away with Eric and pretend that nothing bad was ever going to happen to her again. Tomorrow she'd deal with reality.

'You really mean that?' he said.

'Yes, I do.'

'Good. That's what I needed to hear. So what do you say we have a little toast to our friendship?'

He worked a bottle of sparkling apple juice with a corkscrew and poured a glass for both of them before handing one over to her. 'You do the honours, sweetheart.'

Dana leaned her head back and studied the ceiling for a moment as she came up with the appropriate sentiment. 'Well, I was going to wish for something romantic like world peace or that we'd both find true love and happiness one day, but what the hell.'

She raised her glass in Eric's direction and clinked it against his. 'Here's to you, here's to me, best of friends we'll always be, but if we should ever disagree, fuck you – here's to me!'

And with that she downed her entire glass in one swallow.

Eric shook his head. 'You surprise me, Dana, you really do, but it's good to see a bit of the old Dana back.' Looking her directly in the eye and rising to the challenge, he said, 'And no, fuck *you*, Dana. Here's to *me*.'

Throwing his head back, he drained his own glass in one quick pull.

And they both laughed harder than they had in years.

Finishing up the dinner dishes an hour later, they returned to Eric's living room and popped in a DVD. *Bambi* – one of Dana's all-time favourites.

Snuggled together on the couch, they closed their eyes and fell asleep in each other's arms with Oreo curled up at their feet.

CHAPTER SEVENTY-SIX

Nathan breathed a deep sigh of relief right before he fell asleep. She was still alive. At least for now. Thank God for small favours.

As he slowly drifted away, the narrator of the audiobook continued the list of notorious serial killers in his mind. These ones were from all around the globe.

'Cayetano Santos Gordino. "The Big-Eared Midget" from Argentina killed four children in 1912 before dying in prison in 1944.

'Paul Denyer. "The Frankston Serial Killer" from Australia murdered three women in a Melbourne suburb in 1993.

'Robert Succo. This Italian madman murdered at least five people, including his own parents.'

Nathan hit the stop button in his mind. It was enough for tonight, and it had ended fittingly. Shit, he hadn't seen his own parents in *years*.

Tomorrow morning he'd finally remedy that little situation once and for all.

CHAPTER SEVENTY-SEVEN

When the phone rang at six o'clock the next morning, Eric freed his arm from beneath Dana to answer it. After a moment, he handed it over. 'Bill Krugman,' he said.

Dana removed a silver hoop earring and sleepily brushed a strand of hair out of her eyes before placing the receiver to her ear. 'Hello?'

'Dana,' Krugman said, sounding so alert she was sure he'd been up for hours already. 'Feeling any better?'

'Much. What's up?'

'Good. Well, we're over at the office now. Can you meet us here in an hour?'

'Of course. Make any decisions yet?'

'As a matter of fact, I have. I'm going over to check out an apartment in Rocky River. Apparently Crawford, the killer – hell, I hate thinking it could be him – anyway, he was staying there while impersonating the Son of Sam. You and Jeremy Brown are going down to West Virginia.'

Dana stifled a yawn. 'West Virginia? What's down there?'

'Appalachia is down there.'

'So?'

Krugman paused. 'We received a letter from our killer last night, Agent Whitestone. It had a return address on it.'

Dana sat up straighter on the couch. 'What did the letter say?'

Krugman cleared his throat. 'It didn't say anything, but Liza Alloway's chopped-off fingers were stuffed inside.'

'Was there any DNA?'

'Nope. Not a trace. Get on the road as soon as you can.'

PART V

RESHAPING JOHN WAYNE GACY AND REDEEMING NATHAN STIEDOWE

CHAPTER SEVENTY-EIGHT

Nathan logged onto his Yahoo! Messenger account and looked at his 'Buddies' list.

His target was online, just like he always seemed to be. It was so goddamn irritating how some people had no lives.

He laughed and pecked a message into the chat box. The irony was just too delicious. Pretty soon, this guy really *wouldn't* have a life.

Almost instantaneously, his message popped up in the guise of his online persona with the accompanying chime.

C-townTop: hey big guy. what's up?

The response came less than ten seconds later.

LkwoodBtm: Not much. You?
C-townTop: just horny, as usual
LkwoodBtm: I hear ya. So when are we getting together to take care of that little problem of yours?
C-townTop: little?
LkwoodBtm: LOL. Sorry about that. So when are we getting together to take care of that BIG THROBBING problem of yours?
C-townTop: the sooner the better

LkwoodBtm: How about tonight?

C-townTop: mmm. sounds good. i really want to stick something in you

LkwoodBtm: Sounds hot.

C-townTop: good

LkwoodBtm: And you promise you'll stick something in me?

C-townTop: i will. but it might hurt a little

LkwoodBtm: Don't threaten me with a good time!

C-townTop: it's not a threat

LkwoodBtm: What is it?

C-townTop: that's a promise too ☺

Nathan leaned back in his chair and closed the chat box. Eighty-six per cent of the world's serial killers were heterosexual – and he liked the ladies every bit as much as the next guy, of course – but the time had come for him to take a walk on the wild side. Time to try out the gay thing to see what all the fuss was about.

He laughed again when the chords of 'Lola' by The Kinks suddenly echoed in his mind.

Lola, L-O-L-A, Lola . . .

CHAPTER SEVENTY-NINE

The region of Appalachia in West Virginia is a land that time has largely forgotten. With its rolling green meadows, crystal-clear blue lakes and an expanse of woodland stretching on for hundreds of miles, it is, at first glance, God's country.

Jeremy Brown was at the wheel of a rented Chevrolet as the beautiful scenery whizzed by at eighty miles an hour. Dana came awake with a start a moment later.

She turned in her seat and squinted her eyes against the blinding winter sunlight. 'Sorry about that. I can't believe I fell asleep.'

He looked over at her and smiled. 'No problem, kiddo. You needed the rest. Are you sure you're OK? You had us really worried there for a moment. Thank God for your friend Eric.'

Dana stretched her arms over her head and rolled her neck on her shoulders. 'Yeah, he's the best. I'm fine now. Just want to catch this son of a bitch. How much longer until we get there?'

Brown glanced down at the odometer. 'Twenty more miles until we reach the access road. The cabin's another mile from there. Apparently it's not accessible by car, so I'm afraid we're gonna have to hoof it.'

Twenty minutes later he pulled the car over to the side of the road and popped the trunk. A solitary buzzard circled high in the blue sky above as they shrugged their torsos into bulletproof Kevlar and checked their side arms.

Brown turned to her and handed over the keys. 'You take them, Dana. I'm notorious for losing these goddamn things.'

A fifteen-minute hike along an overgrown trail brought them to a steep ledge overlooking a ramshackle cabin partially obscured by a stand of enormous oak trees. It was the only dwelling in a ten-mile radius, and one of the trees had recently been cut down. Now it was lying on the snow-covered ground like an enormous felled giant.

Brown shook his head when he saw it. 'Looks like our man's something of a lumberjack in addition to his day job of being a deranged serial killer. Very industrious of him, wouldn't you say?'

Before Dana could answer him, the gunshot-sound of snapping branches sounded fifteen yards to their right. She caught a dark flash of movement out of the corner of her right eye as Brown unholstered his Glock in one fluid motion and whipped it around with his finger twitching over the trigger.

He had an eight-point buck dead in his sights.

'Jesus Christ,' he breathed. 'That scared the living shit out of me.'

He stared at the huge buck, which defiantly stared right back. 'What do you think, Dana? Should I drop him or what? I think we're still in season.'

'And kill Bambi's dad? I don't think so.'

Brown smiled at her. 'You're too soft for your own good, Whitestone. A real marshmallow softie, but that's what I love so much about you.'

A moment later the majestic creature lifted its enormous head and gave one derisive snort before suddenly turning and crashing back into the winter woods.

Dana sighed. 'So are you ready for this or what?'

Brown didn't answer her. He was looking at something over her right shoulder. 'What's that?' he said.

Dana turned around and followed his gaze. Even from a hundred feet she could make out the front-page headline stripped across the top of a newspaper that had been nailed to a tree.

WEST PARK COUPLE SLAIN; DAUGHTER SURVIVES

Brown started walking toward the tree.

'Hey, wait up,' Dana said, her stomach churning with nausea as she followed him through the woods.

Brown pulled the newspaper off the tree. His deep brown eyes narrowed as he read quickly through the article. He looked up at her. 'Jesus Christ, Dana. Check this shit out.'

Dana could hardly breathe. She looked down at the paper, at the familiar article recounting her parents' murder in terrible detail. Quick puffs of vapour issued from her mouth. 'Motherfucker,' she said.

Brown took back the paper. 'We could have gotten some useful background information out of this reporter,' he said. 'This . . .'

He paused and ran his eyes over the byline at the top of the article. 'This Jeremiah Quigley.'

Dana's heart almost stopped. 'What did you say?'

Brown frowned. 'I said we could have gotten some useful background information out of this reporter. This Jeremiah Quigley guy. About your parents' deaths, I mean.'

Dana's world went black. Her vision swam out of focus, then she suddenly felt weightless. Brown caught her just before she completed a face-plant on the forest floor.

'Whoa,' he said. 'Take it easy, Dana. You're obviously not well enough. I should have per—'

Dana's brain reeled, unable to process the information she'd just heard. In the hundreds of times she'd read that article, never once had she noticed the reporter's name. She stumbled again.

'What's wrong?' Brown asked as he steadied her.

Dana took a deep breath and tried to regain her bearings. 'Quigley is my mother's maiden name,' she said hoarsely.

Brown's jaw nearly hit his chest. 'But I thought you said you were an only child.'

'I am.'

'Jeez.' Brown toed the ground. 'I guess that's something we'll have to deal with later. Right now we need to get down there and check out that cabin. You OK to do this or what? If not, I'll do it by myself.'

Dana shook herself. 'Absolutely not. I'm fine. Let's go.'

'OK, Dana, but just be careful, all right? This is some dangerous shit we're getting into here. Don't go passing out on me now.'

Dana's glare was hot enough to burn through six inches of solid steel. 'I said let's go,' she hissed.

Stooped over in a half-crouch, they made their way down the slippery ledge and advanced upon the cabin's wide porch gallery before ascending the creaking steps in front. Dana squatted at one side of the door and motioned for Brown to do the same at the other. She flicked off the safety on her Glock and gave him the signal to knock.

He popped up without hesitation, banging on the rickety

wooden door with one fist. 'FBI!' he yelled. 'Open up! We have a search warrant!'

There was no response. Straining her ears hard, Dana heard the low murmur of voices coming from inside.

Somebody was *definitely* in there.

Brown raised an eyebrow questioningly. Dana nodded back, every muscle in her body tensed and ready for action.

Brown rose to his feet and put all his weight behind the kick. The termite-infested jamb splintered as they rushed inside with their guns drawn.

The smell hit them first, like a hard slap across the face. The stifling heat pouring out of a pot-bellied stove in the middle of the room only intensified the unmistakable stench of decay.

The source of the horrible odour wasn't hard to trace.

The elderly couple, both frail and well into their seventies, were propped up at the kitchen table, their wrinkled hands solemnly folded in prayer. An open Bible lay between them, its sliver-thin pages splattered with blood.

Their killer had struck from behind, cutting their throats with the bloodstained butcher's knife that now lay on the table beside the Bible. Dana recognised the precise handwriting on the note under it at once.

LIZZIE BORDEN TOOK AN AXE AND GAVE HER MOTHER FORTY WHACKS. WHEN SHE SAW WHAT SHE HAD DONE, SHE GAVE HER FATHER FORTY-ONE.

A blizzard of black flies buzzed loudly in the cabin. Dana brushed a flurry of them from her eyes and almost gagged when she saw that they'd already laid eggs in the open wounds in the couple's throats. Hundreds of maggots squirmed in their flesh, madly wriggling over one another in their quest for the tastiest bits.

The voices she'd heard from outside were coming from an old transistor radio, its broken dial set to a Southern Baptist church sermon – an angry preacher raging fire-and-brimstone against the evils of fornication.

Dana flipped her cellphone open to call for backup but the reception was too weak inside the cabin for her to get a signal.

She was about to walk outside and try again when Brown motioned to the only other door in the cabin. Presumably it led into the bedroom. 'We need to clear that room,' he said, wrinkling his nose up against the overpowering smell.

Dana nodded and fell into step behind him as they quickly crossed the uneven plank floor. Taking a deep breath, Brown reached out a hand and turned the knob until the lock popped.

The double-barrelled shotgun rigged to a crude pulley system of chicken wire exploded immediately with a tremendous bang, slamming him squarely in the chest and lifting him three feet in the air. The force of the blast tore the black dress shoe off his left foot.

'Jeremy!' Dana screamed.

She covered the few feet between them in a flash, dropping to her knees by his side. She lifted his head off the floor and cradled it in her arms, lightly slapping at his alarmingly pale cheeks. 'Come on, partner,' she said. 'Talk to me, goddamn it.'

Brown only groaned impotently in response. The breath had been knocked completely out of him.

Dana's hands scrambled for the Velcro straps on his Kevlar. She gently eased the vest over his shoulders. What she saw next almost made her vomit.

The Kevlar had only done half its job. It had stopped one of the shotgun blasts but the other had gone clean through. A rapidly expanding circle of blood was soaking into Brown's white dress shirt now as a sucking chest wound tried to eat a small section of the fabric.

'Oh, sweet Jesus,' Dana breathed.

Brown stared up at her blindly, his brown eyes glazing over as the blood pulsed out of his chest with every beat of his badly labouring heart. He opened his mouth and tried to speak, but a thin trickle of blood leaked out instead.

'Hang in there, Jeremy,' Dana said softly. 'Don't try to talk. Just hang in there, goddamn it.'

The veteran FBI agent's eyes fluttered as he lost consciousness.

Dana dug in her pocket for her cellphone again, ripping a fingernail clean off in her haste but not even feeling it. Miraculously, an operator answered on the fourth ring.

'9-1-1. What is your emergency?'

Dana struggled to stay calm as she gave the woman their location. 'Officer down. Single shotgun wound to the chest. I need an ambulance out here *now.*'

She tossed the phone to one side. It rattled across the wooden floor while she pressed two fingers against Brown's throat.

Nothing.

Dana shook her head violently to clear it. They hadn't fallen into his trap *this* easily.

Had they?

She quickly began single-man CPR – fifteen hard chest

depressions followed by two quick breaths. An eternity passed because of the remoteness of the location, but Dana repeated the exhausting series until a large blond man finally pulled her away several lifetimes later.

'Out of the way, ma'am,' the EMT grunted.

He used heavy fabric scissors to cut Brown's bloody dress shirt away and a black man holding a portable defibrillator moved in, the two men's movements as perfectly choreographed as those of ballet dancers. The black man shocked Brown with the paddles once.

'Nothing,' the blond man said, his fingers pressed against Brown's throat.

The black man shocked Brown twice more and looked up at his partner both times, but the blond man only closed his eyes and shook his head in response.

Ratcheting up the dial on the defibrillator finally produced the result that Dana was praying for.

'We've got a pulse!' the blonde man shouted. 'Let's move!'

Two more EMTs moved in to help load Brown's body onto a stretcher for the gruelling trip back to the access road.

When they finally pulled off in an ambulance twenty minutes later – sirens wailing like a thousand tortured souls – Dana fumbled in her pocket for the car keys and jammed the Chevrolet into drive.

She followed the ambulance as closely as she could, gunning the engine hard. The sound it made was eerily similar to the starving howl of a mongrel dog.

CHAPTER EIGHTY

Dana flew into the visitor's lot at forty miles an hour and slammed the car into park mode before heading into the emergency room at a dead run.

She reached the front desk and frantically asked the nurse where Brown had been taken. In response, the woman calmly inquired who she was.

Dana whipped out her badge and shoved it in the nurse's face. 'Just tell me where he is, please!'

The woman rose to her feet with an angry frown on her face. She rested her hands on her wide matronly hips and motioned to the waiting room with an annoyed jerk of her chin. 'Just *sit down*, young lady. All you can do now is wait.'

Chastened, Dana sat down on a plastic chair bolted to the floor and then got up again to pace. She was in the lobby for almost six hours before a doctor finally came out.

'Special Agent Whitestone?' the man asked those in the packed room.

Dana's knees shook. 'That's me, sir.'

He walked her into the hall and out of earshot of the others. 'He's out of surgery, but it's touch-and-go right now. He's lost a lot of blood. We'll know more tomorrow.'

The doctor reached out and touched her arm lightly. 'You might as well go home, ma'am. If he makes it he'll be here quite a while longer. He wouldn't be able to talk to you right now, anyway. I'll call you if there's any change in his condition.'

Dana was little more than a walking zombie as she slowly made her way back through the parking lot and slid behind the wheel of the Chevrolet for the long, lonely trip home. The early-winter night sky moved in as she drove. There was no moon above, no stars dotting the heavens. Only total darkness.

It was pitch black as she made three calls.

The first was to the local police department. The captain on duty there assured her that his force was processing the cabin for any additional clues. The second was to Bill Krugman, who told her to get back to Cleveland as quickly as she possibly could.

Reaching the southern outskirts of Cleveland three hours later, Dana made her third and final call.

'Hello?'

'Hey, Eric.'

Eric sensed the stress in her voice at once. 'What's wrong, honey?'

Dana took a deep breath and filled him in.

'Oh my God,' Eric said when she'd finished. 'I'm so sorry. Are you all right?'

'Not really.'

He paused uncertainly. 'Listen, Dana, I've actually got some company here right now, but I'll send him home so that we can . . .'

The static of a bad connection crackled in Dana's ear. 'What was that, Eric?' she asked, sticking a finger in her right ear and straining to catch his voice. 'Say that again. I didn't hear you.'

But Eric was having troubles of his own. 'Dana? You're breaking up, honey. I can't hear you very well. If you can hear me, I said I'll send my company home so that we can talk when you get here.'

His voice was a disjointed mumble for several seconds before the connection cleared up again briefly. 'I'll tell you how we hooked up later. It's the strangest thing. Remember the other day at the hospital? Turns out I've talked to one of those guys before. *Online*, of all places.'

Just then, the beep of an incoming call sounded on Dana's cellphone. 'Goddamn it, hold on, Eric. I've got another call coming in. I'll switch back over to you in a second.'

She took the second call and said, 'Hello?'

'Dana, it's Bill Krugman again.'

'Yes, sir?'

Krugman cleared his throat. 'Thought you should know – we finally found a link between all the copycat victims. With the exception of Mary Ellen Orton, they all belonged to a computer-dating website called the Lonely Hearts Club. I'll let you know when we find out anything else, but it's looking pretty promising so far.'

Dana was confused for a moment after she hung up with Krugman, then suddenly alarmed by the terrible thought that came next.

Eric belonged to the Lonely Hearts Club, had done for years. Their killer was fixating on her; could he be getting closer than she feared? Was he focusing now on someone she really cared about? It was a frightening thought but she made herself stay with it. This killer was capable of anything. And Crawford knew all about Eric and how much he meant to her.

She tried to keep her voice calm as her connection to Eric was re-established. 'Eric? Listen to me. You need to get out of the apartment right now, honey. No questions. Just get out of there *right now*.'

But her best friend didn't hear her. The phone had already gone completely dead.

CHAPTER EIGHTY-ONE

Nathan closed the bathroom door behind him and pulled the shower curtain shut. He reached into the shower and turned the water up full blast to mask the sound of his voice, twisting only the cold-water handle to avoid fogging up the mirror. The mirror was very important to what he needed to do next.

It was almost over now; redemption was almost his.

Perfection was almost his.

In his possession he had an old black-leather satchel, the kind used by doctors in the long-ago age of house calls. Placing it on the toilet, he unsnapped it and removed the art supplies he'd purchased earlier in the day.

First there was a large jar of white foundation, the type favoured by stage actors. Then there were three containers, one each of pink, red and black make-up. A small circular sponge and a brush with a long tapered handle were positioned on either side of the sink basin.

Nathan used the sponge to apply carefully the white foundation in the shape of a heart around his eyes and over the bridge of his nose, then repeated the motion in a wide arc around his mouth. Ten minutes later he reached back into the satchel and extracted a red clown's nose before positioning it over his own. The final touch was the curly red wig.

Looking into the mirror at the reflection of the man he'd just become, he appraised himself with a critical eye.

Perfect.

As always, he cleared his throat before he began the sacred recitation out loud.

'I am well respected by my community. Everyone who knows me thinks of me as a generous, friendly and hard-working family man. I'm an extremely sharp businessman, and I play a major role in local Democratic politics. Hell, I even had my picture taken with former First Lady Rosalyn Carter once.

'I am many good things, but beneath my carefully crafted veneer I am also a murderous homosexual who cannot for the life of me stop killing teenaged boys and burying their bodies in the crawl space beneath my beautiful suburban home. Painting those pictures in prison never satisfied my thirst for innocent blood. Murder is my *true* medium; my rightful canvas the body of a teenaged boy.

'Society locked me up before putting me down like an animal on 10 May 1994, but now I'm back from the dead and ready to kill again. My last words still ring as true today as they did back then.

'*Kiss my ass.*

'My name is John Wayne Gacy, and I am an eagle.'

Smiling at the reflection of his alter ego in the bathroom mirror, Nathan opened the door and stepped quietly back out into the hallway of the stylishly decorated apartment.

CHAPTER EIGHTY-TWO

Dana roared into the parking lot of her apartment complex at sixty miles an hour and came to a screeching halt in front of the main doors.

She jammed the car into park mode and threw the door open hard, not even bothering to remove the keys from the ignition before covering the few feet to the entrance in a flash.

She fumbled with the magnetic card for the front doors, her hands shaking so violently that she almost dropped it twice before finally managing to coax it through the reader.

Dana's heart slammed in her throat. Never before had she known such an all-encompassing fear, not even on the night she'd witnessed the brutal murders of her own parents. She was a trained law-enforcement official now, not just a scared little girl wetting her pants at the sight of her parents' killer. She'd fought damn hard to get to where she was today, and now she had a personal and professional obligation to protect the man she loved more than anything else in this world.

She mashed the button on the elevator for the fourth floor, but grew impatient after the longest three seconds of her life had passed and took off for the stairwell at a dead run.

She raced up the slippery concrete steps as fast as her frantically pumping legs would carry her. After throwing the fire-escape door open with a violent bang, Dana raced down the hallway and came to a skidding halt outside Eric's door.

D13. Please, God, don't let that be an unlucky number today.

She unholstered her Glock and listened for noises coming from inside, but she was breathing so hard that her ragged gasps were the only sounds she could hear, filling her mind like the howling winter wind outside.

Dana placed her ear directly against the cold surface of the apartment door. Nothing. Only silence. No discernible noises other than her own frantic breathing. She tried the door. Locked.

She flipped back the welcome mat in front of her own apartment and grabbed her copy of Eric's house key. She slid it into the lock and turned the knob until the lock popped. Flinging the door open, she dropped down into a crouch with her Glock at the ready. The door slammed halfway back on her, but no other immediate movement came from inside the apartment.

She rose to her feet and nudged the door with her left elbow. Stepping inside, she swung the Glock back and forth in front of her as she made her way through the dining room, living room and kitchen.

Dana was on autopilot as she cleared the rest of the apartment quickly, her years of training taking over completely now as she stepped inside the bathroom and threw the shower curtain aside. No one there.

The only room left to check was the master bedroom, and that door was closed.

She moved to the outside of Eric's bedroom and heard a low, mournful cry coming from inside – an inhuman wail of pain and grief. Dana stepped back and kicked the door in hard, thrusting the Glock in first to lead the way.

The first thing she noticed was Oreo gently nuzzling the side of Eric's face.

The next thing she noticed was the blood.

Eric was completely naked and was lying on his stomach on the bed. The claw hammer that had been used to cave in his head was covered in blood, bone and little bits of brain tissue and was now lying on the bloodstained pillow beside him, denting the fabric with its heavy weight.

Oreo looked up at her and meowed pitifully.

For one terrifying moment, Dana's heart actually *stopped*. There were no sounds in this new world of hers, no smells, no discernible sensations of any kind. Only an emptiness so complete that it was impossible to comprehend.

Her best friend was *dead*.

The phone jangled on Eric's bedside table, kick-starting her heart back into gear. She raced across the room and picked it up in the middle of the second ring. 'Hello?'

The voice on the other end of the line was unnaturally deep and robotic, computer-altered by a speech-masking device. 'Look out the window,' the voice told her. 'I'd like to say hello to you, my dear.'

Dana stepped to the bedroom window with the cordless phone still at her ear. Her thumb went to the safety of the Glock to double-check that it was off. Looking down into the parking lot, she squinted toward the front doors.

From behind the rented Chevrolet he popped up like a human jack-in-the-box. A man dressed as a clown.

He raised a set of keys and playfully jangled them in Dana's direction, then tossed them into the thicket of overgrown bushes lining the side of her apartment complex.

'Hello, Dana,' the clown said into the cellphone at his ear. 'Long time, no see, sweetheart.' It was the same robotic voice as before.

Dana dropped the cordless phone to the floor and emptied the Glock's full clip through the closed window. Shattered glass rained down on the parking lot below.

But the clown only laughed gleefully at her while he danced across the street, effortlessly dodging the bullets kicking up thick chunks of concrete at his feet.

Jumping into a brown Lincoln parked on the far side of the road, he jammed the car hard into drive and peeled out. The Lincoln's bald tyres squealed as though in agony against the slick pavement as he sped away, the noise echoing in the night like the sound of insane laughter.

And then he was simply *gone*.

CHAPTER EIGHTY-THREE

Eric's funeral three days later was the hardest thing that Dana had ever had to live through – even harder than the night she'd watched her own mother brutally murdered right in front of her eyes. She couldn't help thinking there must have been something she could have done to prevent it. But he had taken her parents away from her so why should she be surprised he'd take the nearest person to family that she'd had since? She didn't even want to think about how Crawford had been like a father to her. It made her feel sick.

She choked back sobs during the entire service, and not even Bill Krugman's comforting arm around her shoulders was enough to take the pain away.

Her head swam with the realisation that her best friend was dead and he was never coming back.

She was all alone in the world.

Again.

The FBI had lifted Crawford's fingerprints off the claw hammer in Eric's bedroom, the final proof that they were looking for. It came as a surprise to absolutely no one. He knew he was better than them, and now he was just showing off to prove it.

Dana returned home directly after the service, knowing that she wouldn't have been able to handle the sight of watching them lower Eric's body into the frozen ground. Outside her apartment complex two Cleveland PD cruisers were parked to provide a visual deterrent should Crawford make good on his threats to come after her. Slumping down on her living-room couch with Oreo curled up in her lap, Dana cracked the seal on a fresh bottle of Captain Morgan's rum and cried uncontrollably for the next hour. Twenty minutes later the phone jangled on the wall in her kitchen.

She picked it up drunkenly and found herself listening numbly to the words Bill Krugman was saying.

'The bastard squeezed off a couple of shots at the graveyard, Dana. Winged me. I'm getting patched up at the Cleveland Clinic now. He also set off an explosion down the street. The security detail assigned to your place was called away to go deal with it. All hands on deck, the chief of police said.'

Dana's head almost imploded with the news. 'Was anyone *killed*?'

'No, thank God,' Krugman said. 'But there is something else.'

He blew out a slow breath but didn't continue right away.

'What is it?' Dana said. 'Just tell me.'

The Director cleared his throat. 'You're off the case, Dana. Things are way too personal for you, were from the start. I should have realised that earlier, but Crawford convinced me to give you a second chance. Now I know why.'

Dana couldn't have been any more stunned if he'd just slammed an aluminium baseball bat across her forehead. She started to protest but Krugman cut her off before she could continue.

'Sorry, Dana. That's final. I'm sending a new security detail to your apartment to watch over you now. Should be at your door in a couple minutes. Other than that, you're done. It's all over for you.'

Dana's mouth went dry. Over? *Done?* How could it be *over*?

She was so shocked that for a moment she couldn't even *breathe*. Everything was coming down on her all at once.

Her stomach gurgled violently from the Captain Morgan's swishing around in her guts. She dropped the phone to the floor and rushed into the bathroom for the toilet, but her left foot slipped on the tiled floor just as a knock sounded at her front door. The security detail.

A split second later Dana's head slammed into the sharp edge of the bathroom sink. Bright white stars danced in front of her eyes.

After that, there was nothing. No grief, no nausea, no pain.

Just a cold black flood of emptiness as the unconsciousness wrapped her brain tight in its freezing embrace.

CHAPTER EIGHTY-FOUR

Numb confusion replaced the nothingness sometime later as Dana struggled to come awake. She had no way of knowing exactly how long she'd been out of it. Might have been an hour but just as easily could've been a month. It felt like someone had stuck a long needle in through her ear and anaesthetised her brain.

Her eyes were still too heavy to open and when she tried to move her arms she found that she couldn't. Her shoulders ached as though they were on fire.

The fog cleared gradually and Dana realised her hands were tightly secured behind her back with some kind of restraining device.

A deep voice came from no more than five feet away.

'Special Agent Dana Whitestone, you are under arrest for the murders of the five little girls in Cleveland, of Mary Ellen Orton in Los Angeles, of the Aiken family in Kansas, of the college students at Loyola University, of the high-school students in the western suburbs of Cuyahoga County, of the young mother and child you interviewed on the east side, of the elderly couple in West Virginia and of your neighbour Eric Carlton. You have the right to remain silent. Anything you say can and will be used against you in a court of law. You have the right to an attorney. If you cannot afford an attorney, one will be provided for you. Do you understand these rights?'

Dana groaned as her eyelids fluttered open. Everything was a blur, as though she was trying to focus through a veil of tears. Wherever she was, though, it was freezing. The lighting was dim, but she could just make out the puffs of frozen air issuing from her mouth with every ragged breath she exhaled. She couldn't seem to hear straight, either.

She could smell all right, though. The scent that filled her nostrils made her want to throw up.

Liquorice.

When Dana's vision cleared finally, she saw that she was tied to a chair in the middle of a cold room. She gave a startled moan when she suddenly realised where she was. If this was a nightmare, it was the perfect setting.

She was in the house of her childhood. Or at least in the *bedroom.*

Dana looked up at the large man standing over her. He was dressed entirely in black and his face was covered with a black ski mask. Dark sunglasses shielded his eyes.

The fear materialised as a lump in her throat. 'Why are you doing this, Crawford?' she stammered. It *was* Crawford, wasn't it? Although it didn't sound like him. She cleared her throat. 'You had everything. You were the best.'

He threw back his head and laughed. 'Before we get to that, Dana, I have a little something to show you. Are you awake enough for it yet? Brace yourself. This will probably come as something of a shock.'

He moved to a large wardrobe three feet away – it was a perfect replica of the one she'd had in her bedroom as a kid – and flipped the latch up. Dana gasped as he stepped to the side and the doors creaked open slowly.

His face blue and his lips black from strangulation, Crawford Bell was hanging by the neck from a length of tightly knotted cord.

'Not exactly your daddy, but I figured he was close enough for my purposes.'

Dana shook her head violently to clear it and stifled a scream. She stared up in horror at the man dressed in black.

'But *how*?' she said, her brain still foggy despite the horrifying vision before her. 'Crawford's prints were on the hammer in Eric's bedroom.'

The man in black laughed. 'Jesus Christ, Dana, finger-prints can *lie*. Don't you fucking know that? You can transfer them with a simple piece of Scotch tape.'

He waved a hand in the air. 'Do you remember the man who gave Crawford a glass of water when you two were in the library at Quantico? The asshole didn't even drink it. Just set it down on the table for my private investigator to retrieve and send to me. Pay the wrong people the right kind of money and they don't ask too many questions. Anyway, some fucking expert *he* turned out to be.'

Dana's mind slammed back to Quantico. She *did* remember the man in the library, but her mind had been too clouded even to consider the possibility. Once she'd suspected Crawford of masterminding the copycat murders she'd held onto those suspicions as tenaciously as a dog with a bone between its teeth and she'd taken everyone with her. She hadn't thought things all the way through – none of them had. And now Crawford had been murdered; it was no comfort to know he was dying anyway.

'Who the fuck *are* you?' Dana rasped.

The man in black smiled and dragged a magnetic easel in front of her. Again, a perfect replica of the one she'd had in her bedroom as a kid. On it, NATHAN STIEDOWE had been spelled out in colourful plastic letters.

'Notice anything familiar about this name, Dana?'

She swallowed painfully. 'No.'

'Well, watch this.'

Dana looked on numbly as he slid the colourful plastic *D* out of his name and started a new row six inches below. Next he slid down the *A*. Then the *N*.

One by one, the letters slowly formed two new words.

Dana Whitestone.

She looked up at him in confusion. 'Another anagram?'

'Precisely.'

'But why *my* name? I still don't understand what the fuck's going on.'

Nathan Stiedowe removed his ski mask and dark sunglasses at last. The story he told brought them both hurtling back to 1976.

CHAPTER EIGHTY-FIVE

Trembling in fear and anger, Dana looked up into those horrible brown eyes for only the second time in her life.

They were demonic and glittering and she knew them as well as she knew her own. She'd seen them only once before – when she'd been four years old – but they'd haunted her nightmares ever since. For more than thirty years those terrible brown eyes had silently mocked her every time she'd closed her own eyes and tried to fall asleep.

The eyes of the man who had murdered her parents.

'You sick son of a bitch,' Dana hissed.

Nathan Stiedowe threw his head back and laughed harshly. 'And you happen to be the daughter of the very same one.'

Dana glared at him. 'What are you talking about?'

The man in black tutted. 'Come now, Dana. Haven't you figured it out yet? I'm your brother, dear. Well, your *half*-brother, in any event. Don't you recognise the family resemblance?'

'Bullshit,' she snapped, the flame of anger building higher inside her. 'You're no relation of mine. You're just a lonely, misguided piece of shit.'

'Ah, but it's true. Have a look at this.'

He removed a thin sheet of paper from his breast pocket before unfolding it and holding it up in front of her eyes.

392

Dana stared at the name at the top. Jeremiah Michael Quigley – the name of the reporter who'd written about her parents' deaths. Then she glanced down to the line below that indicated the identity of the mother.

Sara Beth Quigley. Her mother's maiden name.

'You doctored that,' Dana said weakly. But she already knew he was telling the truth. She'd have to process the information later. There was no time now to rearrange all the shattered pieces of her past to make him fit in somewhere – not when she was tied to a chair in the middle of a cold room that was a perfect snapshot of her worst childhood memory.

'What's your game?' she asked. 'Why didn't you just kill me when you had the chance?'

Nathan Stiedowe refolded the paper and placed it back into his breast pocket. 'Oh, this document is very authentic, Dana. That much I assure you. As for what my game is, I'm surprised you haven't figured out that little mystery as well. I'm very disappointed in you. I watched you graduate – you could have been the best.'

Dana forced herself to concentrate. He'd been there, watching her, even then. Somehow, through her overwhelming fear and anger, she had to switch gears and try to regain control of the situation.

'You recreate the crimes of notorious serial killers,' she said, trying to keep her voice even. Flatter him – that was what all the training told her – keep him engaged. 'And though I don't approve of what you did, I have to admit I'm a little impressed. It takes a focused mind to accomplish what you did. You made very few mistakes.'

Nathan Stiedowe sneered at her, darkening his handsome face. 'Correction, Dana. I made *no* mistakes. Not one fucking mistake at all. Don't you understand what that means?'

Dana inhaled sharply when the connection snapped into place. The weird feeling she was missing something wasn't due to the meticulous attention to detail that he'd been paying while recreating the crimes of other serial killers; it was from what he'd done that was *different*.

He hadn't left his cap behind at the Night Stalker murder scene. He hadn't slipped up with the floppy disk as Dennis Rader had. He hadn't forgotten the Asian girl under the bed as had Richard Speck, and a parking ticket hadn't stopped him as it had the Son of Sam. As John Wayne Gacy, he'd had sense enough to kill his victim – Dana's sweet, sweet Eric – outside the comfort of his, the killer's, own home.

He was fixing their mistakes.

He smiled as he watched the pieces connect in her brain.

'Exactly, Dana. Those assholes were stupid, incompetent idiots. Sadly, I too was stupid once upon a time. I didn't kill you when I had the chance the first time around, but now I'm going to make up for that. You see, my dear, I don't make mistakes. I *correct* them. You know me as the Cleveland Slasher, but I've always preferred to think of myself as The Editor. Sounds much classier, wouldn't you agree? Then again, what the hell's in a name, anyway?'

'What does any of that have to do with me?' Dana breathed. 'I don't even *know* you.'

Anger flashed across his face. 'Jesus Christ, Dana, are you really *that* fucking stupid? You should be dead right now. You never should have survived that night in the first place. You didn't *deserve* the life you were given. You *stole* it from me. You stole it from me, and now I'm taking it back.'

Nathan Stiedowe stepped forward quickly and smacked

her violently across the forehead with the heavy butt of a gun. Dana's brain convulsed in waves of deep purple for a split second before her world plunged into total darkness once again.

CHAPTER EIGHTY-SIX

The needle in the brain again. More fog.

When her world finally limped into existence again several minutes later, Dana's hands were still tied, but now she was lying on the replica single bed of her childhood.

Everything was positioned exactly as it had been on that terrible night in 1976, right down to the Wonder Woman night light over in the corner.

Her brother's eyes glittered madly as he stood over her bed with a long knife in his hand. Bright red drops of blood slid down the silver blade, clinging to the sharp tip for the briefest of moments. One by one the droplets plopped down onto her face like rust-coloured water from a leaking faucet.

Wincing, she realised she'd been slashed across the stomach.

'Nothing too serious, sis,' her brother said, idly placing the bloody knife on the bedside table next to the gun whose butt he'd used to shut off her lights. 'It's just a simple flesh wound. Ten stitches at most will close it up. But that's not something you really need to worry about right now, is it? For what? So you can be a good-looking corpse?'

He shook his head. 'Besides, everything has to be completely authentic if the unforgivable mistake is to be corrected

396

properly, no? I needed your blood since our mother, God rest her soul, isn't here with us any more.'

Dana frantically worked the knots on her wrists behind her back. She knew what the bastard was doing – trying to bait her into doing or saying something stupid – but she wasn't falling for it. The knots were starting to loosen, and she needed to buy herself just a little more time. Adrenalin was helping to keep her focused.

Her brother took a step back and cracked his knuckles. 'Tell me, dear sister, how exactly would you like to die? Shall I slice you up into little pieces like Albert Fish sliced up young Gracie Budd before he roasted her flesh in the oven and ate it, or is there some other storybook ending you'd prefer to emulate?'

He stepped forward again and leaned his face down into hers. The overpowering scent of liquorice on his breath made Dana's stomach churn.

'How exactly would you like to die, Dana? Just tell me and I promise I'll do my very best to accommodate your wishes.'

He straightened back up and reached for the knife on the table just as the knots on Dana's wrists suddenly fell away. She thrust out her right hand and reached the gun a split second before his fingers curled around the wooden handle of the steel blade.

Heart in her throat, she tumbled onto the floor past him in a shooter's roll and knelt on one knee. She levelled the gun directly at his head. 'Freeze!' she screamed in a raw voice.

The look on her brother's face was inhuman as he lifted the knife over his head and took a step toward her, his dark brown eyes glazing over. His deep voice was flat, emotionless, as he spoke. 'Yea, though I walk through the valley of the shadow of death, I shall fear no evil.'

Dana lowered the gun and shot him once in the left kneecap.

No good. He kept advancing, not even the slightest hint of pain crossing his face. She squeezed the trigger twice more just as the sharp silver knife came flashing down on her head.

Two more bullets in his right kneecap finally sent him stumbling backward onto the bed. A huge lungful of air exploded from his mouth in a loud *whoosh* as Dana scrambled to her feet and watched as he stared up at her in utter disbelief.

And then he *smiled*.

'What's so funny?' she demanded.

He was still smiling as she felt in the front pocket of her jeans for her cellphone. She slipped it out and flipped it open. No reception.

Dana tossed the phone to the side in frustration. 'You're through,' she said, breathing hard. 'You'll never hurt anybody ever again. You're going to prison and I'm going to make sure they execute you for this.'

The tight-lipped smile on her brother's face never wavered. 'Oh, I'm not *going* to prison, Dana. And the state's not going to execute me, either. I leave that job up to you. Hell, one out of two of us ain't bad. Still, I was hoping we'd go together.'

She glared down at him, confused. 'What are you talking about?'

In the very next instant he was off the bed and flying through the air at her again, his shattered kneecaps somehow functioning as good as new. He yanked the sharp knife over his head. Dana's finger slipped once on the trigger before she finally squeezed it hard.

Her brother's breath exploded from his mouth in another loud *whoosh* as the bullet slammed into his lower gut. He fell backward onto the bed and finally dropped the bloody knife.

'I told you so,' he gasped.

Dana's mind clouded over. The hot rush of adrenalin coursing through her veins was making it impossible for her to think clearly. 'You told me *what?*'

Rivers of blood spilled through his fingers as he pressed his hands into his stomach. 'I told you that you would be my executioner. But unlike the victims that my brethren and I shared, you can only kill me once. Pity, isn't it?'

He laughed, grimacing from the pain. 'You didn't really think I'd be stupid enough to leave that gun so close to you unless it was *on purpose*, did you?'

He threw his head back and laughed again. 'Anyway, now I can finally be reunited with my murdered wife and daughter. You've done me a favour here, Dana. You've done me a favour and I thank you for it.'

Dana's mouth went dry. Her ears rang. She immediately knew that he was telling her the truth. She'd played right into his hands again, just like she'd been doing the entire time. But what choice had she had?

Her brother jerked a ragged breath into his lungs and relished the expression on her face as though it was a fine wine. Their stares locked briefly, communicating what they both already knew.

He had *won*.

The blood draining out of his cheeks turned his handsome face a ghostly white. 'I know what you're thinking, Dana, but don't worry. I kept our little secret safe. You and I are the only two people left on Earth who know that we share the same blood running through our veins. Soon you'll be the only one.'

He winked up at her and grinned, revealing a set of remarkably white teeth that were now stained bright red with blood. 'See you in hell, Dana. I'll make sure I keep a seat warm for you.'

And with that, Jeremiah Michael Quigley simply ceased to exist in this world.

CHAPTER EIGHTY-SEVEN

An hour later, dozens of law-enforcement personnel flooded into the clearing in the deep north-east Ohio woods where the serial killer known only to himself as The Editor had taken his last ragged breath.

The steady whir of helicopter blades flattened the frozen grass all around Dana as they wheeled her out on a gurney and into the back of a waiting ambulance.

Before they could take off, however, Bill Krugman stepped into the back of the vehicle and pulled the doors shut behind him.

'I'm sorry, Agent Whitestone,' he said. His left arm was encased in a sling. 'We should've protected you earlier. It's my fault.'

Dana swallowed hard. 'Can we talk about it later, sir? I'm really not feeling up to it at the moment.'

Krugman looked down at her. 'That sick son of a bitch pulled the old "suicide-by-cop" routine, didn't he? He left you no choice.'

Krugman stared intently into her eyes. 'That *was* what happened, wasn't it?'

Dana looked up at him and nodded slowly. 'Yes, sir, it was.' It was the truth. Even if he'd *wanted* her to pull the trigger, he'd wanted her to die too. He'd said so.

The Director let out a deep breath.

'Good. That's exactly how it will appear in the official report.'

He paused as a look of sorrow passed across the folds of his face. 'Crawford Bell was my closest friend, Dana. He always thought of you as a daughter. I just thought you should know that.'

And with that Bill Krugman patted her left knee and left the ambulance to go deal with the colossal mess that Dana and her brother had created in the snowy Ohio woods.

EPILOGUE

Dana lay in her hospital bed three days later, recovering. The doctor had insisted that this time she should stay where she was until *he* decided she was well enough to leave.

The most she'd been able to accomplish over the past three days was to arrange for her landlord to take care of Oreo. Everything else was just too hard for her to deal with right now. She'd lost just about everyone she'd ever cared for in her life and everyone who'd cared for her. That would take longer, much longer, to recover from – if she ever could.

A tray of uneaten food lay in front of her. On an extended leave of absence now from the FBI, she doubted she'd ever go back. The time had probably come for her to consider a different career – one where everyone around her didn't wind up dead.

Over the classical musical channel on the radio in the corner, the velvety-voiced DJ announced the next song.

'Next we'll hear from Irish concert-pianist Ashley Ball playing Ernesto Lecuona's "Crisantemo". '

When the phone rang on her bedside table, Dana leaned over gingerly and picked it up, being very careful not to disturb the long row of stitches in her belly.

'Hello?'

'Hey there, good-lookin'. I hear you're holed up in bed too. Can you believe the taxpayers are actually *paying* us for this?'

'Jeremy,' Dana said softly, 'how are you doing?'

Brown sighed. 'I'm still alive. You didn't really think someone with a face as ugly as mine was going to die *that* easily, did you?'

Hot tears sprang up into the corners of Dana's pale blue eyes. He was the one bright, shining spot on the horizon and she wanted to hold onto it. It was all she had. 'Hey,' she said sternly, 'I happen to love that face of yours very much, so you'd better bring it up here just as soon as you possibly can. You still owe me that bite to eat, you know.'

'It's a date, Dana.'

And with that Dana knew she'd be OK. She'd have to be.

ALSO AVAILABLE IN ARROW

Genesis

Karin Slaughter

Someone had spent time with her – someone well-practised in the art of pain . . .

Three and a half years ago former Grant County medical examiner Sara Linton moved to Atlanta hoping to leave her tragic past behind her. Now working as a doctor in Atlanta's Grady Hospital, she is starting to piece her life together. But when a severely wounded young woman is brought in to the emergency room, she finds herself drawn back into a world of violence and terror. The woman has been hit by a car but, naked and brutalised, it's clear that she has been the prey of a twisted mind.

When Special Agent Will Trent of the Criminal Investigation Team returns to the scene of the accident, he stumbles on a torture chamber buried deep beneath the earth. And this hidden house of horror reveals a ghastly truth – Sara's patient is just the first victim of a sick, sadistic killer. Wrestling the case away from the local police chief, Will and his partner Faith Mitchell find themselves at the centre of a grisly murder hunt. And Sara, Will and Faith – each with their own wounds and their own secrets – are all that stand between a madman and his next crime.

arrow books

THE POWER OF READING

Visit the Random House website and get connected with information on all our books and authors

EXTRACTS from our recently published books and selected backlist titles

COMPETITIONS AND PRIZE DRAWS Win signed books, audiobooks and more

AUTHOR EVENTS Find out which of our authors are on tour and where you can meet them

LATEST NEWS on bestsellers, awards and new publications

MINISITES with exclusive special features dedicated to our authors and their titles

READING GROUPS Reading guides, special features and all the information you need for your reading group

LISTEN to extracts from the latest audiobook publications

WATCH video clips of interviews and readings with our authors

RANDOM HOUSE INFORMATION including advice for writers, job vacancies and all your general queries answered

Come home to Random House

www.rbooks.co.uk